BUDDHA'S MONEY

"Martin Limón knows the noir thriller inside
out. . . . Evocative."
—Lisa See

"The story moves as fast as Bascom's ginseng
gum chewing."
—*Tales from a Red Herring*

"A slam-bang thriller . . . Limón keeps the action
coming at a furious pace."
—*Albuquerque Journal*

"Limón writes gritty, tough, unusual thrillers that are
steeped in the Korean culture."
—*The Register-Guard*, Eugene, OR

"Brims with non-stop action."
—Barbara Seranella

"A heck of a yarn."
—*The Orange County Register*

"A real page-turner."
—*Abilene Reporter-News*

SLICKY BOYS

"A smart combination of classic noir thriller and
police procedural."
—*Los Angeles Times*

"Gritty, gripping . . . memorable . . . as pungent as kimchee."
—*Kirkus Reviews*

"The writing is plain and sinewy, the characterizations quietly brilliant. . . . This is writing of the first rank, a truly unusual mystery that's not to be missed."
—*The Oregonian*

"Gritty . . . Combining the grim routine of a modern police procedural with the cliff-hanging action of a thrilling old movie serial, *Slicky Boys* is full of sharp observations and unexpected poignancy."
—*The Wall Street Journal*

JADE LADY BURNING

"It is not often that so impressive a debut as *Jade Lady Burning* appears. . . . Searing in its intensity. Without ever trying to be 'literary,' this novel achieves the stature of literature."
—*The New York Times Book Review*

"An extraordinary book."
—*The Washington Times*

"As gripping as it is disturbing."
—*The Plain Dealer*, Cleveland

BUDDHA'S
MONEY

BUDDHA'S MONEY

MARTIN LIMÓN

BANTAM BOOKS
NEW YORK TORONTO LONDON
SYDNEY AUCKLAND

BUDDHA'S MONEY
A Bantam Book

PUBLISHING HISTORY
Bantam hardcover edition published May 1998
Bantam paperback edition / April 1999

ISBN 0-553-57610-0

Bantam Books are published by Bantam Books, a division of Random
House, Inc. Its trademark, consisting of the words "Bantam Books" and
the portrayal of a rooster, is Registered in U.S. Patent and Trademark
Office and in other countries. Marca Registrada. Bantam Books, 1540
Broadway, New York, New York 10036.

PRINTED IN THE UNITED STATES OF AMERICA

OPM   10 9 8 7 6 5 4 3 2 1

BUDDHA'S

MONEY

THREE MINISKIRTED BUSINESS GIRLS FLITTED AROUND ERNIE like butterflies bothering a bear. He pulled out a packet of ginseng gum, grinned, and passed out a few sticks.

Another business girl, her face as brightly painted as the flickering neon of Itaewon, trotted across the road. I recognized her. Her name was Sooki. She grabbed Ernie's arm and peered up at him.

"You MP, right?"

"CID," Ernie told her. "Criminal Investigation Division. Not MP."

"Same same," Sooki said.

"Not same same." Ernie pointed at his skull. "I use my brain. MPs just beat the hell out of everybody. And anyway, I'm working tonight. So don't bother me."

We were working, all right. The black market detail. Undercover. Wearing our running-the-ville outfits: blue jeans, sports shirts, sneakers, and black nylon jackets with golden dragons embroidered on the back. Trying to catch off-duty GIs trading PX liquor and cigarettes for the charms that only a beautiful young woman can provide.

Red lips mounded into a pout. Sooki slapped polished nails on her out-thrust hip and purred in the voice of a vixen. "MP, CID, all same same. Any GI slicky my ping-pong heart. No bullshit."

The other girls exploded into laughter and chomped on their gum, seeming more like children in a playground than women ready to sell their bodies to the highest bidder.

Through round-lensed glasses, Ernie's green eyes studied the painted business girl. His grin never faltered, just gradually widened at the upturned corners. He's like that. If you're half nuts, he's interested in you. But if you're a sober professional, he'd just as soon see you take a flying leap off the edge of the world.

We were in Itaewon, the red-light district that services American soldiers stationed at the headquarters of the Eighth United States Army in Korea. More than twenty years ago a cease-fire had been signed ending the Korean War but GIs have been here ever since. Thirty thousand of us. Protecting the wire. Staring across the Demilitarized Zone at the 700,000 stone-cold eyes of the North Korean People's Army.

My name is George Sueño. Me and my partner, Ernie Bascom, are agents for the Criminal Investigation Division in Seoul.

Prostitution is legal in Korea as long as you are eighteen years old and you register with the county health officials and you keep the stamps on your VD card up to date. Most of these girls looked as if they'd turned eighteen yesterday. Some of them still wore their hair straight, in short-cropped bangs, the cut required of every uniformed schoolgirl in the country.

Ernie and I were sent out to Itaewon to enforce rules

that both of us thought were stupid. But being in the army kept Ernie off heroin—a habit he'd picked up in Vietnam—and kept me off the streets of East L.A. Not incidentally, being in the army also kept money in my pocket and a clean shirt on my back. From where I'd come—an orphan at the mercy of the Supervisors of Los Angeles County—it was a big step up.

Sooki grabbed Ernie's arm. He jerked it away.

"I told you, Sooki. Don't bother me. I'm *taaksan* busy."

"No way, GI. You come. You help. Something bad happen."

Ernie's brow crinkled. "What are you talking about, Sooki?"

In the center of the cobbled road, a few splats of rain pattered onto dirty slabs of stone. Dust and the odor of rust exploded into the air.

The humidity felt like a warm hand fondling me under my shirt. Cockroaches the size of a hitchhiker's thumb scurried out of stone gutters. In the fading twilight, I could still see dark clouds hovering in the distance.

It always strikes during July and August. A warm current boils up out of the South Pacific, slams into the shallow waters of the Yellow Sea, and fat clouds shove across the low-lying valleys of the Korea Peninsula.

Chol param, the Koreans call it. The seasonal winds. The monsoon.

"GI punch somebody," Sooki insisted. "*Chogi.*" There. She pointed up the dark hill behind the glittering nightclubs. Tin and cement and red tile roofs covered hovels clustered together as tightly as chips on a poker table.

"Go tell the Military Police," I told her.

Her painted face swiveled. "No MP jeep in village now! They still on compound. GI beat somebody up. No have time wait MP!" She turned back to Ernie. "You come. You help. *Bali bali.*" Hurry. "Somebody *apo!*"

Ernie tossed the foil wrapper of his ginseng gum into the gutter. "Who's hurt?"

"How you say?" Her face crinkled in concentration, searching for the English.

"*Hankuk mallo*," I told her. Say it in Korean.

"*Deing deingi chung.*"

Clouds like bad dreams drifted across the silver face of the rising monsoon moon. Ernie pushed away from the damp stone wall he'd been leaning against.

"What'd she say?" he asked me. "Who's hurt?"

"A monk ringing a bell."

"A what?"

"A Buddhist monk."

The monks come to Itaewon to collect money for their temples. Usually during the day, when the GIs are still on compound. Although most of the denizens of Itaewon are pimps or whores or worse, many of them are still devout, and sacrificing some of their ill-gotten gains to the representative of the Maitreya Buddha will buy them credit in paradise. At least they hope so.

"*Bali bali,*" Sooki insisted. Quickly. "You come."

Ernie zipped up his jacket. "We're good guys, Sueño. Can't let anybody kick the crap out of a Buddhist."

I didn't like it. We were on black market detail. Not village patrol. Still, Sooki was right. There were no other law enforcement officers in the area.

Like a quivering rainbow, a jumble of neon signs sparkled to life along Itaewon's main drag. Above us, in a symphony of black and purple, the monsoon night lowered.

"Okay," I said. "I guess we have no choice."

Sooki didn't hesitate but trotted off, her high heels clicking on the slick stone road. We followed her up the main drag of Itaewon, past the open-doored nightclubs blaring out versions of Stateside rock and roll.

When the girls on Hooker Hill swarmed around us, we

straight-armed them and kept our sights on the gyrating butt of the little business girl devotee ahead. Sooki disappeared into a crack in the brick-and-stone walls.

As we ran, pellets of rain slammed onto my head and back. A dim glow emanated from behind oil-papered windows. The edges of tiled roofs leaned above us, sometimes blocking the light of the three-quarter moon.

Water reeking of urine leaked down the jagged stones that paved the walkway. Charcoal gas from the *ondol*, subterranean heating flues, elbowed out most of the breathable air.

Ernie's footsteps pounded ahead of me. Molars rhythmically ground on gum.

The faint remnants of a high-pitched scream drifted through the alley.

"What was that?" I called to Ernie.

"What was *what*?"

"Listen."

The narrow lane was lined with high walls topped with rusty barbed wire and shards of jagged glass. Then we heard it again. Another sound. This one a harsh bark. Male. A shout of rage.

Ernie chomped faster on his gum. "Sounds like somebody's getting their ass kicked."

Sooki didn't slow down.

The female scream again. Ernie heard this one clearly. He turned to me, his eyes blazing with glee.

"We're going to catch some asshole in the act," he said.

Ernie is always in search of something that will make his heart race and his blood bubble. I'm a little less crazy about the wild life. I face trouble when it comes, but I sure as shit don't look for it.

I reached into the pocket of my nylon jacket and gripped the roll of dimes I always carry with me. It felt firm in my hand, adding heft to my knuckles.

2

THE MAN MI-JA BURKOWICZ HAD BEEN FORCED TO CALL FATHER crashed through the rickety wooden gate, stumbled across the courtyard, and bellowed her name.

"Mi-ja! *Meikju kajiwa!*" Bring me a beer!

Mi-ja remained frozen, squatting in front of a pan of laundry. After having worked all day, the muscles of her arms and shoulders quivered from exertion. Still, she pulled off her oversized plastic gloves, placed her hands on her knees, and shoved herself to a standing position.

"Yes, Father," the nine-year-old Mi-ja said in English.

For some reason, this big foreign man liked to holler his orders in Korean and have her answer in his strange American language.

Mi-ja shuffled in oversized slippers to the small refrigerator hooked to a buzzing electrical transformer. She reached in, grabbed one of the cold cans of beer, and brought it to the man who called himself her father.

His body was huge. Gross. Round as a summer melon.

His cheeks bulged and his nose was bulbous. Shockingly bright blue eyes sat recessed in layers of red-veined flesh. He was hard to look at, Mi-ja thought, and he always reeked of sweat, but he was never cruel to her.

Mi-ja popped the top of the can, watched the frothing liquid bubble to the edges. She offered it to her foster father with both hands, bowing as she did so.

No, it wasn't this fat man who was cruel to her. It was his wife, Mistress Nam, the woman who had adopted Mi-ja and brought her here. She treated Mi-ja as a slave. Making her work all day while Mistress Nam was out with her friends smoking and gambling at *huatu*, the ancient Korean flower cards. At night, if she was sober, Mistress Nam would dress Mi-ja in the traditional *chima-chogori*—a gaudy flower-print dress that Mi-ja hated—and parade her around the homes of her neighbors, showing her off, pretending that she herself had given birth to such a fine-looking Korean female child.

But everyone knew it wasn't true. Behind her back, Mistress Nam was called Slicky Girl Nam. Which meant that she had been a thief before, and before that a business girl. A *yang kalbo*, a whore for the foreign troops. The troops who cling to the terrain of Korea like fleas on the hide of a mule.

As Father Burkowicz guzzled his beer, Mi-ja noticed that he had left the front gate open. An unusual occurrence. This area, this Itaewon, is the most dangerous district in Seoul. Right near the American army base, the Itaewon district has the highest crime rate in the city. Thieves congregate here because the Americans put their wealth on display at every opportunity. To be sure, rich Koreans have more money, but they aren't as foolish as the Americans. They pay armed guards to patrol high fences and protect their wealth with unremitting ferocity.

Before she could trot across the courtyard and slam shut

the gate, Father Burkowicz glugged down the last of his beer. With his big hairy fist, he crushed the can into a prickly ball of tin.

"*Do hana kajiwa*," he said. Bring me another.

Mi-ja did as she was told, puzzled as to why he was drinking so fast. Although his appetite was enormous, she'd never seen him toss down beer so quickly. Was he trying to get drunk? Would he start screaming and crying as Mi-ja had seen him do before, when he'd guzzled too much rice wine?

The remaining daylight faded rapidly. Now the narrow alley outside the gateway was completely dark. Anyone could walk right in, Mi-ja thought. And if this big fat American who called himself her father was drunk, the local thieves could steal anything. How could Mi-ja stop them?

She wasn't worried about losing the household possessions. Mistress Nam and Father Burkowicz were rich and they were always buying and selling on the black market, increasing their wealth. But if some thief took anything, even the most inconsequential item, Mistress Nam would punish Mi-ja severely for not protecting it with her life. Mi-ja started for the gate.

Father Burkowicz reached out his big hand and clamped his clammy fingers around her forearm.

"*Anjo*," he said. Sit down.

He'd never ordered her to do this before. Nevertheless, Mi-ja had been trained in obedience since infancy. She folded a pleat in her woolen dress and sat on the narrow wooden porch. Father Burkowicz draped his heavy arm around her shoulders and hugged her close to his side.

Mi-ja cringed and shut her eyes. To lessen her fear, she thought of her real father. A farmer in the province of Kangwon-do. A poor man, but hardworking. He rented five tiny plots carved out of the side of Star Spirit Mountain. Every morning before dawn, her father was out working, trying to coax the rocky land to grow something valuable enough to sell in the county market fifteen *li* from their home. Always, it was the same story. A small crop bringing in little money. But the taxes remained high and every month there was the rent to pay.

Mi-ja's oldest brother, Wol-sok, had been stricken with a disease as an infant, a disease that left him without strength in his legs. He was no help in the fields. Her second brother, Wol-han, was frail and always coughing up blood. Still, he assisted his father as best he could. After the birth of the two sons, Mi-ja's mother had borne only girls. One, two, three, four of them. Until Mi-ja herself was born.

All of the children worked as hard as they could, but there was never enough money. And never enough food.

When the matchmaker had come to their village, Mi-ja assumed that it was to find a husband for one of her older sisters. Instead, the wizened old woman had told of a rich lady in Seoul, with a fabulously wealthy foreign husband, a lady who was unable herself to bear children. Her only wish was to have a daughter that she could call her own.

That had been a year ago.

When Mi-ja left the village with the matchmaker, her father covered his eyes with his big hands and cried. Only Mother's face, of all those in her family, didn't crinkle in grief. Mi-ja could still see it. Gray as ashes. Unmoving. As if the flesh had been exhumed from a grave.

Tin clattered on rock. An empty beer can rolled across the cobbled courtyard. Saliva dripped from the lips of Father Burkowicz. Mi-ja swiveled in time to spot a row of shadows entering swiftly through the open gate. Men. Not Americans. Koreans, she thought. But then she looked again.

They were darker than Koreans and their cheekbones were not as pronounced. Their eyes were cruel and underlined with scars. Foreigners, she thought. What kind, she had no idea.

Soon, six of the men filled the small courtyard. The head of one of them, the tallest, was wrapped in a long strip of linen. This man stepped in front of Mi-ja and slipped a knife from his belt.

The wicked blade glinted in the harsh light streaming from the bulb that dangled in the kitchen. The turbaned man stuck the sharp tip beneath Mi-ja's nose. She straightened her back, lifting her head as high as she could, but dared not breathe.

Slowly, the man's full lips pulled back, revealing yellow blocks of teeth.

Father Burkowicz rose to his feet. The invaders stepped toward him. Mi-ja closed her eyes.

Everything happened fast then. She heard the sharp bark of command, raised voices.

Wood splintered.

Porcelain cracked.

Then she was pulled to her feet, across the courtyard, and into the darkness of the streets.

3

CAPTAIN KIM, THE COMMANDER OF THE ITAEWON POLICE STA-tion, strode into the interrogation room. His blazing eyes pinned me and Ernie and then the gathered policemen with darts of barbed brass. Kim was a stout man, bronze-skinned, with muscular arms and shoulders and a face that could melt granite. It was the first time I'd seen him in civilian clothes—loose slacks and a bright blue sports shirt. His officers had probably called him from home.

In the center of the bare room, keeping her eyes tightly shut, sat a tiny woman wrapped in gray robes. Minute black stubbles dotted the naked flesh of her skull. Across her temple, a cruel purple welt was gradually beginning to bulge. Blood dripped in a thin line from the corner of her mouth.

Ernie was a little bruised up himself but he grabbed some tissue paper, stepped toward the woman and, his face crinkled in concern, dabbed at the red trickle.

Kim barked an order and one of the policemen hustled

over to a first-aid cabinet and rummaged around. When the policeman found what he was looking for, he returned to the bald nun, cracked open a capsule, and waved it in front of the woman's nose. Her face crinkled, her head jerked back, and her eyes popped open.

The first thing she saw was Ernie.

Her mouth opened and she let out a scream. So loud it rattled the windows; a roar of anger rose from the crowd outside. The policemen all looked at us accusingly.

Who were we, two foreigners, to upset this virtuous Bride of Buddha?

AFTER SOOKI HAD LED US INTO THE CATACOMBS OF THE Itaewon alleys, we heard screams and scuffling. Somehow, in the dark, we crashed headlong into a mugger in the act of attacking his victim. Ernie lost his footing on the slick cobbled pathway, then so did I. Still, before I went down, I managed to lay a left hook into the culprit's rib cage. Bone crunched beneath flesh. I was sure of it.

He was a big man and definitely knew how to handle himself in a fight. What with Ernie flailing around beneath me and it being so dark and Sooki screaming and me still trying to regain my footing, he landed a few punches and managed to slip away. I followed him through the Itaewon alleys but it was no use. He disappeared in the maze.

The only thing I could say for sure was that the perpetrator was well above average height and weight and probably a black man. Therefore, he was almost certainly a GI. The number of blacks in Korea who aren't GIs is not worth considering.

A lone mugger in our grasp and yet he'd escaped. Ernie and I were the best two CID agents in the country and we knew it. Still, I wasn't looking forward to the snide comments from the other agents when we returned to the CID office.

We'd have to capture this guy. No question about that.

What surprised me most was the identity of his victim.

"She's a broad," Ernie told me after he examined her. "I know these things. Hands-on anatomy training I received in 'Nam."

I shook my head wearily. "A GI attacking a Buddhist nun. The CG isn't going to like this."

"Fuck the Commanding General," Ernie said. "*I* don't like it. I don't like it at all."

We carried the unconscious Bride of Buddha through the village, Sooki leading the way. In about two minutes flat, word spread through Itaewon like poison filtering through blood.

A GI had raped a Buddhist nun.

At least, that's what they were saying. I doubted that the nun had been raped. There wasn't time. But facts have never been known to stop a rumor. A crowd of angry Koreans formed quickly.

We were called names: *yangnom sikki.* Foreign bastards. And we were spit at and a few people even threw rocks. One business girl bounded out of the crowd that lined the main drag of Itaewon and tried to scratch Ernie's eyes out. While he was shoving her back, a Korean who takes photos of GIs and their girlfriends cuddling in nightclubs snapped a photograph of the scene. He ran away before I could confiscate his film.

A squad of KNPs intercepted us and, wielding their riot batons, escorted us back to the Itaewon Police Station.

When we were safe inside the cement-block edifice, Ernie gave vent to his rage. "Listen to those assholes! You'd think *we* were the ones who jacked up this Buddhist chick."

"Remember what they tell us in training," I told him. "All GIs are ambassadors for America."

Ernie put his hands on his hips and glared at the growing crowd outside. "Fuck some kind of ambassador."

Curses floated through the open windows.

CAPTAIN KIM GRABBED A CHAIR, STRADDLED IT, AND LEANED toward the frightened nun, speaking in soothing Korean. What had a nun been doing here in Itaewon? he wanted to know.

After a few deep breaths, the little nun relaxed slightly and started to talk.

She had arrived this afternoon, by bus from Tobong-san, north of the city, and had visited some of the young women who work in the bars, ministering to them about the Path of the Middle Way.

Many of the business girls were devout. And despite what they had to do to make a living, they often made offerings of money and prayer, trying to assuage the guilt that gnawed at their souls.

The nun's name was Choi So-lan. She was a novitiate at the Temple of the Celestial Void.

Sweat beaded the ghostly pallor of her forehead. Eyeballs rolled up in their sockets until only the whites showed. Still, Captain Kim leaned over her, occasionally blasting her with the smelling salts, whispering gentle questions in her ear.

Ernie didn't understand much but he kept quiet, knowing I had to concentrate to follow the conversation and that I'd translate for him later.

There was no thought of rushing her off to a hospital, or having her examined by a doctor. Nobody was cordoning off the crime scene and bringing in lab technicians. Sophisticated crime-detection techniques were for the rich foreign countries. Not for Korea. Not for just a mugging.

And certainly not for Itaewon. Maybe some effort would be made if a wealthy industrialist had been the victim. But not for a penniless nun.

The young woman shook her head. Tears squeezed from her tight eyes.

"He hit me. I was walking in that dark alley, leaving the home of a good woman, when suddenly the moon was blocked. For a moment I thought it was a monsoon cloud."

She lowered her head again. Captain Kim kept whispering the soft, soothing words. The nun said, "He shoved me and tried to grab the pouch with the offerings. When I resisted, he punched me and punched me again."

She sat up straighter and seemed to steel herself.

"I am small but I am strong. While he held me, I managed to use my legs and my elbows and I kneed him good. Where a man hurts most. He stumbled and cracked his head against the wall.

"I tried to run away but he was too fast. He caught up with me and dragged me back and now he was really angry. I fought back but it didn't help."

Captain Kim pointed at the felt purse clutched in her hands. "But he didn't take your money?"

"No. I wouldn't give it to him. This is Buddha's money. He tried to grab it but I bit his finger. I bit it hard. I crunched bone." Her pale face dripped with tears. She slipped the pouch inside her tunic.

"Then he was on me again, punching, clawing, grunting like an animal, and I started to lose my mind, fading into darkness, and I screamed again and he punched me again. The next thing I knew, other people were there." She looked around, focusing on Ernie, as if seeing him for the first time. "Him. He was there. He chased the evil cloud away."

Ernie shuffled his feet, nervous from the attention. I'd

never seen him this way before. Women like Ernie. Everywhere he goes the best-looking chicks are after him. Something about him. What, I don't know. Usually he takes their attention in stride. But not so the attention of this tiny nun. He looked ill at ease. A schoolboy on his first date.

When I thought about some of the gorgeous chicks he'd been with and compared them to this little, bald, bruised, battered Buddhist nun, it didn't make sense. Of course, most things about Ernie don't make much sense.

That's what makes Ernie Ernie.

He composed himself and reached in his pocket and stepped forward and offered the little nun a stick of ginseng gum. She accepted it but her hands were shaking so badly that Ernie had to unwrap it for her.

She popped the gum in her mouth and then, for the first time, she smiled. The gleam of her white teeth and the radiant beam of her small round face made even the hardened cops in the room sigh with appreciation.

Captain Kim touched the bottom of her chin lightly, tilted her head up, and pointed toward us.

"Did the man who attacked you, did he look like these men?"

"Yes. He looked like them."

"So he was a foreigner?"

"Yes."

"Was he as big as them?"

"Yes. As big as the biggest one." She turned her eyes on me.

"Was he dark like him or light-skinned like the other one?"

"He was dark. Very dark. As dark as the night. As dark as *moktan*." As dark as charcoal.

"Had you ever seen him before?"

"Oh, no. The foreigners frighten me. Whenever I see one, I turn my eyes."

I had to ask a question. To see the crime from her eyes. To make sure my own observations weren't skewed.

"How can you be so sure he was a foreigner?"

When I blurted it out in Korean, she seemed surprised. Her big eyes studied me for a moment, as if seeing something inside that most people don't.

"I am certain he was a foreigner," she answered.

"But it was dark. Maybe he was a Korean man. A very large Korean man."

"No. He couldn't have been."

"Why not?"

"Because he smelled like you." She pointed at me and then at Ernie. "He smelled like meat."

For some reason, that started her crying again. Captain Kim stood up. All the policemen turned their eyes on me, eyes of accusal.

Outside, a howl went up from the mob.

The nun seemed to realize the discomfort she was putting us through, identifying us so closely with her assailant. She reached inside her tunic, pulled out her felt purse, and motioned for Ernie to come forward. She cupped Ernie's hand in hers and plopped the half-full coin pouch into his palm. To our surprise, she spoke in halting English.

"I go hospital now. You save me, so I trust you. You keep this money," she said, patting his hand. "It is Buddha's money. Bring back to me later." With her finger, she pointed to the north. "At the Temple of the Celestial Void. On Tobong Mountain."

Ernie nodded, hefted the bag, rattled the coins inside, and stuffed it into his pocket. "Can do," he said, snapping his gum between his teeth. "Can do easy."

The little nun smiled.

Outside, the mob howled.

BEHIND THE DESK SERGEANT'S COUNTER, CAPTAIN KIM POINTED his stubby finger at my nose. "I want that GI."

Involuntarily, I took a step backward. "We'll find him. Don't worry about that."

Captain Kim nodded and then asked me to fill out a police report. I told him I would.

I sat at a rickety wooden desk and went as far as I could in the form using Korean but switched to English when my vocabulary ran dry. It took about twenty minutes. By then, the nun had been whisked away in a small white ambulance and Ernie was out of ginseng gum and anxious for action. The crowd still loitered outside the Itaewon Police Station. Bigger than ever. Some of them were burning candles now.

Ernie and I walked to the front of the desk sergeant's counter, under the brightly lit fluorescent lights. I slipped the report into a half-filled wire basket. People outside spotted us through the windows and started shouting. They waved their fists. Maybe they thought we had been arrested for the assault. Maybe they weren't thinking at all. Just enraged at the sight of a foreigner.

Outside, the gruff voice of a policeman ordered someone back.

"*Weiguk-nom chuko!*" someone else shouted. Kill the foreigners!

Ernie's eyes widened. He'd understood that. "Maybe I should change my breath mint," he said.

A murmur rose from the crowd. Someone was trying to push his way through. A dark figure burst past the shouting citizens and bulled his way up onto the broad cement porch. The officers tried to hold him back but he shoved forward with tremendous strength and finally, with four sets of hands still clawing at his back, popped free into the Itaewon Police Station.

The man who stood in front of us was built like a bowling ball. Claw marks scratched his bald head. I knew him. He was an old retired First Sergeant, Herman Burkowicz.

Nobody knew exactly what nationality Herman was—some said Polish, some said Hungarian—but he spoke with an accent so everyone just called him Herman the German.

Herman had been in Korea for longer than anybody could remember. A couple of decades anyway. Black-marketing his ass off.

Another army success story.

The KNPs unhooked their riot batons and stepped toward Herman. I held up my hands and shouted in Korean.

"It's all right! I know this man. We'll handle it."

Scowling at the loss of face, the cops stared sullenly at Herman the German. Still, he was an American and Ernie and I had already grabbed him by the armpits and taken him into custody. The KNPs resecured their riot batons and turned back to face the crowd outside.

"For Christ's sake, Herman," Ernie said. "What the hell are *you* doing here?"

Herman's moist eyes scanned our faces. His face was splotched, with large, blubbery lips and a pug nose. The broad brown belt and the creased slacks and the pullover golf shirt he wore were strictly PX. No Paris fashions for Herman the German.

Out front, the cops kept pushing back at the mob.

Crimson rivulets streamed down Herman's ears. He rolled glistening blue eyes up at me and started to open his mouth, but instead of speaking he just gurgled and sputtered bubbles across wet lips.

Ernie realized first that something was wrong. He

reached for Herman. Before I could move, Herman crashed to the floor in front of us. He lay there, moaning and gripping the mountainous bulge of his stomach. That's when I noticed that the entire side of his skull was puffed into a nasty bruise.

I knelt down, rolled him over, and lifted his head up. Ernie squatted and slapped his loose jowls.

"Evening, Herman," Ernie said. "Nasty bump. You have to stop walking into walls."

"It wasn't a wall," Herman moaned.

"What was it?" I asked.

Herman turned his sad blue eyes toward me. His throat convulsed and air rushed out in a croak. "*Doduk-nom,*" he said.

Herman had lived in Korea so long that certain words— the important ones—he remembered only in Korean, the English completely forgotten. *Doduk-nom* meant thieves.

"Where, Herman?" I asked.

"At my hooch."

I started to rise. Herman clutched my forearm with an ironlike grip. "Wait. I'll go with you. Help me up."

Ernie and I hoisted him to his feet. When he finally reached the standing position, Herman tottered like a round-bottomed clown. Ernie towered over him. So did I, being a couple of inches taller than Ernie.

"I don't know," Ernie said, gauging Herman's steadiness. "A simple burglary. The Korean National Police can handle it. What'd the thieves take? All your black market shit?"

"No." Herman was still woozy. Even when he was clearheaded, Herman the German wasn't the most articulate guy in town.

"No?" Ernie asked.

"No. They weren't those kind of thieves."

Ernie's face darkened like the monsoon sky. He was

suspicious now. Smelling a rat in the rice wine jar. "If they don't want stereo equipment and liquor and cigarettes, then what the hell kind of thieves are they?"

"The kind who want people."

"People?"

I thought of Herman's wife. Slicky Girl Nam was one of the oldest hags who had ever worked the streets of Itaewon. Nobody wanted her. It was even doubtful that Herman wanted her.

Ernie lost his patience. He shoved Herman's haunch of a shoulder. "What the hell did they steal, Herman?"

Herman stood perfectly still, his thick arms hanging at his sides. Somewhere in the short gap between his chin and his shoulders, he swallowed.

"Mi-ja," he said.

Mi-ja. A name that in translation is simple and direct: Beautiful Child. The little Korean girl whom Herman's wife had adopted. The girl with the topknot tied by a pink ribbon and the sparkling smile and the bright eyes like black diamonds.

Every day Mi-ja could be seen flitting to and from the Itaewon market. Snatching candy from the business girls, making them laugh. Bantering with the playful GIs. Mi-ja was the mascot of Itaewon. The one fine thing that prompted everyone—no matter how debauched—to remember where they came from. Remember that they were once part of a loving family. Remember that they once had brothers and sisters and wives and parents and children.

Taking in Mi-ja was the only good thing two lowlifes like Herman the German and Slicky Girl Nam had ever done.

No one doubted that Mi-ja was adopted. Slicky Girl Nam had probably had venereal disease so many times that her reproductive tubes were nothing more than a burnt-out memory.

"How old is Mi-ja?" I asked.

"Nine," Herman answered.

Ernie chomped on his gum. "Why would anyone want her?"

Herman wasn't surprised by the question. In Korea, after the devastation of the Korean War, children were an economic burden, not a prize. Especially girls. Not something to be fought over. Even now, more than twenty years later, things hadn't changed much.

Saliva bubbled on Herman's lips. "I don't know," he told Ernie. "But you've got to help me get her back."

"It's a matter for the Korean National Police," Ernie said. "It happened off-post. A Korean was kidnapped so it falls under their jurisdiction. You're here now. Report it." Ernie glanced around at the shoving and hollering and screaming going on outside. "After things calm down a bit."

"I can't," Herman insisted.

"Why not?"

"The guys who took her already told me. They'll kill her if I tell the KNPs."

Ernie scowled. "Don't worry about threats from a bunch of crooks. Kidnappers always say that kind of shit. Doesn't mean nothing."

"No KNPs," Herman said. His round body was frozen like a rock. "This time they mean it."

"How do you know?"

"Because the kidnappers are not Koreans, they're foreigners. Some sort of brown guys, I don't know which kind. And they're after something. Something valuable."

"What? Your new stereo?"

"No." Herman's big moist eyes searched Ernie's soul. "I've seen you guys let people off after busting them. Maybe they gave you a little money, maybe something else. I don't know. But if you don't help me, I'll turn you in. I'll say I saw you taking bribes."

Ernie leapt forward and shoved Herman's shoulders with all his might. The former First Sergeant barely budged.

"I ought to pop you for that remark." Ernie cocked his fist.

Herman stared at the naked knuckles. "If you don't help me now, they'll kill her. And you know as well as me that the KNPs will only be interested in keeping the ransom for themselves."

Herman was right. Kidnapping, especially of female children, is not seen as being the most serious offense in the country. Tragic but not serious. The KNPs would go through the motions but if they didn't solve the case easily, they'd move on to more pressing matters.

When Herman didn't jump at him, Ernie slowly lowered his fist. He turned to me and grinned.

"I've never heard our man Herman here make such a long speech."

The crowd outside was becoming even more unruly. In the back room, Captain Kim shouted into the telephone.

If it had been Herman who was kidnapped, or Slicky Girl Nam, neither Ernie nor I would have bothered. But Mi-ja was an innocent child. She didn't deserve what had happened to her.

Besides, Ernie and I were constantly on the outs with the Eighth Army honchos—for our unorthodox methods, for busting people regardless of their rank. Any formal accusation made against us—even a false one—would make our working life more uncomfortable than it already was.

"It wouldn't hurt to take a look," I said.

"Yeah," Ernie said. "Why not?"

Herman straightened himself and took a deep breath. He stood shakily on his two broad feet, like a bull in the middle of a ring. He snorted in acknowledgment, turned, and stumbled toward the front door.

I grabbed him by his thick forearm. "Hold it, Herman. Let's wait until these folks outside quit discussing religion."

Herman gazed up at me, confused. It was as if he hadn't even noticed the riot going on outside the Itaewon Police Station.

Sirens sounded in the distance. Plaintive wails that grew steadily louder. Headlights converged on the concrete-block walls of the station. Reinforcements unloaded from jeeps. That must've been what Captain Kim ordered on the phone. More troops.

Suddenly, the commander of the Itaewon Police Station stormed out of his office. He pulled a dented metal helmet down low over his eyes and snapped shut the leather chin strap. He gave the pack of policemen at the door a short pep talk and led them out the door. Responding crisply to his orders, they formed up in ranks and unhooked their riot batons. After Captain Kim shouted the command, the policemen charged into the crowd.

People screamed, cursed, and fell back in panic. Over the sea of heads, I glimpsed nightstick-wielding policemen, whaling away. Swiftly, the crowd started to melt into the night.

The policemen surged forward, chasing the retreating foe.

Herman and Ernie and I walked outside. On the wet pavement lay wounded rioters, some in pools of blood.

Ernie surveyed the damage. "These KNPs sure know how to bust up a party," he said.

A battalion of monsoon clouds drifted low, blotting out the gray pallor of the moon. Rain started to pelt down and we hurried through the narrow lanes, swerving always in the direction of Herman's hooch.

My blue jeans and black nylon jacket were soon soaked and clung to my body like bloody sheets on a corpse.

In the distance, far up amongst the jumbled tile roofs that spread like a maze behind the bar district, we heard a shriek. From a shredded voice.

The forlorn wail of a woman in anguish.

4

RUSTY BARBED WIRE COILED ATOP THE STONE-AND-BRICK WALLS that lined the narrow pathway. Rain pattered on upturned tiles. The sound increased in volume when we passed a roof made of tin.

I breathed deeply of the damp air, occasionally inhaling a hint of garlic from cooking pots bubbling in open kitchens. When we passed a *byonso*, I held my breath, hoping to avoid the aroma of lye-encrusted septic tanks festering in soggy ground.

Wooden gates of various colors and thicknesses were stuck in the center of each wall, most of them locked and barred against interlopers.

I held my hand over my head to keep water from dripping into my eyes, but it wasn't working too well.

Ernie strolled along unconcerned, as if the rain drizzling down his round-lensed glasses and his pointed nose concerned him not in the least. Physical surroundings were something Ernie paid attention to only when they interested him. Usually, they didn't.

By now, the shrieks we'd heard earlier had become moans.

Herman ducked through an open gate. When he did, the shrieking started again. I recognized the distinctive bark: Slicky Girl Nam. Mrs. Herman the German.

An address was embossed on a brass plate embedded in the stone wall: 45 *bonji*, 36 *dong*.

A short walkway of flat stone led into a courtyard festooned with scraggly shrubs and an ancient iron-handled pump with a plastic bucket beneath it. On a raised wooden platform, hooches with sliding paper doors faced out at us.

The joint didn't look much different from the whorehouses in the area. In fact, from previous visits I'd determined that a couple of the residents next door were freelance business girls working the local clubs. By Itaewon standards, this was a routine place to raise children.

Holes were punched in the paper in the doors of Herman's hooch. Some of the latticework was splintered. Inside, shards of pottery and smashed glassware and ripped pillows lay strewn across the vinyl-covered floor.

Ernie whistled. "A lot of damage, considering it's not typhoon season."

Elderly Korean women squatted along the edge of the wooden platform, like a patient jury of ghosts. We stepped under the large corrugated fiberglass overhang to get out of the rain.

When she saw Herman, Slicky Girl Nam bounded across the courtyard, long nails bared like a tigress.

"*Shangnom-ah! Tangsin weikurei?*" Born of a base lout! What have you done?

She wore a flower-print blue dress that clung to her quivering belly and rode high above plump knees. Her hair was dyed raven black and ratted into a headdress that would've startled a New Guinea headhunter.

She swiped at Herman's eyes. He stopped, and without moving his neck, leaned his rotund body backward. The claws sliced by his face within inches. The miss threw Slicky Girl Nam off stride; she reeled forward and rammed her shoulder into Herman's stomach. A "whoof" erupted from his blubbery lips and he stumbled backwards. Ernie and I caught him, but just in time for him to open his eyes and see the wild-eyed Slicky Girl Nam charging at him again.

"*Kei-sikkya!*" she shrieked. Issue of a dog!

Ernie jumped between them, grabbed Slicky Girl Nam by the wrists, and tried to hold her. For a moment it was touch and go as to who was going to win the wrestling match. But finally she jerked her hands away, stepped back, and pointed at Herman.

"*Shangnom-ah!* You let them take Mi-ja. What's a matter you? You *dingy dingy*. You no have brain?"

Herman kept his bull-to-the-slaughterhouse blue eyes on her, his aggrieved expression staying perfectly in place. Slicky Girl Nam pushed past Ernie, reached, and rapped two knuckles atop Herman's round head.

"No have nothing inside?" she demanded. "Why you no stop them? Why you let them mess whole house, break everything, and then take Mi-ja? You no man? You no have nothing down here?"

She thrust a claw toward Herman's crotch, but he jerked back in time and managed to avoid her wicked nails. Again Slicky Girl Nam rapped Herman on the side of the head.

"Where she go? You tell me, *where she go?*"

Herman stared at us, ignoring the steady knocking on his head.

"They took her," he said.

"Who took her?" I asked.

He waved his heavy arm towards the hooches. "The guys who searched the rooms."

"What were they looking for?"

"Antiques."

"Antiques?"

"Yes. A special antique. One they thought I have, but I don't."

Slicky Girl Nam let out a low growl, raised her hand, and stepped closer to Herman.

"You *stupid!* You stay black market. Don't need old, what you call it . . . antique. You make enough money. Why you mess with old Korean things? *Pyongsin-a!*"

Herman didn't respond to being called a cripple, any more than he had to any of Slicky Girl Nam's attacks, verbal or physical.

I could only figure it was love.

When Herman the German and Slicky Girl Nam were married, it was the biggest social event of the Itaewon season. They rented the patio on the top of the 7 Club, right in the heart of the strip, and hired a band and a go-go girl and dressed Mi-ja up as a little Korean flower girl. The beer and the chop were free, so they had a pretty good turnout. Ernie and I chipped in and bought the newlyweds a gift, two rolls of quarters for the slot machines at the NCO club on post.

The man who performed the ceremony was the owner of the 7 Club, which was okay because the official wedding between a Korean woman and an American man takes place when you receive a bunch of stamps on a pile of paperwork at Seoul City Hall. Neither Herman nor Slicky Girl Nam was very religious anyway. But superstition, that was different.

They hired a *mudang*, a Korean witch, to chase ghosts away with a torch during the wedding ceremony. Later, the witch performed a few chants until she fell into a trance. After a couple of drinks, the trance must've been working pretty well because the *mudang* grabbed Herman and performed a lewd dance with him in the center of the patio until Slicky Girl Nam got pissed off and punched her in the nose.

All in all, it was a successful party. During the last couple of hours, both Ernie and I went into alcoholic blackout, which is the criteria we use to judge any social event.

Now Ernie strode around the courtyard, surveying the damage that had been done to the hooches. Whoever had decided to search had been thorough about it. Drawers and clothes and kitchen utensils were scattered everywhere.

Slicky Girl Nam glared at Herman, occasionally knocking on his bowling ball skull with her gnarled fists, but she wasn't hysterical anymore.

"Why you no change charcoal?"

"I'm sorry, honey," Herman answered. "I'll take care of that right now."

Herman scurried over to a large metal plate canted into the stone foundation of the hooch. He opened it and, using a nearby pair of metal tongs, reached in and pulled out a glowing cylinder of flaming charcoal. He scooped out the orange-tinted ash beneath it and tossed the refuse into a pile of spent fuel. After reinserting the flaming briquette, and placing a fresh charcoal briquette on top of it, Herman slapped his dusty hands together and closed the lid of the stove.

Koreans call it the *ondol* heating system. Flues carry charcoal gas beneath the hooch, which heats the stones above and the wood-slat floors above that. All in all it's very cozy and Koreans love a hot platform to sleep on, even during the warm monsoon season.

Generally, changing the charcoal is considered to be

menial work, and most people with any money hire some-one to do it for them. Slicky Girl Nam could've afforded a maid. But, apparently, changing the charcoal was another method she used to humiliate her husband.

Three of the old women put on their slippers and sur-rounded Slicky Girl Nam, tugging on her arms, cajoling her to sit down. Slicky Girl Nam let her face slump, now playing the role of the bereaved mother. The old women sat her down on the raised varnished floor and cooed over her. One brought her a glass of warm barley tea.

When Herman finished with the charcoal, I stood in front of him.

"Spill it, Herman. What the hell were you into this time?"

"Nothing."

Ernie, hands on his hips, strode behind Herman and booted him in the butt. Herman didn't jump as I'd ex-pected him to but turned slowly, tears building until his eyes looked like boiled eggs.

"What'd you do that for?" he asked.

"For not talking to my partner. For not spilling it all." Ernie jabbed his pointed nose into Herman's round one. "Your little girl has been kidnapped. You came to us for help. If you don't start talking there's no way anybody's going to find her. So talk!"

For a moment I thought Herman might slug Ernie, but instead he rotated his torso back toward me.

"A skull. Carved in jade," he said. "From some old king. That's what she told me it was. Worth a lot of money, too."

"Who's 'she'?" I asked.

"The chick," Herman said. "The tall chick. The one with the big *yubang*s."

Yubang. Breast. Another important word.

Ernie raised one eyebrow. "What's this chick's name?"

"Lady Ahn."

"*Lady* Ahn?"

"Yeah. That's what she calls herself."

"And these guys were looking for that antique?"

Herman nodded.

"How do you know?"

"They told me." He held up his arm. Fresh round burns had been seared into the flesh above his elbow. I hadn't noticed them before. "They told me they wanted it."

"What'd you tell them?"

"I told them the truth. I don't have it."

"Who does?"

"Lady Ahn. I'm meeting her tomorrow to set up the transfer. So I can get it back to the States for her."

"Hold baggage?"

Herman nodded.

I saw the connection now. An antique dealer with a particularly precious piece she wants to smuggle out of the country. The Korean Ministry of the Interior won't let dealers take some pieces out, especially the ones classified as national treasures. Maybe this jade skull Lady Ahn had was one of them. And even if she received Korean permission to ship it to the States, once it arrived at a U.S. port of entry, a fat customs duty would be slapped on it. Military hold baggage wasn't checked as closely. In fact, it's hardly checked at all. A cursory sniff for drugs and that's about it. The perfect way to ship a prize antique out of the country.

"And once this skull arrived in the States, Lady Ahn was going to buy it back?" I asked Herman.

He nodded. "With a nice markup."

"So you were getting ready to arrange the transfer," I surmised, "but before you received the piece some guys visited you and did this."

Herman nodded again.

"And when you couldn't produce this jade skull, they took Mi-ja."

Herman let his head droop.

"You ought to get a job, Herman," Ernie said. "Earn an honest living. Then this shit wouldn't happen to you."

Herman raised his head and glanced back and forth between us. "We have to get her back."

"No sweat," Ernie said. "We grab this jade bullshit from this chick with the big *yubangs*, hand it over to these tough boys, and they'll give you Mi-ja back."

"But I don't know where the jade is at."

Ernie shrugged. "So we'll find it."

A bell tinkled outside. I heard a kickstand snap open and click against the pavement. A Korean boy in black shorts and a damp T-shirt pushed through the small door in Herman's gate.

"*Chunghua yori chapsuseiyo*," he said in a singsong voice. Please eat Chinese food.

The boy trotted past us, carrying a large tin box slashed with red ideograms. My regular attendance at Korean language night classes allowed me to read it: The Virtuous Dragon Dumpling House. The boy set the box down on the wooden platform in front of the hooches, slid back the metal sides, and pulled out a large plate of steaming dumplings. As he laid out plastic bottles of soy sauce and vinegar and a few paper-wrapped pairs of wooden chopsticks, Slicky Girl Nam roused herself from her grief.

"*Uri an sikkyoso*," she said. We didn't order this.

"*Sonmul*," the boy said. A gift. "*Ohton chingu sikkyosoyo.*" A friend ordered it for you.

Slicky Girl Nam nodded. One of the old women squatted near the plate, grabbed a small table, unfolded the legs, and started to arrange the chopsticks.

The boy splashed past us, ducked through the gate, and hopped on his bike. In a few seconds, I heard the swishing rubber of his tires wheeling away. I turned back to Herman.

"Tell me more about the guys who broke in here," I said.

"They were foreigners."

"Foreigners? Not Korean?"

"Right. But not Americans, either."

Ernie was growing impatient with the slow plodding of Herman's thought processes. "Then what the hell were they?"

Herman shrugged. "I don't know."

"What'd they look like?" I asked.

"Sort of like Koreans, but maybe darker. They all smelled funny, too."

"Like what?"

"Like maybe incense."

"How many of them were there?"

"Maybe a half dozen. I fought 'em but they hit me a few times." Herman rubbed his head.

Ernie was completely disgusted. He knew I had the patience to continue the questioning, so he strode over to the old women and the dumplings.

"Okay," I told Herman, "a half-dozen dark Asian men break in here, demand a jade skull, and when they don't get it they torture you and kidnap your adopted daughter. Is that what happened?"

"That's what happened. When they left I followed them, but I was still dizzy. I lost them in the alleys."

"How long did you search?"

"Almost an hour. Until I found you guys."

"You never saw any of these men before?"

"No."

"And you don't have any idea how to get in touch with them?"

He shook his head sadly.

"I think what we have to do, Herman," I put my hand on his shoulder, "is talk to this woman antique dealer you were working with. She should be able to give us some sort of lead."

A shriek filled my ears.

This one was high-pitched like the others, but male. I turned and saw Ernie sitting on the raised wooden floor, kicking back with his feet, trying to get away from the plate of dumplings as if he'd just seen the flickering tongue of a cobra. I ran over, Herman huffing right behind me.

One of the dumplings had been bitten in two. A sliver of meat lay next to it. The old women held their cupped fists to their mouths, looking like frightened schoolgirls. Slicky Girl Nam's mouth hung open. A croaking sound leaked out.

"What is it?" I asked.

Ernie pointed. "The dumplings. Look at the goddamn dumplings!"

I studied the plate more carefully. The sliver of meat was raw flesh. Curled.

I opened more dumplings, pulling back the soft, doughy crust. Each dumpling contained a similar sliver of flesh. Soon I had all the slivers in a pile in the center of the table and I realized that they fit together like a jigsaw puzzle. Using a pair of chopsticks, I twisted and turned until they formed an odd shape.

Brown and wrinkled, about the size of a silver dollar. A human ear. The ear of a little girl.

Slicky Girl Nam started to screech again. This time the old women joined her. So did Herman.

Ernie crept off behind the hooch and threw up.

I slumped down, staring at the tips of the chopsticks and then back at the ear. After a couple of minutes, I joined Ernie.

5

MI-JA SHIVERED IN THE COLD CHAMBER, HER ACHING BUTTOCKS pressed atop the varnished wood plank floor. But none of it mattered now. The discomfort made no difference. All she could feel was the searing explosion of pain flaming from the side of her head. The side of her head where her ear had been sliced off.

How had it happened so quickly? Her life had been painful before, but nothing like this. Nothing like the nightmare that had befallen her without warning.

Across the room sat the man she had first seen in Mistress Nam's courtyard. He was naked now except for the white rag wound tightly about his head. His eyes were closed, and Mi-ja wondered if he wasn't asleep. But he couldn't be, because his legs were crossed and his back was ramrod straight.

She wriggled on the hard floor. As soon as she did, a bamboo rod snapped out of the darkness and bit into the

flesh of her thigh. Mi-ja winced in pain but clamped her
eyes tightly. She tried not to cry.

How long had she sat like this? It seemed like hours,
ever since her ear had been sliced off. And every time she
moved, the bamboo rod licked at her tender nerves like the
flickering tongue of some ancient serpent.

Across the chamber, a supplicant knelt behind the man
in the white rag. Mi-ja opened her eyelids ever so slightly
and watched, fearing the bamboo rod but wary about what
these men were about to do. The supplicant dipped his
hand into a wooden bowl, brought his fingers out dripping
with oil, and slowly rubbed the fluid over the bronze skin
of the man in the turban.

Why were they doing this? Mi-ja knew about meditation, she knew about monks, but monks always wore gray
robes and covered their bodies from neck to feet. These
men seemed to enjoy their nakedness. And they seemed to
enjoy caressing one another.

Mi-ja tried to push the pain of her severed ear out of her
mind. She thought of the mountains. Of her home. Of her
mother serving her every morning—when there was food.
It was always the same fare: rice gruel, steamed mountain
herbs, a sliver of mackerel flesh when her father's harvest
was particularly grand. A simple breakfast, but hot and filling. Better than the nurungji, the burnt crust of rice at the
bottom of the cooking pot, that she had to scrounge for in
the home of Mistress Nam. The old woman never rose
early but always slept late, her body reeking of perfume
and sweat and cigarettes and rice wine. And if Mi-ja
cooked for herself, the old hag would rouse herself and
shriek out a tirade against wastefulness.

Mi-ja tried not to let her mind stray from the mountains. She thought of the stream near her village that ran
gurgling and swirling over ancient rocks. She thought of
how she used to squat on the flat stones every morning,

beating her father's hemp tunic with a *mongdungi*, a long
wooden stick. And she remembered his baggy pantaloons
and the soap sudsing in the clear water of the pond and her
father's pleased expression when she knelt before him and
presented him with a freshly pressed suit of clothes.

It had been a difficult life, but so much more filled with
joy than life with Mistress Nam and the big American in
Itaewon. But as bad as even that was, it now seemed idyllic
compared to this dank and smelly chamber. Once again,
Mi-ja fearfully studied the man across from her, his oiled
skin glimmering in the guttering light of a single candle.
What were they planning on doing with her?

Finally, the supplicant stopped rubbing his master with
oil. He raised himself off the floor and shuffled across the
meditation chamber toward Mi-ja. Instinctively, she
scooted away. Like lightning summoned by an evil god,
the bamboo rod snapped onto her flesh. Stinging pain
flashed through her body. She froze where she was, hoping
she wouldn't be hit again.

The supplicant knelt beside her, dipped his greasy fingers into the wooden bowl, and began to smear oil over
Mi-ja's body. Fearing the rod, she did her best not to move,
but the oil was slimy and cold and the smell of it disgusted
her. What was it? Something familiar, she decided. Like
the tiny bricks of hardened milk that Mistress Nam bought
in the American PX. What did she call it? Butter, that was
it. But the American butter had only a mild aroma. This
vile potion reeked as if it had been rotting for months.

As the man's fingers slid over her body, Mi-ja's supple
mouth twisted in horror. The bamboo rod snapped
again—and again—but no matter how many times it bit
into her flesh, Mi-ja could not stop quivering at the touch
of his greasy fingers.

Finally, her body was almost completely lathered in
grease. The supplicant's fingers paused for a moment, just

below Mi-ja's navel. Then his hand slid lower until the tips of his fingers touched her in a spot where even Mi-ja knew no one was supposed to touch.

Mi-ja leapt back. The bamboo rod lashed out. She bit her lip, squirming, flinching at the lash of the pliant wood. Tears streamed down her soft cheeks. The supplicant seemed offended that someone had interrupted his work and paused for a moment. When Mi-ja stilled her shaking, he continued.

Soon, every part of her small, unblemished body reeked of the rancid butter. Then the supplicant paused and placed two fingers at the cleft between her legs. Without warning, he jammed them deep into her body.

Mi-ja screamed. She squirmed and kicked away from his pressing fingers. The bamboo rod snapped and sliced again into her flesh.

The pain slowed her for only an instant. The supplicant's breath came hot and close. In a language she didn't understand, he hissed into the gory wound that had once been her ear.

"You will be ready for our master soon, Little Sister. Ready to assist our Master Ragyapa in praising the Lord Mahakala. The Lord of the Demons."

He reached for her. Mi-ja flinched backward. Again the bamboo rod lashed out, running its fiery tongue along her quivering flesh.

The slimy hand grabbed her arm, slipped, and grabbed again.

This time it held firm.

6

HERMAN AND ERNIE AND I TRUDGED UP A SHORT HILL. THE clang of unsyncopated rock music, the harsh barking of GIs, and the lilting laughter of business girls drifted through the walled lanes. *Dok Yong Mandu Jip*, the Virtuous Dragon Dumpling House, was stuck back in an alley in the maze behind the Itaewon bar district.

Flimsy glass panes rattled as Herman slammed open the sliding door.

Korean customers gazed up at us—openmouthed— from steaming bowls of noodles. With Ernie and me behind him, Herman must've looked as ominous as a Mongol horde.

We strode into the kitchen. It was tiny, with charred metal woks atop cement stoves filled with glowing charcoal. The odor of burning peanut oil seared into my nostrils. Half-moon dumplings sizzled in popping grease.

An old man looked up from the flames. Worry creased his wrinkled face.

"Koma oddiso?" I asked. Where's the boy?

The old man didn't answer. But his head turned slightly toward the back door.

The entire alley was a sea of mud. The boy stood next to his bicycle, tying his sheet-metal carrying box to the rack above the back tire. He swiveled when he heard our footsteps. The smooth, even features of his face bunched in terror. Stepping back, he held up his hands.

"Na kuriqu an hagosipposo!" I didn't want to do it!

Herman either didn't understand or didn't listen. He grabbed the boy by his narrow shoulders and slammed him up against the brick wall. As thick fingers clutched his neck, the boy started to croak. Rivulets of rain ran from his short black hair, puddled in his eyes, and streamed down his cheeks.

Ernie shoved Herman. "Let him down! George will interrogate him."

Herman hesitated, glaring. Finally, his fingers curled open and he eased the boy to the mud. I made Herman back up a few steps and then leaned over.

"Orini oddiso?" I asked the boy. Where's the child?

He answered in quavering Korean.

"I don't know of any child. All I know is that men came and forced my grandfather to make dumplings, using the meat they gave to us."

"Did you know what kind of meat that was?"

The boy shook his head. "I don't know. I don't know."

The shout came from behind us. *"Manji-jima!"* Don't touch him!

We all turned.

The old cook stood in the doorway, a huge meat cleaver in his hand, his face twisted like the mask of a demon.

Herman seemed not even to notice the cleaver. He sloshed forward through the mud, heading directly toward

the cook. The old man raised the heavy chopper. Herman
stopped.

"We've had enough!" the old man said in Korean.
"This is the second time today foreigners have tormented
us. No more!"

Herman stared at the old man and the blade. Then he
suddenly lunged forward, ramming his big round head
into the man's narrow chest. The blade slammed down,
twisting in midair, thudding onto Herman's back.

The two men crashed back into the kitchen. Pots clattered onto cement, sizzling oil splashed against flesh,
smoke and flames leapt up toward the ceiling.

The boy screamed.

"Christ, Herman!" Ernie yelled. He glanced toward me,
a smile starting to curve across his lips. "That guy's crazier
than I am."

We ran into the kitchen and pulled them apart. I
grabbed an earthen jar of barley tea and poured it over the
burning spots where hot oil had splattered onto their arms
and necks. Using a can of flour, Ernie put out the small
fire. In the serving area, all the tables and chairs were
empty, customers vanished, plates of hot food abandoned.

We jerked the two combatants to their feet. Ernie had
the old cook shoved up against the wall, his forearm pried
beneath his wrinkled neck. Herman stood huffing and
puffing, his eyes watery as if he was about to cry. In Korean, I yelled at the old man.

"Who were the men who brought the meat? Who told
you to make the dumplings?"

The old man shook his head. "I don't know. Foreigners."

"Americans?"

"No. At first I thought they might be Japanese, but they
spoke some strange language. Not Japanese."

The cook was old enough to have lived through the

occupation of Korea that ended with the Japanese surrender at the close of World War II. He'd know if the foreigners were Japanese. They weren't.

"Had you ever seen these men before?"

"Never. It was as if they were demons who floated in on the monsoon clouds."

"From Asia then?"

"Maybe."

"How many of them were there?"

"Five. Maybe six."

"How did they talk to you? How did they tell you what they wanted done?"

"In GI talk."

"You understand English?"

"No. Just a few words. Mostly they pointed, gave me the meat. Made me make the dumplings."

"How did you know where to deliver them?"

"When the dumplings were finished, they took them, and took my grandson."

I turned to the boy and jabbed a thumb toward Herman.

"How did you know where he lives?"

"I didn't." The boy's lips started to tremble. I turned back to Ernie.

"Let the old man down," I said. "But keep an eye on the hatchet."

Ernie reluctantly released his hold on the cook and even helped him straighten his grease-splattered tunic. A sense of hope entered the boy's dark eyes. Herman breathed more heavily. The boy tensed again.

"If you didn't know where this man lived," I asked him, gesturing toward Herman, "how did you know where to deliver the dumplings?"

"They went with me."

"All of them?"

"Just one. The one with the thing wrapped around his head." The boy swirled his forefinger in a circle above his skull.

"The thing? A hat?"

"No. Rags."

A turban, I thought, but I didn't know the Korean word.

"So this man with the rags on his head guided you to the home and ordered you to deliver the dumplings?"

"Yes. And he waited outside while I delivered them."

I translated for Ernie. His eyes widened slightly. Mi-ja's kidnappers—at least one of them—had been close. Very close.

"Did he pay you?" I asked the boy.

"No." The boy seemed surprised.

"Then why'd you do it?"

"They were going to hurt my grandfather."

At that, the old man rolled up his sleeves. His underarm was lined with cigarette burns, the same type of wounds the kidnappers had branded on Herman.

Out front, the door slammed open. We heard voices. Korean voices. Men.

"KNPs," Herman whispered. "Let's get out of here."

I was reluctant. The Korean National Police would interrogate the dumpling house owner and his grandson thoroughly. They might learn something we hadn't. Something useful.

Herman yanked on my arm. "Come on," he urged. "Those guys'll kill Mi-ja if I don't keep the Korean police out of this."

I allowed him to pull me through the back door of the kitchen. Ernie followed.

In a few seconds, we were lost in the catacombs of Itaewon. A police whistle sliced through the rainy night.

———

WHEN WE REACHED HERMAN'S HOOCH, SLICKY GIRL NAM WAS holding her hair out to the sides of her head with splayed fingers. Screaming. Her eyes were glazed. A teenaged girl stood next to her. Cringing.

Herman strode up to his wife and shouted, "Nam!"

When she didn't stop screaming, he slapped her with his fat, rough hand.

The flesh of Nam's face shook and she looked up at Herman, surprised.

"What happened?" he asked.

"*Chonhua*," she answered. Telephone.

Herman looked at the girl. She wore a black skirt and white blouse and black tunic. A middle-school uniform. Her glossy hair was in braids. The girl motioned toward the gate. All of us, including Slicky Girl Nam, followed her outside.

"She's the daughter of the pharmacist on the corner," Herman explained to Ernie and me. "That's where the phone is."

A red telephone was hooked onto a pole beneath the awning in front of a wooden shack with a big red sign in front that said "*Yak*." Medicine. The receiver was off the hook. It dangled on its metal cord.

Slicky Girl Nam held her fists to her mouth, staring at the phone as if it were about to explode. Herman's face was a round mask of worry.

"You'd better answer it," I told him.

Ernie strode toward the plate glass window and began studying the rows of medications. Even though he'd kicked the heroin habit, he couldn't give up his hobby—pharmaceuticals—altogether.

Herman snatched up the dangling receiver. "Hello?"

He held the phone away from his ear. A shrill wail erupted from the mouthpiece. A little girl's voice, screeching in pain.

Slicky Girl Nam backed up as if she'd heard a demon from hell. Herman stiffened his arm, holding an asp by the neck. Ernie stopped studying the medications and squinted at the phone, probably trying to decide whether or not to punch it into submission.

I grabbed the receiver from Herman's hand.

"Hello?" I said in English. "Hello?"

The voice that answered sounded as if it were ground out by metal gears.

"I will give you five minutes . . ." it said. The English was clear but thickly accented. But an accent I couldn't place. ". . . to climb to the top of Hooker Hill. Someone has been paid to give you a message. Do not bother her. She knows nothing. If policemen are following you, the fat man's daughter will be killed."

As I listened, a blade of ice slid along my spine. The words were pronounced precisely, like a mortician expressing condolences to a bereaved family. The accent seemed Asian but didn't sound like anything I had ever heard. Not in East L.A., anyway. And not in Seoul.

I shouted into the receiver. "We can work something out. I know you want the jade skull, but—"

The line clicked and went dead.

Herman and Ernie stared at me.

"What'd he say?" Ernie asked.

"We have five minutes to get to the top of Hooker Hill."

7

HOOKER HILL IS THE NAME GIS HAVE GIVEN TO THE NARROW lane that stretches about forty yards, from the Lucky 7 Club on the main drag of Itaewon up to the Roundup Club on a rise overlooking the entire village. The pathway is lined with chophouses and hole-in-the-wall bars and wooden gates behind which lurk hooches jam-packed with Korean business girls. At night the women flood onto the street. Trap-door spiders searching for prey.

When business is slow, a GI with a pocketful of money is lucky to take two steps before one of the denizens of Hooker Hill latches onto him. Wrapped in a web of sensuality, most of the hapless GIs are quickly tugged back into the business girl's lair, there to be devoured at the spider lady's leisure.

Ernie and I didn't want to have anything to do with the women of Hooker Hill. Not now. Not when we were in a hurry. The problem was that it was a week before military payday, and although the rain had slowed somewhat, a steady drizzle was still keeping most GIs inside the cozy dryness of the nightclubs lining the main drag. As a result, Hooker Hill was so crowded with desperate business girls that a eunuch with an empty wallet would've had trouble wriggling past them.

Normally, Ernie enjoyed himself on this street, playing grab-ass with the girls, giving them eighteen reasons why he was broke and wouldn't be able to accommodate them. Tonight was different.

"Get your hands off me!" he bellowed.

The pack of girls just giggled.

"Ernie, why you go fast? You no want catch me?"

"No time," Ernie told them. "I have business to attend to."

Flesh slapped on flesh. "That's *my* crotch . . ."—Ernie's voice—". . . and I'll use it the way *I* want to."

I was making better progress: Keeping my face somber, my eyes focused on my destination, and straight-arming every overly made-up business girl who had the courage to approach me.

Herman had fallen behind in the alleys but now, here on Hooker Hill, he was making up for lost time. The girls backed out of his way, moving so quickly that it was like Moses parting the Red Sea.

All he needed was a long beard and a staff.

I had almost made it to the top of the hill when a business girl wearing tight blue jeans and a brightly striped knit sweater sprinted out of the crowd. I recognized her immediately. Sooki. She had changed clothes. Not an unusual thing for a busy business girl to do.

She bumped into me, twirled, and jammed a wad of stiff paper into my hand. I tried to grab her but missed and watched her escape down Hooker Hill.

Business girls hung on Ernie like fronds on a palm tree. Still, when I whistled he caught the signal and lunged for the darting Sooki. He grabbed her arm. She tried to wriggle free, but with Herman's help Ernie kept his grip on her and dragged her over and stood her in front of me.

I held the note under her nose.

"Who told you to deliver this to me?"

Sooki pouted. She scanned the heavily lined eyes in the crowd, apparently finding nothing there to be afraid of.

"Some guy," she told me. "A foreigner."

"From which country?"

"I don't know."

"Asia?"

"Yeah. Maybe. He look like a Korean."

I twirled my forefinger around my head. "Did he wear a turban?"

Her eyes widened. "How you know?"

"Did this guy also pay you to tell me and Ernie about the Buddhist nun?"

She shrugged. "Maybe."

Herman lunged forward. Ernie held him back. Sooki studied Herman's protruding lower lip and his clenched fists.

"Same guy," she told me.

"Where can I find him?"

"I don't know. He stop me in alley, told me to tell you about the little nun. Pay me five dollars GI money."

"And the second time?"

"Same." Sooki straightened her shoulders, glancing proudly at the curious business girls clustered around us. "But this time he pay me ten."

A sigh of appreciation arose from the women.

I kept interrogating Sooki, but it quickly became apparent that she knew nothing else. I pointed my finger at her nose. "If you're lying to me, I'll find you."

She slapped her painted nails on her hip. "No sweat,

GI. Anytime you want to catch Sooki, can do easy. Only need this one."

She rubbed her thumb and forefinger together.

Sooki had been hired twice in the same night to carry a message to us. Maybe by sending us after the mugger of the little nun, this foreign man had been trying to get me and Ernie—the only two CID agents in Itaewon—out of the way. To divert our attention from Mi-ja's kidnapping. But he'd been fooled. Even though there'd been a riot outside the Itaewon Police Station, Herman the German had managed to break through to us.

Herman shoved his huge body in front of me.

"What the hell does the note say?"

I ignored Herman and scanned the dark skyline. Two- or three-story buildings. A few *yoguans*, Korean inns, hot-bed operations for GIs and the girls they picked up. Most were apartments. Housing business girls and the families of those Koreans who did legitimate—or semilegitimate—work here in Itaewon.

Beyond the buildings, between drifting rain clouds, the tristudded belt of Orion glimmered with a faint glow, no match for the glare of the Itaewon neon. Still, the pale stars seemed somehow heroic. I swiveled slowly in a 360-degree turn, scanning high and low. The three-quarter moon was rising. No sign of observers. But they were there. We were being watched. I was sure we were.

Because I had stopped moving forward, the business girls pressed in on me, breathing their hot breath on my arms, clutching my elbows. I shrugged them off and unwrapped the note.

"What's it say?" Herman demanded.

I showed it to him.

"That's Chinese." Herman looked back and forth between me and the note. "I can't read it."

So many business girls had their arms laced around

Ernie that he looked like a man towing an acrobatic troupe. "You couldn't read it anyway," Ernie told Herman, "even if it *was* in English."

The business girls giggled.

Herman just stared at Ernie. Amazed. Not by what Ernie had said but by the stunning fact that we wouldn't be able to read the note. Herman could only work on one problem at a time. Ernie's sarcasm couldn't break through.

"I can read the note," I said.

"You can?" Herman leaned over the paper, blocking my light.

"Yes." I pointed to the three characters at the top. "These are simple. The name of the district we're in: Itaewon."

Herman peered at the paper. So did Ernie.

"And this is the character for temple."

"Temple?" Herman said. "There's no temple in Itaewon."

"Then we'd better shit one," Ernie said.

Sooki stepped forward again. "Yeah. There's a temple in Itaewon. GI never go there. GI *babo*." Stupid. "GI don't know."

Herman grabbed her soft arms. "Where is it?"

Sooki leaned as far back as she could. "Sooki show you. But cost ten dollars."

The surrounding business girls cackled in glee. Herman backed off as if Sooki had suddenly become radioactive.

"There's one more thing that has me worried," I said.

"What?" Herman asked.

"The three characters down here on the bottom of the note."

"What do they say?"

"*Oh bun hu.*"

"What the hell does that mean?"

"It means they've given us five minutes to get to the temple."

Herman let out a *whoof* of air. "We've already used three."

"Maybe four. We don't have time to be dicking around," I told Herman. "Pay her the ten dollars."

"I'm broke."

I couldn't believe it. Herman's daughter had just been kidnapped and the asshole was still trying to stiff me for a measly ten dollars. I reached in my pocket, dug out a wrinkled Military Payment Certificate, and slapped it in Sooki's hand. "Here. Let's go. *Bali bali!*" Quickly.

Sooki smiled, slipped the money in the top of her bra, then trotted off into one of the alleys that led off from the top of Hooker Hill.

Ernie flapped his arms like a flamingo preparing for flight. About three business girls fell back. They pouted and straightened their skirts.

Without hesitation, Herman rolled forward after Sooki. This time I kept score. He bowled over nine business girls. But didn't have time to try for the spare.

DURING THE WEEKDAYS, WHEN ALL OF THE GIS ARE ON COMpound, the Korean business girls have a life of their own. They gossip and play *huatu*, Korean flower cards; they visit the public bathhouses with their friends; they smoke cigarettes and eat chop. The fact that there was a temple in Itaewon shouldn't have surprised me. A place to worship Buddha would fit right into the business girls' routine.

But what surprised me most was that I didn't know about it. Maybe none of them wanted to tell a GI about their secret temple. I didn't blame them. We Americans have a habit of ruining everything that's good.

Sooki wound through the alleys like an expert. I wasn't sure if we could trust her, but with only a minute or two until our rendezvous, I had no choice but to take a chance on her. I didn't have to explain this to Ernie. He was alert. Watching for a trap.

Up here above Itaewon the lanes became even narrower and darker. Even the clangs of rock and roll from the main drag faded into silence. All I heard was heavy breathing and our footsteps sloshing through the mud.

Finally, Sooki stopped and crouched at the corner of a tall stone wall. I squatted down next to her and she pointed, whispering. "The Dream Buddha," she said. "That's His temple."

"The Dream Buddha?"

"Yes. We call him Maitreya."

I'd read about Maitreya. The Buddha of the Vision of the Coming Age. A Buddha who has not even been born yet in his human form but who still manages to help mortals in the here and now. It makes sense when you think about it. All Buddhas are eternal. Neither the future nor the past is a barrier to their will.

Ernie and Herman crouched next to us, breathing heavily. I peered around the wall.

It was a small pagodalike temple. Made of wood, painted blue, with red and gold filigree along the tile of the layered roofs. A few candles shone inside, illuminating a gold-plated Buddha. His enigmatic smile beamed out at the world. The odor of incense wafted through the gentle rain.

"Nobody's there," Ernie told me.

"They're here," I answered. "Somewhere."

Herman motioned for us to keep quiet. "Listen," he said.

We heard creaking in the pagoda. Up high. Through the mist I saw another stone wall, looming behind the pagoda, almost as high as the highest roof.

"Somebody's up there," Herman said.

"Sounds like it," I answered. "Okay. They want us in the temple, so we go in the temple. Me and Herman. Ernie, do you think you could work your way around behind?"

Ernie chomped on his ginseng gum. "Can do easy."

"Good. That'll give us an extra measure of safety if they try anything."

A high-pitched moan sliced through the rain.

We all froze, looking toward the top of the temple. Sooki shivered, rubbing her bare arms. She stood. "Sooki go now."

Herman grabbed her elbow and yanked her back down. "If you mess us up," he told her, "I'll come looking for you. You *alla*?" You understand?

Sooki swallowed and slowly nodded her head.

"Good." Herman released his grip and Sooki rose and trotted down the dark lane.

Ernie waited until her footsteps faded. "Scared the shit out of her, Herm baby." There was admiration in his voice.

Herman grunted.

"Come on," I said. "Let's get this show on the road."

"Right." Ernie scurried off through one of the side alleys, happy as a drunkard in a saki factory. There was nothing like the prospect of violence to brighten up his outlook on life.

Ernie'd spent two tours in Vietnam. Driving trucks and hiding in bunkers from rocket attacks and buying vials of heroin from the snot-nosed boys who sold it through the wire. And he'd run the ville there, too. But Vietnam was a lot more dangerous than Itaewon. Bar girls turning tricks at night and selling military secrets in the morning. Still, Ernie loved it. The lying, the hatred, the intensity.

When I asked him about the Vietnam War he said, "There will never be another sweet one like that."

After Ernie's footsteps faded, I slapped Herman on the

shoulder. "Looks like you and me are going to have to talk to these assholes."

Even in the darkness, I could see that Herman's features were bunched into wrinkles of worry.

"Follow my lead," I told him. "But if you see a chance to grab Mi-ja, take it. Better to have her and to fight for her—no matter what happens—than to let them keep her."

Herman nodded. "What if they have guns?"

"Not likely. They're foreigners."

In Korea, gun control is absolute. No nonsense like the bad guys have guns but the good guys don't. No way. In Korea, nobody has guns. No one except the Korean National Police and the military. And each weapon is tightly accounted for, from manufacture to dismantling. No black market for guns exists in Korea. And if anybody tried to start one and was caught, the sentence would be death.

The chances of a group of foreigners managing to buy small arms once they arrived in-country was slim to none. Knives, though. Clubs and axes. That was a different matter. What happened next in the temple could get rough. But I knew that Ernie wouldn't let me down. And something told me that, in a fight, Herman wouldn't be any slouch, either.

When we'd busted him for black-marketing, I'd seen Herman's military record. He'd been a straight-leg grunt in the Korean War and an infantry platoon sergeant in Vietnam.

I pulled the roll of dimes out of my pocket and clenched them in my left fist. Herman adjusted a short cudgel beneath the belt behind his back.

We stepped across the cobbled street to the Temple of the Dream Buddha.

———

IT WAS DARK INSIDE, I KNEW IT WOULD BE, BUT THERE WAS NO way to hide our entrance. The old varnished boards creaked with every step.

I felt bad about not taking off our shoes at the entrance—it seemed like a great sacrilege—but with a little girl's life at stake we couldn't add the disadvantage of being barefoot to all the other disadvantages we were facing. The golden Buddha seemed to recognize our breach of religious etiquette: Somehow the corners of his smile had lowered into a frown.

The heavy sting of incense pricked its way up my nostrils. I snorted a couple of times. So did Herman.

Brightly painted statues of saints and demons flanked the Buddha. In the darkness, some of their faces seemed almost human. Something moved. Herman grunted. I swiveled.

A man, a dark Asian man, stood next to the red-faced effigy of a snarling demon. The man's arms were crossed, he wore a heavy jacket and wool slacks, and his head was shaved bare. He smiled at our surprise. With one finger, he pointed up the stairs in front of us.

I turned and looked. It was dark up there.

As if on cue, another high moan drifted down from the upper floors. Mi-ja.

Herman took a step toward the man. I grabbed his arm.

"He's just a lookout," I told Herman. "If we beat the crap out of him, they could hurt her. Our only choice is to go upstairs, listen to what they have to say."

Herman was breathing heavier now. He didn't answer me but turned and followed me up the stairs.

The only light was the glimmer from the candles below. The stairs were so narrow that I had to cant my shoulders to squeeze through. Helpless, I thought. And the kidnappers are waiting for us. I felt my heart beating wildly in my chest, pumping blood up through my throat.

Finally, a shaft of moonlight revealed an open chamber. I stepped into it. Men pressed around me. All of them Asian, burly, their arms crossed. Knives stuck in broad sashes around their waists. I scanned the room for Mi-ja. She wasn't there.

One of the men stepped forward. I raised my fists but he paused and held up his open palms. Then he made patting motions. He wanted to frisk me.

Another moan drifted down from upstairs. "She's up there," Herman said hoarsely.

"And they won't allow us to see her," I told him, "unless we allow them to frisk us."

"No sweat," Herman said, glancing at the tough faces around the room. "My little cudgel wasn't going to do much good, anyway."

"Okay," I said. "But be careful when they get close. It could be a trick."

I stepped away from Herman and raised my arms, signifying that I would allow them to search me. The dark Asian man who had approached me patted me down quickly, stepped back, and pointed upstairs.

I was free to go.

That was fine but I didn't particularly want to go alone. I pointed at Herman.

The man shook his head.

Herman understood. "They only want you to go up there," he told me. "Don't worry. If anything happens, give out a holler. I'll be up there lickety-split."

I gazed around the chamber. "There's six of 'em, Herman."

"They won't be able to stop me," he said, "if they start to hurt Mi-ja."

Hollow words. I knew we were playing right into their hands. No weapons. Our strength divided. And I sure as shit didn't want to climb those last stairs alone. But what choice did I have? These foreign thugs were holding Mi-ja and they'd already proven that they'd do anything, including slicing off her ear and sending it special delivery to her mother, if we didn't follow their instructions exactly.

I started up the creaking steps.

THE TOP CHAMBER WAS THE SMALLEST OF ALL. THE ONLY LIGHT was moon glow filtering through oil-papered windows. A dark figure sat in the center of the wood-slat floor. Against the far wall, a shadow moved slightly and whimpered.

I could barely make out who she was: Mi-ja.

I could kick the shit out of this guy, grab Mi-ja, and carry her downstairs. But how far would I get? All the thugs downstairs looked tough and determined, and all of them made a big display of the leather-handled knives stuck in their waistbands. I wouldn't get far. But if it came to that, I'd have to try.

Better to try talking first.

The dark figure in the center of the chamber rose straight up, almost as if he were levitating, until he stood on two feet.

He was a husky man. Not as tall as me, but he exuded an aura of strength. Dark. Asian. Everything outsize. A big-boned man of raw power. He wore trousers and a tunic, like the men downstairs, and dirty linen wrapped around his head.

"Where is the jade skull?"

The voice cut into me like a blade. I took an involuntary step backward and cursed myself for showing weakness. It was the same voice I'd heard on the phone. In English. The voice that sounded like grating gears.

"We don't have it," I said. "The girl's father doesn't have it. He's never had it."

There was a long silence. "Then you must acquire it."

I pointed at the small figure cowering at the edge of the

wall. "Let her go. You can get your jade skull without hurting her any further."

Stray beams of light shone into the man's eyes. For a moment it was as if two tiny moons were floating in the center of the chamber. I thought I heard something, along the outer wall. A scraping. If he heard it, too, he showed no sign.

"Do you have any idea how valuable this jade skull is?" he asked.

"Not as valuable as a little girl's life."

He barked a harsh laugh. "You are a fool. The jade skull is the most valuable antique in the *world*!" His eyes blazed brighter. Muscles in my face must've twisted. He noticed and stared at me quizzically. "You think I'm mad, don't you?"

I didn't answer.

"Then let me show you." He leaned over and lit a small oil lamp. The guttering flame cast eerie beams into the thick darkness. He reached atop his head, grabbed at the dirty linen, and ripped the turban off his head. Laughing crazily, he bowed. The flickering light showed a thousand scars crisscrossing the top of his head like some sort of nightmarish spider's web.

He rose and his mad eyes stared into mine.

"Do you know *why* these lines were etched on my skull? Do you have *any* idea?"

I realized that my mouth was open. I closed it.

"These scars are a badge of honor," he continued, "designed to remind me that my mission in life is to find the jade skull! They were put there when I was a boy, by the monks who trained me. Monks who trained me for high position. Why me? Why the son of a common Mongol yak herder? Why should I be trained for high position? Because the monks had determined that inside here . . ." he pounded his gnarled fist on his chest. ". . . inside here resides a great soul. The reincarnated soul of a great man. The reincarnated soul of the emperor who had once owned the jade skull!"

I suppose he mistook my stupefied expression for understanding. He lowered his voice, as if we were conspirators.

"My name in this life is Ragyapa." He waved his hand dismissively. "Don't bother to write it down. You will find the name Ragyapa on no passport. It is my religious name only, not my official name. But centuries ago, while wearing a different body, I was known by the name of Kublai Khan, grandson of Genghis Khan and the Emperor of the entire Central Kingdom!"

He laughed through yellowed teeth.

Kublai Khan was a conqueror greater even than Napoleon. In addition to his native land of Mongolia, he ruled China and Burma and Vietnam and Korea and Tibet. He tried twice, without success, to invade Japan. The fact that this man called Ragyapa believed he was the reincarnated soul of Kublai Khan convinced me—beyond a doubt— that he was insane.

"So you see," Ragyapa continued, "I am only trying to reclaim my own property. And regain the jade skull of Kublai Khan for its rightful owners, the people of Mongolia!"

His eyes narrowed.

"Many men have died for possession of this jade skull, Agent Sueño . . ." How did he know my name? Probably through Sooki. Or anybody else in the village, for that matter. Ernie and I were famous in Itaewon. ". . . and many more will die soon unless I gain possession of what is rightfully mine!" Once again, he thumped his fist on his chest. "The dead will include this undisciplined child, if you don't produce my jade skull for me."

"I told you, I don't have it."

"Then get it!"

Ragyapa's voice roared so loudly that for a second I thought he had suddenly transformed himself into a beast of the jungle. The sound thundered, filling the room.

"You have until the full moon," he told me. "If you do not turn the jade skull over to me by then, Agent Sueño, I will wring her scrawny neck. And each time I think you are not making progress in finding the jade skull, I will send her old hag of a mother another gift. Another gift such as the one she received in the plate of dumplings. Do you understand?"

Rage made my arms start to quiver. Why not punch out this creep right now? He was only another nut case. As mad as any bum wandering the streets of East L.A. What was holding me back? Fear. Yes, that was it. Fear. And in my entire life only one thing had ever allowed me to overcome my fear. And that was rage. This man of such greed and such brutality, this man who could hurt a child who had never harmed anyone, was filling me with that rage now. I fought it back. If rage blinded me, I would act foolishly.

"I understand," I said. "We will find your jade skull. But while I'm looking," I pointed at the cowering figure against the wall, "you will not mistreat this child. Do you understand *me*?"

Before he could answer, something crashed through the oil-papered window. Something black. Something huge. A giant raven smashing into the chamber. Wood splintered everywhere.

I knew what it was immediately. Ernie.

I lunged at Ragyapa.

It was my rage and my desire to free Mi-ja that made me move in on him so quickly. Still, his reflexes were those of a Siberian tiger. Something whizzed out of the darkness. Not his fists because I had my eyes on those. But his foot. Somehow I sensed it coming and twisted out of the way at the last moment. The toes slammed into me like blocks of iron, missing my crotch but ramming full force into my stomach.

Air exploded out of me. I fell to the floor, clutching my stomach, floundering for breath like a giant catfish.

Ernie was stunned by his crash through the window and crawled on all fours on the wood-slat floor. Ragyapa shuffled forward and kicked him hard in the ribs. Ernie let out a groan and rolled over.

A herd of footsteps charged up the stairway. If any of them belonged to Herman, he'd be greatly outnumbered.

Whistles shrilled through the night. The KNPs. They were downstairs. Ragyapa and his Mongolian thugs would be trapped.

I still couldn't breathe. I tried to rise. It wasn't working.

Ragyapa snatched up Mi-ja, shuffled through the darkness, and pushed on something that creaked and let out a groan. Suddenly starlight streamed through a rectangle in the temple wall.

As the herd of men trampled over me, I raised myself up and took a swing at one of them but all my efforts got me was a thump on the side of the head. I fell back down.

Ernie was on his feet now, bouncing around like a marionette, throwing jabs and neat combinations. One of the thugs noticed, stepped inside his punch, and elbowed him neatly in the throat. Ernie crashed to the floor.

I heard more footsteps downstairs. Boots. Maybe it was Sooki who'd notified them. Whoever it was, the KNPs would save us. I was sure they would.

I tried to crawl toward Mi-ja. If I could hold her, protect her, maybe I could keep these foreign thugs off of her until we were rescued.

But when I looked up, she was gone.

A large plank had been laid down outside of the rectangular hatchway in the side of the pagoda. I dragged myself along the floor until I could see that the splintered board reached to the top of the stone wall, more than twenty feet across a dark chasm.

Ragyapa scurried across the plank, holding Mi-ja under his arm.

I bellowed in anger. None of the thugs even looked back. One by one, they tiptoed across the narrow causeway.

We had been so close. Why hadn't I brought my .38 to Itaewon tonight? We never carried arms on the black market detail, but if I'd only made an exception this one time. I wanted to blow their brains out. Each one of those arrogant bastards.

Still, I admired their planning. A wooden plank through a secret opening in an ancient Buddhist temple.

No way I could've picked up on that one.

Soon, all of Ragyapa's thugs had crossed to the safety of the stone wall. I heard gruff cursing in Korean and then the cops started upstairs. I crawled toward the plank.

If I could just hold it, I thought, so the KNPs could use the plank to cross the chasm and chase those Mongols down. We could get Mi-ja back.

Still barely able to move, I slithered closer to the edge, reached out with both hands, and grabbed on to the plank. At that moment, two thugs atop the stone wall gave it a mighty tug. I held on as tightly as I could but the wood slid through my grip. A splinter needled my skin and, as they pulled, sliced deeper into my flesh.

I screamed.

The plank slid through my fingers, tearing my flesh, and fell into the chasm, clattering to the cobbled road below. The last of the dark figures leapt off the far side of the stone wall and disappeared.

Ernie crawled over to me, clutching his side. Perspiration streamed off his forehead.

"Was that her? Was that Mi-ja?" he asked me.

I watched drops of blood squeeze past the splinter in my hand. "That was her."

Ernie spat into the night. "Next time, I'll blow me some asshole's brain out. Right through that pile of rags he calls a turban."

8

BLOOD FROM THE FIRST SERGEANT'S NECK RAN UP THE VEINS behind his jaw, reached his gray sidewalls, and began to pulse.

"*Kidnapping?* And you didn't *report* it?"

Ernie shrugged. "Herman the German didn't want us to."

"Herman the *who?*"

"Herman the German. An old retired lifer."

The First Sergeant of the Criminal Investigation Division paced around his desk, reached the coffee counter, and fumbled with a thick porcelain mug. He was a thick-shouldered man and always wore his dress green uniform to work, unlike Ernie and me, who were required to wear civilian coats and ties during regular duty hours. We both sat in straight-backed army-issue chairs. The ones we always sat in when we received our ass-chewings.

The First Sergeant returned to his desk, placed the half-full coffee mug in the center of the immaculately white blotter, and leaned toward us.

"A Korean National Policeman was injured! Hospitalized with a severe concussion. His M-one rifle was stolen." The First Sergeant shook his head, not sure whether the injured man or the lost weapon was more important.

After Ragyapa and his thugs escaped from the Temple of the Dream Buddha last night, Ernie and I caught holy hell from Captain Kim, the Commander of the Itaewon Police Station. When Kim was given the report about the shenanigans at the Virtuous Dragon Dumpling House, he figured it was me and Ernie. And when he discovered that an abduction was underway in his precinct, he was incensed that he hadn't been informed. Later, he followed the wide swath we had left up Hooker Hill and, with a few of his men, surrounded the Temple of the Dream Buddha. Somehow, before the foreign thugs escaped, they managed to surprise one of Kim's men in an alley, beat him, and steal his M-1 rifle.

The Korean National Police were on the case now— with a vengeance—crawling all over Herman the German and Slicky Girl Nam. With one of their own hurt, the KNPs had a particularly strong reason to bring the foreign kidnappers to justice.

"Eighth Army is catching hell from the ROK Government." The First Sergeant stared into our eyes, searching for something, not finding it. "And you aren't authorized to keep the kidnapping of a military dependent secret, no matter what the reason."

"Mi-ja is not a military dependent," Ernie said. "The adoption wasn't legal. Slicky Girl Nam just bought the kid from some poor farm family who couldn't afford to feed her anymore. Herman never got her a military ID card."

The First Sergeant slammed the desktop. Murky fluid erupted from the mug.

"I don't *give* a damn! When something as important as a kidnapping happens and you become involved, you report it, Sergeant Bascom. You understand me? You — report — it!"

Ernie didn't seem in any way fazed by the First Sergeant's hollering. He sat back in his chair, legs crossed, coat open, as calm as a deacon in a private pew.

"Look, Top," Ernie said, picking lint from his pants leg, "have you been to the one-two-one Evac lately?"

"What the hell are you talking about, Bascom?"

"About your blood pressure. You really ought to have it checked."

The First Sergeant's knuckles whitened around the coffee mug. "Listen, Bascom. You, too, Sueño. Don't you two worry about my goddamn blood pressure. You just do your jobs. And when there's a kidnapping, you *report* it. You understand me?"

Ernie looked over at me. "Did you jot that down, George?"

I had a small notebook out, notes I'd taken on the case. I ignored Ernie's remark and gazed into the First Sergeant's gray eyes.

"We had reason to believe," I said, "that they'd murder the little girl if the Korean National Police were notified." I held up my hand before the First Sergeant could interrupt. After returning to the barracks last night, I had carved out the splinter in my palm and patched and medicated the wound as best I could, but it still ached with a dull throb. "You're right. I realize now that with KNP help we might've been able to rescue the girl last night. But we'll never know for sure. Too many cops, and the kidnappers might not've shown themselves. Anyway, that's over now. Herman's filed a formal complaint at the Itaewon Police Station."

My businesslike tone of voice seemed to calm the First

Sergeant somewhat. Ernie slouched in his seat. He knew what I was doing. Ruining his fun. He loved nothing better than to antagonize the First Sergeant. Like poking a dragon in its lair.

"What's your next move on the case?" the First Sergeant asked.

I was a little surprised by the question. Usually, the First Sergeant tries to control every aspect of our investigations. This time, he apparently realized that he would only get in our way. All the principals, other than Herman the German, were Koreans or Third Country Nationals. The First Sergeant couldn't speak Korean, didn't know anything more about the country than what he learned on the military base, and once he was out in the Korean villages, he had no more idea of how to proceed than the Man in the moon. Ernie and I, however, had proven our ability to work off-post. I spoke Korean. Ernie had an almost instant rapport with people of any nationality—when he chose to. We were the best investigative team the First Sergeant had. And he knew it.

And the pressure was on him. The honchos at the Eighth Army head shed were raising hell. Now that the word was out that a military dependent—even an unofficial one—had been kidnapped, the howls for revenge were rising. The secret fear of every American colonel and hotshot diplomat is that some sneaky Korean will some day swipe their child. It had never happened before, but now something close to it *had* happened.

The American community in Korea wanted blood.

And that wasn't the only case Eighth Army was barking about.

The First Sergeant reached into his desk drawer, pulled out a Korean newspaper, unfolded it, and slapped it down on his desk in front of us.

"Anybody here look familiar, Bascom?"

The photo was grainy, but the image was unmistakable. Ernie. Manhandling the business girl who had tried to claw his eyes out last night. Behind him, I emerged from the black and white shadows, carrying the little nun. We looked like pirates preoccupied with rape and pillage. The headline said it all: *GI ATTACKS BUDDHIST NUN.*

Nothing else was on the front page. Only feature stories about the riot that followed and the outraged reaction from the Temple of the Celestial Void, the little nun's home base. And a short bio of Choi So-lan. Who she was. How she came to be a Bride of Buddha.

"It hasn't hit the television yet," the First Sergeant said. In Korea, the government doesn't allow the TV stations to start broadcasting until five P.M., after the end of the working day. "But it will tonight, and then Eighth Army's going to be in a world of waste."

Ernie spread his fingers. "A little bad publicity, Top. We've been through it before."

"Why were you attacking that whore?"

"I wasn't. She was attacking me."

"Sure. And now that she has this photo to back her up, she'll probably file a charge against you and try to settle for big bucks."

"No way, Top."

The First Sergeant raised his gray eyebrows. "Why not?"

"She's an Itaewon business girl. They all love me. That was her method of showing affection."

"My ass. The Community Affairs Officer at Eighth Army's about to shit a brick over this. He and the Commanding General want you both to stay away from cameras. You got that?" The First Sergeant turned to me. "What do you have so far, Sueño, on the mugging of that nun?"

"We spotted the perpetrator, but didn't get a positive ID

on him because of the poor lighting. I do suspect, however, that he might be reporting into sick call for a broken rib."

I held up my left fist. Ernie guffawed.

The First Sergeant jotted a note. "I'll have somebody check with the medical command. Anything else?"

"And you might also have them check on a damaged finger," I told him. "The nun claims she chomped down on him pretty hard. Drew blood."

"Will do," the First Sergeant said. This is what he liked. Crisp police work. What I added to my report brought a frown back to his face.

"The perpetrator appeared to be a black GI," I said.

"Shit! That makes it more complicated."

Ernie's eyes shone at the First Sergeant's discomfort. "Why's that, Top?"

The First Sergeant either didn't notice Ernie's enjoyment or didn't care. He lowered his head, still talking but lost in thought.

"Because the CG has been trying to improve race relations in the command. This will just complicate things."

"Why?" Ernie asked. "She was a Korean nun, not a white nun."

"Still, some of the blacks might think we're just pinning it on them."

"Meaning we have to arrest somebody?"

"The Korean government is demanding it."

"Whether it's the right guy or not?"

The First Sergeant looked up. "I didn't say that! Of course, it has to be the right guy."

Ernie grinned. "Sure it does, Top."

The First Sergeant pointed his finger at Ernie. "Don't go twisting my words, Bascom."

Ernie spread his hands. "I didn't. I just repeated them."

I stood up. Action's the only way to stop their bickering.

"We have two hot cases. Which one do you want us to start with?"

"Neither," the First Sergeant answered.

"Neither?"

"That's right. The mugger of the Buddhist nun will be a snap to pick up. Ask a few questions in the barracks, check with the medical clinics, somebody will pop."

I wasn't so sure about that. Amongst the black troops of Eighth Army, the distrust of the CID ran deep. Especially with some of the ham-handed methods most of the agents used: Just ask questions of some GI, while all his buddies are watching. Ernie and I went more direct. We gathered evidence of lawbreaking on somebody and then forced them to tell us what we needed. Snitching or the stockade, that's what it came down to. They always chose snitching.

The First Sergeant had no such doubts, however. He tapped a ballpoint pen on the top of his desk.

"It's this kidnapping that has me worried," he said. "But the KNPs are on it now and you can bet they'll do a thorough job. Anyway, it falls under their jurisdiction since the victim is a Korean citizen."

"They won't turn jurisdiction over to us?"

"Not on your life. Not after the anti-GI feeling these newspaper headlines are causing. Still, the head shed wants us to assist in any way we can."

I saw where he was going with this. "They want insurance," I said. "In case the KNPs don't find the kidnappers."

"Exactly. I've already checked it out with the Provost Marshal, who's cleared it with the Commanding General."

Ernie rose halfway out of his seat. "You want to pay the ransom to these clowns?"

"Only as a last resort."

"But the kidnappings will never stop, then."

"Yes, they will. The kidnappers will never leave the

country. We'll see to that. And once they're apprehended, Eighth Army will formally request that the Korean government treat the case as an international incident."

"Meaning we'll cut their foreign aid if they don't give them the prison sentence that we want?"

The First Sergeant spread his fingers. "That's up to the ambassador, Sueño."

Ernie slumped back down in his chair. "They'll do it," he said. "The Koreans will do whatever we ask them to do. Including executing these guys, if that's what it takes."

"The punishment will be up to them."

"Sure it will," Ernie said.

The economic and military foreign aid provided to South Korea by the United States Government runs into the hundreds of millions of dollars each year. With a case as serious as the kidnapping of an American dependent— even a dependent of unclear legal status—you can bet that Eighth Army would flex its muscles and tell the Korean government how it wanted the case handled. And what they wanted done would be done quietly—so everyone saved face—but it would be done. That was certain.

I took a deep breath. "So you want us to find the antique jade skull," I said, "in case we have to trade it for Mi-ja."

"That's exactly what I want."

"Piece of cake," Ernie said. "When we find it, do we get a bonus?"

"The only bonus you'll get," the First Sergeant said, "is not getting court-martialed for dereliction of duty."

"Hey," Ernie said, "I finally wheedled something out of the old skinflint."

The First Sergeant glared at him. "That's right. You'd better get busy. And I want to see all your reports—on my desk—before anybody else sees them."

"Of course, Top," Ernie answered. "What do you think? We're going to send them to Dear Abby?"

As we stepped toward the door, the First Sergeant called us back.

"By the way, once you find that skull, if possible, try to use it to bring that little Korean girl back alive. The head shed doesn't want to see her dead. Bad for everyone concerned."

Ernie chomped on his gum. "Especially her."

We strode down the long hallway toward the CID Admin Office. All I could think about was the deadline Ragyapa had given us. Until the full moon. I shook it off and shoved Ernie's shoulder.

"Why are you always messing with the First Sergeant? You're going to give him a heart attack one of these days."

"Not possible."

"But his blood pressure's high."

"When that old lifer had his guts issued, the supply sergeant was fresh out of one important internal organ."

"Let me guess."

"That's right," Ernie said. "The source of all tender emotion. The human heart."

Back in the Admin Office, Miss Kim, the fine-looking Korean secretary, was pecking away at her Remington electric. Staff Sergeant Riley, the Admin NCO, sat hunched over a stack of paperwork.

"How's it hanging?" Ernie asked.

"Okay," Riley growled. "You found that jade skull yet?"

At the mention of the jade skull, Miss Kim stopped her typing and swiveled in her chair. She nodded to me and smiled at Ernie.

Ernie sat on the edge of her desk and offered her a stick of ginseng gum, which she accepted. As they chomped happily, Ernie reached into his jacket pocket, pulled out a felt purse, and flopped it down on top of Miss Kim's type-writer.

I recognized the purse. The Buddhist nun had given it to Ernie last night at the Itaewon Police Station. Ernie pointed to the embroidered Korean lettering.

"What's it say?" he asked Miss Kim.

Miss Kim picked up the little felt pouch in both hands, holding it as if it were a sacred artifact.

"It say, 'Choi So-lan,'" she answered. "Everybody talk about her. Last night some GI knuckle-sandwich with her."

Miss Kim balled her small fist and swung it sharply through the air.

"That's right," Ernie said. "And me and my partner here, George Sueño, we were just about to kick his ass when he ran away."

I knew what Ernie was doing. Gathering brownie points. To help him in his long-standing campaign to invade Miss Kim's panties.

Miss Kim looked up at him. "May I open?"

"Sure. Why not?" Ernie answered. "All that's in there is Buddha's money."

Ernie studied Miss Kim's red-tipped fingers as she fumbled with the leather drawstring of the purse. A bubble of saliva formed on his lips. Ernie has two fetishes: manicured hands and unshaven armpits. Both drive him to distraction.

Miss Kim turned the purse upside down and a handful of bronze coins and wads of crinkled bills clattered atop her desk. The last thing out was a jade amulet. While Miss Kim fondled the amulet, Ernie counted the money.

"Three thousand five hundred and eighty won," he said. "About seven dollars U.S. This is what that little nun risked her life over?"

Miss Kim nodded vehemently. "Oh, yes," she replied. "It is Buddha's money."

She held the jade amulet up to the light. A calm-looking Buddha, his eyes half closed, sat on a floating cloud. One leg was folded beneath him in the lotus position and the other leg pointed down. The lowered foot held back a snarling demon who was trying to claw his way up toward heaven.

The workmanship seemed exquisite to me. This amulet had to be worth a lot more than the three thousand five hundred and eighty won that the little nun had collected from the business girls in Itaewon.

"What is it?" I asked Miss Kim.

She cooed softly while fondling the pale green amulet in her long fingers. "The Buddhist nun who give this to Ernie, she really like Ernie."

"How do you know?"

"If she no like, she no give him this." Miss Kim pointed to the figure at the top of the amulet. "This is Maitreya, the Buddha of the Future. Below is Mahakala, the Lord of the Demons. This jade amulet, it will protect Ernie. Make sure nobody hurt him."

Ernie snapped his gum. "Good. I could use a little protection."

Reluctantly, Miss Kim handed the amulet back to Ernie.

"You take very good care of this," she said.

"Are you kidding?" Ernie said. "I take good care of *everything*."

WE WALKED UP ITAEWON'S MAIN DRAG, PAST THE UNLIT NEON signs and the flatbed trucks unloading beer and ice. A light smattering of rain filled the morning air, but not enough for us to bother with a raincoat or an umbrella. The workers were half naked, the muscles of their shoulders and arms steaming with exertion.

Clusters of Korean women lined the sidewalk, some of them arranging flowers, others holding a black-and-white blowup of a face I recognized: Choi So-lan, the Buddhist nun who'd been attacked by the American GI.

"They're turning her into a saint," Ernie muttered.

"Looks like it." I was worried that some of the demonstrators would recognize us from the photo in the Korean newspapers, so I kept Ernie moving through the big double doors of the Itaewon Police Station.

The waiting room was jammed with citizens inquiring about their loved ones who'd disappeared after last night's riot. Ernie and I pushed through the crowd and demanded to speak to Captain Kim.

The surly Desk Sergeant shook his head. "No way, he's busy." When he saw that Ernie was about to jump over the counter, the Desk Sergeant slipped me a sheaf of brown pulp. "He say give you this," he said.

It was the official police report on Mi-ja's kidnapping.

Deciphering it from the Korean was difficult without my dictionary, but I managed to pick up the main points.

Sooki had been brought in for questioning and asked about the man who paid her to deliver the messages to us. As I suspected, she had little to add to what she'd already told us. She was paid, told to do a job, and that was it. The description of the man who'd paid her was clear enough. Big, burly, turban on his head. Ragyapa. The same guy I'd seen last night in the Temple of the Dream Buddha.

The most interesting part of the report was the interrogation of the caretaker of the temple. He had been bound and held against his will by Ragyapa and his thugs. The kidnappers were Buddhists, the caretaker said, but they were followers of an obscure sect. Definitely not worshipers of Maitreya, the Buddha of the Vision of the Future.

I explained all this to Ernie.

"Then who are these assholes?"

"The caretaker can't be sure. But he traveled outside of Korea in his youth and he made a guess."

"Which is what?"

"They're Mongols," I answered.

"Mongols? You mean like in the Mongol hordes?"

"Exactly. They worship a five-skulled deity known as Mahakala."

"The same dude who's in that amulet the little nun gave me," Ernie said.

"Right. His official title is Lord of the Demons."

Ernie pulled out another stick of ginseng gum and stuffed it into his mouth. "The Lord of the Demons. Good. About time he arrived in Itaewon. Don't know what's keeping him."

9

ERNIE EASED THE JEEP THROUGH THE SWIRLING SEOUL TRAFFIC.
Herman the German sat in the front seat—because he was
too fat to fit in the back—and gave directions: Mukyo-
dong, the high-rent boutique and nightclub district in
downtown Seoul. Herman was bruised and battered from
the beating the Mongol thugs had given him last night in
the Temple of the Dream Buddha. But he stared stolidly
ahead into the rain. Unmoving.

The time limit until the full moon had been gnawing at
me all day. The almanac we kept on the bookshelf in the
CID office told me how long we had: five days. Five more
days and four more nights until the full face of the moon
rotated once again toward the earth.

As I thumbed through the slick pages of celestial calcu-
lations I remembered the carved stone calendars of the
ancient Mexicans. When I was a child in East L.A., I'd
seen pictures of these calendars in books and read about
their amazing accuracy. I asked my schoolteacher about

these wonders, but my questions irritated her. Their accuracy wasn't proven, she told me, and it would be better if I stuck to my textbooks instead of reading about ancient calendars and UFOs and the like.

Later, I found out how wrong she'd been. The calendars were accurate. And useful to the people who'd created them. But I resented the years I'd been allowed to believe that nothing of value had ever been produced in the country of my ancestors.

The jeep rattled through the rain of Seoul, swerving in and out of speeding traffic. With the tips of his fingers Ernie kept a light touch on the steering wheel, and chewed nonchalantly on his wad of gum. I forced my mind back to the job at hand.

Actually, I was surprised the kidnappers had given us five days. But at the time we'd made the deal, they hadn't known that the KNPs would be breathing down their necks. If they believed that we'd betrayed them to the cops, Mi-ja might already be dead. But I was hoping that their greed for the jade skull would keep her alive. Nothing to do now but search for the skull, wait for further word, and hope for the best.

I leaned forward and spoke to Herman.

"This Lady Ahn, what kind of setup do you have to contact her?"

"She contacts me. Last time we talked, she scheduled this meeting." He glanced at the watch on his hairy wrist. "She said noon. It's almost that now."

The next question I left unasked. If this antique was so valuable, would Lady Ahn be willing to give it up? Even to save the life of a child?

We would see.

The rain hit the windshield in a drizzle. The herd of red taillights before us clumped tighter as Ernie bulled his way into the traffic of downtown Seoul.

Herman had told us that Slicky Girl Nam's hooch was crawling with Korean police. "They smell a buck," he'd said. A cop had been stationed at the pay phone outside the pharmacy on the corner, waiting for it to ring again with a message from the kidnappers. But so far this morning, nothing.

With a screech of tires, Ernie pulled over in front of a long taxi queue.

A thick chain was welded onto the floorboard of the jeep in front of the driver's seat. Ernie lifted it, wound the chain loosely through the steering wheel, and padlocked it. With the short chain looped through the steering wheel, no potential car thief would be able to make turns and therefore wouldn't be able to make a getaway. Like most military vehicles, the jeep didn't have an ignition key, just an on and off switch that anyone could use.

We piled out. Both Ernie and I were wet. So was Herman, but he didn't seem to mind.

We waded through the crowd: businessmen on their way to working lunches and women bundled in raincoats, umbrellas over their heads, clutching string-handled bags with the logos of upscale shops emblazoned on them in glossy print. A wrinkled crone dressed in rags pushed a cart carrying a hot pan. She wailed out her message as we passed.

"Bam sajuseiyo!" Please buy chestnuts!

Even in the gray afternoon dimness, neon spangled the main road of Mukyo-dong and lit the narrow side alleys jammed with dress shops and coffeehouses and pool halls.

We rounded a corner and Herman stepped down a flight of broad marble stairs. The steps led into what seemed to be an explosion of jogging shoes hanging by their laces. A cloudburst of rubber and canvas.

Pushing with our hands, we bulldozed our way through the hanging shoe garden and emerged onto a walkway illuminated by a row of overhead fluorescent lamps. All around us were stands packed full of T-shirts and leather bags and thick silk blankets and mother-of-pearl-inlaid jewelry cases. Men on bullhorns hawked their wares.

"Shopping," Ernie grumbled. "Somehow I always end up goddamn shopping."

We had burrowed our way into an underground market.

After another twenty yards or so, the lane widened and a sign pointed the way to a well-lit corridor. *Ji Ha Chol*, the sign said. Subway.

Here, stands sold newspapers and snacks and cups of iced coffee to go. Pedestrians streamed back and forth. In the middle of the intersection stood a tall woman in a light blue raincoat and matching broad-brimmed hat.

Long fingers with wickedly red nails held the blue raincoat clutched across her chest. Pale skin was pulled tautly across a face chiseled with high cheekbones. Her lips were full and clamped tightly. Her eyes were black, blazing with defiance.

A goddess, I thought. A goddess like I'd seen in the National Museum, carved in bronze, floating in silk robes across the face of the moon.

Ernie chomped on his gum. "Not a bad-looking chick."

Herman stopped a few feet in front of the woman, peering up into her unblemished face. A medieval serf paying homage to a feudal princess.

I realized now why she'd chosen this place. Commuters streamed past but none of them did more than glance in our direction. They were busy. In a hurry to get to work or squeeze in some midafternoon shopping or finish whatever errand seemed pressing enough to bring them out on this rainy monsoon day.

We were surrounded by people, and yet we were alone. No one was listening. Even an overweight fireplug of a retired American infantry sergeant and two dripping wet

GIs and a statuesque Korean woman in a tailored blue raincoat weren't enough to garner more than passing interest.

Herman stood with his fists clenched at his sides, his blue eyes watering like peeled grapes. The Moon Goddess gazed down at him and began to speak.

"Why you bring two men?"

Her voice was low and strong, used to projecting command. The English was well-pronounced, with a hint of an accent that seemed almost French. A few words were left out of the sentence but not enough that you couldn't understand her meaning.

Slowly, she turned toward me. The eyes of a she-wolf burned into mine. Under their challenge I almost stepped back. I forced myself to hold my ground.

Usually it's Ernie who attracts all the feminine attention. The excitement he generates seems to enflame every female nerve ending within a hundred yards of his antics, as if his hormonal system was steadily broadcasting waves of magnetism. But Lady Ahn seemed immune.

She stared only at me.

Herman glanced back at us, his blue eyes suddenly befuddled, as if he'd forgotten we were following him.

"They're helping," he told the woman. "I have a problem."

Lady Ahn's tapered eyebrows lifted slightly. "I don't know about your problem. You and I, we only do business. That's all."

"But this is more important than business," Herman insisted. "Someone stole my daughter."

Lady Ahn took half a step backward but quickly regained her composure. Long fingers rippled across the buttons of her raincoat.

"I am sorry," she said courteously, "but that is not my problem."

"The men who took her," Herman persisted, "they want the jade skull."

"No!" Lady Ahn shook her head. "They cannot have it. I only pay you to have an American ship it to the United States. That's all."

Herman held his stubby body still. "These guys are Mongols. Not Koreans. You must sell the skull to me now. These foreigners want it. If they don't get it, they will kill my daughter."

Lady Ahn clutched her raincoat even tighter and looked from side to side, as if contemplating an exit.

"I am sorry," she repeated. "I am sorry if this business has caused you trouble. But I cannot turn over the jade skull to foreigners. It is too important. More important than you can possibly know."

"It's just a piece of artwork," Herman said.

"No!" Lady Ahn snapped. "It's more than that. It is the key to everything. The key to the restoration of my country."

"But I need it *now*!"

The sudden rage in Herman's voice startled Lady Ahn. It startled Ernie and me, too. Before we could react, he'd lunged toward her.

She stepped back swiftly, but Herman was too quick for her. He grabbed Lady Ahn by the elbows, lifted her off her feet, and carried her back toward the small coffee stand with white-smocked girls milling around filling orders.

Lady Ahn's beautiful face twisted in rage. She shouted: *"Salam sollyo!"* A person needs help!

Ernie chuckled. "Goddamn Herman knows how to negotiate, doesn't he?"

I slapped him on the shoulder. "Come on!"

We rushed forward and grabbed Herman's arms, but still he managed to shove Lady Ahn up against a cement pillar. She was kicking back now, screaming at him, her long red claws slashing at his eyes.

Herman screamed, let go of her, and clutched his forehead. Lady Ahn started to run but Ernie jumped in front of her, holding his hands in the air, hopping from side to side as she tried to dodge past him.

"Wait now," he said. "A little girl's life is at stake. More important than any goddamn antique. We have to talk about it."

Lady Ahn continued to scream: *"Salam sollyo! Salam sollyo!"*

A crowd gathered. In the distance I heard the heavy tromp of boots, then a police whistle.

No sweat. Once I flashed my CID badge and explained the situation, the Korean police would interrogate Lady Ahn thoroughly, possibly arrest her for trying to smuggle a valuable national treasure out of the country, and help Herman get his daughter back.

Everything would be under control.

I tried to push through the growing crowd, ready to help Ernie hold on to Lady Ahn.

A broad-shouldered Korean man in a business suit stepped out of the throng and shoved Ernie. Instead of just taking it and concentrating on doing his job, Ernie swiveled on the man, bristling, ready to throw a punch. Lady Ahn took advantage of the interruption and made a break for it. I yelled.

"Ernie! She's getting away!"

Ernie slammed past the Korean man and lunged for Lady Ahn, but she turned and swiped at his face with her nails. Ernie was expecting it: He raised his forearm just in time to ward off the red razors.

Lady Ahn stepped forward, embraced him, then kneed him in the balls.

Like a deflating balloon, air exploded out of Ernie. He

bent over, blue-faced, cheeks bulging, green eyes threatening to pop out of his head.

I ran forward. Lady Ahn sprinted away.

Whistles and pedestrians converged on us from every direction. Lady Ahn was still screaming as she ran: "*Salam sollyo! Salam sollyo!*"

Two more Korean men stepped out of the crowd and lowered themselves like rugby players. I was running full speed, hemmed in on either side, and couldn't make a turn or come to a stop fast enough. As I crashed into the men, they rose up and head-butted me. I knocked them down, but sprawled on the floor after them.

I scrambled to my feet, breathing hard. But I was only fast enough to see Lady Ahn's blue raincoat fading into the sea of sneakers and handbags and leather jackets.

Behind me, a pack of Korean police were arresting the struggling Herman. Piling on. Finally, one of them managed to snap the handcuffs on first one big hairy wrist and then the other. Soon they had him down and stood over him like a tribe of Eskimos surrounding a blood-soaked polar bear.

I trotted away from them, through the catacombs of the shopping maze, trying to catch my breath. At a few stalls I stopped and asked the proprietors if they'd seen a tall woman in a blue raincoat. Each time they looked at me as if I were mad.

Finally, I found my way outside and stood in the drizzling rain. The afternoon overcast revealed nothing but tired commuters, their heads bowed, trudging through monsoon mist.

I ran back and forth between the alleys. Searching. Finding nothing.

No blue raincoat.

No tall woman.

No beautiful Lady Ahn.

10

AFTER FLASHING MY EIGHTH ARMY CID BADGE, I PLEADED WITH the KNPs not to arrest Herman. They took us to the Mukyo-dong Police Station, unlocked Herman's handcuffs, and made him sign a statement accepting full blame for the incident. What finally convinced them not to arrest him, however, was that the victim, Lady Ahn, had disappeared without filing a complaint.

When we left the police station, Ernie bopped Herman on the head. "Why don't you learn to act like a civilized human being, Herman? Always attacking people. What are you, some kind of a caveman?"

Talk about the critic being guilty of the crime.

Standing on the busy sidewalk, Herman seemed oblivious to the sting of Ernie's knuckles. Flesh crinkled on his sloping forehead. "What'll we do now?"

"We'll find Lady Ahn," I said.

"How?" Herman asked. "I don't have any way to contact her."

"She found you once, didn't she?"

"Yes."

"Then *we* can find *her*."

Herman looked up at Ernie, puzzled. Ernie slapped Herman on the shoulder. "Believe him," he said. "George Sueño can sniff out a kimchi jar in a field of garlic. He's Mexico's answer to Sherlock Holmes. Maybe not a very good answer, but an answer nevertheless."

Herman stared at Ernie, still confused.

The drizzle turned into a steady patter. I grabbed Herman's arm and walked him toward the jeep.

"Where are we going?" he asked.

"To meet some of your partners in crime," I answered, "and ask them a few questions."

WE SPENT THE AFTERNOON IN DOWNTOWN SEOUL, TALKING TO various antique dealers. The way I figured it, when Lady Ahn went looking for an American who would be able to ship a valuable antique to the States, she would've talked to Korean businessmen in the trade. The only ones able to guide her to the right man. Namely, Herman the German.

Once we found the dealer who had tipped her off to Herman, we could backtrack from there.

If we found her, I could get a better handle on what was so valuable about the skull. Once I understood that, I might be able to understand what would bring men thousands of miles from Mongolia to Korea to lay claim to a piece of carved jade. And why. And knowing why could lead to us finding them.

First I had to know more about Herman's business. He was reluctant to tell us—a couple of CID agents—since his business was mainly illegal. After Ernie rapped him on the skull a couple of times, however, he opened up.

Herman and Slicky Girl Nam had been running a thriving black market business for years. Buy the duty-free goods in the PX and the commissary on-post, sell it to the Koreans off-post. Double your money. But that hadn't been enough.

In Itaewon, a lot of shops catering to international tourists had started to spring up over the last few years. The shops specialized in name-brand products—sneakers and jackets and blue jeans—that were produced here but shipped overseas to be sold at inflated prices. Since Itaewon purchased factory-direct, the goods cost about half what you'd pay for them in America or in Europe. Itaewon also specialized in brassware, handcrafted leather goods, and, more to the point, antiques.

In recent years, so many ancient chests and vases and statuettes had disappeared from Korean estates that the government had started to clamp down. Many shipments were turned back, the owners fined—even jailed. Certain items, such as handcrafted celadon vases, couldn't be shipped out of the country at all. The translucent green pottery was considered irreplaceable and as such, a treasured national artifact.

But household goods shipped out of the country by United States military and diplomatic personnel were never inspected by ROK customs personnel. Only by GIs deputized as U.S. Customs agents. For the most part, these inspectors were either incompetent, lazy, corrupt, or all three. And they definitely weren't worried about stopping Korean national treasures from leaving Korea.

Therefore, if you wanted to ship a valuable antique out of the country, placing it in a GI's household goods shipment was the safest—and cheapest—way to go.

That's where Herman came in.

Somewhere along the line some smart Korean antique dealer had contacted him and asked him to set up an outbound shipment. Herman had agreed, contacted a GI on his way out of the country, and a price was set for him to ship the item in his household goods. Later, the Korean dealer would have somebody in the States contact the GI and retrieve the smuggled item—and ship it on to the ultimate buyer in the States or Europe or Saudi Arabia.

Everybody made out. The GI was paid for his trouble, half in cash up front, half when the shipment arrived in the States. Herman raked off a percentage. And the antique dealer didn't have to worry about being arrested by the Korean Ministry of the Interior.

Word spread. If you wanted something shipped out of country, Herman the German was the man to contact.

Through the overcast monsoon afternoon, Ernie and Herman and I moved from antique dealer to antique dealer. Ernie usually waited in the jeep, since parking in downtown Seoul is mostly impossible. Herman and I talked to the dealer. Seeing if he'd sent any referrals Herman's way lately. Describing Lady Ahn as a last resort.

After twelve joints, we'd found nothing.

"You have a hell of a thriving business," Ernie told Herman.

Herman gazed through the rain-smeared windshield of the jeep. "A guy's got to eat."

Ernie glanced at Herman's belly. "You're getting plenty of that done."

No matter how you insulted him, Herman never responded. His watery blue eyes stared straight ahead. His expression stayed worried.

The gray sky darkened as if someone had pulled a shade. The rain fell harder. Herman guided us to another antique shop and Ernie stopped in front, waving with his free arm for the honking cabs behind us to pass.

"This is the last one," Herman said.

"Good," Ernie said. "We still have time to make Happy Hour."

"No way," I said. "We have an ancient jade skull to find and not much time to find it. Sobriety could prove useful."

Ernie groaned, flicking his wrist for us to hurry. "Make it quick, will you?"

Herman and I clambered out of the jeep, crossed the sidewalk bobbing with umbrellas, and pushed through a beaded curtain into the cool confines of a dimly lit shop.

At first I thought he was one of the statues. A long-faced man, wrinkles sagging from limp cheeks. He wore a jade-colored tunic, gray pantaloons, and soft-soled cloth shoes.

Then the statue opened his mouth and said, "*Oso-oseiyo*"—please come in.

Herman came right to the point. "You send somebody to talk to me, Papa San? A woman?"

The old dealer gazed back and forth between us, his face calm, almost smiling.

"Yes," he said. "I did. A beautiful woman."

Bingo! I stepped forward. "Why did she want to talk to Herman?"

The old man turned away from me, upset by my passion.

"*Kulsei*," he said. It's that way.

I stepped back, lowered my voice. I didn't want to frighten him into silence.

"We've lost contact with this woman," I told him. "That's all. We're just trying to find out why she wanted to talk to Herman in the first place."

Maybe my English was too complicated for him, maybe he just wanted time to think. But when he didn't respond right away I repeated what I had told him in Korean.

He turned back to me, his face somewhat offended, and spoke in clear English.

"She told me she wanted to talk to an American. An American who can send something Stateside."

"Did she tell you what she wanted to ship?"

"No."

For once Herman seemed to grasp the situation. The old man was clamming up, not sure whether I was a cop or if Herman wanted him to talk to me or what. Herman opened his big fists and spread his fingers.

"Where is she now, Papa San? I need to talk to her. It's important."

The old man studied Herman.

"You don't want to talk to her."

"Yes, I do."

The old man shook his head. "No. She is a dangerous woman."

At the corners of Herman's mouth, drool started to bubble.

The old man shuffled over to a glass counter filled with intricately painted porcelain artifacts.

"First, I no want tell her about my friend." He pointed at Herman. "But she told me she would go to police. Tell them I do black market with Americans." He shrugged his narrow shoulders. "So I told her about this man."

I still didn't see it. "What makes you think she's dangerous?"

"The way she talks."

I waited.

"She's from the south. She has . . . how you say? *Ssaturi.*"

"An accent," I said.

"Yes. But more than that." The old antique dealer looked at me, his eyes defiant, daring me to laugh. "This woman," he said, "is a *yangban*."

The *yangban*. The educated Confucian elite of the country. The landowners. The people who for centuries had been the only class who could read and write and therefore ran the politics and economics and cultural life of Korea.

"You're afraid of this woman because she's a *yangban*?" I asked.

The old man chortled at that. "No. *I* am *yangban* also. She's more than that."

"Then what is she?"

"She is *Sung Cho*."

It didn't compute. "You mean *Yi Cho*," I said. From a prominent family of the Yi dynasty, the dynasty that had ruled Korea for over five centuries.

The old man waved a withered hand. "No. *Sung Cho*." From the Sung dynasty.

"In China?"

He nodded.

For a moment I thought he was kidding me. The dynasty of the Sung emperors in southern China had been overthrown by the Mongols more than seven hundred years ago.

I let that sink in. In 1911 the Japanese had deposed the last king of the Korean Yi dynasty. The Crown Prince was taken against his will to Japan and forced to marry a Japanese woman. Later, he renounced any claim to the throne, and when Korea became a republic in 1945 the issue of nobility was long dead and buried. Maybe it was odd, in this day and age, to be worried about nobility. But that some people would still claim royal blood didn't seem strange to me. Every other person with a foreign accent in the United States claims to be related to a king or a count or a rajah.

"All right," I said. "So this woman has some blood from the rulers of an old Chinese dynasty. What's the big deal?"

The old man let his head sag. "You don't understand."

"Then explain it to me."

"Some people haven't given up." The leather of his neck quivered and he sat down on a stool. "They still think they can get it all back."

"Get what back?"

"The Dragon Throne. They think they can overthrow the Communists in Beijing and seat someone of royal blood on the Dragon Throne of China."

BACK IN THE JEEP, ERNIE WAS PISSED THAT WE WEREN'T GOING to Happy Hour. But the old antique dealer had given us the name of the *yoguan*—the Korean inn—where Lady Ahn had been staying. We had to check it out. And check it out now.

"It's in the Sodae-mun District," I told Ernie. "It'll only take a minute."

"Damn," Ernie muttered. "All the hors d'oeuvres will be gone."

He jammed the jeep in gear and the wheels swished through the wet streets.

For over four thousand years, Korea had been a separate country, at least by Western standards. What wasn't widely understood was that throughout that time, sometimes to a greater or a lesser extent, Korea had snuggled beneath the protective wing of the Chinese emperor. Although the Korean monarch ruled his kingdom without interference, Korean foreign policy always was conducted while looking over the royal shoulder for the approval or disapproval of the emperor sitting on the Dragon Throne of China. Even in official documents, Korea proclaimed itself a "little brother" of China. Their relationship was a filial one. The subordinate to the superior.

To give this relationship concrete form, the Korean king, every year, sent a convoy of dignitaries to the Dragon Throne in the Forbidden City in Beijing. The dignitaries presented tribute to the Chinese emperor consisting of thousands of *taels'* worth of magnificent goods.

During much of the Yi dynasty, before 1911, the Koreans were probably as independent as they'd ever been. But this was because of the growing power in the Far East of Japan and Russia. And the weakness of the Chinese Empire, which was being carved up by foreign powers and ravaged by the scourge of opium.

When the antique dealer had told us that Lady Ahn was from nobility that predated the Yi dynasty, he was speaking of traditions that were ancient indeed.

THE WOODEN STAIRS CREAKED AS HERMAN AND I WALKED UP the short flight of steps that led to the Beik Hua Yoguan, the Inn of the White Flower.

Immaculate varnished floors and railings led to a small foyer with a vase of white peonies and a display with a black-and-white photo of someone's ancestor in traditional dress. The odors of incense and ammonia wrestled in the dust-speckled air. We found the owner squatting on the vinyl floor, scrubbing nonexistent dirt with a *kullei*, a thick hand towel. She was a husky woman, with black hair tied back by a white bandanna. People spent their lives in places like this. Scrubbing floors, changing bedding, suffering obnoxious customers. This woman looked as if she had. Rising easily, she gazed calmly at Herman and me.

"*Bang pillyo heiyo?*" she asked. Do you need a room?

I answered in Korean. "We don't need a room. We're looking for a woman who is staying with you. A tall woman. Young. Maybe twenty-two. From the south. She calls herself Lady Ahn."

The woman broke into a broad grin, as if satisfied about something. "Ah," she said. "The good lady."

"Is she here now?"

Her brow wrinkled. "Who are you?"

I showed her my badge. "*Mipalkun honbyong.*" Eighth Army Military Police.

She gazed at the badge for a moment, then looked up. "What has she done?"

"Maybe nothing. We just want to talk to her."

"Not possible now. She left over an hour ago."

Herman's shoulders sagged.

"Did she say where she was going?" I asked.

"No."

"Show us her room."

It was upstairs on the third floor and just as fastidiously clean as the other rooms. It told me nothing.

"Show me the guest register."

Back at the counter, the woman pointed a finger at Lady Ahn's signature. *Ahn Myong-lan*, it said. *Ahn*, one of the venerable family names in Korea, and *Myong-lan*, meaning Bright Orchid. Her Korean National Identification card number was there, too. I copied it down. Every place of lodging is required to record them. Place of residence: Taejon, a major city halfway down the peninsula. But no other address.

I looked at the innkeeper. "She must've said something about where she was going next."

"No. She kept to herself. She was out a lot."

"Doing what?"

"I don't know. But she never brought a man back with her."

"You called her 'the good lady.' Why?"

"Because she treated me, and everyone, as if we were servants."

"And she has a southern accent?"

"Yes. Cholla Namdo, I would think." South Cholla Province, two hundred miles away.

"But according to this she lives in Taejon, farther north than that."

"Yes. She received a couple of phone calls from there." The woman pointed to the heavy black telephone, which rested on a knitted pad.

"Who called her?"

"A woman."

"Did you get the name? Her address? A phone number?"

"No."

"But you must remember something."

"Yes. When the good lady talked to that Taejon woman she did not seem so arrogant. In fact, she called her 'onni.' And she even laughed."

Onni means older sister. But Korean women who are friends often refer to the older woman in the relationship as *onni*. It doesn't necessarily mean that they are actually related.

"What else did they talk about?"

"About old things. Buying. Selling."

"Antiques?"

"Yes. And the place where this Taejon woman was calling from sounded like a business. I heard a bell tinkling in the background, people talking. It didn't sound like a home."

So Lady Ahn was getting calls from an older woman who owns an antique shop in Taejon. It was something.

"When this Lady Ahn checked out, how did she act?"

"In a hurry. She came in and I heard her packing, getting ready to go. She called me from my cleaning to settle the bill."

"Did she say anything to you?"

"Not to me. But she caught a cab right across the street. He asked her where she was going."

"What did she answer?"

"Seoul *yok*." The Seoul train station.

Herman looked confused. Even though he'd lived in Seoul for years and knew a lot of words and phrases, his Korean was still not able to keep up with complicated sentences. Of course, neither was his English. I thanked the woman and we started down the flight of steps toward the front gate.

The owner stood at the top of the stairs, arms folded.

"There's one more thing," she said.

I turned. "What's that?"

"The entire time she was a guest here, there were men waiting across the street. After she left, they left."

"They were watching her?"

"No. I don't think they were watching her."

"Then what were they doing?"

"They were old men. Sages. Disciples of Confucius. I think they were worshiping her."

WHEN WE ARRIVED BACK AT THE JEEP, ERNIE WAS CURSING.

"Goddamn Happy Hour is *over* already," he told us. "By the time we get back, there won't even be one deviled egg left."

Herman checked his wristwatch. "Shit! I'm late."

"Late for what?" I asked.

"To change the charcoal. Nam will kill me if I let it go out."

The pressed charcoal briquettes of the *ondol* heating system have to be changed every few hours or the fire sputters and dies. It's an involved process to start it up again.

"You're pussy-whipped," Ernie said.

Herman didn't answer.

"We'll drop you off," I told Herman.

The rain kept up a determined drizzle and Ernie kept up his bitching, all the way back to Itaewon. Lady Ahn had escaped. She was our only connection to the jade skull and the jade skull was our only connection to Mi-ja. We had to keep searching. Taejon, where Lady Ahn's *onni* lived, was our best bet.

Ernie didn't know it yet, but he was going to miss out on a lot more than just a few chicken drumettes.

After grabbing some chow at the Eighth Army Snack Bar, we went straight back to the barracks, packed our overnight bags, and headed to the H-101 Helipad on Yongsan Compound South Post.

Now the rain was being whipped back and forth by wind gusts of up to eighty miles an hour. All flights other than emergency aircraft were canceled until further notice. I argued with the NCO in charge and flashed my badge and even threatened to call the Provost Marshal, but it did no good. No choppers were lifting off unless it was a life-or-death situation.

"There is some good news," the sergeant told us. "The weather's expected to break sometime tonight."

"And you'll put us on the first thing smoking?" I asked.

"You got it," he promised.

Resigned to our fate, Ernie and I grabbed a couple of cups of coffee and tried to make ourselves comfortable on the wooden benches in the tiny waiting room.

I leafed through a magazine. Ernie bitched about missing Happy Hour. We waited.

IT WAS ALMOST MIDNIGHT, AND I HAD STARTED TO DOZE OFF, when the Flight Control Sergeant shook me awake.

"Call for you."

Rubbing my eyes, I stumbled to the counter and grabbed the telephone. It was Herman. In the background I heard a woman shrieking. Slicky Girl Nam.

"We received another package," Herman said.

"From the kidnappers?"

"Yeah."

"What's it say?"

"It doesn't say nothing. It's a clipping from a newspaper or something. A picture of the full moon."

Nam was crying and gnashing her teeth so loudly in the background that I could barely hear Herman.

"They're reminding us of the deadline," I said. "That's it? There was nothing else in the package?"

"Something was wrapped in the paper."

My stomach started to churn. Herman's voice seemed eerily calm.

"What was it, Herman?"

"A part of a finger. Mi-ja's. Two knuckles' worth."

I heard something plop on wood. The phone line crackled. Slicky Girl Nam's wailing increased in volume. Herman came back on the line.

"Sorry," he said. "I dropped it."

I swallowed through a dry throat but managed to speak. "Have the KNPs come up with anything?"

"*Nada*. Not a goddamn thing."

"Keep a grip, Herman," I said. "Ernie and I are on our way to Taejon."

I hung up the phone.

Ernie was still stretched out on the wooden bench, his head propped up on his overnight bag, his hands laced across his stomach, snoring calmly. He slept with the clear conscience of a Catholic saint.

Three hours later the rain slowed and the wind stopped. I shook Ernie awake and the two of us clambered aboard a roaring Huey helicopter.

As we lifted into the sky, the stars emerged from behind drifting monsoon clouds. They sparkled brightly, as if each one had been polished by the hand of God.

11

STEEL NEEDLES OF AGONY SHOT UP FROM MI-JA'S SEVERED FIN-
ger. The pain from her missing ear had long since settled
into a pounding ache. Still, all these sensations had gradually spun into an unbreakable cocoon of misery. A cocoon
Mi-ja was coming to accept.

Mi-ja was most worried about whether or not her legs
would work. A couple of times she'd raised from her squat
on the cold cement floor, but she managed only a few
faltering steps. Yet she must find strength in her legs and
she must find it now.

Every time she moved the chain rattled. She had to be
careful, because if she made too much noise one of the
men would come in to check on her.

Her face was just a few feet from the commode, the
chain attached to her neck wrapped around the pipe that
ran into the cement floor. The toilet hadn't been flushed
since she was brought here, and Mi-ja was glad of that

because she was afraid that if anyone tried to flush it, rancid filth would overflow onto the floor.

The stench bothered her not at all. She had more important things to worry about.

All night, as she faded in and out of consciousness, she had heard the voice of her mother. "Hardship is the lot of women like us, Mi-ja. You must be a strong girl, even if it means you have to leave us and go far away to live with someone else."

She had promised her mother she would be strong—and now she would prove it.

Mi-ja had a plan.

Footsteps approached. She held her breath. Now was the time. She would be allowed only one chance.

The door of the *byonso* crashed open. Mi-ja flinched. Dim light filtered in, slicing into her eyes. She covered her face with both hands.

One of the foreign men stomped across the cement floor. Roughly, he grabbed the chain and jerked it upward, almost choking Mi-ja in the process. He reached in his pocket, pulled out a key, and unlocked the padlock that held the chain. With the side of his boot, he kicked Mi-ja back away from the commode.

Mi-ja kept her eyes tightly shut, cowering against the cement wall. Within seconds she heard the steady stream of urine splashing into the waste-filled porcelain bowl.

Slowly, she leaned backward on her haunches, flexing the stiff muscles of her thigh, testing their strength. Flesh quivered in protest. Still, her body must obey her commands. Her legs *had* to work. It was vital that everything proceed in one unbroken motion.

The stream of urine was steady and hard. The reek of it drifted into Mi-ja's nostrils. She forced herself to take a deep breath, opened her eyes, and launched herself forward, twisting behind the urinating man, slamming her thin shoulders against the far cement wall.

The chain around her neck slipped and clattered to the floor. The urinating man swiped his hand backward, but his fingers slithered off the flesh of Mi-ja's upper arm. She hit the wooden door—squirming, turning, running— pushed through, and burst out into the outside room.

Men squatted on a large vinyl-covered floor, tossing oddly-shaped wooden sticks into a pile between them. They looked up as she ran past them, scattering dried bones in her wake.

Men shouted. Men reached out. But none of them moved quickly enough. She was already at the front door. She slammed into it and pushed but it wouldn't open.

Frantically, Mi-ja twisted the handle. It slid downward and she pulled the door ajar. She stepped out into the hallway, glancing both ways. A window. People on a street far below. The voices of children. Men and women selling fresh produce. The sounds of Korea. The sounds of home.

She heard footsteps behind her and sprinted with all her strength toward the window. Too high to jump out. A stair- way. She ran toward it.

Mi-ja was naked, she knew that, but her mind had no care for modesty. Only freedom. Only real air. Like an animal escaped from its cage, that was all she could think of.

As she rounded a corner she saw it. A metal grillwork door blocking the stairway. She grabbed the tightly woven bars, rattled them. They wouldn't budge.

Trapped.

The footsteps of the men were in full pursuit now. No way to slip under the grillwork, but she could climb over it. There was enough space at the top for her to slip through. But there wasn't enough time. Her pursuers would be on her in seconds.

In the hallway behind her she spotted a small wooden hatchway. It probably led to a storage shed for charcoal.

She stepped back up the stairs, pushed the door. It held at first but then, just as she was about to surrender to despair, it shifted slightly. She pushed harder. The door popped open. Flat back. She was right. The dank space was filled with charcoal dust. She crawled inside and shoved the small hatch back into place, holding it with her trembling hands.

The footsteps exploded above her. A herd of men. All shouting. All tromping down the stairs. Angry sounds. None of which she could understand. She dared not breathe; she prayed her strength would last long enough so that she wouldn't lose her hold on the wooden door.

Someone shouted again and metal clanged on metal. A key. And then the creaking of the grillwork gate as it swung open. Footsteps pelted down the stairway.

They'd been fooled! They thought she'd climbed over. Mi-ja listened. All was quiet.

She dared not believe it at first but now she must. The men were gone. Now was her chance to escape. They would be back soon, once they discovered that she wasn't out on the street.

Scraping her shaking fingers against the splintery wood, she pulled back the small hatchway and crawled out. Silently, she crept back up the steps, back toward the room where she had been held hostage. Cautiously, she peered inside the open door. No one was left inside.

She scurried down the hallway until it turned and turned again. The doors in the long corridor were shut tight and all was silent. Then she saw it. A back stairway.

She crept down, taking one step at a time. Listening. No sound.

At another window she could see below. This stairway led to a back alley lined with large crates of refuse. She must hurry before the men searched back here. She sprinted down the stairway but before running outside she stopped, squatted low, and glanced both ways. The alleyway was perfectly still.

Freedom at last, she thought.

With a great burst of breath, Mi-ja leapt out into the alleyway and ran as fast as her shaky legs would carry her, past the line of crates. Only a few more steps and then she would be on the main street. Others would be there. Street vendors, shop owners, maybe—if she was lucky—even a policeman.

Only a few more steps.

She was about to reach the last crate when a demon emerged from the shadows.

Even as Mi-ja's mind flooded with terror, her small body kept moving.

A turbaned man—not a demon—leaned toward her and, with a great paw, swiped out at her naked body. Fingers like iron spikes bit into the soft flesh of Mi-ja's arm, pinching bone.

The fingers softened and wriggled and slithered around her like curling pythons.

Mi-ja howled.

Not in pain but in anguish. Anguish for the freedom that had been so near.

The man in the turban slapped her hard across the side of her head. He slid his enormous hand across her mouth, covering her nose. Choking, Mi-ja kicked and struggled, but it did no good.

The turbaned man's lips slid back, revealing blocks of yellowed teeth.

He hoisted Mi-ja into the air, tucked her beneath his arm, and sauntered nonchalantly down the alleyway. He kicked open the creaking back door and reentered the endless darkness of the ancient wooden building.

12

# #

Ernie squinted through a tinted visor. "Prepare for heavy swells."

"What?"

I couldn't hear him above the roar of the helicopter engine. We were in the back compartment, behind the pilot and the copilot, wearing helmets and loose flight crew overalls.

Ernie leaned toward me. "I say it looks like a world of shit is about to roll down on top of us!"

I gazed out at the gray overcast of the Taejon city skyline, a jumble of brick and cement-block buildings—nothing over three stories tall—in a sea of traditional Korean homes with blue and red tile roofs. Off toward the Yellow Sea, a solid wall of black clouds rolled steadily inland. Occasionally, a spark of lightning flashed out of the roiling mass.

Looked like we were arriving just in time. The monsoon

was about to hit hard, and all military flights were sure to be canceled.

The chopper dove through the mist, bounced a couple of times, and came to rest on a cement helipad. We were on Camp Ames, an American compound on the outskirts of Taejon. We took off our gear, folded the overalls neatly, and thanked the crew chief for the ride.

After flashing our identification to the MPs at the front gate, Ernie and I stepped out into the streets of the city. As we walked down the brick sidewalk, I felt as if we'd stepped back into a different era.

The city of Taejon had been leveled during the Korean War. What had been rebuilt was done, for the most part, in a traditional Korean style. Each hooch was surrounded by bushes sprinkled with purple *mukunghua*, the Korean national flower. Long-faced men on three-wheeled pedicabs rolled solemnly through the narrow lanes.

There wasn't even much hustle outside the GI compound, a spot which had to be a major source of income for this slow-moving city. No bars. Only a couple of tailor shops and souvenir emporiums. A short row of pedicab drivers waited patiently outside them for passengers, and didn't run up offering "special deals" for Americans.

One driver looked surprised when I spoke Korean to him.

"Yes, you want to go downtown," he said, "but where downtown?"

"*Chungang*," I replied. The center.

The driver smiled at that and I asked him how much and he told me. Ernie and I piled into the back of his pedicab. We paraded through the quiet lanes toward downtown Taejon.

Unlike Seoul, where everything is cement and exhaust fumes, the streets of Taejon were lined with elm trees rustling in the morning breeze. Shop owners splashed buckets of water on brick sidewalks and scrubbed away filth with long-bristled brushes. A few cars wound through the traffic, but mostly the thoroughfares were filled with women on foot, carrying bundles over their heads, and men on bicycles, clanging out warnings of their whereabouts with the ringing of tinkling bells.

The leather sandals of a bevy of robed Buddhist monks slapped past us. The monks strode up ancient stone steps toward an intricately carved and brightly painted wooden pagoda. Schoolchildren in yellow caps crossed the street and bumped into each other every time the teacher brought their centipedelike procession to a halt.

The pedicab driver dropped us off in front of the August Moon Yoguan. When I paid him he said *"Komowo-yu,"* ending the verb with a *"yu"* instead of a *"yo"* as they would've said in Seoul. It was an accent that I was to hear often in these southern realms.

Ernie stood on the sidewalk with his bag draped over his shoulder, glancing around, chomping on gum.

"Nice place they got here," he said.

I wasn't sure if he meant the city of Taejon or the August Moon Yoguan, but whatever it was I had to agree.

The August Moon Yoguan was a ramshackle two-story building made of darkly aged lumber. Through the red-lacquered gate of the inn was a small garden filled with roses and tulips camouflaging rows of earthen jars pushed against the outer brick wall. A woman in a long blue cotton dress and rubber slippers with upturned pointed toes stepped out to greet us. She bowed.

"Oso-oseiyo." Please come in.

The rooms were cheap, and larger than what we were used to. Each had a sleeping mat with a bead pillow, a two-foot-high writing desk, a black-and-white TV, and a bathroom. Hot water in the early morning and in the evening from eight to ten.

We ordered chow.

A boy from a Chinese restaurant brought in a tin box and Ernie and I stared at it suspiciously. But when the boy slid up the side panel and pulled out a plate of *chap chae*—fried noodles laced with beef—and two steaming bowls of shrimp fried rice, we relaxed, paid him, and commenced to wolf down the food.

We didn't speak as we ate. We were both thinking the same thing. How in the hell were we going to find this Lady Ahn in a city we didn't know? How in the hell were we going to keep little Mi-ja from having her throat cut by the scar-headed Ragyapa and his Mongol horde? And what the hell was this all about?

I glanced out the window. The first plump droplets of monsoon rain hit the sidewalk so hard that they bounced like Ping-Pong balls. A steady patter tapped against the wooden roof. I wondered about the moon. It would be more than three-quarters full tonight.

We finished our chow, went downstairs, told the *yoguan* owner we'd be out, and pulled our jackets over our heads. Splashing through puddles, we trotted into the bustling center of downtown Taejon.

A WISE MAN ONCE SAID THAT THE WAY TO GET RICH IS TO ASK A bunch of tomfool questions and listen well to the answers.

Apparently, this wise man had never been an American CID agent in the Korean city of Taejon. Most of the people we talked to didn't have answers. They were just frightened.

There isn't a very large American military presence in Taejon, and tourism in these parts is unknown. We might've been the first long-nosed foreigners many of these people had ever encountered.

Ernie wasn't helping matters much. He was impatient and surly, and the more people acted as if we'd just landed in a spaceship from Mars, the more Ernie felt compelled to feed into their neuroses and act weird.

At one shop that specialized in porcelain, he grabbed a teacup and sipped on it, slurping loudly. Of course there was no liquid inside. Ernie wiped the dust out with his tongue. At an antique furniture shop, he rummaged through an ancient hand-carved cabinet as if he'd stashed something there and forgotten where he'd left it.

It hadn't been a big problem finding the antique shops themselves. Most were clustered in the upscale shopping area downtown. At each place, I described the type of jade-carved skull we were after but every time I did, I received puzzled looks. No one had heard of such a thing.

I also described Lady Ahn. Everyone seemed intrigued by a woman so tall, so gorgeous, but no one had any leads for me. Until finally the face of one old crone puckered at the description. She pointed. A shop. Two blocks down the road, she said.

"The owner is very famous," the old woman said in Korean.

"Famous how?" I asked.

"Famous in nightclubs."

Her wrinkles drew in so tight around her lips that I was worried that her face might turn inside out.

Ernie looked at me quizzically, knowing something was up. "We have a lead," I said in English and switched back to Korean for the old woman. "What's the name of this shop?"

"Rising Phoenix," she replied. "Very easy to find. The outside is as brightly painted as the owner's face."

"What's her name?"

"The Widow Kang. But she never calls herself that."

"What does she call herself?"

"Fifi."

"Fifi? You mean like a Frenchwoman?"

"Yes. She thinks she's too good for Taejon." The old woman shook her forefinger at me. "But she's not. We're too good for *her*."

On the way down the road I explained to Ernie what the old woman had said.

"Fifi? You've *got* to be shitting me."

"No way. That's what she said. Fifi."

"And this gal, this Fifi, is hooked up with this Lady Ahn?"

"Looks like it."

BY THE TIME WE REACHED THE SHOP, ERNIE AND I WERE BOTH drenched. The front was ornately carved, each wooden knob painted with vivid splashes of color. A shimmering bird lifted off of the branch of a cherry tree, scattering pink blossoms in its plumed wake.

"Damn," Ernie said. "This Fifi would fit right in on Madison Avenue."

"She's not exactly a bashful maiden."

We pushed through the door. A bell tinkled.

An attractive young woman in a short skirt and silk blouse stepped out from behind a glass counter and bowed. "*Oso-oseiyo.*" Please come in.

She must've been about nineteen, short hair, cute as one of the hand-painted dolls lining the shop's shelves. After a long day of interviewing sullen merchants, Ernie couldn't help but grin.

He ran his hand through his short hair, flicked monsoon rain onto the wood-plank floor, and pulled out a package of ginseng gum. He offered her a stick. She took it in her soft hand, smiled, and bowed again.

"Fifi *oddiso?*" I asked. Where's Fifi?

The girl shook her head. "Fifi's not here. Can I be of service to you?"

I decided not to translate that for Ernie. Vulgar retorts we could live without.

"It's very important that I talk to Fifi Kang immediately," I told her. "It has to do with Lady Ahn."

The color in the girl's cheeks began to fade. She shook her head.

"Fifi is not here now. If you give me your calling card I will be sure that she contacts you."

I glanced at Ernie, rolling my eyes. A look of disappointment descended on his face as he deciphered the signal—I suppose he had been looking forward to being nice to this girl—but he shrugged and shook the expression off almost as soon as it appeared. His eyes darted around the room, searching for something to smash.

"We must talk to Fifi," I told the girl. "If we don't, my friend will become very angry."

Her slim fingers began to quiver. "You can't talk to Fifi," she said. "She is busy. She must not be disturbed."

Ernie snatched up a crystal carving of Kuan Yin, the Buddhist goddess of mercy. Her long robes draped gracefully to her feet. Her face was as calm as the face of an eternally youthful goddess should be. No expensive salves. No face-lifts. Just eternal beauty. She would put Max Factor out of business.

Ernie surprised me. He didn't pulverize the statuette immediately. Instead, he walked slowly up to the frightened girl and faced Kuan Yin toward her blinking eyes.

"Do you know who this is?" he asked.

I translated. *"Nugu inji allayo?"*

When the girl didn't answer, Ernie continued. "It's *you,*" he said, "and if you don't tell us where Fifi is, this is what's going to happen."

As soon as the last word of translation had emerged from my mouth, Ernie flicked his wrist and slammed the goddess into the glass counter. Shards of crystal exploded into the air. The girl leapt away, shoving her cupped fists against her mouth, her eyes wide with fright.

"Fifi *oddiso?*" I shouted. Where's Fifi?

"The bathhouse," the girl stammered. "In the alley behind the shop. Not far."

"And Lady Ahn?"

"Yes," she said, nodding, pressing herself up against the wall, as far away from Ernie as she could get. "She's there, too."

Ernie looked at me.

"Jackpot," I said and started toward the back door.

He gazed at the still intact Kuan Yin, kissed her on the top of her tiny head, and set her very carefully down on what was left of the shattered counter.

13

SINCE THE KOREAN WAR, PLUMBING HAS COME A LONG WAY. But in many areas of the country it's still primitive. People don't drink tap water, not unless they boil it first. Cold water service is provided almost everywhere, but hot-water heaters are still something few people in Korea can afford.

For bathing, people go to bathhouses. It's cheap and convenient and for many people somewhat of a social event.

Unlike the Japanese, Koreans don't take community baths. Women use one side of the bathhouse, men the other.

The Seven Luck Bathhouse was a long cement-block building painted powder blue. At the entrance sat a young woman nursing a baby.

The woman leaned back in fright when Ernie and I emerged from the rain. Her long bruised nipple popped out of the infant's moist mouth. Immediately, the child began to wail, grasping with its tiny claws until the mother regained her composure and managed to shove her breast back into the baby's greedy reach. All was quiet again.

"Kang *Kuabu oddiso?*" I asked. Where's the Widow Kang?

The woman glanced toward the entrance marked *yoja.* Women. "In there," she said.

Ernie understood and started to push through the swinging door. The young mother shouted. "Women only!" She pointed. "Men must enter on the other side."

Ernie looked back at her, smiled, then pushed on through into the steaming darkness.

I slapped two thousand won, about four bucks, onto the rickety table in front of her.

"Police business," I said. "It will only take a minute. Don't worry."

The woman's face was still crinkled with concern but she grabbed the wrinkled bills and slipped them into a pocket in her long dress.

I pushed through the women's entrance and felt the steam grab onto my face.

The bathhouse reeked of mint-scented lather. At first I couldn't see Ernie. But my eyes became accustomed to the darkness and I made out his shadow down the long hallway. As I stepped down the corridor I felt the spongy spring of wooden slats beneath my feet. The walls were made of cement, and in each large room, water spit freely from nozzles onto women in various stages of undress. They were all busy. Scrubbing themselves with pumice stones, shampooing hair in great billowing cathedrals of suds, or drying themselves carefully while seated on short wooden benches.

Up ahead, Ernie stopped at the entranceway to each room and peered in, studying something carefully. I caught up with him. He glanced back over his shoulder.

"Checking the whazoos," he said.

"What?"

"Whazoos. When I find breasts large enough, I'll know we've found Lady Ahn."

What an investigator.

The women inside the bathhouse were so preoccupied with their own cleanliness, none of them had noticed us yet. We moved down the hallway. At the end, we heard wood slapping on flesh and the voices of two women. Laughing.

As we approached the room at the end of the hall, the slapping became louder. So did the laughter.

Inside, two tall Korean women, completely naked, were beating one another with willow branches. Both had their hair knotted up inside of white towels. With each slap, the women laughed louder, and each slap was delivered with more fervor. More joy.

Ernie and I stood mesmerized.

He mumbled through wet lips. "The whazoos," he said. "I'd pick 'em out of any lineup."

Lady Ahn was built like Venus, only better. Her limbs were long and straight, hips round, waist narrow, breasts heavy and ripe. At the V between her legs, jet black pubic hair stood out straight and lush with no hint of curl.

The other woman wasn't bad looking either. A little older, a little thinner, not quite as tall. Fifi Kang. She had a right to be proud of her figure, too. Still, she looked skeletal compared to the ravishing Lady Ahn.

The two women twirled, still beating one another with the quivering twigs. I was worried they might actually cause bruises, even cuts, on their golden flesh. But their swats were practiced. The flicks of the wrist delivered with just the right amount of snap. It was clear they'd enjoyed this ritual before.

Finally, Fifi Kang stopped, standing perfectly still, her

eyes wide. She lifted the white towel higher up on her forehead.

Lady Ahn, waiting for the next blow, turned when she didn't receive it. She saw Ernie and me standing in the doorway.

I was beginning to sweat. It was hot in here, and I felt like taking off my shirt. In fact, after soaking up the beauty of Lady Ahn, I felt like taking off my shirt and my pants and everything else.

The four of us stood frozen, staring into one another's eyes. Neither Fifi Kang nor Lady Ahn made any movement to cover their nakedness. I expected one of the women to scream. Instead, Fifi Kang raised her willow branch and rattled it at us.

"Dumb GI don't know this lady shower?" She waved the twig. "You go man side. Not here."

I started to speak but instead of words coming out I just croaked. Lady Ahn had me more worked up than I realized. I tried it again and managed something slightly better than a squeak.

"We're here about the jade skull," I said.

Lady Ahn stepped backward. Fifi Kang continued to brandish her twig.

"You go back my shop. You look at jade there. Plenty of jade. You no bother lady in bathhouse."

Ernie stepped into the shower room. Keeping his back close to the wall, he leaned in and switched off the water.

"What you doing?" Fifi Kang said. "You *kara chogi!*" Get out of here!

Ernie grabbed her twig and held it. Fifi Kang struggled for a moment but stopped when she realized struggling was useless. Ernie gazed deep into her eyes.

"Answer the questions," he told her.

By now, people had started to realize that two men were

in the women's bathhouse. Behind us, we heard footsteps, concerned chatter, shower spigots turning off.

"We want the jade skull," I said. "I know it's valuable, but we're willing to pay for it. Without it, a little girl in Seoul will be killed. She's already been hurt badly. You must help us save her life."

I pointed at Lady Ahn. "You knew about this, but still you ran away."

She turned away from me, angry now, over her shock, for the first time realizing her nakedness. She snatched a towel from a peg on the wall.

"Why you follow me?" she demanded. "Why you bother me? Why you don't leave me alone?"

"I can't." Not sure what I meant by that. Maybe something about the case. Maybe something else. "A little girl has been hurt. We heard her scream."

Ernie tilted the end of one of the benches, lifting it into the air. What the hell he was planning to do with it, I didn't know. Fifi Kang caught on quickly, however. Whatever it was that Ernie was planning wasn't going to be good.

"Okay," Fifi agreed. "We will talk. In my shop. You go outside wait. We get dressed."

"We'll wait here," Ernie said.

The smooth skin of Lady Ahn's forehead crinkled in rage. She'd had enough. She stormed forward, straight-armed Ernie out of the way, and pounded out the door past me. I gazed after her in admiration. All by herself, almost naked, she was as imposing as a royal procession. Unstoppable.

Fifi Kang, like a lady-in-waiting, scurried after her, droplets of water spraying in her wake.

Ernie dropped the bench with a bang and he and I followed. Ahead, soft flesh wiggled.

The dressing room had a plastic drape slid across it, and

Ernie and I waited as the two women dried themselves and got dressed.

Back at the entranceway, a door slammed. Gruff male voices barreled down the corridor. Boots pounded on planks.

Ernie glanced at me and lifted his eyebrows. I shrugged. Whoever it was, now that we'd gone to all the trouble of finding Lady Ahn, I wasn't leaving. Not until we obtained the jade skull.

The footsteps grew closer. From the cloud of steam, dark figures emerged. Khaki-clad. Visored caps. Nightsticks slapping at the seams of their trousers. The Korean National Police.

Maybe the girl at the Rising Phoenix antique shop had called them. Or maybe the young mother guarding the entranceway to the bathhouse. Whoever it was, it didn't matter now. The KNPs clearly had our number.

There were four of them, and they came to a halt a few feet in front of Ernie and me. The leader had a dark, mottled face, and his mouth was open, his eyes wide, staring up at me, amazed that two grown men would somehow make their way into a women's bathhouse. I spotted the insignia on his collar and read the engraved plate on the flap of his breast pocket. Lieutenant Ho. Central Precinct.

Ernie thrust his chest out, tugged up on the belt around his waist, and chomped loudly on his ginseng gum. The four policemen formed themselves into a semicircle around us, hands on the hilts of their nightsticks.

Lieutenant Ho jerked his thumb toward the front door. "*Pak ei ka!*" he snarled. "*Bali.*" Go outside. Quickly.

Ernie snorted. "No way, Charley. We're here on official police business."

Lieutenant Ho didn't understand but he knew Ernie

wasn't planning on following his order. His face flushed red. *"Jikum!"* he shouted. Now!

Ernie laughed.

It was too much. One of the policemen stepped in and grabbed Ernie's elbow. As if he'd been raked by claws, Ernie spun, launched his knotted fist, and backhanded the cop up against the wall.

"Tangsin weikurei?" Lieutenant Ho shouted. What the hell's the matter with you?

All the policemen unsheathed their nightsticks.

I leapt in front of Ernie, fumbled in my pocket, pulled out my CID identification.

"Jom kanman," I said. Relax. *"Uri Mipalkun honby-ong."* We're from Eighth Army.

I thrust the badge in front of me, waving it from side to side, as if it were a crucifix and I was trying to ward off a pack of vampires.

Lieutenant Ho clutched his nightstick, his knuckles turning white, his face burning crimson. Still, he somehow managed to control himself. He studied the badge carefully.

When he was finished, he gruffly told Ernie to show him his. Ernie bounced on the balls of his feet and puffed out his chest again, but I told him to cool it. Finally, he pulled out his badge and flashed it in front of Lieutenant Ho.

Lady Ahn and Fifi Kang stepped out into the hall. Both wore cutoffs and T-shirts and rubber thongs, routine garb for a trip to the bathhouse. Lieutenant Ho swiveled his attention to them.

"What is it with you?" he asked them angrily. "These two Americans, how do you know them? What are you doing with them?"

Lady Ahn stood taller and began to answer but the lieutenant cut her off, firing more questions at her. Ernie didn't like it. When he took a step forward, two of the policemen angled their nightsticks for a quick backhand to the skull if he came any closer. Ernie stopped, clicking furiously on his gum.

Lieutenant Ho was talking nonstop now, shouting, all his anger at not being able to arrest Ernie and me—at having his authority lessened in the eyes of his men; by foreigners yet!—focused now at the two women.

Fifi Kang fidgeted, smiled, and bowed, attempting to soothe the sputtering Lieutenant Ho. But Lady Ahn stood her ground, no longer even attempting to answer his questions, staring down imperiously at the furious policeman.

Lieutenant Ho was talking so rapidly I was having trouble following him, but I understood enough to see where he was heading. He was accusing the two women of consorting with foreigners, a crime if you're not a registered prostitute.

When Fifi Kang tried to explain that it was us who barged in on them, Lieutenant Ho shouted even louder. Finally, he barked out an order. The three other policemen slipped their nightsticks into their holders, stepped forward, and took Fifi Kang into custody.

It was more than Ernie could take. He shot forward like a Doberman on the attack and stood nose to nose with Lieutenant Ho.

"You can't do that!" he shouted. "They're our suspects. We found them and we're the ones who are going to interrogate them."

This was territorial for Ernie. He hunted down these women, they belonged to him.

The policemen started to drag Fifi toward the entranceway. Ernie grabbed her elbow and jerked her back.

There was no way shouting was going to solve this. The more Ernie embarrassed Lieutenant Ho, the less likely that the lieutenant would give in. I shoved Ernie against the wall and whispered urgently into his ear.

"Mellow out, pal. Let me try it my way."

When the first policeman reached for Lady Ahn, she slapped his hand. "*Manji-jima!*" she shouted. Don't touch me.

Fifi wiggled herself free from the policeman who was holding her and scurried over and embraced Lady Ahn.

"You'd better hurry," Ernie told me. "I'm about to knock me some KNP out."

I pulled out my badge again.

"We're here on official business," I said to Lieutenant Ho in Korean. "A case concerning the kidnapping of a child. A case that has the attention of the Eighth Army Commander and has the attention of your own Ministry of National Defense." I pointed toward Lady Ahn and the Widow Kang. "We *must* interrogate these two women. You are making that impossible."

Doubt flickered, for the first time, in Lieutenant Ho's eyes. Still, his face hardened.

"You interrogate them in prison."

Someone screeched behind me. A policeman. Four rivulets of blood ran down the side of his face. Fifi Kang stood in front of him, red nails bared. The injured policeman snapped open the holder of his nightstick and belted Fifi on the flesh of her arm. She screamed, and suddenly Ernie was in the middle of everything, windmilling one punch after another.

A KNP leapt on Ernie's back. Without thinking, I hopped forward and smashed the cop's head with a sharp left jab. He flopped to the ground like a sack of barley.

Another KNP came at me. I crouched and punched him in the stomach, and then I was shoved against a wall and I saw Ernie barreling toward the door, pushing the women in front of him.

Lieutenant Ho charged me with his nightstick. I hooked one of the wooden benches with my foot and slid it in front of him. The lieutenant crashed into it with his shins, howled, and slammed face-first onto the floor. As the other policemen started to close in, I picked up more of the short benches, tossing them into the narrow corridor, forming a barricade, and then I was backing out the door.

Through a curtain of rain, I saw Ernie and Fifi Kang and Lady Ahn disappearing down an alley. Ernie waved for me to follow.

I did. Sprinting at full speed.

We sloshed through the alleys, making dozens of hairpin turns, the heavy footsteps behind us gradually fading.

All four of us were breathing heavily when we finally stopped long enough to look back and catch our breath. Rainwater ran in rivulets down my face.

"We lost 'em," Ernie said.

"Great," I wheezed. "But for how long?"

Ernie caressed the raw knuckles of his right fist and grinned. "But it was worth it, wasn't it?"

I could never figure why he loved trouble so much. We were in deeper shit now than we had been since we first heard about this kidnapping two days ago, but Ernie seemed elated.

The two women seemed a lot more worried than Ernie.

"*Bali wa*," Fifi Kang said. Come on. "We go my hooch. Policemen no catchy up there."

"Yeah," I said. "You bet. Policemen no 'catchy up' there."

Ernie slapped me on the shoulder.

"You worry too much, George. Think positive." He pointed to the side of his skull. "That's the secret."

As we wound through the narrow pathways of Taejon,

rain slamming down on our backs, Ernie offered the two women a stick of ginseng gum.

Fifi Kang accepted. Lady Ahn stared at him as if he were a piece of dragon dung. Even with her hair sopping wet, she looked regal. Ernie grinned sheepishly and stuck the gum back in his pocket.

14

LADY AHN SAT ON A PLUMP PILLOW, THE PALE BLUE SILK OF HER billowing skirt spread before her. Her *chima* was embroidered in red and gold with the Chinese characters *su*, for long life, and *bok*, for good fortune.

Fifi, the Widow Kang, knelt on the floor and bowed, placing a lacquered wooden table in front of Lady Ahn. The table was laden with handleless porcelain cups and a steaming pot of imported Black Dragon tea. Shuffling backward, Fifi waited, her hands on her knees, until Lady Ahn poured steaming tea into the cups and handed them to Fifi, who in turn handed them to us.

Royalty doling out favors.

I'd heard a lot about royalty when I was growing up. Mexicans, like most people, are slightly in love with it. I was told proudly about Maximilian, the red-bearded Austrian archduke who'd been appointed by Napoleon III to become Emperor of Mexico. I was told somewhat less proudly about Quatemoc, the last emperor of the Aztecs, who'd been murdered by the treachery of the Spaniard Hernán Cortés.

I'd heard plenty about royalty, but I'd never seen it up close. Not until now.

Lady Ahn looked gorgeous on her low dais. Anybody's idea of a queen, or an unfortunate princess stranded amongst commoners.

Ernie chomped on a pecan cookie and slurped on his barley tea. "You have any *soju* around here?"

Fifi Kang shot him an evil look. "You wait for *soju*. You drink too early, pretty soon too much stinko."

"Hey," Ernie objected. "The sun's almost down."

I knew what he meant. Back at Eighth Army headquarters it was Happy Hour. The go-go girls were dancing, the cheap booze flowing. We both missed it. But my aching need was eased every time I gazed at Lady Ahn. The skin of her face was as smooth as the handcrafted porcelain cup I held in my hand.

She looked so gorgeous, so serene, that I almost didn't want to bother her with my questions. Still, questions had to be asked. I took a deep breath.

"Lady Ahn," I said, "tell me about the jade skull."

She tilted her head toward me and her eyes tightened slightly. "Why should I?"

Her English was pronounced expertly. No doubt that she'd been well educated.

"You know why you should," I answered.

I reached in my pocket and pulled out what even Ernie didn't know I had, a clump of red-stained newspaper. I tossed it on the table next to the tea. Slowly, the crinkled sheets opened, revealing the gore inside: crusted blood, shredded flesh, the shriveled remains of a little girl's ear.

Lady Ahn's face paled.

Fifi screeched, recoiled, but recovered quickly.

"What's the matter you?" she hollered. "Why you do that? Your brain go TDY?"

TDY. Temporary duty, when GIs are sent for short periods of time to assignments away from their base camp. With that one slip of the tongue, I learned a lot about Fifi Kang. She'd dealt with GIs before. Extensively. She knew our jargon. Maybe she worked on the compound as a clerk or a waitress. Maybe she dealt on the black market. Or maybe she had been a business girl.

A woman alone, building up the capital to open her own antique shop. Unless she were an heiress, the fastest way to do that was by becoming a professional girl. Looking at Fifi Kang, that's where I'd bet my money.

Ernie picked up on it, too. He chuckled and bit back into his pecan cookie.

Lady Ahn couldn't keep her eyes off the slivers of mottled flesh. Slowly, her face drained of blood. Pulling out my handkerchief, I picked the shredded ear up again and tucked it back into my pocket.

"That ear," I said, "belonged to an innocent child. The men who are holding her have already cut off one of her fingers. If we don't give them the jade skull by the full moon, they will kill her."

Trying to keep her hand from shaking, Lady Ahn reached for her tea. She sipped on it daintily.

Fifi Kang swung her mane of black hair toward me. "You bother her *too* much, GI. Why don't you shut the mouth?"

Ernie growled at her. Fifi tightened her lips.

"What I need," I said, still addressing myself to Lady Ahn, "is the jade skull. If I give the skull to these men, they will let the little girl go."

Lady Ahn didn't answer.

"We're willing to pay for it," I continued. "Between the

two of us," I nodded toward Ernie, "we could probably raise a few hundred dollars."

For the first time Lady Ahn laughed. The soft derisive laugh of a queen.

"Yes," she said. "You will pay for it. Everyone pays for the possession of the jade skull."

I waited for her to go on. She didn't. I leaned forward. "Tell us about it, Lady Ahn."

Ernie shot a warning look at Fifi. For once, she kept quiet. Lady Ahn sipped once more on her tea and cleared her throat.

"I don't have the jade skull," she said.

"But you made arrangements with Herman—"

She held up the soft flesh of her palm to quiet me. "Yes. I made arrangements. With something as valuable as the jade skull, one must make all arrangements in advance. Even before the piece comes into your possession."

Lady Ahn stared out the sliding paper door that led onto a narrow balcony. The gray pallor of the sky was darkening. A light rain began to fall. If it kept up, I wouldn't be able to see the moon tonight. How close was the silver orb to full? Too close. And getting closer.

We were on the top floor of a three-story brick building. Fifi had led us all up here the back way so the neighbors wouldn't see her bringing in two foreign men. She'd also called the girl at the antique shop and told her to lock up and go home and under no circumstances to tell anyone— especially the Korean National Police—the whereabouts of the apartment.

It was a nice joint. Plenty of antiques, a few paintings, everything immaculately clean. Ernie felt right at home. He was used to having women take care of him. He expected it. His attitude didn't seem to bother Fifi though.

Lady Ahn spoke again. "The skull was carved from one solid piece of jade during the Yuan dynasty."

I clicked it through my memory bank. Ernie was always laughing at me for checking out books from the post library on the history of the Far East. He said it was a waste of time.

"What are you going to *do* with it?" he often asked.

I never really had an answer for him. Until now.

The Yuan were the first foreign dynasty of China. The Mongols. Established more than seven centuries ago. Contrary to popular belief, Genghis Khan didn't conquer China. He conquered some of the northern provinces, but the conquest was completed, and the great Southern Sung dynasty finally defeated, by his grandson, Kublai Khan.

I said the name aloud, hardly aware that I was speaking. Lady Ahn's eyebrows lifted slightly. In approval, I hoped.

"That's right," she said. "The jade skull belonged to Kublai Khan."

My heart flushed with pride. I was glad this woman realized that I wasn't just some dullard who did nothing but drink beer and watch football games.

From what I'd read about Kublai Khan, he probably would've fit right in at Eighth Army headquarters during Happy Hour. He was a drinker. Not of beer or liquor but of *kumiis*, fermented mare's milk. As a matter of fact, most of his biographers say he died of alcoholism. It was something a lot of the Mongol conquerors had a problem with, although they didn't see it as a problem in those days.

Ernie was having trouble taking all this in. "Okay," he said, "you have some jade skull that belonged to an old Chinese king. So what's the big deal?"

Lady Ahn looked at Ernie as if he were a clump of night soil. But to give him his due, it wasn't a bad question. She must've realized that because she answered it.

"There is a very 'big deal' about this jade skull," she said carefully. "The design was not exquisite. Not that Kublai Khan minded. He was a Mongol, a warrior, a rough man.

They say that the green jade carving of the skull is so ugly it looks like a pockmarked face."

At the words, Fifi Kang flinched. Every vain woman's worst fear. Facial blemishes.

"But the skull served more than one purpose," Lady Ahn continued. "Kublai Khan, it is said, used the skull to drink his *kumiis*. Some even said that the skull was a replica of his grandfather's skull."

In my surprise, I made a gurgling sound. Graciously, Lady Ahn turned to me and nodded.

"So they say. But it was more important than just an unusual drinking cup. In fact the purpose was so important, Kublai Khan kept the skull near him always. Even sleeping with it."

Her gleaming black eyes searched Ernie's face, then Fifi's. They finally rested on mine.

"The carving disfiguring the top of the jade skull . . ." She twirled her fingers above her head. ". . . was actually a map. How do you say it in English? A map with bumps?"

"A topographical map," I said.

"Yes. A topographical map. A map that shows the way to the burial place of Kublai Khan's grandfather."

A silence followed Lady Ahn's pronouncement. I tried to catch my breath. I thought of Ragyapa and the scars etched into the top of his head. The monks who had trained him as a young boy had molded him into a living replica of the jade skull. A constant reminder of his one mission in life: to find the jade skull and the precious map on it.

Fifi Kang bowed her head as if in respect for revered ancestors. Ernie swiveled his eyes, studying our expressions.

"Okay," he said. "A map to the grave of his grandfather. So like I said, what's the big deal?"

Lady Ahn sipped on her tea, through talking for the moment. I explained it to Ernie.

"Kublai Khan's grandfather was the greatest conqueror the world has ever seen. No one, even to this day, comes in a close second. His empire stretched from Korea to Poland, from Russia to Persia.

"That jade skull," I told Ernie, "is carved with a map to the Tomb of Genghis Khan."

Ernie still didn't seem too impressed. But he sipped on some more tea and held the fragrant fluid in his mouth for a while. Savoring it.

BEAMS OF RED AND BLUE AND GOLD GLINTED FROM THE MIL-lion tiny mirrors that formed a beach ball–sized globe. The globe spun atop the dance floor of the Lucky Dragon Cabaret and Beer Hall.

Ernie was truly happy now. We had cold liters of Oriental Beer in front of us and a plate of sliced chestnuts and radishes and an occasional shot of imported brandy to wash it all down with.

I was pretty happy myself.

Lady Ahn had changed into a black lace evening gown, and if we had been in America, every man in the place would've been spending half the night ogling her. I'm not sure if it's from politeness or merely from male self-absorption, but in Asia, ogling of women is rare. Even one as statuesque and as beautiful as Lady Ahn.

Fifi Kang wore a tight red blouse and a miniskirt with knee-high leather boots. Ernie kept staring at the stiletto heels, occasionally rubbing his crotch. I think he was formulating some sort of plan.

The band was too loud but stuck to Korean pop songs. At least I could tune out the meaning and not be nauseated with American rock and roll lyrics.

As it was, I kept my concentration on Lady Ahn. I didn't

want to stare, so I did my best to keep her entertained, so we'd have a reason to look at one another. I borrowed a paper and a pen from a waiter and wrote the various Chinese characters for *Yuan dynasty* and for *jade skull* and for *Mongolia* and for *tomb*. Occasionally, I missed a stroke or two, and with a serious expression, Lady Ahn took the pen from my hand and wrote the symbol correctly.

After a couple of sips of brandy and cola, Lady Ahn filled me in on her background.

She claimed to be royalty. Not Korean but from the Chinese dynasty known as the Southern Sung. It had taken the Mongols many decades to finally defeat the fierce Chinese warriors of the Southern Sung. Lady Ahn's ancestor, an admiral in the Imperial Navy, had been a nephew of the great emperor himself. After the capital city had been stormed by the Mongols, near the end of the thirteenth century, the admiral was one of the last survivors. He and his family sought refuge in the hinterlands of the mountainous province of Szechwan.

Later, his great-grandson, a man called Ahn the Righteous Fist, led a rebel band against the Mongols. Revolution spread throughout China. When the dynasty collapsed, Lady Ahn's ancestor Ahn was able to break into the fortress of the last Mongol emperor and spirit away as much treasure as he and his men could carry. The most valuable piece of loot was the jade skull of Kublai Khan.

In the chaos that followed the collapse of the Mongol dynasty, no one was safe. Ahn the Righteous Fist, along with his entire clan, fled in ships to Bian-do, a remote island off the coast of Korea.

That was six centuries ago.

Ahn the Righteous Fist found a suitable hiding place for the jade skull and some of the more valuable pieces of their treasure trove. Afterward, he and his followers settled on a nearby island, an island more suitable to agriculture.

Their goal was to bide their time and eventually return to China and reclaim the throne of the Sung dynasty. But with constant warfare in China—and a new dynasty in power called the Ming—the moment never seemed auspicious. In the years that followed, the men of the Ahn family took Korean wives. Life went on. The grandiose goal of reclaiming the lost Dragon Throne was forgotten.

More than a century later, a monastery of devout Buddhist monks was established on the island of Bian-do. The monks took it as their mission to protect the jade skull, along with the remaining Sung artifacts. The ones they could find, anyway. Some of the riches had been so cleverly concealed that all memory of their whereabouts had been lost.

The descendants of the admiral, Lady Ahn's ancestors, stayed on, becoming farmers and fishermen like everyone else in the area. But they never forgot their heritage, their lineage that led directly to the emperor of the mighty Sung dynasty.

From generation to generation, they kept their secrets. Lady Ahn's family always had relatives in the monastery who kept them apprised of the monks' activities.

Occasionally Japanese pirates landed, stealing many of the remaining treasures. Over the years, the monks became adept at fending off the pirates. But for the last couple of centuries it seemed that nothing of the riches of the Sung had escaped the thievery of others. And the jade skull of Kublai Khan appeared to have been lost. Or at least that's what everyone thought—until a few months ago.

A young monk had been excavating a new meditation chamber beneath the mountain of Bian-do. Buried beneath a giant rock, he discovered an iron box that contained the jade skull of Kublai Khan.

The monks of Bian-do are honest men, unconcerned

with the wealth of the world. But inevitably, word of their precious discovery reached the nearby islands.

It was commonly believed that the Tomb of Genghis Khan held enormous riches, many of them looted from the Chinese people. Looted, even more specifically, from the Sung dynasty.

When he died, Genghis Khan's body had been carried back to Mongolia by trusted lieutenants. These lieutenants went far into the plains and beyond the mountains, searching for the ideal spot to bury the great Khan and his wealth. After the burial, most of the warriors who had accompanied Genghis Khan to his final resting place were executed, along with thirty "moon-faced" virgins, to service the great Khan beyond the grave. The secret of the whereabouts of the Tomb of Genghis Khan had been buried with them.

The only map that remained was the etchings on the jade skull.

Why had none of Lady Ahn's ancestors retrieved the skull and claimed the riches of Genghis Khan for their own?

For one thing, over the years the Buddhist monks of Bian-do had become fierce in their protectiveness of their holy artifacts. They allowed no one on their island, and myths of strange beasts protecting their wealth had sprung up amongst the fishermen on nearby islands.

And Lady Ahn's ancestors had become complacent. They prospered and lived well as *yangban*, the educated landowning class. None of her ancestors had had the nerve to risk it all and go off after the treasure of Genghis Khan.

And this lack of nerve had caused her family to weaken. Now, all that was left of a once-proud clan was her frail old mother, living alone on Sonyu Island, and herself.

But she wasn't weak, Lady Ahn said. And when I saw

her smooth jaws set in place like cement, I knew she wasn't.

Ernie grew bored at her long-winded explanation, and his liver was crying out for poison. Before I could ask all the questions that were tumbling through my mind, he waved down a waiter and ordered another round.

After that, Ernie and Fifi pretty much stayed on the dance floor. Unless Ernie could talk her into returning to the table so he could quaff down about half a liter of suds. I'd never seen him dance so much for any woman. But apparently, Fifi, with her knockout looks and her sinister, almost evil way of looking at a man, had clamped a firm hold on Ernie's gonads. She seemed to be sizing him up as if she were preparing to eat him.

Lady Ahn and I danced only once. A slow dance. My hand felt so good on the back of her waist, and her body fit so perfectly against mine, that I became feverish with desire. What with the lack of sleep and the booze, I barely managed to stay on my feet.

Almost a month ago, when Lady Ahn had first approached Herman the German in Seoul, her plan had been to set up an escape route for the jade skull. Once she possessed it, she could slip the skull past Korean customs without being noticed. She never intended to cause Herman so much grief. She never intended for Mi-ja to be kidnapped.

Who were these men who had kidnapped Mi-ja?

Her unblemished face crinkled. She wasn't sure, but she thought that these men were her fault, too. When she had started making inquiries about the best way to smuggle an antique out of Korea, people were naturally not willing to open up to a stranger. So she'd explained about the value of the jade skull, keeping her stories as vague as she could. Apparently, they weren't vague enough.

Over the centuries, fabulous legends concerning the

Tomb of Genghis Khan had circulated through the antique markets of the Far East. Once Lady Ahn's story hit, the word spread swiftly. To Hong Kong. To Singapore. To who-knows-where.

Apparently, Ragyapa and his Mongolians had taken the rumors seriously. When they located Herman, they believed he possessed the jade skull. Or if he didn't, he would know where to get it. In some sense they were right. Herman did know how to get in touch with Lady Ahn. Ernie and I were living proof of that.

Where was the skull now? I asked Lady Ahn.

Still on the island of Bian-do.

How was she going to get it? Lady Ahn hadn't decided yet. She had still been formulating a plan when all this happened.

When Fifi's high heels finally started to dig into her foot bones, she came back to our table, sat down, and allowed Ernie to rest for a while.

I gave him a rundown of all I had learned from Lady Ahn. He sipped on his beer and watched her.

"If we help you latch onto this skull thing," he said, "will you turn it over to these guys in exchange for the kid?"

Lady Ahn lowered her eyes. "I will have to think about that," she answered.

"After we free Mi-ja," I said, "we'll go after these kidnappers with the entire U.S. and Korean police forces backing us up. They'll never be able to slip out of the country. We'll trade the jade skull for Mi-ja and then we'll retrieve it. We'll return it to you."

"No one will allow you to return it to me," she said evenly.

She was right about that. Once officialdom sniffed that much wealth, there was no way they'd return it to a private citizen.

I looked at Ernie, asking silently for a decision. He thought for a moment, then nodded. I turned back to Lady Ahn.

"They won't have to know," I said. "We'll keep the cops out of it. Once we free Mi-ja, Ernie and I will catch these Mongols and retrieve the jade skull for you."

Lady Ahn gazed deeply into my eyes, measuring my willingness to go through with such a risky plan.

"I will consider your offer," she told me.

WHEN WE RETURNED TO FIFI'S HOOCH, I FELT AWKWARD BE-cause sleeping arrangements hadn't been settled. Ernie didn't hesitate. He scooped up Fifi, carried her into the bedroom, and slammed shut the paper-paneled door.

Lady Ahn and I looked at one another. I took a step forward. She held up her hand.

"You sleep here." She pointed to the stuffed cotton mat in the center of the *sarang-bang*, the main room of the hooch. "I will sleep in the kitchen."

And she did. Unrolling a straw mat on the cement floor and covering herself with a comforter.

When she turned off the lights, I lay down. But I didn't sleep very well.

Ernie's and Fifi's giggling didn't bother me much. But later, when the Widow Kang started moaning—and then screaming—it became a little difficult to drift off into dreamland.

I listened intently but Lady Ahn didn't seem to move. I couldn't even hear her breathe.

IN THE MORNING, FIFI KANG BOILED A BIG BRASS POT OF WATER and we took turns in the outside *byonso* using the toilet and washing up.

Ernie was the last to rise and emerged from the bed-room unshaven and red-eyed, buckling up his pants.

Something fell out of his back pocket. The felt coin purse, the one the little nun had given him.

"You're pretty careless with that thing," I said.

"What thing?" Ernie asked.

"That felt purse on the floor."

He looked down. "Oh, that thing."

"We forgot to return it to the little nun."

"I guess we did," Ernie said wearily.

The contents had tumbled out and Ernie knelt and picked up the coins. He counted them out and smoothed the wrinkled bills.

"Buddha's money," he said. "All three thousand five hundred and eighty won of it."

Not even seven dollars U.S.

Something else was poking out of the felt purse. Ernie pried it loose from the felt and held it up to the light. The jade amulet.

Lady Ahn walked into the room at that moment and her mouth fell open. She was staring at the amulet. I snatched it from Ernie's hand and handed it to her.

She studied the smooth-bodied Maitreya Buddha, a deity as much revered here in Korea as any Catholic saint. The little figure was still perched on his lotus blossom and his face was still serene, but one foot stomped down on the supine figure of a snarling, long-fanged demon with six arms.

Lady Ahn snapped at Ernie.

"Where did you get this?"

Ernie scratched his tousled hair, his eyes still bleary, and looked at me.

"Where the hell *did* I get it, pal?"

"From the Buddhist nun. The one who was attacked in Itaewon."

"A nun was attacked?" Lady Ahn asked. Apparently, she

hadn't been reading the newspapers much. It was the first time I'd seen her lose her composure.

"Yeah," Ernie said. "And a good thing we saved her, too, or that GI might've done a real number on her."

Fifi Kang, eyes wide, stepped forward and hugged Lady Ahn. She, too, stared at the amulet as if it were a scorpion about to snap.

Lady Ahn handed the amulet back to Ernie, an expression of defeat on her face. "Yes," she murmured. "I understand now."

"What do you mean?" I asked.

"The Korean Buddhists, the followers of Maitreya, are searching for the jade skull. That's why that nun was in Itaewon. And she carried this amulet to protect her from the followers of Mahakala, the demon who is the lord of the Mongolian Buddhists." She shook her head. "The Mongolian Buddhists must be the ones who kidnapped Mi-ja. And the man who attacked your Buddhist nun must've been one of them."

"No way," Ernie said. "It was a GI who attacked her. We saw him, didn't we, pal?"

I nodded.

"Who you saw," Lady Ahn said, "was a Mongolian, and a follower of Mahakala, who is trying to discourage the Korean Buddhists from searching further for the jade skull."

"A follower of Mahakala?" Ernie asked. "That would be a first for a soul brother."

I didn't like him mocking Lady Ahn. I knew my feelings for her weren't helping me conduct an objective investigation. Still, I had to protect her.

"So maybe it wasn't a GI," I said. "It was raining. And it was dark."

Ernie snorted. I ignored him and turned to Lady Ahn. "Then a lot of people are after the skull?"

"Yes," Lady Ahn answered. "Many people. Some of them Mongolian followers of Mahakala, the Lord of the Demons. And some of them Korean followers of Maitreya, the Buddha of the Vision of the Future."

Ernie rubbed his chin. "In that case, I'd better shave."

AFTER COFFEE, LADY AHN BUSIED HERSELF PACKING HER SMALL suitcase. She'd made her decision.

"You will go with me," she told me. "So will he." She pointed at Ernie. "The Widow Kang will stay here."

Fifi didn't complain. She looked haggard after last night's session. Ernie sat cross-legged on the warm vinyl floor, smiling contentedly as Fifi stirred his coffee for him and ladled in more sugar. "So where we going?" he asked.

I already knew the answer but I let Lady Ahn say it. She stopped packing and turned and stared at him.

"To the Monastery of the Sleeping Dragon," she replied. "On the island of Bian-do. We're going to recover the jade skull of Kublai Khan."

"Why not?" Ernie lifted his coffee and sipped noisily. "I don't have anything else to do today."

Ernie admires a bold chick.

So do I.

"But first you must know this." Lady Ahn pulled a stiff piece of paper out of her handbag and tossed it on the floor between us. Ernie picked it up, frowned, then handed it to me. It was a photo. Of a mutilated body, neck slashed, lying spread-eagled on a rocky beach.

"What is this?" Ernie asked.

"A man," she answered. "A skilled commando."

"Yeah?"

"This man was the last person to reach the Monastery of the Sleeping Dragon and attempt to steal the jade skull."

Ernie set down his coffee, staring at it sourly, and spoke

gruffly to the Widow Kang. "There's not enough sugar in this."

Fifi hurriedly dumped in two more mounds of bleached granules.

I stared down at the grainy photo. The neck of the commando had been savagely ripped, his head almost completely sawed off.

I touched the mutilated ear in my pocket and tried not to think of Mi-ja—and what she must be suffering. I tried not to think of what might happen to her if we didn't save her before the moon became full.

15

IT HADN'T BEEN EASY TO FIND A HORSE IN THE CITY OF SEOUL.
These people live together like packed rats, Ragyapa
thought. Not like Mongols, who make their homes in
yurts, felt tents, on the endless steppes and trackless mountains of his homeland, Mongolia.

It was past midnight curfew, and Ragyapa and his band
of followers stood near a children's amusement park. The
horse they'd found was only a pony, caged in a wooden
pen. Nearby was the small carousel the pony pulled during
the day, with smiling ducks and geese and swans for the
children to ride on.

Ragyapa patted the little horse on the neck. Its brown
eyes rolled up at him nervously.

What a paltry specimen, Ragyapa thought. Not much
smaller than the Mongol ponies he had known all his life,
but there was no strength in this animal. His legs were
spindly and his haunch and forelimbs had no heft to them,

not like the muscled creatures who ran wild across the upper plains of the Mongolian heartland.

Still, Ragyapa needed horseflesh and this creature would have to do.

Ragyapa climbed up on the back of the pony. The animal whinnied and staggered beneath his weight. A few of Ragyapa's men smiled at the horse's weakness but none of them laughed. Laughter is not the way of the nomad.

Ragyapa fondled the pony's mane, feeling along the vertebrae beneath the short hair. He pinched when he found the correct spot and felt the vein pulsing beneath his fingers. Deftly, Ragyapa unsheathed his gleaming blade and sliced a thin line through the horse's hide. He squeezed, forcing blood out, then bent and sucked the warm fluid into his mouth.

One of Ragyapa's disciples handed him a wooden bowl. When Ragyapa's mouth had filled with blood, he spit it into the bowl, and leaned down to suck out more.

This was the method Mongol warriors had used when they'd ridden for many hours and had no time to forage for food. They would feed off the blood of their horse. Leaning down, even as they rode, sucking up the life-giving fluid. In this way, they could ride for many hours—even days. And if the horse died, they'd switch to another. A disciplined troop of Mongol warriors could cover as many as seventy to ninety miles a day.

But now, in these modern times, Ragyapa and his warrior monks would use the blood not for sustenance but for ceremony. To launch the beginning of a great enterprise.

Word had come concerning the whereabouts of the Americans. Ragyapa's disciples were about to be given a mission: Follow the Americans, wait until they found the jade skull of Kublai Khan, and then take it from them.

It was risky and it was difficult but, if the plan failed, Ragyapa still had the kidnapped girl as a hostage. With the girl, he could still force the Americans to turn the skull over to him.

Ragyapa himself would stay in Seoul and guard the pampered child known as Mi-ja.

His lips curled in disgust at the thought of her.

As he sucked up more of the pony's blood, Ragyapa remembered his early days in the monastery, high in the mountains of Mongolia. His mother had given him up when the arthritis had finally overtaken her. He remembered sitting naked, in the lotus position, on a hard wooden floor. And he remembered the yellow parchment of the rolled scroll of the ancient text and how he was forced by the elder monks to sit with his back straight and balance the scroll on his head for hour after hour, without once ever allowing the scroll to fall. And he remembered how there was always someone else in the room. Someone he couldn't see. The old monks used to tell him it was Mahakala, the six-armed Lord of the Demons, watching him to see if he was devout. To see if he could keep the ancient text balanced on his head. Or if he was just another weak soul who would surely fall away from the true path. Fall away from nirvana. Fall toward the sins of the flesh.

And when the aching hours mounted one on top of another, his muscles became tense and his entire body quivered. Finally, the parchment always fell. That's when Ragyapa would feel the whiplike rod, again and again. And when he whimpered, like the undisciplined child known as Mi-ja, the punishment was even more severe. The encircling of the flame until the flesh of his arms began to sizzle. And the cure, which was worse. Embracing the snows outside the monastery, all through the night, until the monks found him blue and nearly frozen in the morning.

All for discipline. Everything for discipline.

Still, no matter how they tried to teach her, the girl Mi-ja kept whimpering.

Ragyapa sucked more blood and spit it out. The bowl was half full now.

Mi-ja was an ugly child. All the contours of her little face even and smooth, nothing distinctive about them, nothing to set her apart from other people. But now she looked better.

The jagged scab where her ear had been seemed to make her skull slightly tilted. Off balance. Yes, a great improvement.

Just as Ragyapa's looks had been improved when a hot knife etched the lines of the ancient jade skull into the top of his head.

A disciple hissed. "Someone is coming."

Ragyapa spat out the last of the blood and slid off the pony. His fellow Mongols crouched in the shadows behind the equipment of the amusement park. Footsteps scraped on gravel. A man appeared beneath the stone archway.

He wore a khaki uniform and a visored cap. Cautiously, he scanned the park. Fondling his big metal whistle, he stepped forward.

Ragyapa couldn't call out, but he knew that his trained monks would take the action that was necessary.

The policeman strolled slowly toward the pony and the small carousel.

As he passed the wooden replica of a small train engine, a man slipped out of the darkness, moving with all the quickness of death itself. Ragyapa saw the flash of the blade and then the policeman's head being jerked viciously backward. There was a gurgling sound and in the glow of the almost full moon, blood spurted across stiffly starched khaki.

"Hold him!" Ragyapa commanded.

He rushed forward, holding the wooden bowl, blood sloshing over its edges.

As the other Mongols held the struggling policeman, Ragyapa lifted the bowl up to the cruel gash in his neck and caught the hot, squirting gore.

The policeman slumped to the ground. One of the Mongols dragged him into the caboose of the wooden train. Ragyapa stared down at the full bowl, satisfied.

When his disciples gathered around him, Ragyapa raised the bowl up to the almost full moon.

"Nothing will stop us," he said, "from finding the jade skull of our ancestor, the Great Khan Kublai."

"Nothing will stop us," the men intoned.

"All power to the Lord Mahakala!"

Ragyapa lowered the bowl to his lips and drank deeply. He handed the bowl to the Mongol standing next to him, who drank and passed it on.

Ragyapa fumbled inside his tunic and pulled out six train tickets. He handed one to each man.

Embossed on each ticket in Korean and English was the name of their destination.

Taejon.

16

CLOUDS BOILED ATOP THE PEAKS OF THE BOMUN MOUNTAINS, far to the south of the city, watching us.

At the Taejon bus station, the milling crowds of Koreans stared at the three tall people moving amongst them. We carried overnight bags slung over our shoulders and the three of us—Lady Ahn, Ernie, and me—all wore blue jeans and sneakers. Ernie and I topped this outfit with bland-looking PX-bought sports shirts, but Lady Ahn brightened up the whole world with a shimmering red silk blouse.

I had trouble keeping my eyes off of her. Although I did my best not to make my attention obvious, she noticed. But I don't think she minded much.

At the ticket window, Lady Ahn purchased three express bus tickets to Ok-dong. I'd never heard of the place but she assured me it was on the coast of the Yellow Sea. When I tried to hand her a few bills, she pushed my money away.

"No," she said firmly. "You help me, I pay."

Ernie leaned against a cement pillar, gazing intently at the women in the crowd. When he occasionally found one he liked, he zeroed in on her like radar honing in on a North Korean fighter jet.

Sometimes the women noticed and turned away. Sometimes they noticed and giggled. But whatever their reaction, it made no difference to Ernie. It was his right to stare, he figured. And until someone hit him in the forehead with a two-by-four, he'd continue to do it.

Before we climbed on the bus, Ernie stopped at a snack stand and bought four double packets of ginseng gum. If we were heading for the wilds, he needed proper provisions.

OUTSIDE THE WINDOWS OF THE BUS, THE CITY OF TAEJON faded into warehouses and factories and finally into broad fields crisscrossed with the wet patchworks of rice paddies. The bright sunshine turned the tender rice shoots emerald green. Straw-hatted farmers, pant legs rolled up, waded through the muck, hunched over their work as intently as physicists peering through electron microscopes. White cranes rose from the paddies, lifting lazily into the blue sky.

I sat next to Lady Ahn and Ernie sat right behind us, next to an old lady eating watermelon seeds. She popped open a few seeds, sucked out the nut inside, and after a while offered some to Ernie. He accepted gladly and soon she had accepted a stick of ginseng gum in return.

She chattered away happily in Korean, Ernie smiling and nodding occasionally, not understanding a word she said. Actually, she was telling him about her grandchildren, but Ernie didn't give a damn one way or the other.

Lady Ahn was silent for the first part of the trip, the smooth flesh of her forehead crinkled slightly in concentration.

At the front of the bus sat a uniformed stewardess who occasionally made trips down the aisle handing out warm hand towels or lukewarm cups of barley tea. I used the towel to wipe down the back of my neck, because without the rain the morning was beginning to become a little warm.

Lady Ahn looked as cool as a chilled melon.

One thing we Mexicans know about is patience. I didn't push her. I didn't badger her with questions. I waited.

About an hour later, it paid off.

She turned in her seat and studied my face.

"You're not an American," she said.

"Yes," I answered. "I am an American."

"But your family, they come from another place."

"My parents were both born in Mexico."

"Aah." She nodded gravely. "Mexico."

Lady Ahn seemed to be weighing something in her mind. Finally, she spoke again. "I have question about Mexico."

"Shoot."

"Why is it a poor country?"

That one stumped me. Mexico had been poor, was poor now, and probably always would be poor. But why, I had never thought about. Lady Ahn continued.

"Mexico is bigger than Korea, isn't it?"

I nodded.

"And it has many mountains and gold mines and much land to grow rice or corn or whatever people want to eat."

I nodded again.

"So why is it poor?"

I thought about the Spanish legacy, the corruption, the overcrowding, the millions of acres of land that would never be irrigated. I tried to formulate an answer for her but it didn't hang together. So I told the truth.

"I don't know why Mexico is poor, Lady Ahn."

She studied me for a while longer, that same serious expression on her perfect features.

"Your family, did they come from Spain?"

I didn't know exactly. Most of the explanations I'd received from my relatives had been pretty garbled but I gave her the most accurate answer I was aware of.

"Some," I said.

She leaned forward slightly, excited now. "Were they conquistadors?"

How did she know that word?

"Conquistadors? I don't really know. After the conquest a lot of regular people came. Farmers, priests, merchants, sailors. I don't know if my ancestors were conquistadors or not."

"But not all of your family is from Spain?"

"No. Part of my family is Indian."

She pulled back slightly. "They are the poorest people?"

"Usually. But in some cases they are the only ones who are free."

"What do you mean?"

"My mother's side of the family, we have much blood of the Yaqui Indians. The Yaqui were never beaten by *los conquistadores*. They are still free, a separate nation. They've only signed a peace treaty with the Mexican government."

"So you are one of these free people?"

"Part of my blood is."

"One of your grandfathers?"

"Maybe a great-grandfather."

"And was this great-grandfather a chief?"

Has anyone ever been descended from an Indian who wasn't a chief? "Of course," I replied.

Lady Ahn seemed to think about this long and hard,

holding her gaze on my face. I hadn't a clue as to why it was so important to her.

"Then you are a prince," she said at last. "A prince of the people known as the Yaqui."

I fiddled with my hand towel. "I suppose you could look at it that way."

Lady Ahn sat back in her seat, satisfied for some reason. After a few minutes of silence, however, she sat up suddenly. "What does Sueño mean?"

"It means dream."

She smiled. "That's nice. I like to dream."

Lady Ahn reached out and squeezed my hand. Her flesh felt as cool as I had imagined. As cool as a mountain spring.

"I like to dream, too," I said.

When she let go of my hand, I was disappointed. She turned away from me and curled up slightly and gazed out the window.

I let her dream.

OVER THREE THOUSAND ISLANDS LIE OFF THE COAST OF KOREA. Almost every one of them is inhabited by seafaring people.

Koreans aren't usually thought of as seafarers. If anyone in the West thinks of them at all, it is as rice farmers or merchants or tae kwon do instructors. But Koreans have been sailors and fishermen since before history began. The islands of Japan were settled by Koreans in ancient times. In fact, the Japanese and the Koreans are nothing more than cousins who have been separated for a long time. Their languages have the same grammatical structure, although few words still sound alike.

The culture on the islands off the coast of Korea is a world of its own. People fish, they harvest seaweed from the sea, and they worship ancient gods who have never been banished by any foreign invasions. Not by Buddhism, not by Confucianism, and not by Christianity.

These islands have often been used as a refuge. During the Mongol invasion of Korea seven hundred years ago, the entire royal court moved from Seoul to the island of Kanghua. There, the Koreans negotiated with the Mongol generals, gave up most of their sovereignty, but managed to keep the royal court fundamentally intact.

Before Lady Ahn, Ernie, and I reached the coast of the Yellow Sea, our bus crossed a small mountain range. Down the steep cliffs of winding roads were lush green valleys, so narrow and rocky they didn't appear to have ever been cultivated.

We entered a long tunnel carved in granite and when we emerged, the magnificent panorama of a curved coastline opened before us. On the beach near a wooden quay sat the ramshackle blue-tile-roofed buildings of Ok-dong. At the end of the pier bobbed a ferryboat. Beyond that rose the rocky outcroppings of mist-shrouded islands.

Ernie grabbed the back of my seat and leaned forward. "I gotta piss like a racehorse."

Lady Ahn pretended not to hear.

"Soon you'll have a whole ocean out there to do it in," I answered.

"By the time I get through," Ernie said, "it really *will* be the Yellow Sea."

We pulled into the Ok-dong station and climbed off the bus. Ernie made a beeline to the public *byonso* and I stretched my legs while I waited for him to return. After we had all relieved ourselves, Lady Ahn guided us down the main drag of the city, heading downhill toward the pier.

The farther we traveled from Seoul, the farther back in time we seemed to be going. Here in Ok-dong the road was lined with shops with old metal scales and woven hemp bags bulging with rice, and wooden stalls teeming with mackerel and squid and octopus. The tang of salt air rose up from the ocean and bit into my sinuses.

People gazed at us politely but no one stared. I think they'd seen so few foreigners around these parts that, at the sight of us, all the natives went into a mild state of shock.

Ernie clicked loudly on his gum and strutted down the wood-planked road.

"So where's the beer hall?" he asked.

"No time," Lady Ahn told him. "The ferry will leave soon."

A foghorn ripped through the air. We started to run.

By the time we reached the loading dock we were pretty much out of breath. I pushed my way to the front of the ticket booth and pulled out some wrinkled Korean bills. When the ticket vendor asked me which island, I turned back to Lady Ahn.

"*Majimak*," she said. The end of the line.

I turned back to repeat the instruction to the vendor, but she had already slid our tickets forward and slapped a few bronze coins down as my change. We moved toward the loading ramp.

What I saw there made my heart leap. A counter manned by uniformed representatives of the Korean National Police.

Ernie elbowed me. "You think they received the report of us punching out those cops in Taejon?"

"I don't know," I said. There was no way around them. "We'll find out."

Why would the KNPs have an inspection counter at a ferry loading dock?

Since the Demilitarized Zone dividing Communist North Korea from the South was protected by six infantry divisions and about a jillion land mines, it was a little difficult to cross it whenever you wanted to. As a result, the North Korean commandos often raided South Korea by sea. The offshore islands were the perfect hiding spot for them. The South Koreans had set up hundreds of military bases and thousands of observation posts, the location of which North Korean spies would be delighted to know about. So the offshore islands were a sensitive area militarily. The KNPs checked people out before allowing them to travel in this area.

Lady Ahn stood between Ernie and me. "Don't talk," she told us. "I talk."

It sounded like a good idea to me.

The Korean police inspector had a sunburned face and bored but suspicious eyes. Those eyes widened, though, when he saw us. He seemed shocked to see such a gorgeous Korean woman with two American GIs.

"*Wein ili issoyo?*" he asked Lady Ahn, a hint of incredulity in his voice. What business do you have?

Lady Ahn gazed steadily at the policeman. "My mother lives on Sonyu Island," she answered. "I am going to visit her."

The policeman studied her National Identification Card, looked up, and pointed at Ernie and me. "And what of these two?"

Lady Ahn wrapped her arms around my elbow and hugged her soft breasts against me. "I am going to marry this one. He must meet my mother first. The other is his commander."

Her statement had the desired effect. The policeman's mouth fell open and he jerked back as if he'd been stung. "Are you registered to consort with foreigners?"

"No." She pointed at her ID card. "I'm a student, as you can see. But we are to be married. It is legal for me to be with him."

The policeman flapped out his hand toward Lady Ahn. "Your fiancée paperwork," he demanded.

I started speaking in English. "Hey, wait a minute.

What's going on here?" I turned to Lady Ahn. "Is everything okay, honey?"

"He says we must have our engagement paperwork," she said in English.

"Wait a minute!" I gaped at the policeman. "You've got to be kidding! All that paperwork requesting marriage approval is back at the compound." I pulled out my regular army ID card, not my CID badge, and held it in front of the inspector's face. "I'm Eighth Army. You *alla*? Eighth—Army."

Ernie started speaking even louder than I had. "Who the hell does this guy think he is? We're just trying to get on the damn boat! What *is* this shit?"

The crowd of Koreans behind us waiting to board the ferry began to mumble. The foghorn blasted through the air again. The rest of the policemen wandered over, wanting to find out what all the fuss was about.

Lady Ahn resumed speaking in Korean to the policeman. "You can't stop us from visiting my mother," she said, "just because we didn't bring our engagement paperwork."

The policeman's face was very red now. Obnoxious GIs and stubborn Korean women weren't something he had to deal with every day.

A policeman with more gold braid on his shoulder than the inspector strode over, his face calm, his arms behind his back, acting as unperturbed as a Confucian scholar strolling through a grove of flowering plum blossoms. The first cop turned to him and explained rapidly. "They don't have their engagement paperwork."

"We forgot it," Lady Ahn said in Korean.

The honcho ignored her and pointed to me and Ernie. "Are they soldiers?" he asked the red-faced cop.

"Yes."

"Let's see their identification."

Lady Ahn translated and both Ernie and I flashed our military ID cards.

The honcho studied the ID cards intently. Then with a flick of his wrist, he waved us through. He sauntered off.

We scurried onto the ferry.

IT TOOK THE REST OF THE DAY TO REACH THE ISLAND OF Sonyu. A tiny village clung to the feet of a jagged cliff. The hooches were made of driftwood and roofed with straw thatch. Nets hung drying from the rickety wooden quay and women squatted in the shade of cherry trees, weaving straw mats. There weren't many boats along the quay. All were out fishing.

The three of us stood along the railing.

"Your mother lives *here*?" Ernie asked Lady Ahn.

"Yes. My family has lived here for six centuries."

Ernie whistled. "Not much business for the van and storage boys."

Lady Ahn pointed to the gray-shrouded distance. "See that island there?"

I could barely make it out on the western horizon. Craggy rocks rose straight out of the sea. "Yes," I said.

"That is Bian-do," she said. "That is where the jade skull is hidden."

"*That's* where we're going?" Ernie asked.

"Yes," Lady Ahn said happily. "Tomorrow at dawn."

"Bian-do," I said. "The Island of Mysterious Peace."

Lady Ahn swiveled her head. "Yes, Agent Sueño. You are correct."

Her pleased expression was worth more to me than all the gold in Genghis Khan's tomb.

LADY AHN'S MOTHER BOWED AS WE ENTERED THE SMALL courtyard of her home. It was a large ramshackle building on a hill overlooking the village of Sonyu, much too large for one old woman. It had been an ancestral home, built originally by Ahn the Righteous Fist in the fourteenth century, and rebuilt repeatedly over the years.

Within minutes we were seated on the polished wood-slat floor and a table was placed before us spread with rice and kimchi and *kalchi*, a scabbard fish found only in Far Eastern waters.

The food was delicious and both Ernie and I were famished. We polished off every plate in short order. As was ancient custom, the women ate in the kitchen and later came in to clear our plates.

Lady Ahn seemed to be glowing, as if returning to the island of her birth had infused her with a strength of spirit that made her even more impressive than she was on the mainland.

She wore traditional Korean clothing. A long white skirt called *chima*, tied high up along the ribs, and a short powder-blue *chogori* vest coat with long flowing sleeves. Her short hair was brushed back but fell forward and caressed her smooth cheeks when she bent to pick up the small serving table.

The sun was almost down now, and Lady Ahn's mother fixed one of the many rooms for Ernie and me. Ernie hit the sleeping mat almost immediately. Lady Ahn and I strolled down to the beach and watched the fishing boats sail in, floating across the red glimmer of a sinking sun.

The moon started to rise and I held my breath. But it still wasn't full. Not quite. We still had time.

As Lady Ahn outlined her plan to me, I realized that she'd been setting it up for years. Her scheme was brilliant and in it all of us would have our roles. And, as she told me more about the island and the mythology surrounding it, I realized that by taking such a bold step as to defy the monks of Bian-do, she was overcoming many of her own misgivings.

Still, she was a modern woman. Not one to be awed by superstition. A great beast supposedly protected what was left of the Treasure of the Sung. But as I pointed out to her, whatever this creature was, it hadn't been able to stop ancient Japanese pirates. Hadn't she told me they had looted most of the treasure?

She agreed. The monster was probably just something conjured up by the monks to keep adventurers away from the monastery.

Still, the corpse of the commando in the photo she'd shown me had been carried to the shore of Sonyu Island by the current from Bian-do. The dead man's wounds were clearly not from a knife or a bayonet.

In fact, if I had to guess, I would have to say that the wounds were from claws.

17

FISHERMAN YUN, LADY AHN'S THIRD COUSIN, STOOD AT THE stern, rough hands gripping the thick oar that both propelled and steered the little skiff. He leaned forward and then pulled, creating a rhythm that moved us through the sea like a wriggling snake.

Ernie sat on a splintered wooden plank, clicking loudly on his ginseng gum, scanning the darkness before us. What he was looking for, I wasn't quite sure.

A blanket of clouds swept across the sky. For an instant a gap opened in them and I spotted the nearly full moon. Not much time left to turn over the jade skull to Ragyapa and his Mongols. Not much time to save Mi-ja's life. Then the clouds closed and opened again on the other side of the cosmos. The vast panorama of the Milky Way glittered above us. I wasn't used to stars being so bright, or so close. In East L.A. the only contact with heaven I had was reaching up and touching the smog inversion layer.

Out here, on the Yellow Sea, heading for the remote

island of Bian-do, the air was fresh and laced with salt, as if it had been created yesterday—solely for our enjoyment.

It seemed like a good time for a burial.

I reached into my jacket pocket, pulled out the bloody handkerchief containing Mi-ja's ear, and dropped it into the cold, choppy waters. The white linen swirled. Then it sank into an endless world of water.

Before we'd left Taejon the day before, I'd placed a call to the pharmacy in Itaewon because I wanted to find out if the kidnappers had contacted Herman again. Slicky Girl Nam had picked up the phone. She was hysterical.

"Most tick full moon! They will cut Mi-ja again! This time they will kill!"

I tried to calm her down. She kept jabbering.

"You find old jade head they look for?" she shrilled.

"We're going for it now."

"You find *bali bali*." Quickly. "Maybe they call soon. I go now."

She hung up on me.

Lady Ahn shifted her weight in the boat and gazed at me with her shimmering black eyes. Her face was scrubbed clean, and she was wrapped in the gray robes of a Buddhist nun. Her legs were enfolded in white linen, laced with string, her feet bound tightly in leather sandals.

She tapped Ernie on the shoulder. He swiveled and the three of us went over the plan one last time.

LADY AHN HAD BEEN PAYING HOMAGE TO THE MONKS OF THE Monastery of the Sleeping Dragon since she was a little girl. She came as a supplicant and worshiped in their temple carved out of the side of Bian-san, the Mountain of Mysterious Peace.

Through the years she had gained the monks' trust. They were aware of her descent from the imperial court of the Sung. They treated her with the respect due one of a royal line, even if the line had fallen centuries ago.

She had found many opportunities to inspect the monastery and committed much of its layout to memory. It was a vast complex, expanded over the years and connected to a network of volcanic caves that honeycombed Bian Mountain.

Deep in the tunnels of the old volcano, the last relics of the Treasure of the Sung were hidden. That's where we'd find the jade skull of Kublai Khan.

In a few minutes, Fisherman Yun would be dropping Ernie and me off on the back side of the mountain, on a rocky cliff remote from the main buildings of the monastery. Lady Ahn would continue in the skiff. She'd arrive at the entranceway to the Bian Temple in about an hour. Just in time to make the predawn call to meditation with the monks.

Ernie dipped his palm into the cold sea and splashed a handful of salt water onto his face. Grumbling. As if to remind us that he wasn't pleased about the early hour.

Lady Ahn ignored him and continued her explanation.

The Dragon Throne of China had been stolen from her family. As far as she was concerned, any possessions of the Mongol rulers, including the jade skull, were nothing but ill-gotten booty. She had no qualms about stealing it back.

But the monks who had protected the treasure all these centuries didn't see it her way. They were aware of the power of the skull. Of the untold riches it could lead to. And although they had taken a vow of poverty, they knew of the allure that wealth held for most men.

The monks had taken an oath to protect the stolen relics in their possession. And they had sworn to allow the Great Khan Genghis to rest peacefully in his tomb, hidden far away on the mainland, high in the hinterlands of the vast steppes of Mongolia.

When Lady Ahn explained this, Ernie piped up. "So you're saying that if they catch us trying to rip off the skull, they'll jack us up royally."

Lady Ahn turned to me for translation.

"They'll fight," I said.

She nodded her head solemnly.

Our goal was to sneak in, snatch the jade skull, and creep back out without being noticed.

Lady Ahn went over the instructions again.

The morning meditation lasted an hour. That would give Ernie and me time to enter through a tunnel in the back of the mountain and make our way deep into the earth, to a vast chamber where lay entombed the relics of Buddhist saints. There, we would wait for Lady Ahn. Her job was to make sure that no one would be working in the back caverns. Once she slipped away from the monks, she would find us and lead us to the skull. Then we'd grab it and slip out a back entrance. Outside, Lady Ahn's cousin, Fisherman Yun, would be waiting for us with his boat.

"Piece of rice cake," Ernie said. Then his brow furrowed. "What about this commando who got sliced up?"

Lady Ahn shook her head. "He was not careful."

"Not careful about what?"

A rock-strewn shoreline burst into view in the swirling mist. The roar of the breakers filled our ears. The skiff bobbed high in the air, but Fisherman Yun guided us expertly past the churning waves. Once we hit land, Ernie and I hopped out. We dragged the little boat up onto the pebbled shore.

Before we left, Lady Ahn touched my hand and stared into my eyes. It was a look of promise, I thought.

Of what, I wasn't sure.

Fisherman Yun shoved the boat back into the water, hopped aboard, and, like the great seaman he was, soon had the rickety little craft sporting proudly through the waves. In seconds, their silhouettes disappeared into the dark mist.

"Do you think that chick is going to come through on all this?" Ernie asked.

"Damn right she is."

We trudged through heavy brush. A pathway led toward a cave that sat high on the side of the cliff wall.

THE CREATURE COULD SMELL THEM BEFORE IT HEARD THEIR footsteps. Vibrations quivered through the soil, up the trunk, and through a sluggish body. *Predators.* A surge of fear rushed through its flesh. The creature hugged the heavy branch tighter, claws clicking free, ready to swing.

Were they coming closer? No. The pounding moved away. And then it heard rocks sliding, grunting, and finally silence.

The monsoon wind rustled through the thick foliage of the jungle.

The intruders were gone. Slowly, the fear seeped from the creature's body. It reached for food and chewed, weak eyes glazing over, gradually drifting back into the stupor that was its beloved natural state.

Before fading completely into sleep, it felt what seemed like footsteps again. It opened its eyes again but swiftly closed them. The sound was not footsteps. Merely the first droplets of rain, pelting rocks and trees and leaves. A flash of lightning tore the sky. Thunder roared. An entire ocean of wetness fell from the heavens.

The creature lay soaked, clinging to the branch, steam rising from rancid fur. It thought of nothing.

After an hour, hunger stirred. There was no food left on the tree. It decided to reposition itself.

ERNIE CURSED AS WE CRAWLED THROUGH THE NARROW tunnel.

"You got to be *shitting* me. This tunnel leads nowhere, Sueño. You must've taken a wrong turn."

We'd been crawling through bat shit for half an hour. I was just as fed up as Ernie was. Still, I wasn't going to admit it. Lady Ahn would be waiting and I couldn't let her down. And I mustn't let Mi-ja down.

As we rounded a corner, a red light glimmered up ahead. I motioned behind me for Ernie to be quiet.

Sweat poured down my forehead. I wiped it with the back of my hand. Quietly, I inched closer to the light, stretched forward, and peered around the granite wall.

A skull grinned into my face.

I leapt back. Ernie grabbed me.

"What the shit?"

"Quiet!"

I crept back to the corner. When nothing moved, I rose and stepped out into a small cavern.

In front of us, cross-legged, sat the skeletal remains of a man, draped in tattered gray robes. In front of him, guttering softly, was the flame from a small oil lamp. Next to that sat a bowl of fruit. I pinched the pear and the persimmon.

"Both fresh," I told Ernie. "The monks make regular offerings."

Behind the cross-legged skeleton loomed a silk screen painting of ancient Buddhist saints engaged in various struggles with the powers of evil.

Ernie reached down, grabbed the pear, and took a bite. "Who the hell is this guy, anyway?"

"Maybe one of their leaders. From the past."

He crunched on the pear. "From the past is sort of obvious, George."

We left the ancient monk and wandered into another tunnel, much larger than the one we'd been crawling through. This one was high enough so that by bowing our heads, we could walk almost upright. As the light from the oil lamp faded behind us, I switched on the heavy flashlight Lady Ahn had provided.

"We must be getting close," Ernie said.

There was less bat shit on the ground. Someone had been cleaning this portion of the tunnel network regularly.

In another open cavern, we found pools of water. Ernie almost stepped into one but I stopped him in time. I pointed the beam of the flashlight into its depths. The water was clear but agitated by the pebble Ernie had kicked into it. Still, we could see down at least ten feet before the pool faded into darkness.

"How far down does this thing go?" Ernie asked.

"I don't know. This mountain is porous. Filled with tunnels. And water."

"That's interesting," Ernie said, "but do you know where in the fuck we are?"

I glanced at the sketch map Lady Ahn had given me. After the myriad turns and twists we'd been through, the diagram had long ago stopped making sense.

"Sure," I said. "No sweat. We're almost there."

Ernie sighed. "We'd better be."

I pointed the beam of the flashlight back into the water. The ripples had settled now, and the light probed to a depth that must've been at least thirty feet. That's when we saw them. Shimmering and white. Globes of death.

Human skulls.

"For Christ's sake," Ernie grumbled. "These damn monks aren't as peaceful as Lady Ahn makes them out to be."

I resisted the urge to cross myself. "Maybe this is just the way they bury their dead."

"Maybe, but I don't think so. Some of those skulls have been crushed."

He was right. Deep gouges slashed into the bony craniums. Other bones lay snapped in two, as if some great beast had feasted on human marrow.

"Come on," I said. "Let's keep moving."

Ernie didn't argue. He just followed me deeper into the catacombs. Anything to get away from that pile of the macabre.

Ernie pulled out his pack of gum and offered me a stick. This time I accepted. The stuff was bitter and tart in the mouth, but at least the juices started flowing again.

Finally, we reached another cavern and another shrine. Instead of a skeleton, this one featured a bronze statuette about three feet high. Of our old friend Kuan Yin, the goddess of mercy. I sighed with relief.

"This is where we're supposed to meet Lady Ahn," I said.

Ernie flopped down at the naked feet of the goddess and glanced around. Disappointed. "Doesn't this little gal rate any pears?"

"I guess not."

I sat at the entrance to the tunnel leading deeper into the mountain and leaned my back against granite. When we were both settled, I flipped off the flashlight. The darkness became absolute. All we could hear was the steady drip of water on rock and the occasional squeak of a bat.

Ernie spoke in a voice of reverence. "This is like being high," he said. "Not on booze. But on the real stuff. Pure China White."

"Cheaper though," I said. "And easier on the liver."

"Maybe so," Ernie answered. "Unless those damn monks show up."

THE SOFT FOOTSTEPS JOLTED ME OUT OF A DOZE. THE FOOT-steps stopped just a few feet from us. When I realized it was only one person, I rose to a crouch and switched on the flashlight.

Lady Ahn covered her eyes.

"They're following me," she said.

"Who?"

"The monks. Come. We must hurry."

Ernie was up and right behind us, molars grinding on stale gum.

We wound through passageways for what must've been twenty minutes. Finally, we stopped in another cavern, this one with a pool much larger than the ones we had seen before.

Lady Ahn pointed. "It's down there. The jade skull of Kublai Khan."

Ernie peered after the beam of my flashlight. "Must be a little soggy."

"No. There is a chamber," Lady Ahn said. "There. See the dark spot on the water's bottom? It leads back up toward the surface. And there is a dry area with an airhole. Many of the remaining artifacts of the Sung Treasure are still there. Along with the skull."

"Cute," Ernie said. "How do we get in?"

"I will swim." Lady Ahn began to unknot her robes.

Ernie stood back, arms crossed, a half-grin on his face. Prepared to observe.

I grabbed her arm. "No. I will go in."

"You can swim?" she asked.

I remembered the plunge on Slauson Avenue. Free on Thursdays. Compliments of the L.A. County Board of Supervisors. Half the kids there to swim were black. Half the kids were Mexican. About every third week, someone drowned.

"I can swim," I told her.

"Hurry, then. I had to make sure that the monks weren't planning any ceremonies back here today. They weren't but they missed me as soon as I slipped away. They have already started their search."

I stripped down to my undershorts; Lady Ahn calmly folded every article of clothing as I handed them to her.

Ernie gazed at the golden cross on my chest. "I didn't know you wore that."

"Only when I break into heathen temples." I glanced at Lady Ahn. "Sorry," I said.

No expression showed on her face.

I tested the water. Icy as hell. I splashed some of it on my chest and arms. My body exploded with pimpled flesh.

Lady Ahn knelt down and grabbed a handful of mud. "Here. Rub this on. It will keep you warm."

"No time." I took a deep breath and, feet first, leapt into the pool.

The shock almost collapsed my lungs. I felt as if a huge fist of ice was squeezing my heart out of my rib cage. Everywhere, my skin burned. Not with fire, but with a searing flame of cold as intense as a blowtorch. Somehow, I managed to keep the blood pulsing through my body. Still quaking with cold, I continued to sink into the water. At the bottom, I followed the beam of light Lady Ahn held steadily on my target. Reaching the narrow cave entrance, I slithered in.

Inside, after a few feet, it became pitch-dark again. I rose quickly, expecting to break water, but nothing happened.

My lungs ached with stale air. I let it out in a steady stream of bubbles. Soon, my lungs were empty, and screaming to be refilled.

I must've swum up half the depth of the pool, maybe twenty feet. Still no air. Panic churned inside of me. I fought it down.

I kept swimming, frantic to breathe again. Maybe I should turn back?

I stopped, swiveled around, started to kick back the way

I had come. But then I stopped. No way. I'd never hold my breath that long. I had to go on.

I turned and continued up through the darkness. Reaching forward, groping for the surface, praying for it to arrive. My chest writhed in agony.

I had to have air and I had to have it soon.

Something slimy grabbed my arm.

I wrenched at it. A poisonous eel? The tentacle of a great squid? Whatever the hell it was, I jerked it from my arm, my fingers sinking into mushy flesh, and broke free.

Just some plant. Was this chamber clogged with seaweed? Or filled to the top with water? Had the airhole Lady Ahn mentioned been caved in centuries ago?

I kept swimming upward; a blind creature thinking only of air. Suddenly my head smacked into rock. I almost passed out. I clawed upwards, fingernails shredding against the roof of the stone chamber. No air. I had to go *back*!

I groped blindly, my lungs searing with the sharp prick of a dozen daggers.

Air! I needed air!

I kicked, trying desperately to turn myself around. I'd have to swim back down to the bottom again, out of this tunnel, and then back up to the surface of the pool.

But how would I make it? There was no way I could stand this flaming pain in my chest any longer. I needed air now!

Suddenly, my flailing arm broke through to open water.

The rock wasn't a roof after all. Just an outcropping. I shot up past it, an explosion of pain searing my lungs. The opening from the rock wall to the outcropping was very narrow; rock scraped the flesh of my chest as I pushed through.

And then I felt it. The surface.

I exploded up like some demented sea lion; roaring,

gasping for air. I inhaled greedily. My lungs filled with dust and decay but also with air. Sweet air!

I inhaled and exhaled with conscious effort. Savoring the sensation.

In the darkness which surrounded me, I groped along a craggy limestone wall and found a ledge. Propping my elbows atop it, I pulled myself onto dry land.

I crawled forward, still groping. Objects. Some made of wood. Some of metal. Some box-shaped, others like teapots or vases or delicately carved icons. Some were cool to the touch. Smooth. Carefully varnished.

What treasures these must be if I could only see!

Finally, I found what I was after. Even though it was larger than I expected, there was no mistake.

It had the smooth, solid feel of jade. Curved, its surface pimpled with details. All along the inner and outer surface, it was intricately crafted with minute design. Not a pattern. Everything slightly different. Never repeating itself.

I'd found the jade skull.

I hefted the skull in both hands, turned it upside down, imagined it filled to the brim. I could almost smell the biting, rancid odor of the fermented mare's milk Kublai Khan used to drain from it seven centuries ago.

The skull made me feel oddly powerful. Any man who could drink from an object such as this had to be a man amongst men. A king. An emperor. Definitely a standout at Eighth Army Happy Hour.

Something slithered against my thigh. I recoiled instinctively and reached down. A snake! No, whatever it was wriggled out of my grasp. A lizard, I decided. Maybe a salamander.

No sense waiting down here to find out what other types of critters might be intrigued by a warm body. I took three deep breaths, then lowered myself back into the icy water. Sinking down with the jade skull was easier than coming up. I knew what to expect now and wouldn't panic. I'd make my air last longer. When I reached the bottom, I cradled the antique in my arms to protect it from jagged granite. As I swam back into the bottom of the pool, I was almost blinded by the quavering beam of the light far above. Soon, I could see her. Lady Ahn. Crouched forward. Ernie hovering behind her.

When I hit the surface I gasped for air and sputtered. Ernie clamped his hand over my mouth, leaned forward, and hissed: "Monks."

I eased out of the pool, shivering. I rose and held the jade skull in front of my chest.

As the beam of Lady Ahn's flashlight ran through it, an expanding aura emanated from within. The skull glowed eerily, shooting off emerald rays into the darkness, filling the world with its green-toothed grin of death.

Lady Ahn's face remained impassive but tears ran down her smooth cheeks.

Ernie sneered, as if to say, "What's the big deal?"

In the distance I heard men talking, footsteps.

Motioning for me to grab ahold of the hemp rope around her waist, Lady Ahn also made it clear to Ernie that he was to keep track of me by grabbing the elastic band of my shorts.

My body rattled with cold. Lady Ahn tucked the bundle of my clothing under my arm, switched off the flashlight, and moved forward. The voices followed us through the maze of tunnels like whispers in a nightmare.

Lady Ahn knew the tunnels well. She never faltered. She never slowed.

Soon, we were running.

WHEN WE FINALLY EMERGED FROM THE MOUNTAIN OF MYSterious Peace, I blinked, blinded by the light. Actually, the morning was heavily overcast and almost as dark as night.

The cloud cover above rolled fast, pushed by an impatient wind. Still, nothing could make me go back into the dank bowels of the volcano from which we'd escaped.

We hadn't heard any monks behind us for some time, so we stopped, and I enjoyed the luxury of slipping into dry clothing.

"Let me see this damn head," Ernie said.

Lady Ahn offered the skull to him and he held it up to the sky. Its grin was sinister, as if it came from the wickedest man in the world. But even in this shadowed world, it was clear that the etchings circling the jade sphere were of an exquisite quality.

Lady Ahn stared at Ernie nervously, probably afraid he might drop the skull.

"Come on," she urged. "We have much jungle to cross before we reach the boat."

We were about a half mile from the spot where we had originally entered Bian Mountain. After gently prying the jade skull from Ernie's grasp, Lady Ahn led us through an opening in the thick foliage. The passage was narrow, overhung with branches, and seemed more like a game trail than a pathway for humans.

"I hope they don't have any warthogs around here," Ernie complained.

"Are you kidding? People would've killed them off for bul-kogi centuries ago."

"I don't know," Ernie grumbled. "I don't think many of the locals are dumb enough to come to this island. Only us."

We must've been less than a hundred yards from the shore when the clouds opened and rays of sunshine filtered to the ground. Lady Ahn paused long enough to smile back at me, both of us appreciating the golden slivers of light.

Above her, crossing over the path, loomed a large knotted branch. She ducked under it, and Ernie was just about to follow when the knot quivered.

I'm not sure what warned me, but somehow I knew that this wasn't good. I shouted and leapt at Ernie's back.

I slammed into his spine, tackling him forward, and his head jerked down toward the ground.

"What the—?"

As we fell, two wickedly curved spikes of brown ivory swished down in a vicious arc. By a fraction of an inch, the spikes missed Ernie's skull. We crashed into the ground. I rolled and watched the dark knot unravel itself from the bark. As it dropped from the sky, I realized that the spikes I had seen weren't spikes at all but claws.

The creature thudded on top of Ernie.

He grunted, air exploded from his lungs, and then he screamed.

I scrambled to my feet. The beast, whatever it was, was large and furry and brown. A bear? A giant monkey? No time to think about it now. I grabbed a rock.

The creature shrugged when the rock hit but made no sound. It didn't release its grip on Ernie's neck. Again I slammed it with the rock: It just seemed to cling tighter.

Lady Ahn was back now, a sharp branch in her hand. Screaming. Poking at the beast.

It rolled Ernie over and I realized what had fallen on him. It had a tiny face and huge hairy arms, longer than a man's. A short body. Clicking claws dug into Ernie's back.

A sloth! A goddamn giant sloth.

Ernie had a grip on its paws and with all his strength was barely managing to keep the big ivory spikes from ripping his face apart.

I grabbed one of the arms and pulled. No dice. The thing was incredibly strong.

Ernie's face was blue from lack of oxygen.

I crouched and grabbed a better hold, with two hands, on one of the sloth's arms. Bracing my feet against a rock outcropping, I managed to slowly force the arm away from Ernie. Once I was above the open arm, I leaned down on it, letting my weight do the work. It took forever.

When I finally shoved the big clawed limb to the ground, I stepped on it, pinning it firmly with all my weight. Bone and ligament crunched beneath my heel but the ugly beast didn't let out so much as a whimper.

The other furry arm was still wrapped around Ernie. I grabbed it. As it started to budge, Ernie croaked out a choking sound.

Lady Ahn dragged Ernie away.

But now I had a giant sloth spread-eagled between my feet and my outstretched arms. How in the hell was I going to get out of this?

The sloth kept trying to close his powerful arms. I held him back, but my strength was ebbing. His hadn't lessened at all.

Menacing beetle eyes watched me, huge curved claws twitching and clinking together, just waiting for the chance to slash my neck.

Lady Ahn knew what to do. As soon as Ernie was safe, she grabbed her sharp branch. When she jabbed the creature's neck, the arms spasmed. Stumbling at the unexpected movement, I almost lost my grip. Lady Ahn stabbed down with the stick again. The ferretlike face beneath me twisted from side to side, trying to avoid the sharp point of the probing spear. A slice opened in the sloth's neck. Shoving down, arms straining, Lady Ahn jabbed the stick deep into the creature's throat.

Hot blood squirted upward, splattering my pant legs. Droplets splashed across Lady Ahn's muddy linen leggings.

The sloth strained with its long muscles one more time, so violently that I almost fell. Finally, it shuddered and lay still.

I watched the sharp claws slap into the mud. Lady Ahn stepped back. She grimaced at her bloody spear, then tossed it into the foliage.

Still rubbing his neck, Ernie stumbled to his feet.

"What the fuck was that?" he wheezed.

"Just a teddy bear," I said when I could, breathing heavily. "It wanted to hug you."

Lady Ahn took three quick breaths, scooped up the jade skull, and started down the trail. Ernie and I glanced at one another, amazed at her resilience. Then we turned and followed.

AS I HEARD THE FIRST CRASH OF BREAKERS ON THE SHORE, I noticed Lady Ahn's shoulders were heaving. I hurried forward. Her cheeks were wet with tears. When I tried to speak to her, she turned her face away.

At the tree line we finally halted. There, on the pebbled incline along the beach, stood Fisherman Yun next to the prow of his ancient skiff.

Nothing ever looked so wonderful.

The three of us rushed forward.

As we stumbled across the rocks, Fisherman Yun's weathered face broke into a broad smile. Just as suddenly as the smile had appeared, however, it faded. Yun gaped.

Out of the trees emerged a line of seven men with shaved heads and long robes. They strode quickly toward us. Lady Ahn moved behind me, covering the jade skull with her hands.

Ten feet away, the men stopped.

"*Anyonghaseiyo*," one said. Good day.

18

THE SLOTH, I FIGURED, WAS AN IMPORT.

It was a dangerous, slow-moving tropical animal that would never have survived in Korea during all the thousands of years the peninsula has been populated by aggressive hunters and rice farmers.

The species must've been brought to the island of Biando by Lady Ahn's ancestor, Ahn the Righteous Fist, to help protect the treasure hidden deep in the bowels of the mountain. Who knows what other sorts of creatures lurked in the thick foliage of Bian Island? I didn't want to find out.

As we stood on the rock-strewn beach gaping at the mouth of the AK-47, Ernie decided to act nonchalant. He stared at the monks, like a punk on a street corner trying to intimidate the gang from another block.

One of the monks stepped forward. His head was shaved, and the brown leather of his skin stretched tightly across high cheekbones.

"*Chosim heiya ji,*" he said. You must be careful. "*Yogi ei dongmul manhayo.*" There are many animals here.

I translated. Ernie nodded toward the automatic weapon still pointed at us. "You ought to be careful with that thing, too."

The leathery monk barked an order. The AK-47 was lowered.

Lady Ahn stepped forward, arms wrapped around the jade skull, head bowed. Gracefully, she lowered herself to a kneeling position on the beach.

"We have greatly bothered you," she told the monk in formal Korean. "For that I am full of regret."

Ernie fidgeted, not liking all the groveling, even of a formal kind, but I shot him an evil look, warning him to shut up.

It was our only chance. Koreans have to work these things out in their own way. Ways that have been mapped out by thousands of years of culture.

While they talked, Ernie and I moved a few feet farther apart. If we had to charge, one of us might be able to reach the gunman.

The leather-faced monk narrowed his eyes at us. "*Umjiki-jima!*" he said. Don't move. Ernie and I froze.

He spoke to Lady Ahn in rapid Korean. So rapid I had trouble following it all. But in general he was berating her for having stolen the skull, for not coming to him and explaining why she wanted it. He knew of her descent from the last emperor of the Sung dynasty; he knew, too, that the precious jade skull held the key to untold wealth.

Lady Ahn raised her voice and interrupted him. Ernie grinned. I held my breath. Pissing the monk off was a gamble. This guy held all the aces. Nobody even knew we were on this island.

"If I had come to you," Lady Ahn said, "would you have turned the jade skull over to me?"

The monk thought about it for a moment. "No. I would not have."

"Then I had no choice. I had to devise a plan. I had to seek help. Not from Koreans. It would be too tempting for a Korean to betray me and keep the wealth for himself. So I had to seek help from these foreigners, who have no family here. Who have no ties to ancient clans or to secret societies. Had I asked for the jade skull, you would've laughed at me."

"No." The monk shook his bald head. "I would not have laughed. I understand your desire to see the Sung dynasty rise again. To see a fully Chinese emperor once again sit on the Dragon Throne. Not a Mongol. Not a Manchu. Not some intellectual with political ideas stolen from the West. But a true Chinese leader of royal blood. Don't you think we have wanted the same thing, too?"

Lady Ahn raised her head, staring up at the monk, her jaw clamped tightly. The monk continued.

"But where would we find such a leader? The answer is simple. No one can find such a leader. Such a leader must rise by his own strength. No matter what the obstacles. So the answer is no. Had you asked for the jade skull, I would have turned you down. But you didn't ask, you *took* it!"

The other monks murmured in assent.

Fisherman Yun crouched silently in his boat, a look of grave resignation on his face, as if he expected to be executed any moment. Ernie's teeth clicked madly on his ginseng gum, his eyes darting like two bumblebees swarming from a hive. He was about to make a move, no question about it, and there was nothing I could do to stop him.

The monk turned to his own men. "She *took* it," he said again. "And with a bold plan. With fierce warriors performing daring feats at her command!"

The monks murmured again, a little more fiercely this

time. Ernie didn't understand enough Korean to follow this. The monk with the AK-47 raised it slightly.

The chief monk turned back to Lady Ahn and held out his open palm. "Rise, Lady Ahn," he commanded. "Rise!"

Ernie picked this moment to dart for the shore. A monk stepped in front of him.

Ernie flung out his elbow, catching the monk square in the jaw with a loud crack, slamming his bald head back.

Everyone on the beach exploded into action. One monk leapt at Ernie and grabbed him by the ankles; another snatched the skull out of Lady Ahn's hands. Three more swarmed toward Ernie. They piled on until he lay on his back punching and cursing and kicking.

I tried to pull them off of him, but somebody threw me to the ground with a deft judo move. When I looked up, the monk with the rifle held the barrel on me. Smiling.

After a few well-placed karate chops, Ernie lay silent on the blanket of pebbles. I watched his chest rise and fall. He slept as soundly as a lifer after Happy Hour.

The monks dusted off their robes and resumed their positions behind their leader.

During the fight, Lady Ahn had risen to her feet. She now stood staring solemnly at the leather-faced monk.

He motioned. A young monk stepped forward. Holding the jade skull out with two hands, the monk said, "You earned the jade skull." He offered it to Lady Ahn. "It is yours, good lady. Do with it as you wish."

She accepted it, then bowed. He barked another order. The monk with the rifle pulled out the curved ammunition clip, switched the rifle to safety, and tossed both the rifle and the clip to me. Startled, I barely caught the weapon before it hit the ground.

The chief monk spoke again, this time in English.

"The rifle belonged to the man who tried to invade our island two weeks ago. He wore the uniform of a North

Korean commando and carried one of their weapons, but he wasn't one of them." The monk waved his arm behind him. "This island has no military value. The man was a mere thug. His mission was to sneak into our temple and steal the jade skull. However, he was careless, and the brown sloth caught him before he could complete his job." The monk turned and stared into Lady Ahn's eyes. "The man was hired by another foreigner who stalks our land. This foreigner is a Mongol, a member of a people who have plagued our peaceful country before. This foreigner knows of the Tomb of Genghis Khan and he knows of the jade skull. He is ruthless; he will stop at nothing to possess it. We have no use for that rifle. But if you and your soldiers insist on keeping the jade skull, you will need it."

Lady Ahn bowed until her head was level with her waist. "We are grateful, Honored Monk."

She stood upright and the monk looked her over one last time. "Make your ancestors proud," he said.

With that, he barked a final order and he and his entourage disappeared into the trees and shrubs that lined the shore.

Ernie came to and jerked his head up.

"Where are they?" he said. "I'll knock me some bald-headed monk out."

"Relax, Ernie," I said. "They're gone."

We were in the boat now, Fisherman Yun rhythmically pulling on the oar, Lady Ahn sitting forward, clutching the jade skull, staring into the distance.

Ernie rubbed the back of his head. "What happened?"

"You got your ass kicked."

"I mean, besides that."

"The monks decided they liked Lady Ahn's style. They let her keep the skull."

"What do you mean they let *her* keep it? We *all* stole it, right? Fair and square."

Lady Ahn didn't move, although she must've heard Ernie's comment.

"She still plans to trade it for Mi-ja," I answered. "Don't worry about anything else."

This time I noticed her back tense a little. Maybe she was having second thoughts about releasing the jade skull after all she'd gone through to possess it. I had no such doubts. The skull had to be traded for Mi-ja. I'd see that it was. One little girl's life was more important than all these bitter squabbles over ancient treasure.

Mi-ja was real. And she needed our help. And she needed our help now.

I decided to keep an eye on Lady Ahn.

Not that I hadn't before.

LADY AHN'S MOTHER WAS SO SAD TO SEE HER DAUGHTER GO that she couldn't hide her tears. As we left on the ferry, Lady Ahn held hers through what seemed to be a massive display of will.

After the ferry stopped at the first island on its way back to the mainland and picked up a few more passengers, Lady Ahn told us about the KNP inspection routine at the dock in Ok-dong.

"They don't inspect every bag," she said. "Just the ones that might produce a tip for them."

A bribe is what she meant.

Plenty of smuggling went on in these islands. Foreign products not stamped by the Ministry of Customs were illegal. A few hundred won, however, would convince most KNPs to look the other way. But they wouldn't look the other way for an AK-47 automatic rifle. Or an antique of such obvious value as Kublai Khan's jade drinking cup skull.

Our problem was how to slip both items past them.

Lady Ahn shoved the jade skull deep into a twenty pound sack of unhusked rice, threw away some of the excess grain, and slung the heavy bag over her shoulder. The sack looked big and awkward. It might work. It might not.

Ernie had dismantled the stock from the main firing chamber of the AK-47. The disassembled mechanism fit easily into the bottom of his leather bag.

Still, it was a big risk. Either item, if discovered, would set off alarm bells from here to Seoul. The first thing that would happen is that they'd be confiscated. The second thing that would happen is we'd be thrown in jail.

Ernie and I would almost certainly be court-martialed for carrying a Communist-made weapon. I thought of getting rid of it. In fact, I damn near told Ernie to toss it over the side. But finally, I reconsidered. Now that we had the jade skull, there was no telling who might be after us.

At the time, I figured I was just paranoid.

The skull was a bigger risk than the machine gun. The Korean government would take possession of it and we'd never see it again. And then we'd have nothing to use to bargain for Mi-ja's freedom.

Once they knew they weren't going to obtain the jade skull, the kidnappers would only want to cover their tracks. Killing Mi-ja was the sure way of doing that.

Leaning on the rail of the ferry, the three of us talked it over.

The sky was gray. Gulls swooped into the choppy waters of the Yellow Sea. The crisp air reeked of fish.

Lady Ahn thought we should be prepared to pay a large bribe.

Ernie objected. "No way. I'm not coughing up no more money to no more KNPs." He waved his hand dismissively. "You just leave it to me. I'll get this stuff past them."

Maybe he would. Still, I counted out the dollars I had

on me. Less than forty. Lady Ahn had about fifteen thousand won, almost thirty bucks.

That might work. But it would leave us broke and with no money to make it back to Seoul.

The worst case was that it would only be enough money to piss off the KNP, and instead of letting us off the hook we'd be charged—in addition to arms smuggling and theft of national treasures—with attempted bribery of a public official.

Ernie occupied himself with trying to hustle three college girls wearing caps and backpacks and hiking boots. He passed out ginseng gum all around, and soon the four of them were laughing.

Lady Ahn and I went to the galley and bought two tin cans of iced coffee. We walked back up on the deck. As we sipped, the lush islands of the Korean west coast floated by.

She wore a freshly pressed pair of beige denim slacks, a sky-blue blouse, and a brown windbreaker with a snap-on collar like the race car drivers wear. Shades would've completed the picture, but Lady Ahn was too busy studying the world to allow anything to intervene.

As she breathed slowly, I watched her and thought of reaching for her hand. Somehow, I never quite worked up the courage.

THE CROWD DEBARKING FROM THE FERRY PUSHED AND shoved. Everybody shouted, trying to reach the narrow exitway past the Korean National Police inspection counter.

Some of the women with bundles atop their heads had to stop and open them. Others were waved through by white-gloved policemen.

When it came our turn, Lady Ahn went first, followed by me and then Ernie right behind. The fat policeman pointed at Lady Ahn's bag. He told her to drop it on the counter.

Ernie stepped forward. "Wait just a minute, honcho," he said. "I saw that little lady in front of us and you let her squirt on by without so much as a howdy-do."

The fat policeman stared at him blankly, not understanding a word he said. Ernie leaned forward, jabbing his forefinger into the palm of his open hand.

"You have to understand here, *chingu*. Us *Miguk* people, we don't put up with this kind of treatment. No, sir."

Ernie pounded on his chest like a gorilla from the Congo.

"I'm an American, you *alla*? Born and bred in the U.S.A. No, sir. We don't put up with this type of treatment. We're here defending your country and we demand to be treated with some serious respect!"

The line behind us came to a complete halt. People craned their necks to see what was going on and still kept shoving forward. Soon, some of them started to yell.

"I want to see your boss!" Ernie roared. "I want to see your honcho and I want to see him right now!"

The Korean National Policeman was still confused, not sure what was going on. Most people just followed his orders. He wasn't used to some big-nosed foreigner shouting loud English at him.

Other cops yelled at him to keep the line moving. Someone in an office behind the counter with its big plate-glass window finally noticed the commotion. A man dressed in a neatly pressed khaki uniform under a brass-braided cap strolled out.

The same officer who had waved us through when we boarded the ferry two days ago.

When the officer saw Ernie, his face crinkled as if he'd bitten into a sour persimmon. The KNP looked at him for instruction.

"*Migun itjiyo?*" the honcho shouted. Aren't they GIs?

"Nei." The fat cop nodded. *"Migun ieiyo."* Yes. They're GIs.

The honcho impatiently waved his hand. *"Kurum ka. Bali ka!"* Then let them go.

The KNP waved us forward. Ernie glared at the cop for a moment, shifted his bag on his shoulder, thrust out his chest, and sashayed past the inspection counter.

Lady Ahn and I stayed right with him.

ON THE MAIN DRAG OF OK-DONG, WE STOPPED IN A NOODLE shop and ordered three bowls of *meiun-tang.* Spicy noodle soup, the broth flavored with a few tiny clams and the head of a mackerel.

Lady Ahn slurped delicately on her noodles. I asked Ernie about the college chicks he'd met on the ferry.

"They're from some university out near Suwon. They gave me their phone numbers, but I don't think I'll call them."

"Why not?"

"Because they only want to go out with me one at a time."

"So?"

"When I meet 'em in a group, I want them to stay in a group. All the way into the sack."

Lady Ahn's cheeks turned pink. I changed the subject.

"Looks like rain," I said.

A few drops slapped against the pavement.

"Yes," Lady Ahn said. "We must hurry."

We paid the bill, shouldered our bags, and trooped through the narrow pathways of Ok-dong, heading for the bus station.

LOOKING BACK ON IT, THERE WERE SIGNS I SHOULD'VE NO-ticed. The local villagers didn't stare at us, as they would normally when encountering foreigners. Instead, they turned their heads away.

Men loitered near wooden carts, squatting and exchanging cigarettes. Nobody loiters in Korea. Especially not in a remote fishing village, where scratching out a living is a full-time occupation.

And the leather-faced monk on Bian Island had warned us. Other people were after the jade skull.

THE REEK OF SALTED FLESH FILLED THE AIR, MINGLING WITH A dry mist of sawdust kicked up by our feet.

We had decided to take a shortcut through the Ok-dong market.

Ahead, huge glass tanks swarmed with fish. On either side, damp wooden stalls wriggled with purple-veined squid and piles of reddish crabs pinching madly into nothingness. Above us, a sea of canvas blocked the sky.

Two men stepped out from behind glass tanks. Three more appeared behind us.

All wore the loose pantaloons and soiled vests of farmers. But in their hands each man held a short heavy club or the wickedly curved sickle used for harvesting grain.

They were sunburned men and not Koreans. I knew right away who they were. Mongols. Ragyapa's thugs.

I pushed Lady Ahn behind me until her back was pressed against a stall crawling with crustaceans. Ernie dropped his bag, unzipped it, and started scratching through it frantically.

Searching for the AK-47.

19

SHORTS AND SOCKS ERUPTED INTO THE AIR. BUT NO MATTER how many of them he tossed out of the bag, Ernie still couldn't pry out the AK-47. As the five men closed in, I snatched up a handful of slimy squid and flung it at them. They backed up for a second, covering their eyes. But when the limp flesh flopped into the mud, they bared their teeth in sinister grins.

I didn't have a weapon. No clubs, no tree branches, no loose rocks lying about. I braced myself, prepared to use my fists and my feet and, if necessary, my teeth.

Ernie tugged and cursed and started to rip the leather bag apart.

From the corner of my eye, I saw Lady Ahn slide behind the crab stall.

Ernie had the AK-47 out of the bag now and was fumbling with the ammunition clip, holding it upside down, twisting it, trying to ram it home.

One of the men near the fish tank raised his sickle, let out a blood-curdling scream, and charged.

The world started to tilt. For an instant I felt as if I was suffering from vertigo. Then I realized that it was the glass fish tank, slowly toppling over.

Before the man with the sickle could reach us, a tsunami of water and fins exploded out of the top of the tank. The wave crashed onto his back, followed by glass and metal rods and about a jillion shimmering sardines. The attacker was swallowed up in the deluge.

Lady Ahn stood behind the tank, still shoving, her face glowing with rage.

The men behind us closed in.

I grabbed a handful of crab, flung it, and hopped forward, kicking with the upturned toe of my sneakers. A swooshing club missed my forehead by an inch. My foot caught rib, the man grunted, and I followed with a left jab. The punch landed on his chin.

Something slammed into my arm. Fire exploded from my elbow to my shoulder blade. The canvas above me swirled madly. I remember punching and gouging, but I'm not sure who all this fury was aimed at.

Again something rammed into my back. I realized it was one of the stalls. It was flattened, and I was lying on top of it. Crabs pinched my neck.

Above me a sickle whistled through the air. I rolled. The curved blade slammed into the dust.

And then a blast filled the air. An unmistakable rat-a-tat-tat and a sinus-cleansing burst of gunsmoke.

Suddenly Ernie stood above me, his face red, cords bulging in his neck, screaming, spraying the poles and canvas rooftops of the market with a stream of lethal AK-47 pellets.

Just as suddenly as it began, the firing stopped. Ernie's

hand reached down, I grabbed it, and he yanked me to my feet.

"Out of ammo," he said. "Let's un-ass the area."

"By all means," I said.

Amidst the splintered stalls and tattered canvas and flopping fish, Lady Ahn appeared at my side. I grabbed her and pulled her close.

"Let's go!"

We ran out of the market, away from the bus station, through the narrow pathways of Ok-dong. Not sure where in the hell we were going.

Near the edge of the town, where the vast expanse of green rice paddies began, we finally stopped, panting for breath.

"Did I lay it on 'em, pal? Or *what*?" Ernie yelled.

Lady Ahn peered around nervously, at the rickety shacks behind fences of splintered slats and rusted chicken wire.

"Quiet down, Ernie," I said. "The assholes might still be in the area."

"No way," Ernie said. "We lost 'em. Once I pulled out this baby . . ." he patted the AK-47, ". . . no way they were going to follow."

I wasn't so sure about that. "You didn't kill any of them, did you?"

"Naw. Shot over their heads. But I should've blown a few of them away." He mimed firing the automatic weapon once again. "Rock and *roll!*"

What Ernie needed was a sedative. Or a couple of shots of bourbon.

Lady Ahn tugged on my arm. "We must leave. Quickly!"

"Yes," I agreed. "But they'll be watching the bus station. And there aren't any taxicabs way out here."

"We will find a way," she said. "I will show you."

TWENTY MINUTES LATER, WE STOOD INSIDE A TIN-ROOFED shack peering at a small tractor with a square wooden platform bolted behind the driver's seat. Designed for transporting fifty-pound bags of grain.

A snaggle-toothed farmer grinned at us. He'd never in his life seen such an entertaining display as the three of us. "How much does he want?" I asked.

"Ten thousand won," Lady Ahn answered. Twenty bucks.

"And he'll take us all the way to Taejon?"

"On the back roads only. He'll let us off near the outskirts. Not in the town itself."

"Okay," Ernie said. "It's a deal."

The farmer also threw in three bowls of rice gruel and some turnip kimchi, which we ate while hiding inside the tin shack.

When night fell, the moon rose almost full but not quite. If we were going to save Mi-ja, we had to reach Seoul by tomorrow. The three of us crammed ourselves into the back of the tractor, the cackling old farmer at the wheel. The farmer fired up the engine and we drove off down the bumpy country road, heading once again toward the provincial capital of Taejon.

MY LEGS HAD CRAMPED INTO KNOTS AND MY BUTT WAS AS SORE as a bad boy's rump at a corporal punishment convention. The ancient tractor bounced up and down with every rut. The straw-hatted farmer stared straight ahead into the night. Ernie kept up a steady stream of cursing.

To make matters worse, the heavens opened up as if they had only one last chance to water a parched planet.

Lady Ahn snuggled up against me, clutching the skull in the soaked burlap bag, and I held a plastic sheet over our heads. Ernie had lost everything in the fight in the fish

market and sat with his arms crossed, hugging the AK-47.
Rain ran in rivulets down his straight nose and puddled on
cursing lips.

I had offered him the use of my shirt or the underwear
in my bag but stubbornly he had refused. Finally, he gave
in and grabbed my overnight bag and set the whole thing
atop his head. It didn't provide much shelter.

I thought about the Mongols who had attacked us, trying to bring the memory of their faces vividly into my
mind.

They were tough rascals. Dark-skinned and wiry and
with an apparent relish for combat that only men long
used to violence could attain. They held Mi-ja, and she
was totally at their mercy.

The tractor slammed down hard into a pothole. Soil
reeking of septic tank splashed up and engulfed us in a
rancid wave. Ernie emitted a particularly colorful series of
expletives but the old farmer just kept churning forward.

Soon the rainwater had washed much of the mud off of
us. Through it all, Lady Ahn sat next to me. Uncomplain-
ing. As long as she held the skull in her hands, she seemed
happy.

Streetlamps started to appear at the side of the road.
And then huts and buildings and even a two-story *yoguan*
with a rain-soaked wooden sign over its door.

The farmer stopped the tractor, turned off the ignition,
and the engine coughed, sputtered, and died.

"Yogi isso," he said, still smiling. Here you are.
"Taejon."

I unraveled my legs in sections, stepped out onto the
pavement, and shakily brought myself to the standing position. Ahead in the distance lay a sea of more lights and
even high-rise buildings. Bright blue and yellow neon sparkled through the rain and I could make out the tiny letter-

ing atop one of the skyscrapers. The Pyong-an Tourist Hotel.

Luxury. But much too far away. We'd settle for this small establishment in front of us. The Somun Yoguan. The Westgate Inn.

I paid the farmer. He started up the engine of his tractor, and waved to us as he drove away. Still grinning.

Easy money, he was probably thinking. If we were foolish enough to offer it, he was damn sure going to take it.

We pushed through the heavy oak door of the inn. After a couple of minutes, the chubby woman who owned the Somun Yoguan overcame her shock at seeing two rain-drenched Americans accompanied by a soaked-to-the-skin Korean woman of regal beauty. We paid for two rooms. The owner led us down creaking wooden hallways. Rounding a corner, she slid back a paper-paneled door.

It was a little square room with no beds, just folded sleeping mats and wood-slat floors heated by steam ducts running beneath the foundation.

The owner left Ernie and me, guiding Lady Ahn to her quarters. She returned a few minutes later with a metal tray piled high with hot rolled hand towels and steaming cups of barley tea. When I rubbed the towel on the back of my neck and sipped on the tea, a semblance of color started to return to my shriveled skin.

Ernie was the last to use the *byonso*. While he was gone, Lady Ahn tiptoed down the hallway. Without a word, she took me by the hand and led me to her room.

We slid the door shut and turned off the light. The rain had stopped and the clouds were beginning to disperse. Beams of moonlight drifted through an open curtain. Instead of appearing beautiful, the light from the almost full moon filled me with dread. Dread for what would happen to Mi-ja if we didn't reach Seoul soon.

Lady Ahn sensed my discomfort. She undressed me and

wiped my cold skin with a warm towel. I forgot all worries and did the same for her.

I knelt in front of her. Ministering to royalty. Ministering to beauty.

THE NEXT MORNING ERNIE WASN'T EXACTLY MOROSE, BUT HE wasn't happy either. Usually, he's the one who makes it with the chicks. I'm not sure why. Maybe it's because he doesn't try. He just does whatever crazy thing comes into his demented mind and women find it exciting. Unpredictable.

Personally, I could live without the unpredictable part.

We ordered breakfast in the room: *jiggei peikpan*, white rice with kimchi and bean curd soup. After we ate, we stuffed the AK-47 into my overnight bag and stepped out into the already bustling city of Taejon. Our clothes were still damp.

We waved down a cab, clambered in, and Lady Ahn gave directions. The Rising Phoenix Antique Shop in the district of Chungku.

When we pushed into the shop, the familiar bell tinkled above us. The same young clerk Ernie and I had frightened last time stepped out from behind the still-splintered glass counter. Wide-eyed, she bowed at the waist.

"Kang *oddiso*?" Lady Ahn asked. Where's Kang?

The clerk stood upright and raised her fingertips to her lips. Tears welled up in her eyes.

"*Mullasso, onni?*" You don't know, older sister?

"What?" Lady Ahn asked. "What is it I don't know?"

"The Widow Kang was found in her apartment." The young clerk turned her face, tears streaming easily down the soft skin of her cheeks. "She had been tortured. And cut many times."

"Cut? Is she still alive?"

"No, older sister. They cut her throat." The young

woman clutched at her thin neck convulsively. "Cut it so deep the policeman said they carved into the bone."

I translated for Ernie but somehow he'd already figured out what was going on. "It's Fifi, right?" I nodded. "I think we'd better get out of here," he said. "Now."

Lady Ahn's face was blank from shock. I grabbed her and the three of us slipped out the back door and down the alleyway.

No one followed. At least I don't think they did.

WE PUSHED DOWN THE SIDEWALK, PAST CHILDREN IN BLACK uniforms carrying heavy book bags over their shoulders. In the street, men in loose pantaloons wheeled carts piled high with giant cabbages.

"They'll be watching the trains," I said.

Ernie nodded. "And the bus station."

Lady Ahn's voice was hoarse but her words were strong and clear. "We must hire a car," she said.

"That'll cost money."

"Not much. I know a place."

We walked rapidly, none of us talking, chewing up the kilometers. Red-striped municipal buses roared past us, spewing out diesel fumes. Korean army convoys honked their horns and rolled haltingly past seas of pedestrians and bell-chiming bicycles. We were nearing the downtown area.

At a big circular intersection, we stopped under the awning of an open-front store.

"People who need gas money for a long trip congregate here," Lady Ahn told us. "You wait. I will search for someone traveling to Seoul."

"I'll come with you."

"No. If they see an American face, the price goes up. And they might not even want to travel with you."

"Okay," I agreed. "But stay out on the sidewalk where I can see you."

For the first time since we'd learned of the Widow Kang's murder, Lady Ahn smiled. "I will."

After she left, Ernie sauntered into the store and bought two packs of ginseng gum and three small tins of guava juice. I thanked him when he handed me one, popped open the top, and drank it down quickly. I was more thirsty than I thought.

"Maybe those dudes are watching this area, too," Ernie said.

"Maybe. But I doubt it. They're foreigners like us. They won't know about this place. An unofficial rendezvous for people seeking transportation."

"I hope not." Ernie glugged down his guava. "I heard you last night."

"Heard what?"

"I heard you *and* I heard her."

"You know Korean custom. You're supposed to pretend that you didn't hear."

"Hey, I'm still a *Miguk*. Or almost, anyway."

"American, maybe. But you're getting as bad as Strange."

Strange was one of our information contacts back in Seoul. Although a pervert in his personal life, he was the noncommissioned officer in charge of all the Top Secret documents at Eighth Army Headquarters. Appropriate, when you thought about it.

"I'm just looking out for your welfare, pal," Ernie told me. "There's something weird about this Lady Ahn. She hasn't told us everything."

"Maybe not," I snapped. "But she's told us enough."

"Okay," Ernie said. "Just commenting."

I filled Ernie in on what Lady Ahn told me last night while we lay together in the Westgate yoguan. The first thing I asked about was her reaction to the jade amulet the little nun had given Ernie.

"It frightened me," she explained. "Because it proved that many people are now looking for the jade skull."

"How so?"

"Maitreya is the most important saint for the largest Buddhist sect in Korea. On the amulet, he is fighting Mahakala, the god of the Mongols. The Mongols practice a different kind of Buddhism. Some of them are very good. But some of them like to fight."

"And you think that both Buddhist sects, the ones who control Korea and the ones who control Mongolia, are now after the jade skull?"

"Yes. That is why the little nun was in Itaewon. Her temple must've heard rumors about me. And about Herman. The nun was a spy, trying to learn what she could about the jade skull."

"And someone attacked her because of it?"

"Of course."

"Will the Buddhists who rule Korea send men after us also?"

"No. They are much too powerful for that. They will try to steal the jade skull, but they won't kill us. Not out in the open anyway."

Okay. It made sense. But I had one more question.

"If these two important groups of Buddhists are after the jade skull, why did the monks on Bian-do let us go free?"

"Because the monks of Bian-do have lived alone for many centuries. They belong to neither sect, and they are true Buddhists. Not concerned with money."

"And if you retake the throne of the Sung dynasty . . ."

"Yes," she said. "I will honor the monks of Bian-do and give them the chance to spread their faith amongst millions of people."

While we stood in the little shop, I explained all this to Ernie.

"These religious guys are just as greedy as all the other bastards," he said.

"I don't know," I said. "Maybe they think they have a right to the jade skull."

Before I could explain further, Lady Ahn trotted back into the store. Ernie polished off his guava juice and handed her a tin.

"I found a car," she told us. "It belongs to a gambler who lost all of his money at the casino at Songni-san. We'll have to buy the gasoline."

"No sweat," Ernie said. "Can do easy."

Before we left, Ernie loaded up with some puffed rice disks and some dried cuttlefish and four bottles of sparkling apple cider. And another pack of gum, just in case.

The gambler pulled his little Hyundai sedan up next to the curb and flashed us a toothy grin. We clambered in, Ernie riding shotgun, Lady Ahn and me in the back.

The gambler told us his name was Mr. Peik. As he wound through the Taejon traffic, he described how bad his luck had been at the roulette table. We stopped and bought gas. When we rolled onto the Seoul-Pusan Expressway heading north, I paid the toll.

Mr. Peik kept up a steady chatter in Korean until Ernie reached into my overnight bag and pulled out the AK-47. Peik's hands tightened on the steering wheel, his head swiveled, and his Adam's apple started to bob while his eyes bulged halfway out of his head.

Ernie pointed straight down the highway and said only one word in English: "Drive."

Mr. Peik, the gambler, stepped on the gas pedal, pressed his nose up against the top of the steering wheel, and kept his bulging eyes glued to the white lines slashing beneath our tires on the pavement below.

WE ONLY MADE ONE PIT STOP DURING THE ENTIRE TRIP. THIS time Ernie bought papaya juice and we drank that down and munched on dried squid tentacles that tasted a lot like beef jerky.

Mr. Peik lived in Seoul, and had no trouble navigating the maze of roads when we crossed the Han River. Ernie told him to take us to Itaewon, so the guy hung a right at the Samgakji Circle, cruised past the Ministry of National Defense, and had to slow for traffic in front of Yongsan Compound, our base camp and the home of the Eighth United States Army Headquarters.

We heard chanting up ahead. I saw picket signs waving. It was then that we realized we'd chosen the wrong route.

"*Demo*," Mr. Peik said. Demonstration. He was more concerned now with the angry mob up ahead than with Ernie's AK-47.

He kept rolling forward, searching for a spot to make a U-turn, but we were hemmed in by rows of cars on either side. Most of the vehicles were managing to squeeze past the shouting crowd by decelerating and creeping along in the extreme right lane.

The demonstrators were mostly college kids. They wore white headbands slashed with Chinese characters. A few were inspecting each car as it rolled past, peering in the windows, waving each driver forward.

Mr. Peik kept glancing frantically to his left, looking for a chance to turn around, but every other driver was thinking only of rolling past the demonstration safely, before Molotov cocktails started flying. The other cars wouldn't let him turn.

"*An dei*," he said. "*An dei*." No good. No good.

"What's the problem?" Ernie asked. "We'll creep past 'em like all the other cars."

Lady Ahn was leaning forward now, scanning the situation. "But the students are checking each car."

Ernie swiveled around. "So?"

"So all the other GIs are already back on the compound. We are the only car out here with Americans in it."

I suddenly realized that she was right. That's why the students were searching each car. They were looking for foreigners.

I made out the lettering on some of the picket signs.

"Avenge the nun!" the signs said. "Be the strong fist of Buddha!" "Throw out the foreign louts!"

"She's right," I told Ernie. "They're looking for *Miguk* faces." In unison the students chanted. A volley of rocks flew over the compound gate, clanging against metal roofs on the far side of the wall.

"Looks like we could use some quick plastic surgery," Ernie said. He shifted in his seat, rolled down the window, and slapped the side of the AK-47. "Or one of these babies."

He stuck the barrel of the rifle out the window.

"Knock off the bullshit, Ernie," I said. "You don't even have any more bullets. If we're peaceful, they might let us by."

But it was too late.

Three burly young men, students with headbands, strode down the line of cars. One of them spotted us through the windshield, yelled at his comrades, and pointed. The students forgot about the other cars: They headed toward us.

Mr. Peik started blubbering loudly, pounding his fist on the steering wheel. "*An dei. An dei. An dei.*" No good.

Ernie leaned out the window, held the rifle leveled at the students, and shouted.

"Freeze, assholes! Hold it right there or I blow your goddamn skulls off!"

"Damn it, Ernie!" I grabbed for him. He tried to swat my arm and the barrel of the rifle pointed toward the sky.

The students saw their chance. One yelled back for reinforcements. The others charged toward us.

Before Ernie could turn, someone had snatched the rifle, yanked, and jerked it out of his hands. Ernie cursed and leaned out the window, but it was too late. The AK-47 had vanished.

In a moment the students were kicking the doors of our car, rocking it back and forth on creaking springs. With a mighty lunge, the car teetered and almost tipped over. Lady Ahn cradled the jade skull tightly. Miraculously, at the last moment the car rolled back and crashed firmly onto all four wheels.

I started to breathe easier.

Until a baseball bat smashed the front window.

20

"TRY TO DRIVE!" I SHOUTED. "GET THIS THING MOVING."

I figured our best chance was to stay in the car, keep it rolling forward, try to break loose from the crowd. But Mr. Peik was a complete wreck. He was crying and moaning, and the little sedan still idled in park, a stationary target for the enraged students now surrounding us.

Ernie reached across Mr. Peik, popped open the door, and began shoving the gambler out of the car. "Move!" he shouted.

Mr. Peik clawed at Ernie in terror. Ernie propped his back against the far side of the car and, using the soles of his dirty sneakers, kicked the gambler out onto the street. The protesters pounced. But when they realized their prey was Korean, the punches and kicks stopped. By then Ernie had slammed the door and slid into the driver's seat. He popped the clutch: The little Hyundai sedan lurched through the sea of students. We moved like a giant frog, leaping a few feet forward whenever Ernie found a small opening.

Demonstrators swarmed toward us. We were the center of attraction for the mob now. Ernie gunned the engine, ground the gears; swerving, slamming on the brakes, and cursing all the while.

Lady Ahn sat rigidly still, the bag containing the jade skull strapped around her neck.

Glass splintered into the car. Lady Ahn let out an involuntary murmur but quickly composed herself.

"Get down on the floor!" I shouted.

She sat up even straighter. "No. I will not kneel to these people."

The road ahead was clogged with students. Those in front—even if they wanted to—would be unable to move because of the surging crowd pressing behind them. Ernie swerved again, a confused bull surrounded by picadors.

Like a tidal wave, the bodies engulfed us. More windows smashed; hands reached into the car. I slapped at them, punched them, twisted them, broke them, but still more hands seeped in. Tentacles from a thousand-armed beast.

Fingernails scratched me everywhere. Blood started to trickle down my forehead into my eyes. Blinded, I felt Lady Ahn being pulled from me. I hugged her waist but there were too many arms pulling against me. She was dragged across the jagged shards of broken glass and out through the window.

That's when I got pissed off.

I jumped out of the car and started punching and kicking, feeling the hard rock of skull and bone against my flailing fists. A few demonstrators backed off. That gave Ernie enough space to back up the Hyundai. While he did, I leapt at the students holding Lady Ahn. I was screaming, clawing, slavering at the mouth, insane with panic and anger.

They let go of her for just a second. I kicked one, he went down, and I yanked her back toward the sedan.

Ernie had managed to clear some space and was driving in a tight circle. We moved into the center of the circle and Ernie kept moving around us, gunning the engine fiercely, widening the gyre, backing off the sea of shouting students until Lady Ahn and I stood in the center of a human whirlpool.

Ernie screamed for us to hop in.

"Oddiso?" Lady Ahn said, patting her chest. Where is it?

The grain bag with the jade skull was gone. Before I could stop her, she sprinted into the crowd. The mob watched Ernie spinning the Hyundai sedan like a mad top. Lady Ahn darted from person to person searching for the bag. Finally, she found it.

A couple of loud punks had turned the heavy burlap bag upside down, were grabbing handfuls of grain, and tossing them mindlessly into the crowd. In a few seconds, I knew, the jade skull would come tumbling out.

Lady Ahn charged the two men, shoved one back, snatched the bag from the other's grasp. Someone grabbed her by the arm. Without a second's hesitation, she whistled her small fist through the air and smacked him in the chops.

The man's head snapped back, his eyes filled with rage, and he reached for her. I attacked.

I ran full force into him. Cursing, he went down, Lady Ahn screamed, and about a million paws reached out of the crowd and clawed at me.

I punched and kicked and head-butted anyone who came near but it wasn't doing any good. There were just too many of them.

A wave of shouting rippled through the crowd. The people around me slowed their assault. Lady Ahn grabbed me, holding on.

"*Bikkyo!*" someone yelled. Make way!

Male students sliced like a phalanx through the mob. People backed up for them, and miraculously, attention shifted away from us.

A dozen bald-headed monks emerged from the chaos, all garbed in loose robes the color of red rust. In their midst was another bald person, a woman, draped in dirty white hemp garments. The hue of mourning.

When the woman in white came closer, I recognized her: Choi So-lan. Small Orchid Choi. The little nun Ernie and I had rescued in Itaewon.

The crowd hushed as she approached. Most people took an involuntary step backward. Many bowed.

I'd never seen Koreans show such reverence to anyone.

The engine of the Hyundai was still churning, Ernie still making his tight little circles, still trying to keep the mob at bay.

The little nun and her entourage reached the edge of the crowd and watched Ernie making himself dizzy. Finally, Ernie realized that no one was attacking. He slowed, stepped on the brake, and turned off the engine.

When no one charged, Ernie climbed out of the car, set one elbow on the roof of the sedan, and smiled over at the little nun.

"Thought you'd never get here," he said.

She turned to one of the monks. "*Mullah gu?*" What'd he say? The monk leaned down to whisper in her ear.

I pulled Lady Ahn closer to the little nun.

The crowd seemed to come alive, and many started shouting again. "Kill the foreigner!" "Avenge the little nun!"

The monk next to the nun raised his naked arms in the

air, slowly turning in a circle. Again, the crowd grew quiet. The monk shouted in Korean.

"These men helped the good nun. These men are not our enemies. Choi So-lan says they must be protected!"

A murmur of confusion rippled through the mob. The monk shouted again.

"They are the ones who saved her from her attacker!"

This time heads nodded and the murmur was higher pitched. Approval.

Like magic, small towels were offered out of the crowd. I took one, handed it to Lady Ahn, and took one for myself. The cuts on my forehead stung as I wiped them down. A woman in a light blue smock with a red cross on her vest emerged from the forest of torsos. She produced a bottle of purple ointment and dabbed the stinging potion onto our cuts.

Ernie hadn't been hurt at all. He sauntered over to the little nun and offered her a stick of ginseng gum. Smiling broadly, she accepted.

Over by the main gate, the chanting began again. "Down with the foreign louts! Avenge the nun! Go back to America!"

Ernie kept smiling. Lady Ahn clutched the grain bag to her chest. I spoke in Korean to the little nun. "You have become very famous."

The monk standing next to her ignored my Korean and answered me in English.

"Yes. She is a symbol now to all Koreans. Of our resistance to an American occupation that would allow one of your soldiers to brutalize one as innocent as this."

He sounded like a propaganda recording. "We did not allow it," I told him. "The man who attacked her is a criminal."

"But you haven't turned him over to the Korean authorities yet."

My surprise must've shown on my face. The monk started to smirk.

There was no reason why Eighth Army CID couldn't have picked up the culprit by now. Ernie and I had left all the information any good investigator would need. What was holding them up?

"I'm sure he'll be turned over soon," I said.

The monk shook his bald head. "No. Your superiors claim they haven't even captured him yet."

Haven't captured him yet! No wonder the Korean students were mad.

The little nun was paying no attention at all to us. She kept chomping on her gum and smiling up at Ernie. For his part, he scanned the crowd, occasionally pointing at somebody with their hair tied up by their white headband or their face smeared with paint, making faces, imitating them.

The nun laughed like a little girl.

"Why is she wearing a hemp robe?" I asked.

The monk crossed his long arms. "You know nothing of Korean custom?"

"Hemp robes are the sign of mourning," I said.

"Yes."

"So who died?"

"No one yet. In two days someone will."

I waited. He smiled.

"The virtuous nun," he said. "The little one you see before you."

"What are you talking about?" I asked. "She's young. Healthy. What's going to kill her?"

"Fire. At a rally in downtown Seoul. If the attacker is not caught and turned over to us, this good nun, Choi So-lan, will pour gasoline over her body. She will set herself aflame."

A holler erupted from the demonstrators. People closed in and started shoving.

Down the street, emerging from the high stone gate of the Ministry of National Defense, slithered a long row of helmeted riot police, waving their batons.

The students hooted and tossed stones.

Ernie turned to me. "Time to un-ass the area."

The monk smiled. "I will see to that." He raised his arm. A few monks scurried away and in less than a minute a long American-made station wagon nosed its way through the throng. It was ancient, almost twenty years old, and the outer walls were paneled with revarnished wood. A "woody," they used to call it back in Los Angeles.

Ernie took one look at it and grinned. "Shit. And here I am all out of surfboard wax."

The station wagon pulled up next to us and two monks jumped out and opened the doors. The elder monk motioned with his arm.

"Please. Be our guest."

Ernie shook his head. "I'll walk. Itaewon's just a few blocks from here."

Lady Ahn preferred walking, too. With the jade skull strapped in a bag over her shoulder, she didn't trust these Buddhists at all.

They both looked at me. "Yes," I said. "We prefer to walk."

"Ah," the monk said, "but we insist."

A dozen tough-looking monks closed in on us in a tight circle. Behind them were hundreds of angry demonstrators. The police near the Ministry of National Defense started to scrape their batons along the tops of their riot control shields.

It was an eerie sound. Like Roman legions preparing to clear a square.

The monk motioned again for us to climb into the station wagon. Ernie ignored him and stepped away. Before I could move, three monks hoisted Ernie into the air, and shoved him into the backseat of the woody like a flailing side of beef.

We were outnumbered. There was nothing else for us to do but comply.

Lady Ahn clutched my arm but kept her face set in stony aloofness. Regally, she stepped forward and entered the car. I followed.

21

WE CRUISED IN THE WOODY THROUGH DOWNTOWN SEOUL TO A temple located at the rear of the grounds of Doksu Palace. The palace had been built during the fifteenth century, burned down a time or two by Japanese invaders, and each time rebuilt by the tradition-loving patriots of Korea. The front part of the palace was open to tour groups. But back where we were, hemmed in by elm trees and rows of spruces, no one could hear us.

Even if we screamed.

But it wasn't a dungeon we were brought to. It was a tile-roofed pagoda in the center of a small island, in a placid pond infested with lily pads, frogs, and elegantly floating swans.

Three monks shoved Ernie into the center of the main floor of the pavilion, amidst comfortable couches and cela-don vases filled with flowers and ancient embroidered silk screens covering the walls.

Ernie cursed at his captors and straightened his shirt. "This place sucks," he said.

Actually, this place had been the summer retreat of a king. But Ernie's only impressed by free-flowing booze, sawdust on the floors, and hot and cold running women.

Lady Ahn acted as if she'd been born here. Still clutching her burlap sack filled with rice and the priceless jade skull, she slipped off her shoes, strode toward one of the handcrafted couches, and sat carefully in its center.

I sat next to her, checking out the odds against us. They weren't good. Besides the half dozen or so monks who had accompanied us in the woody, on the way in I had seen ten more monks arrayed around the residence. Extra security.

A novitiate brought a tray holding a teapot painted with white cranes rising from reeds. He poured us each a cup of jasmine-scented tea.

If it hadn't been for the evil-looking monks watching him, Ernie probably would've smashed his teacup and the pot and everything else on the varnished coffee table. Lady Ahn didn't touch her tea. Instead, she sat with her back ramrod straight, gazing into the distance as if pondering great thoughts.

I was the only one who drank the tea. It tasted good. Besides, I was thirsty.

Choi So-lan, the little nun, and the elder monk sat down on the divan across from us. The monk spoke.

"My name is Bo Hua," he said, "the Protector of the Flame. Thank you for accepting our hospitality."

"You can take your hospitality and shove it," Ernie said. He paced the varnished slat floor behind us, unwilling to sit down.

The little nun frowned and stared at the floor.

"The reason we brought you here," Bo Hua continued, "is that we seek the jade skull of Kublai Khan."

Lady Ahn's facial expression didn't change. But her breathing stopped and the knuckles on the hand gripping the burlap bag grew white.

"We have been searching for it for many centuries," Bo Hua said. "I will let Nun Choi explain."

The little nun looked up. She took a deep breath and began to speak Korean in her high, lilting voice.

She had been assigned by her superiors, she explained to us, to collect alms in the Itaewon area. When word of the discovery of the jade skull of Kublai Khan reached her temple, she was further instructed to investigate the possibility that an American might somehow be involved in smuggling the precious skull out of Korea. Investigate she did. During her inquiries she uncovered two names: Slicky Girl Nam and Herman the German. After watching their hooch for two days, she had been assaulted without warning by the American who Ernie and I managed to chase away. She had no idea who the men were who had kidnapped Herman's daughter, Mi-ja, but the fact that the abduction happened wasn't particularly surprising. The word was now out that the precious jade skull had reappeared. Many bad people would be after it, she assured us softly.

"That is why you should turn the skull over to us," Bo Hua added, once the little nun was finished with her dissertation. "You will surely be robbed. There is no way the thieves of the world will allow you to keep something as valuable as a skull with a map to the Tomb of Genghis Khan."

But the little nun wasn't finished yet. She interrupted him, and as she did so, Bo Hua turned to her slowly, amazed at her temerity.

"The jade skull is the key to the Tomb of Genghis Khan," the little nun said. "And all the riches of Genghis Khan's tomb belong to Buddha. They were stolen by the

Mongols, stolen by Genghis Khan, and came from the Buddhist temples of China and Korea and other lands. The wealth was meant to do the work of Lord Buddha. To help the unfortunate. To build a bridge for everyone to the land of the infinite. That wealth does not belong to the Mongols or anyone else. It is Buddha's money."

She spoke with such passion that even Ernie stopped his pacing and stared at her, although he could understand little of what she said.

Finally, embarrassed by her outburst, the little nun's face turned crimson; she bowed her head.

"Yes. Quite," Bo Hua said. "We are not thugs. We are not thieves. We only ask that you turn the skull of Kublai Khan over to its rightful owners. The church of the Lord of the Vision of the Future. The church of the Maitreya Buddha."

At last, Lady Ahn spoke, using rapid Korean. "Have you no shame?" she demanded. "You know who the rightful owner of the jade skull is. Me! It was my ancestor, the great emperor of the Sung dynasty, who owned every bit of this wealth you describe. Some of it he allowed to be borrowed by the Buddhists, since he was a tolerant man. But ultimately all the wealth belonged to the emperor! Not to you!"

Bo Hua started to argue, but Ernie jumped in. "Knock off the bullshit! That jade head goes to get Mi-ja back. All this squabbling over who owns what don't mean *jack* to me!"

The little nun closed her eyes. Still keeping her head down, she scurried from the room. Ernie and Lady Ahn and Bo Hua started screaming at one another.

So much for civil discourse.

I finished the last of my tea and poured another cup.

Even the monks guarding us were involved in the argument, leaning forward, hanging on every word. Tough guys, but not exactly disciplined security guards.

I rose from my seat and sauntered toward the far side of the foyer where the little nun had disappeared. The monks ignored me. Figuring, I guess, that as long as they kept an eye on the burlap bag containing the jade skull, they had nothing to fear from me.

I found the little nun squatting on the tile floor of the kitchen. Crying.

I knelt down in front of her and reached for her chin. *"Ul-jima,"* I said. Don't cry.

Her wet, crinkled face looked up at me. "But it's Buddha's money," she said.

I nodded. "Yes. I believe you. But that little girl, Mi-ja, she also belongs to Buddha, doesn't she?"

The little nun nodded. "She does."

"Then help us escape from here. Help us save an innocent child's life."

"Escape?" The nun's liquid eyes flashed wide with terror. "I could *never* help you do that!"

That's what I was afraid she might say.

"Okay," I said. "You don't have to."

I stood and glanced out the window. The sandy shore that led to the pond had been carefully raked. There had to be gardening tools around here somewhere. I rummaged in a storage shed behind the kitchen and found them. One rake. One shovel. Perfect.

I walked back to the little nun and knelt down again. *"Kokehong ha-jima. Na da halkei."* Don't worry. I'll take care of everything.

I tested the heft of the rake and the shovel. I liked the shovel better.

When I walked back into the main sitting room, I didn't give the first monk a chance. Swinging the shovel in a full arc, I slammed the metal spade into his spine. A *whoof* of air erupted from his mouth.

Mid-shout, Ernie turned. The monks turned. I tossed Ernie the rake and managed to clobber two more monks before they had a chance to react.

Ernie started swinging. Lady Ahn knocked over a flower vase, grabbed the wooden stand, and clobbered Bo Hua on his bald head.

We fought our way to a paper-covered latticework doorway and smashed through it. Splinters and oil-paper confetti splattered everywhere.

Ernie thrust the rake into the face of one of the guards. The monk screamed and clutched his eyes.

"The bridge!" Ernie yelled.

"No. It's too well guarded," I said. "Into the pond."

Lady Ahn didn't hesitate for a second. She dived, twisting at the last second before hitting the water in order to protect the jade skull. Ernie waded in after her, waving his rake at the enraged monks who followed.

Splashing in up to my waist, I threw my shovel at the closest monk, dived into the water, and swam after Lady Ahn.

The monks floundered in the water, some of them going under and sputtering back up for air.

On the shore, pressing a rag to his bleeding head, stood Bo Hua, shouting orders. Waving his monks back toward the bridge in hopes of cutting us off.

When I reached the far shore, Lady Ahn pulled me to my feet in the slippery mud. Then she helped Ernie up. The pack of monks was crossing the half-moon bridge now, about forty yards behind us.

We sprinted into the tree line.

Ernie shoved branches out of his face, still jabbering. "You did a goddamn *number* on that monk, George! No warning, just *whomp*! I didn't know you had it in you."

Neither did I. Not until greed stood in the way of a little girl's life.

We emerged onto a manicured lawn with cobbled walkways and statues and more palaces in the distance. Lovers strolled arm in arm. Women pushed baby carriages.

Dripping wet, we sprinted across the lawn and hopped a low wire fence. Lady Ahn hurdled obstacles like a trained runner.

We zigzagged through the crowds, Lady Ahn leading the way, until I realized where she was headed. A tourist bus had just pulled up in front of the statue of Saejong Daewang, the fifteenth-century king who had invented *hangul*, the Korean writing system.

I glanced back. The monks had broken through the trees and were sprinting straight for us.

The tourists piling out of the bus all wore identical caps and jackets. Each seemed to have about a dozen cameras strapped around his neck. Japanese.

Lady Ahn elbowed one out of her way and shoved another. Stepping up into the bus, she swung her fist and punched the Korean bus driver on the side of the skull. Ernie tossed him down the steps. I managed to slow his fall. Still, he twisted and sprawled face-first onto the pavement.

Lady Ahn stood behind Ernie, shouting at him to drive. But Ernie couldn't seem to get the hang of how to operate the little Korean bus. The monks were so near that I could see the rage in their red eyes. I grabbed the handle and pulled the bus door shut. Two monks slammed into it. I jammed the sole of my foot against the door and held them back.

"Start the goddamn bus, Ernie!" I yelled.

"There's some trick to this ignition," he shot back.

Lady Ahn ran through the bus, slamming every window shut. Monks started to climb up the walls. Ernie twisted something, pushed a button, turned the key. Nothing happened. He cursed and tried it in a different order this time. The engine roared to life. Ernie jammed the bus into gear, let out the clutch, and it lurched backward.

Reverse. The engine died.

Swearing, Ernie started it again. He rejammed the gears, and this time we leapt forward. The two monks banging on the door had to step back. Others still clung to the side of the bus.

"Shake 'em off, Ernie! They're still hanging on."

"Can do easy," he said.

Pedestrians leapt out of the way as we swerved through the park. Up ahead loomed a great stone gate with an upturned tile roof. The five-hundred-year-old entrance to the Doksu Palace grounds.

A low wire fence spanned the round arch. Behind it stood rows of uniformed schoolchildren, lined up patiently behind fluttering banners. Ernie honked the horn. People glanced at us, but no one moved.

Ernie pounded his palm on the horn. "Move, goddamn it! Move!"

Ernie swerved around more pedestrians, and the wheels of the bus squealed. Finally, schoolchildren pointed and started to step out of the way.

Instead of bursting right through the center of the arch, Ernie aimed the bus for the two-yard-thick stone wall. The monks still clinging to the bus realized what was going to happen. Ernie was going to scrape them off the side. One by one, they dropped off the bus like fleas abandoning a mutt.

Ernie kept blasting his horn. Panicked schoolteachers waved their arms and blew their whistles, trying to shoo children out of the way.

We slammed into the side of the arch with a great crunch. The metal partition in front of us shot forward like shrapnel from a grenade. The last of the schoolchildren screamed and scurried out of the way.

The bus swerved through the open blacktop area in front of the entranceway. Turning the steering wheel madly, Ernie careened into traffic.

Horns honked. Tires screeched.

"Anybody left hanging on?" Ernie asked.

I looked back. One lone monk clung like a pinned moth to the rearmost window.

"Just one," I said.

I walked back, pulled down the window, and punched the monk in the face.

He fell back, bounced twice on the asphalt, and rolled until he slammed up against the concrete curb.

"No more monks," I called back to Ernie.

"Pesky devils," Ernie said.

Lady Ahn sat on a vinyl seat in the middle of the bus, rocking the jade skull, cooing to it softly.

As if it were her own precious baby.

22

IT WAS ALMOST DARK BY THE TIME WE REACHED THE OUTSKIRTS
of Itaewon and found a spot to ditch the bus. We hoofed it
through the narrow back alleys. The sight of a beautiful
Korean woman with wet hair clutching a burlap bag as if it
were stuffed with gold dust and two American GIs still
shaking mud and lily pads off their butts was enough to
make every pedestrian we encountered gawk in wonder.

Going to Herman's hooch was out of the question. I
figured the kidnappers would be watching. Our job was to
exchange the skull for Mi-ja. Not just turn it over to them.

Instead, we found a tiny *yoguan* hidden in a narrow
alley. After paying for a large room with bath, we washed,
sent out for bandages, and patched ourselves up as well as
we could.

Lady Ahn had suffered the fewest cuts but still she was
impatient with my careful washing and disinfecting.

"*An apo,*" she objected. It doesn't hurt.

Ernie was okay and so was I. Scratches, bruises, hurt pride, but that was it.

"There're two things we have to do," I told Ernie. "First, we set up a meet with the kidnappers so we can trade the skull for Mi-ja."

Ernie nodded. "Right."

"And second, we collar the guy who beat up the little nun so Eighth Army can turn him over to the ROKs."

Ernie scowled up at me. "What's wrong with those dorks over at the CID Detachment? Why didn't *they* pick him up?"

"You know how they are. Take an MP escort with them when they go down in the ville. Wear their suits and ties so the First Sergeant won't accuse them of screwing off. They scare the hell out of everybody they need to talk to."

"Yeah," Ernie said. "Nobody tells those dickheads shit."

"So apparently this guy who beat up the nun has found out that we're looking for him and he's decided not to make it easy."

"He can't leave the country. Not without a phony passport, and he probably doesn't have any idea about how to buy one of those. We'll pick him up eventually."

"But we can't wait."

"Why not?"

I told him about the nun.

Ernie almost leapt out of his chair. "You're shitting me! She's going to toast herself?"

"The day after tomorrow. In downtown Seoul. In front of the TV cameras and everything."

"She's too young!"

"Right. So let's find the jerk who mugged her. Lock his ass up."

"Okay."

"And we have to get Mi-ja back."

Ernie paused. "You're right. Should we have chow first?"

FROM A PUBLIC PHONE IN A BACK-ALLEY STORE, I MADE A CALL to the pharmacy near Herman's hooch. The pharmacist's daughter answered. She told me that Slicky Girl Nam was at home being cared for by the old women from the neighborhood. The kidnappers hadn't called and no, she didn't know how to locate Herman. I told her I'd call back every hour until the midnight curfew.

Just before the witching hour, the pharmacist's daughter still hadn't seen Herman and she still hadn't received a call from the kidnappers. They wouldn't call after curfew. Movement through the streets of Seoul is impossible once the police shut down the city.

On the way back to the *yoguan*, I gazed up at the rain clouds scudding past the monsoon moon. The silver orb was almost full. Only a sliver of darkness along its edge held the difference between life and death for a small girl named Mi-ja. But tomorrow, even that slender hope would be gone. The moon would be full. And we would have our last chance to save her life.

Back in the room, I spread out a sleeping mat and, without taking my clothes off, plopped down on the floor next to Lady Ahn. Looking back on it, Ernie and I should have taken turns pulling guard duty, but nothing bad happened that night. God must watch over fools.

AT DAWN I WASHED MY FACE AND SHOOK LADY AHN AWAKE. When I tried to pry the jade skull out of her grasp, she shoved my hands away.

"You no *touch*," she said.

I tried to remain calm, explaining to her that two powerful sects of Buddhist monks were now after the skull and it wouldn't be safe here in the *yoguan*. She couldn't protect it by herself. Ernie and I had to return to the compound and find the mugger of Choi So-lan. Otherwise the little nun would burn herself to death and Korea, too, would erupt in flames.

Lady Ahn shook her head. "Nuns have burned themselves before. We Koreans are used to it. Whatever Choi So-lan does, she doesn't get the jade skull."

I stared at the burning fierceness in her eyes, waiting for it to die. It didn't. I spoke anyway. "What about Mi-ja?"

She took a deep breath, turned away. "You can save her somehow. Without the skull."

I let that sit, allowing the silence to grow, until we both knew her statement wasn't true. Ragyapa and his Mongolian Buddhists were ruthless. I wouldn't be able to save Mi-ja. The kidnappers would stop at nothing until they had the skull.

"We only need the skull for a few hours," I said. "Once we make the exchange, and have Mi-ja back, Ernie and I will make sure that Ragyapa doesn't leave the country with the skull. I promised you in Taejon, we'll get it back for you. We won't let the Korean police know about it. We won't let Eighth Army know about it. No government official will confiscate the jade skull. We'll get it back for you. No matter what we have to do."

Lady Ahn looked at me. Then she looked at Ernie. "No matter *what* you have to do?"

Ernie grinned. "That's the easy part. Once I check my .45 out of the arms room, and we have Mi-ja, those Mongol assholes won't be safe anywhere."

"Once you have Mi-ja," Lady Ahn asked me, "are you willing to *kill* to recover the jade skull?"

I almost flinched. Her eyes flamed like the eyes of a tigress. I thought of the yellow-toothed grin of Ragyapa, the man who'd kicked me in the stomach in the Temple of the

Dream Buddha. I thought of the frightened child whimpering in the corner. I thought of the severed ear.

Would I kill for the jade skull? No. But would I kill for Mi-ja, to save her life? That was easy. The answer was yes. Many times yes. And would I kill for this gorgeous woman who sat in front of me? This woman known as Lady Ahn? This woman as beautiful as any goddess carved in ivory?

The answer to that, too, was easy.

"What they did to Mi-ja," I answered carefully, "deserves killing."

Lady Ahn sat with her head slumped for a long time. She breathed slowly, as if working up courage. Finally, she released the strap from her grip. She shoved the burlap bag across the floor. I picked up the jade skull of Kublai Khan, smiled a reassuring smile, then slung it over my shoulder.

WE STOPPED AT THE BACK-ALLEY STORE SO I COULD USE THE pay phone again. Ernie rummaged through the candy rack, searching for his favorite brand of gum. Out front, Koreans milled about, some pushing carts, some carrying loads knotted to wooden A-frames on their backs. Others with pans resting on their hips, filled with towels and soap and shampoo. On their way to the bathhouse.

I kept an eye on them all.

I waited on the phone line. It took about five minutes for the pharmacist's daughter to fetch Herman.

When he picked up and grunted hello, I said, "I got it."

"Where?"

"In a safe place." Actually the skull was still hanging over my shoulder, in the burlap bag half full of wet rice.

"When can I see it?" Herman asked.

"When we meet with the kidnappers. Have they called again?"

"Not yet."

"They will. Tonight's the full moon. When you talk to

them, set up the meeting. Tell them we have the antique. Tell them we're ready to make the exchange for Mi-ja."

"They better call soon. Nam's going nuts. She knows the full moon is tonight and she can't hold still. Been clawing at me all morning. Where you staying?"

"At the *yoguan* behind the Dungeon Club."

I wondered why he asked. Before I could inquire, the wind picked up, ruffling the awning. Ernie had purchased his gum and stood leaning against a pole, staring up at the sky, which had suddenly darkened. He turned back to me. "We'd better *bali*, George."

The first splats of rain hit the muddy pavement.

"Okay, Herman, I have to go. Call me at the CID Detachment if something breaks."

As if the monsoon sky had been holding off beyond endurance, lightning flashed, thunder rolled, and the clouds opened up with a pelting deluge.

Ernie and I ran to the compound.

THE FIRST SERGEANT STOMPED BACK AND FORTH IN THE CID office, his hairy arms waving in the air.

"Where in the hell have you two guys *been*?"

Ernie hung up his soaked jacket, smiled at the secretary Miss Kim, flashed a thumbs-up to Admin Sergeant Riley, and flopped into a padded vinyl chair.

"We *told* you, Top," he said. "We went down to Taejon to pick up that antique."

I draped my jacket over a chair and plucked at my dripping wet shirt in an attempt to unglue it from my body. I started pouring the wet rice from the burlap sack into a metal trash can.

"Five days it took you? Five *days*? Just to pick up some damn old piece of jade?"

The First Sergeant looked sharp in a neatly pressed Class B uniform shirt and slacks. Riley wore his usual fatigues starched to a cardboard consistency. Miss Kim wore a tight skirt and blouse that accented her delectable figure.

They were all dry, which is what made me jealous. Ernie and I were wet and scratched and bruised and — looked like a couple of stray tomcats. Outside, thunder boomed.

The First Sergeant turned his gray eyebrows on me.

"Sueño, what's the story? You don't usually goof off on me. Not this much, anyway."

"We didn't goof off." I held the jade skull up to the fluorescent light.

Miss Kim swiveled on her typing chair and gaped at the shimmering green glow. Even Riley stopped scratching at his pile of paperwork and adjusted his horn-rimmed glasses to take a better look.

"It wasn't easy getting ahold of this jewel," I told them. "Not exactly on sale in your usual five-and-dime."

Miss Kim rose from her seat and clicked over in her high heels. She stood in front of the jade and held out her manicured fingers. "May I see it?"

I handed it to her. She fondled it. Slowly. Sensually.

The First Sergeant propped his butt on the edge of Riley's desk and crossed his arms. "So you have the exchange set up for the girl?"

"We're working on that. When the kidnappers call Herman, he'll set it up."

Miss Kim examined the intricate carving. Tiny pearls of drool bubbled on her red lips.

Ernie bounded out of his chair, walked over to the counter, and drew himself a cup of coffee from the stainless steel urn. It was boiled as black as ink so he poured about a half a cup of sugar and cream into it. As he stirred the concoction, I knew he was working up some mischief.

I was right.

"Seems like the rioting outside the gate has made the head shed a little nervous, eh, Top?" he asked.

The First Sergeant's fingers tightened beneath his biceps. "We've been through this shit before. In 'Nam. We know how to handle it."

"How's that?"

"Bust some heads. That's how."

Ernie and I were both thinking the same thing. Busting heads wouldn't stop the nun from burning herself to death. In fact, it would ensure that she'd go through with it. There was only one way to stop her: Find the man who had attacked her in Itaewon.

"What about the mugger of the little nun?" I asked.

The First Sergeant's fingers clenched the flesh of his arms more tightly. "What the hell do you think I been waiting for you two guys for? The information you gave us before you left was for shit."

Ernie sloshed coffee when he swiveled. "You mean you haven't caught him yet?"

"That's right, Bascom. We haven't caught him yet."

"We gave you a complete description before we left. You have six other CID agents besides me and George. All any investigator would have to do is bust some heads and ask some questions out in Samgakji. Pick up the mugger in no time."

Samgakji was the Korean nightclub district that catered to black GIs.

"What the hell do you think we've been doing, Bascom? We identified the guy the first day. All it took was gathering some information and checking some old blotter reports. His name is Hatcher, Ignatius Q., Private First Class."

"*Ignatius Q?*" Ernie asked.

"That's right. Ignatius Q. But all the bloods out in Samgakji call him Bro Hatch."

Ernie sipped on his coffee. "Beats the shit out of *Ignatius Q.*"

"The problem with picking him up," the First Sergeant said, "is that as soon as he got wind that we were looking for him, Hatcher went AWOL."

"Of course he went AWOL, Top," Ernie said. "He's probably hiding out in Samgakji. Didn't you send anybody out there?"

"Do you think we've had our thumbs up our butts, Bascom? I've had agents in Samgakji day and night. They've come up with zilch."

"White agents or black agents?"

The First Sergeant glared at Ernie. We all knew the answer to that. The Eighth Army CID Detachment didn't have any black agents.

Admin Sergeant Riley buried his nose deeper into his paperwork, worried that Ernie might go too far. Riley was a bureaucrat and a lifer. He wasn't going to take a no-power lowlife staff sergeant's side against the First Sergeant, the top noncom in the CID Detachment.

Miss Kim paid attention only to the jade skull. She was used to GIs arguing over things that couldn't be changed. Since English wasn't her first language, it was easy enough to tune us out.

Not easy for me. I figured I'd better back Ernie off or the First Sergeant was going to grind his teeth so hard his molars would pop out. Top hated admitting that he couldn't get a job done without me and Ernie to help.

"Who'd you send out there?" I asked.

"Burrows and Slabem," he replied.

Ernie groaned. "Not those two dorks!"

The First Sergeant's face reddened. "They're good investigators."

"They're two white nerds," Ernie said. "The soul brothers out there in Samgakji aren't going to have shit to do with them. And the Korean business girls, less."

"And you two can do better?"

"You *know* we can do better. We speak the language of the night. That's why you been waiting for us to get back. So somebody can go out to Samgakji and collar this mugger once and for all."

Ernie was right. All the other CID agents in the Detachment prided themselves on staying away from the drunks in the bars and the dopers dealing drugs and the Korean prostitutes who swarmed through the GI villages. Ernie and I thrived in that environment. And we were known out there. And trusted. When you needed something done in the red-light districts of Korea, Ernie and I were the investigators to see. The other CID agents couldn't sniff out a correct quote on the price of kimchi.

The First Sergeant was silent for a long time. His fists clenching and unclenching, his jaw working away as if he were gnawing on a bone. Finally, he nodded.

"All right. You two are such hotshots. Get your butts out to Samgakji, like right now. And find this asshole for me. The honchos up at the head shed are about to shit a brick because we haven't been able to pick up the GI who jacked up that Buddhist nun. So you guys are back. So you're the experts on the Korean villages and the biggest ville rats in Eighth Army law enforcement. So you set down those mugs of coffee and you put on your jackets and you hop in your jeep and you get your asses down to Samgakji. Right now! You understand me?"

The First Sergeant stabbed his forefinger into Ernie's face and then into mine. "Do either of you have any questions?"

"Yeah," Ernie said.

The First Sergeant swiveled on him. Glaring.

Ernie's face was as relaxed as that of a Buddhist saint. "What's for chow?"

After Riley pulled the First Sergeant off of Ernie, he escorted him down the hallway, whispering soothing words into the old sergeant's ear. When he returned to us, Riley shook his head.

"Ernie," he said. "You have to stop messing with the First Sergeant like that. He's going to burst one of his blood valves some day."

Ernie swallowed the last of the coffee in his cup. "Not to worry. Army medical coverage is a hundred percent."

Trying not to laugh, I managed to pry the jade skull from Miss Kim's soft hands. Riley filled out a receipt for it, handed me the pink copy, and slid the original into his files.

He had written: *Skull, jade, ancient, one each.*

I wrapped the skull in some brown pulp hand towels. Riley opened the big wall safe behind his desk and slid the precious antique onto the widest metal shelf.

He slammed the door, cranked shut the handle, and twisted the dial.

BEFORE GOING TO SAMGAKJI, WE CHECKED WITH A COUPLE OF our contacts on the compound. The first one was scared shitless when we mentioned the mugging of the Buddhist nun, and he wouldn't tell us anything. The second snitch, a small-time dope dealer known as Brother Andrew, was foolish enough to provide us a little leverage.

Ernie didn't smoke much marijuana, but when he had the urge he always bought the reefer from Brother Andrew. When Ernie asked him about copping some shit, Andy didn't hesitate. As soon as the transaction was complete, I entered the barracks and read Brother Andrew his rights. As I did, he wheeled on Ernie.

"You wouldn't *do* this to me."

"Watch me, Bro," Ernie answered.

Andrew had a shaved head shaped like a peanut and a neatly trimmed goatee. The goatee was allowed by the doctor because Andy suffered from folliculitis and couldn't shave. It drove the lifers mad, but they couldn't do anything about it.

Ernie folded his arms. "Tell me about the guy who jacked up the Buddhist nun."

Andy wouldn't tell us anything at first. Apparently, the guy who had attacked the nun had a lot of people terrorized. We had to actually handcuff him, shove him in the back of the jeep, and drive him down to the MP station. When Andy was finally convinced that we were going to book him, he started to talk.

"His name's Bro Hatch," Andy told us.

"We already know that," Ernie told him. Bored.

"He hangs out with a fine-looking sister. Everybody says she's half white and half Korean. Name's Sister Julie."

"Where's she work?"

"In Samgakji. The Black Cat Club."

"Is Hatcher there now?"

"I don't know. But once you take a look at Sister Julie you'll realize that no man in his right mind would stray far. She's one fine hammer."

Ernie leaned back and unlocked Andy's cuffs. "All right, Andy. You can go."

"Hey, you're not going to tell Bro Hatch that I told you how to find him, are you?"

"Depends on how I feel," Ernie answered.

"Feel good," Andrew said. "I got a life to lead here."

BACK IN THE BARRACKS, WE CHANGED INTO CLEAN BLUE JEANS and nylon jackets with embroidered dragons on the back. Fresh running-the-ville outfits.

I called Itaewon and spoke to Herman. Still no word

from the kidnappers. I told him we'd be out and I'd call back in an hour.

This afternoon we would go out to Samgakji and find Bro Hatch, the big GI who'd mugged the Buddhist nun. It shouldn't be hard. Not if Andrew was telling the truth. And not if Bro Hatch wasn't quite as tough as people seemed to think he was.

I grabbed the roll of dimes in my left pocket, enjoying its heft as I slammed my fist into my open palm. After thinking about it, I dropped another roll into my right pocket.

Samgakji is definitely a two-roll kind of place.

23

SAMGAKJI IN THE AFTERNOON IS LIKE A GHOST TOWN. SALOONS
and muddy streets. Upturned red tile roofs. A skinny old
man pushing a cart down the center of the road, lifting a
dirty canvas sheet, hoisting a shimmering blue block of ice
into one of the gin joints.

The front door of the Black Cat Club was locked, so we
walked around to the back. A beaded curtain led into a
narrow hallway bordered by the latrines. Inside the main
room, metal chairs were turned upside down on round
cocktail tables. A boy swabbed the cement floor, the odor
of disinfectant bubbling in the air. An old woman sat beneath a bent lamp, studying the wrinkled pages of a ledger
as if they were bamboo tablets carried across the Himalayas
by a Buddhist scholar.

When we walked into the bar, the woman glanced up.

"*Ajjima, tangsin yogi ei junim ieyo?*" Aunt, are you the
owner here?

She nodded her wrinkled face. Ernie wandered through

the forest of upturned chairs in the ballroom, hands in his jacket pockets, checking for an enemy ambush.

The boy stared at us for a while, but when he saw that we weren't going to cause any trouble he went back to his mopping.

I propped my elbows on the bar and spoke to the old woman. "My partner and me," I said, "are looking for a business girl called Sister Julie."

The old woman didn't flinch, as if she'd been expecting my question. She answered immediately.

"I remember her. But she gone now. Quit work. Two days no come back."

"Where'd she go?"

She waved her hand. "Business girl come. Business girl go. Nobody know where."

I turned to Ernie and translated. "She says Sister Julie left two days ago."

Ernie strode toward the bar. "I believe her. Absolutely. Just for the hell of it, though, how about we check upstairs?"

"Capital idea."

We started toward the narrow wooden staircase when we heard the click of footsteps descending. First appeared a shapely high-heeled foot. Long legs sheathed in black leotards followed. Then round hips, a narrow waist, and a frilly white blouse filled out with extra helpings of female pulchritude.

Her face was a slightly flared oval, her skin smooth as a dark olive, lips full, hair glossy black, curled tightly, exploding straight out from the skull.

She moved like a cobra ready to strike.

Ernie sucked in his breath.

She reached the bottom of the stairs, turned, and sashayed across the ballroom floor toward us, staring right into my eyes.

Brother Andrew was right, she appeared to be half white. The eyes were blue. As blue as light gleaming from a block of glacial ice.

We couldn't move. Even Ernie kept his mouth shut. She stopped a few feet from me. Her scent enveloped us in a cloying hug.

"You look for Sister Julie?" she asked.

I nodded.

She ran red-tipped fingers from her waist down toward her thighs, stuck out her hip, and sneered.

"You lucky today, T-shirt," she said. "Sister Julie be here."

Her accent was perfect. The ultimate soul sister.

"Where's Hatcher?" I asked.

Her lined eyes widened into mock innocence. "I don't know. I no see. Two, maybe three days."

She breathed in and breathed out, letting us enjoy the full magnificence of her warm brown flesh.

Ernie looked but shook it off. He slipped behind Sister Julie and stepped quietly up the stairs.

Sister Julie spun her head. "Where he go?"

"He has to use the *byonso*."

"*Byonso* downstairs."

I shrugged. "He'll find it eventually. Why'd you hook up with Bro Hatch?"

"*He* hook up with *me*. All man want to hook up with Sister Julie."

I didn't argue with that. "Why'd you choose him?"

"He big. Strong. Before, I have 'nother boyfriend. Bro Oscar. He be fine dude, but not strong like Bro Hatch."

"What happened?"

Sister Julie allowed herself a smile. "Bro Hatch knuckle sandwich with Bro Oscar."

"Who won?"

"Be cool, T-shirt. You know who won."

Sister Julie looked and talked and moved like an American black woman. Close enough, anyway, for being seven thousand miles away from the nearest American ghetto. Smears of dark makeup clung to the folds of her neck just above the collarbone.

Under the dim barroom light, once she was fully made up, cooing into the ear of some lonely black GI, who would know the difference? Who would care?

If this woman wanted to be black, the soul brothers would allow her to be black.

Not an attitude shared by their white compatriots.

I had trouble keeping my eyes off her low-cut blouse. With an effort, I gazed into her eyes, shocked again by the startling clarity of their blue light.

"You're half American, aren't you?"

She shrugged her elegant shoulders. "So what?"

"But not half black. Half white."

"The white rapist been doing evil to black women for long time."

The line was memorized. Like propaganda.

"I'm not a T-shirt," I said. "I'm Mexican. And nobody in my family ever raped anybody."

"So?"

"So nothing. Why don't you like white GIs?"

"Before I work T-shirt club. White GI all the time bother me. All the time want to touch *jiji*." One hand slithered up toward a breast. "All the time no want to pay. Complain about Korea all the time. Act like little boy. I no like."

"And it's better here in Samgakji?"

"Black GI like Sister Julie. Sister Julie like them."

"And your white father, he left you?"

Sister Julie's eyes flared with anger. "Of course he leave me! And my mother. And my brother. You think I work here if my daddy take care of me?"

One of the rules of interrogation is to keep the conversation moving in one direction, preferably an emotional one, then switch directions when your subject least expects it. Sister Julie was about to slash my face with her crimson nails. Time to change direction and spring the question.

"Why did you tell Hatcher to beat up that nun?"

For the first time creases appeared on her brow. "What you talk about, T-shirt?"

"I'm talking about how you took Bro Hatch out to Itaewon and told him about all the money the Buddhist nun would collect from the business girls. The nun's purse would be full, you told him. And she's just a small woman. No Korean thief would ever touch a nun. Easy money, you told him."

Her eyes crinkled in anger. "You got a big mouth, T-shirt. Too damn big."

Something crashed upstairs. A door slamming shut. Or slamming open. I heard a grunt. Pounding footsteps and then Ernie hollering. Cursing.

Sister Julie's hand was back on her hip and she was smiling again.

"Sounds like some white boy be getting his ass kicked."

I grabbed her shoulders. "Hatcher's upstairs," I said. "You lied!"

"What lie?" She smiled even more broadly. "Maybe he come back. Looking for Sister Julie."

I shoved her away and ran up the stairs.

Metal clanged on metal, something else crashed, and I heard the wrenching, ripping sound of wood splintering like toothpicks.

Ernie lay flat on his butt, a flimsy wooden door beneath him. The latticework paneling fronting someone's bedroom had been smashed open. Tattered strips of oiled paper fluttered like the tentacles of a squashed squid.

Ernie shook his head, still dazed, a disoriented look in his eyes. I stretched out my hand to help him to his feet.

"Let me refresh your memory," I told him. "You were looking for Hatcher. All hell broke loose and somebody shoved you through that wall."

Suddenly, Ernie came back to his senses. His head whipped back and forth. "Come on!"

He sprinted down the hallway and shot down a stairway that emerged onto the alley running behind the Black Cat Club.

Walls made of stone and wood and ancient lumber lined the gloom. Water trickled down the center of a cobbled lane, reeking of human waste. But no sign of Hatcher.

Ernie glanced around, turned completely, and then looked up. I followed his eyes.

Like a huge bird, something floated from the rooftop of the Black Cat Club over to the red brick of the next building. With a great thump, the raven landed.

"He went upstairs," Ernie said.

We ran into the back door of the brick building next to the Black Cat Club.

It was a series of hooches. A nightclub downstairs. Broad cement hallways and rooms full of business girls upstairs. One woman wore shorts and a light green T-shirt and was bent over filling a pail of water from a rusty spigot. Ernie almost plowed into her.

"How do we get to the roof?" he shouted.

The girl turned, her face pocked, her eyes wide. "*Mullah gu?*" What did you say?

"Shit!" Ernie tore off down the corridor. At the end he found a stairway and charged up, taking three steps at a time. I followed.

The stairway narrowed and ended at a wooden door. Ernie kicked it open.

Out on the roof, the skyline of Samgakji was visible.

Tile-roofed hooches clustered around the main drag of bars and chophouses and *yoguans*. In the distance were the neat manicured lawns of ROK Army Headquarters and beyond that, the Eighth United States Army. Behind us, vibrating with the low rumble of the endlessly charging herd of *kimchi* cabs and three-wheeled trucks, loomed the elevated traffic circle for which Samgakji was famous.

We were three stories up. Since this was a skyscraper—by Samgakji standards—our view of the village was unobstructed. I circled the ramparts, scanning the streets below. No Hatcher.

The sky was overcast, no rain, but dark clouds on the horizon, cavorting with the jagged peaks north of Seoul.

Ernie shouted, pointing, leaning over the edge. "Got him! The son of a bitch took the damn fire escape!"

Before I could try to reason with him, Ernie was rappelling down the creaking metal ladder like a monkey on his way to a coconut feed.

Whenever we're after a suspect, and we have the full weight and authority of military law enforcement behind us, Ernie is joyous. Knowing that at the least sign of resistance he'll be able to vent all the violence that is constantly bubbling inside of him. And that no matter how badly he mauls the hapless victim, the honchos at Eighth Army will back him up. The honchos aren't particularly in love with all that Stateside civil liberties stuff, anyway.

Hatcher, though, was a hard case. If Ernie ran head first into him alone, he might be ground into dust before I had a chance to help. And, if we lost Hatcher, the nun would burn herself to death.

I reached the edge of the roof and peered down. Hatcher had dropped the last few feet to the alleyway, hit, rolled, bounced to his feet, and was sprinting toward the neon-decorated heart of the ville.

Ernie was already halfway down the fire escape. Rusty

bolts creaked under the strain. Figuring they wouldn't hold my weight, too, I ran back to the stairwell.

Bounding down the steps, I made pretty good time and when I burst through the nightclub downstairs, hit the front door, and emerged on the street, I could still see Hatcher rounding a corner about two blocks down the road. Ernie was a few yards behind him.

In front of the Black Cat Club, Sister Julie, the owner, and the boy with the mop stood watching.

I ran down the street, twisted down a couple of alleys. Up ahead, metal clanged, canvas tore, water splashed, and voices were raised in a cacophony of cursing.

What I saw first was a *pochang-macha*, a cart that sells soup and dried cuttlefish and *soju*, tipped over on its side. A rubber wheel spun madly. Feet stuck up in the air. Two men rolled in the mud, punching one another.

Ernie and Hatcher. Kicking and gouging. And Ernie was getting the worst of it.

The owner of the cart, a woman with a bright pink knit cap pulled down over her ears, stood with her hands splayed at the side of her head. Screaming.

Without thinking, I was on Bro Hatch. Punching, mauling, slamming my kneecap into ribs as sturdy as tree branches. I rolled on the ground seeing only grunting flesh and sweaty male bodies.

Ernie's sneakers scraped against gravel. I realized that he had pulled away. Now it was only me and Bro Hatch grappling with one another, rolling on the ground.

As we twirled, I saw a large heavy black pan lift in the air. I never saw it fall. Bro Hatch tugged and whipped me over, and I felt the iron slam into my back. I went limp.

Bro Hatch managed to pull a fist out of somewhere and ram it into my jaw. I almost laughed. Not much power for such a big guy but, of course, he wasn't able to launch his best punch while wrestling on the muddy streets of Sam-gakji.

The black pan orbited above us and slammed to earth once again. This time it found its mark. I heard a bong and felt it reverberating through the thick skull pressed against my shoulder. The pan raised again and crashed once again into bone.

This time, Hatcher's bloodshot eyes rolled back. He lay still.

As Ernie fumbled with the handcuffs attached to the back of his belt, I unwrapped bearlike arms from around me and raised myself unsteadily to my feet. I inventoried the damage. A few more cuts. A few more bruises. Nothing serious.

After the world stopped spinning, I gazed down at Bro Hatch.

He lay on the ground, his hands cuffed securely behind the small of his back, gnashing his teeth, cursing.

Ernie checked the snugness of the cuffs, straightened, and grinned.

"This is one seriously bad dude," he said.

I nodded, still trying to slow my breathing.

We hoisted Hatcher to his feet and walked him through the village back toward the Black Cat Club.

I checked my jaw. Not busted. A little bruised. It would heal.

Business girls in shorts and workmen carting crates of Oriental Beer into nightclubs gaped as we passed by. Sister Julie swayed her round butt out into the center of the street and stood with her hands on her hips.

"You think you take Bro Hatch?" She sneered at us. "No way."

Hatcher was still groggy, his head lolling between his massive shoulders. Ernie shoved Sister Julie out of the way.

"We got him and we're taking him in," he said.

"He make you pay later," Sister Julie smirked, following close at our heels. "When he get out of monkey house, he punch *lights* out on two T-shirts."

"We'll risk it," I said.

Hatcher submitted meekly as we shoved him into the backseat of the jeep.

Ernie trotted over to an open storefront, dropped a ten-won coin into the public phone, and dialed the number for the Eighth Army Military Police Desk Sergeant. It took a while for the Korean operator to connect the call to the on-post military phone exchange, but finally Ernie got through.

"Suspect in custody," he said. "Private First Class Hatcher, Ignatius Q."

Even from this distance, I heard shouting on the other end of the phone line.

"No," Ernie said. "No problem at all. Piece of rice cake."

A small crowd began to gather around the jeep, staring curiously. All Koreans. GIs were on compound at this time of the duty day. Working. At night, arresting Bro Hatch amidst a teeming mob of half-drunk soul brothers would've been impossible.

Hanging up the phone, Ernie strode back, poked his head into the back of the jeep, and grabbed Hatcher's limp paw. Immediately, Hatcher jerked his hand away. But not before Ernie spotted the tooth marks on his knuckle where the little nun had chomped into him during the attack. Ernie leaned into Hatcher's face.

"There ain't no way out of it, blood. We know everything about it. We got the word from the little nun out in Itaewon herself."

Hatcher's head had apparently stopped ringing. He looked up at Ernie.

"You ain't got shit."

His expression was sullen, wary, and I had the impression that the lines on his still-youthful face were set there in stone at a very early age. But no matter how much he'd been pushed around when he was a child, nobody was pushing Ignatius Q. Hatcher around now. Not without a fight. He was a big man, no question about that, and must've spent a lot of time lifting weights. Even in defeat, he let out a palpable air of menace, an aura of violence that glowed around his bulky shoulders.

Ernie ignored it. He wasn't much into auras.

"Sure we do," Ernie told him. "We have the bite marks on your fist and the identification from the nun and the eyewitness testimony of my partner here. He saw you running away."

"Don't mean nothing."

Ernie jerked his thumb over his shoulder, toward the sullen Sister Julie. "And we even have the word from the woman who was there when you beat up the nun."

Hatcher's head jerked back. "Sister Julie won't tell you shit."

Ernie was an expert interrogator. Hatcher had just confirmed that Sister Julie was a witness to the crime. Not even for a second did Ernie allow himself an expression of triumph.

Ernie had been purposely speaking low and rapidly, so Sister Julie wouldn't be able to hear all he said. But she heard her name. With red-tipped claws, she grabbed his arm.

"What you say about Sister Julie?"

Ernie swiveled on her. "Why'd you take him to Itaewon?"

Red lips pulled back from white teeth. "I no take."

"He says you did."

She peered into the canvas-covered back of the jeep.

I spoke up. "Spill it all, Hatcher. The more you hold

back, the more the whole weight of this thing is going to fall on you. If you don't tell us about everyone who was involved, they'll walk away free. Laughing at you for taking the entire hit by yourself."

Hatcher turned his red eyes on Sister Julie. "You tell him about that man who made us do it," he said. "You tell him."

Ernie kept his eyes riveted on Sister Julie. "Who was this guy?"

She shrugged creamy shoulders. "Some guy."

"What'd he tell you to do?"

She looked back and forth between us and then gazed at the glaring visage of Bro Hatch. She swallowed.

"He told us to go to Itaewon. A little nun works out there, collecting money for temple. Business girl, you know, they like to give lots of money to Buddha. Maybe help next life."

"And you don't?"

"Not Sister Julie. No way. I no chump."

Hatcher growled. "Tell him about the guy."

"Yeah. He say he want us to rob Buddhist nun. Take all money. Korean slicky boy, they *taaksan* believe Buddha. Don't want to take her money. So maybe this nun, she have a lot of money."

"But you never found out because we showed up?"

"Yeah." A puzzled look crossed Sister Julie's face. "How you get there so fast?"

"Good police work," Ernie answered. "Why'd you do what this guy told you to do?"

"Usual reason."

"What's that?"

"He pay me."

Bro Hatcher lunged forward off the canvas seat but was stopped by the metal roll bars. "You never *told* me that! How much did that fuck pay you?"

Sister Julie backed away, covering her fright by twisting her lips in a tight sneer. "Be cool, Bro. Most tick I was gonna tell you."

"How much?" Hatcher roared.

"Twenty thousand won."

About forty bucks. For beating up an innocent servant of Buddha. And Hatcher was only angry because he hadn't received his share.

Ernie shoved him backward against the seat. "Shut up unless I ask you a question."

Hatcher stared at him sullenly. Ernie turned back to Sister Julie.

"This guy, was he an American or a Korean?"

"Not American. Not Korean." She waved her hand. "Some outside guy."

"Outside guy?"

"Yeah. Foreigner."

"Which country?"

"I don't know. He look like Korean, only maybe he out in sun too much."

A chill ran through my body. Without thinking I stepped forward, looming over Sister Julie.

"What did he wear, this guy?"

She stared up at me. Her sneer disappeared. "Chump-change clothes. Like he farmer or something."

I reached for the top of my skull. "And on his head . . ."

"Yes. He wear something wrapped around." She twirled her finger around her exploding hairstyle. "Like *kullei*."

"Like a rag? Wrapped around his head?"

"Yes."

A sunburnt Asian man wearing a turban. I turned to Ernie.

"Sounds familiar," he said.

"Sure does."

I turned back to Sister Julie. "What was his name?"

"Rag something." She frowned and then snapped her fingers. "Ragyapa. That was it."

The man who had paid Sister Julie to convince Bro Hatch to attack and rob the little nun was Ragyapa. The same man who had kidnapped Herman's daughter Mi-ja.

When the MPs arrived, Sister Julie hugged Bro Hatch and kissed him and told him that she wouldn't let any other man touch her while he was gone. After the MPs drove away with Bro Hatch, Ernie grabbed Sister Julie by the soft flesh of her upper arm.

"You're right about not letting any other man touch you while he's gone." She tried to tug away from him but he held tight. "Unless it's a KNP," he said.

We turned Sister Julie over to the Korean National Police for her collusion in the mugging of the Buddhist nun. We filed charges and filled out a report and asked her a few more questions. When we left the little Samgakji Police Station she was still cursing, waving a red-tipped finger, promising to get even with us.

Ernie's molars clicked on a new stick of gum. "Righteous sister," he said. "Especially when she's angry."

USING SISTER JULIE AS HIS GO-BETWEEN, RAGYAPA HAD PUT BRO Hatch up to attacking the Buddhist nun. He had even paid Sooki to inform Ernie and me.

Why had he done this?

To divert our attention? Probably. But more important, to divert the attention of the entire United States Army. With riots against our presence in Korea sweeping the country, we'd be less worried about some kidnapped Korean orphan and an old jade skull that had been lost for centuries.

But was that it? To divert our attention? Or was there some other reason?

Maybe he also wanted to divert the attention of the other Buddhists in the country. The Buddhists who the little nun represented.

If that was his intention, he had succeeded admirably.

NOBODY NOTICED US WHEN WE SAUNTERED INTO THE MP STA-
tion. Now that the Provost Marshal had Pfc. Ignatius Q. Hatcher in custody, they had no time to acknowledge the two CID agents who'd made the arrest. Typical bureaucrats. Basking in the glory of somebody else's hard work.

Ernie stood in the hallway, watching the shimmering blue water bottle glug. Inside an oak-paneled office, the Provost Marshal and the First Sergeant and Lieutenant Roh from the ROK Liaison Office hashed out Pfc. Hatcher's future.

"The Korean government demands custody of Hatcher," Lieutenant Roh said. "Right now."

"You're out of bounds, Lieutenant," the Provost Marshal answered. "There are clear procedures to be followed, outlined in the Status of Forces Agreement, when a U.S. serviceman is to be turned over to ROK authorities."

"You have the power to waive those procedures," Lieutenant Roh insisted. "In this case you must."

"We *must* do what is in the interest of the United States Government."

Ernie glanced over at me, raising his eyebrows. I leaned toward him and whispered. "The Eighth Army honchos must be pissed about all the demonstrations. Maybe the Korean police didn't crack down fast enough. Maybe some colonel caught a rotten egg in his puss."

"If they hold Hatcher," Ernie said, "there will be more demonstrations."

"Maybe the Provost Marshal doesn't give a damn."

Outside of the MP Station, a crowd of Koreans had gathered in front of the main gate. MPs and a chain-link fence held them back. A few were chanting anti-American slogans, trying to encourage everyone to join in. Somehow they already knew we had the nun's attacker in custody.

A rock whistled through the air, launched high into the gray monsoon sky. Ernie watched it soar, reach the top of its arc, and sail down and clatter harmlessly against the blacktop in front of us.

"Incoming," he said.

"Yeah," I agreed. "Prepare for heavy swells."

WE EXITED THE COMPOUND BY A SIDE GATE WHERE NO DEMON-strators had yet gathered. Crossing quickly over the big stone block that composed the sidewalk, we reached the jumbled stalls and shops of Itaewon. Leather bags and sneakers and jackets hung from wooden rafters in mad disarray. Signs touting espresso shops and beer halls peeked out of the swirling collage, punctuated by an occasional obstetrics clinic promising help for venereal disease or pregnancy.

"There it is again," Ernie said. "The smell."

I knew what he was talking about. The aroma of spiced cabbage fermenting in earthen pots. Raked earth, damp from the monsoon rain. Bubbling septic tanks waiting to be drained. Perforated charcoal briquettes, smoldering out their last red gasp.

I breathed in deeply. "What's that?" I asked.

"What's what?"

"Smoke."

"Charcoal?"

"No," I said. "More than that."

I gazed above the skyline, about a half mile ahead to the bar district. A steady plume of black smoke rose into the gray sky, like a signal from Apache renegades.

"Something's on fire," I said.

24

THE FIRST SPLATS OF MONSOON RAIN SLAPPED INTO MY FORE-head as we ran toward the *yoguan*. Children in stiff-necked school uniforms scurried out of our way and a cabbage vendor wheeled his cart frantically to evade our onslaught. But the obstacles in the road meant nothing to me. All I could see was Lady Ahn. The high contours of her cheekbones, the stony set of her eyes, the pursed lips as she gazed down upon a world that had never quite met her exquisite royal standards.

She had become an obsession with me. But it was an obsession that made me happy to be young and male and alive. An obsession that I had no desire to break.

The rust-flavored wetness of a sudden monsoon sprinkle moistened the cobbled road. I slipped, quickly regained my footing, but Ernie surged past me. Up ahead the flames shot out of windows and engorged themselves in a brighter red.

Possibilities flashed through my mind. Maybe the fire

was just a freak happenstance. Maybe it had nothing to do with Lady Ahn or with the skull or with Herman the German or with the kidnapped Mi-ja.

Maybe. But I didn't think so. I'd been a cop too long. Things didn't happen by coincidence.

As I ran, I steeled the inside of my gut. Lining it with iron. The same protective covering I'd used every time life presented me with a kick in the ribs.

Nothing good could come of this.

The Itaewon Fire Department was already on the scene, their fat red tanker truck wedged into the alley leading to the *yoguan*. Ernie clambered over it, ignoring the shouts of the firemen, and I followed.

The top floors of the *yoguan* were burning pretty good. Outside, the woman who had rented us our rooms stood screeching at the top of her lungs, pointing that there were more people upstairs.

Ernie didn't even slow down. He charged into the blackness of the front door.

But I hesitated for a moment, gazing up, searching for the small window of Lady Ahn's room. The window was totally engulfed in flames, more than any other spot in the building. The conflagration had started there. Of that I was sure. If she was still in that room, we were too late. I squeezed down the side alley, heading for the back entrance.

I kicked old boxes stuffed with trash out of the way and shoved open the wood slat doorway. The smoke wasn't bad back here.

Before I reached the second floor, however, the smoke was too thick to continue. Footsteps pounded down the stairway. Something black loomed above me, then burst out of a cloud of ink.

Ernie, tugging on an old woman wrapped in a long cotton dress.

I heard the swoosh of fire hoses; water started cascading against the walls above us. Outside, as if the rusty old fire station apparatus had primed something, the heavens opened and rain pelted down with a fury. As the old woman coughed and retched I sat her down on the varnished floor near the back door and shouted at her in Korean.

"Is there anyone else upstairs? A young woman?"

She gazed up at me, her eyes blank with fright. "They took her."

"Who did?"

"Those men. Those foreigners. She fought with them. She wouldn't let them in. They broke down the door. She fought them. I think it was she who started the fire."

"And these men took her out before the flames grew?"

"Yes."

"Where did they go?"

"Out back. The alleys. She was struggling so hard that they all had to hold her."

Ernie was bent over, leaning against the wall, spitting and wiping his eyes with the back of his hands. I slapped him on the back a few times to clear his lungs.

"Ragyapa's taken Lady Ahn," I said. "Come on!"

Ernie hacked and spit up some phlegm. "Son of a bitch!"

We rushed out into the narrow maze of alleys behind the *yoguan*, pushing past the gawkers watching the fire. The rain fell in steady sheets.

A group of men carrying a struggling woman must've left some sort of trace. We scurried like rats in a maze, twisting and turning, having no idea which way they might've gone. Through the mist, light glowed inside the homes we passed. Rain splattered on tin roofs. The soil beneath our feet rapidly turned into a muddy quagmire.

I stopped two pedestrians and shouted questions at

them. We were drenched, our faces still covered with soot, our eyes enflamed with a frantic madness. The first person could only stutter. The second insisted he knew nothing.

We ranged up the hill, getting farther and farther away from the main nightclub district of Itaewon.

Finally, beneath the canvas awning of an open-front grocery store, I spotted a Korean policeman. He wore a long raincoat and a plastic hood pulled over his cap, and he was hunched over, listening intently to a woman who gestured wildly. We ran up to them. The KNP was so absorbed in the woman's story that he didn't glance over at us. I could make out most of the woman's rapid Korean.

A group of men—foreigners, she thought—were wrestling with a woman. The woman was bruised and bloodied and kept shouting for help. But there were no men around in these rain-drenched alleys. No one who could help the poor woman. I'm only a housewife, she said. I have children. What could I do?

I interrupted the tirade.

"Where did they go?"

Both the policeman and the housewife stared at me. I pulled out my badge.

"*Odi kasso?*" I shouted. Where did they go?

The woman pointed. "Down there. Toward the car park behind the *Unchon Siktang.*" The Driver's Eatery.

"I tried to stop them," she said. "But what could I do? I am—"

But Ernie and I were already sloshing away in the rain, heading downhill toward the road that wound through the nightclub district and back to the main road. Once Ragyapa and his boys reached that, they'd have access to all the major thoroughfares in Seoul. And once they reached the main road, catching them would be impossible.

"They must've stashed a car behind the Driver's

Eatery," Ernie said. "And then they walked through the back alleys to the *yoguan*."

"Looks like it."

"But how did they know where Lady Ahn was?"

"No clue," I said. "We'll have to worry about that later."

"And why would they kidnap her?"

"They figured she had the jade skull," I said. "When they realized she didn't, they decided to take her as a bargaining chip."

Ernie swore. "Isn't one kidnap victim enough for these guys?"

"I don't think anything's enough for them," I said. "Not until they hold in their hands the jade skull of Kublai Khan."

The muddy parking lot behind the Driver's Eatery must've held about twenty small taxis. There were also a few three-wheeled flatbed pickup trucks. Ernie took one side of the lot and I took the other. We checked each vehicle closely. When we finished, we met behind the eatery. Tired drivers sat behind steamed windows, slurping on bowls of wet noodles, sipping on barley tea.

"Zilch," Ernie reported.

"Me, too. Nothing." I looked inside the eatery. "Somebody in there must've seen something."

Ernie pushed through the door.

The little restaurant was cramped, and reeked of human sweat and boiled cabbage and charcoal gas. A couple of the drivers stared up at us, unevenly burning cigarettes hanging from brown lips.

I pointed back to the parking lot and spoke in loud Korean.

"Some men brought a woman down here," I said. "She might've been struggling. They put her in a car and drove away with her. How many of you saw it?"

There was silence. I repeated what I had said, careful of

my pronunciation, trying to make sure that everyone understood me. No answer.

Ernie strode over to the heating stove in the center of the room. He hoisted a large brass pot of barley tea and held it at chest level, and when he had everyone's attention he tossed hot tea out of the spout and let it splash on the floor. Then he turned slowly in the center of the rickety tables.

"Who saw it?" I asked.

Still no answer. Ernie sloshed steaming water onto the Formica-covered table in front of him. Three astonished drivers sprang to their feet, slapping the steam rising from their trousers. As one, they all started cursing.

Ernie sloshed more water at the drivers. They kicked their chairs back and leapt out of the way.

"Who saw the men who took the woman?" I shouted.

A burly young driver stepped toward the kitchen and grabbed a butcher knife from a wooden chopping block. An older, gray-haired man noticed him, turned back to me, and started to speak.

"It wasn't a car," he said.

I turned to him, waiting. Ernie stopped sloshing tea.

"It was a truck," the man said. "Three wheels. The back seemed to be loaded, but they shoved the woman in there."

"Was she struggling?"

"No. I thought she was asleep. Or drunk."

"Where did the truck go?"

"Down the hill." He jerked his thumb toward the nightclub district. "It was a blue truck."

That didn't narrow it down much. Almost every truck in Korea was either blue or green or gray.

"Did you see the license plate number?"

"No reason to look."

"What was the truck loaded with?"

"Garlic." The driver with the butcher knife pushed himself past some of his irate comrades, edging closer to Ernie. The gray-haired man noticed him and spoke again. "If you had arrived two minutes earlier, you might have caught them."

The guy with the knife lunged at Ernie. I shouted. Ernie swiveled and tossed the brass pot at him. Steaming water exploded into the air, splashing into the driver's face. He screamed.

I grabbed Ernie, shoved him forward, and kicked open the front door. We dashed out into the pelting rain. Behind us, a gaggle of drivers stood in the doorway, staring. But none of them looked too anxious to follow. They had lives to lead. Money to make. Families to support.

I hoped that the guy who received a faceful of tea wasn't hurt too badly.

Ernie turned back and flashed the drivers the finger.

"Dickheads," he said.

We searched the roads of Itaewon but there was no sign of a blue truck loaded with garlic.

And no sign of Lady Ahn.

25

I LEANED OVER STAFF SERGEANT RILEY'S DESK, BREATHING down the collar of his starched fatigue shirt.

"You must have *something* for me, Riley. Don't the Koreans keep goddamn records?"

Riley leaned away from me. "Back off, Sueño. Of course they keep records. Give me some breathing space and maybe I'll find something."

We were back in the CID office. Ever since Ragyapa and his thugs had taken Lady Ahn, I'd been badgering everyone—the KNPs, the MPs, even Sergeant Riley—to find me some sort of lead so I could nail those bastards.

Before Ernie and I left Itaewon, we'd stopped in the Police Station and questioned Captain Kim on his progress on the Mi-ja kidnapping case. He admitted there hadn't been much.

"Too much *demo*," he said. Demonstrations. "Ever since Buddhist nun beat up, whole country crazy."

The madness that was sweeping the country—and espe-

cially Itaewon—over the mugging of Choi So-lan, the
Buddhist nun, had all Kim's cops working double shifts.
Devotees bearing flower bouquets and a huge photo of the
little nun dotted the Main Supply Route leading out of
Eighth Army Headquarters. What with the occasional altercation between GI and demonstrator, and the nightly
rallies, there was little time left to investigate the kidnapping of a little girl.

I filled out a police report on the abduction of Lady
Ahn. Kim thanked me and filed it away.

"I want *action* on that!" I said.

Captain Kim nodded. "When I can. When I can."

Ernie had to pull me away.

Now, back at the CID office, Ernie was still working on
keeping me calm. Talk about a switch. He poured two
cups of coffee out of the metal urn and handed me one. I
slurped it without tasting it.

A map of Seoul hung on the wall of the CID Admin
office. Usually, I was fascinated by it. All the ancient palaces and gateways and temples. But today, it depressed me.
A city of eight million people. How in the hell was I going
to find Lady Ahn?

I shouldn't have let her stay alone. I should have known
better. Either Ernie or I should've stayed with her. Or we
should've brought her along.

Ernie slapped me on the back. He'd been peering at
me.

"It's not your fault," he said.

"It is."

"No way. Those assholes were after the skull, not Lady
Ahn. And they already had one hostage. Who would've
thought they'd take her, too?"

His attempts to make me feel better didn't do any good.
I sipped on a little more of the bitter coffee and then tossed
the rest into the trash can.

Sergeant Riley slipped the pencil out from behind his ear and tapped the triangular eraser on a sheaf of papers.

"Here it is," he said. "I knew it was in here. The dope for the last two months on all foreigners entering Korea." Riley pushed his sleeves up along his skinny forearms. "Foreigners, most of them businessmen, broken down by nationality."

He started slashing Xs along the list.

"We can ignore all these *Miguks*." The Americans. "And all these pansies from Europe."

"Cross out the Japs, too," Ernie said.

"Right you are." Riley slashed vigorously. "Out with the Eastern dwarfs."

Riley claimed not to have any interest in Korean culture, other than chasing the business girls and guzzling rice wine. But he had somehow picked up all the cuss words—even a few I didn't know—and every racial epithet in the book.

"Now what we have left," Riley told us, "is a few from Africa . . ." He slashed these out. "And a few more from South America." His pencil continued to work. "And that leaves a whole shitload from Indonesia and Taiwan and Malaysia and Singapore and—"

"Cross those out, too," I told him. Riley glanced up at me. I said, "Concentrate only on the states of Northeast Asia."

"Which are?"

"Mongolia, China, Manchuria, and the Soviet Union. Korea and Japan I've already eliminated."

Riley glanced back down at the paperwork. "Nothing from any of those places. The South Koreans don't issue visas to Communists. If these guys are from one of those countries, they must have phony passports."

"So this list isn't going to do me any good?"

Riley shrugged.

"Is this the only list they gave you?" I asked Riley. "Nothing else?"

"Well, there is one more thing." Riley slid a sheaf of paper out from the bottom of the pile. "The guy at Korean Customs told me I didn't really need it, but since I was paying him, I told him to throw it in anyway. By the way, you owe me forty thousand won."

Ernie's head jerked up. "Eighty bucks just for some lousy paperwork?"

"Hey. We didn't go through channels. My man was taking a risk."

"Shit," Ernie grumbled. "Take it out of petty cash."

"You find a way to fool the First Sergeant and I will."

"Don't worry," I said. "You'll get your money on payday."

That seemed to satisfy Sergeant Riley. He slapped the slender list on top of the other. "You see why he didn't think you'd need it."

The title had been translated into crude English: *Entry into Korea by Persons of Organizations Religious.*

My heart beat harder. Even Ernie leaned closer.

A few minutes later, we knew how Ragyapa and his boys had entered Korea.

Using Riley's list of foreigners entering Korea, we figured that the most likely method of entry for Ragyapa and his thugs was by means of a convention that was being hosted here by the Pacific Rim Buddhist Association. About five thousand Buddhists from all over the world were attending. The festivities included elaborate ceremonies at some of the most holy Buddhist shrines on the peninsula. Worship and conferences were scheduled in many sites, and if anyone attended all the events, he'd have to spend over two months in Korea. The exact location of all the attendees was unknown even to the government.

The honchos of the host organization, the Pacific Rim Buddhist Association, were the only ones with that data.

"Where is this association located?" Ernie asked.

"Chong-ro," Riley answered. "Downtown Seoul."

Ernie lifted his eyebrows at me.

It took ten minutes to switch from the Eighth Army phone net to the civilian lines in Seoul. Once I got through, all I heard was a steady ringing.

I slammed the phone down. "No answer."

Ernie glanced at his watch. "Most of the world's already closed up shop and gone to Happy Hour."

"You want me to check with the KNP Liaison Officer?" Riley asked. "See if he can contact them?"

I thought about it. "Wouldn't do any good. Even if these Buddhists had a line on Ragyapa and his boys, they wouldn't be staying in the same hotel. They would've moved by now. Probably two or three times."

I paced the room. Two sets of eyeballs following me.

"Besides," I said, "tonight is the full moon."

Ernie unwrapped a new stick of ginseng gum. "Our last chance to save Mi-ja."

SLICKY GIRL NAM WAS IN HER GLORY. A DOZEN OLD WOMEN from the neighborhood had gathered at her hooch and everyone watched as she stood in the center of the court-yard and screamed at us.

"Where you *been*? Why you no find Mi-ja? Why you no bring jade skull?"

I held up both hands. "Calm down, Nam. We're here now. Where's Herman?"

"I don't know. That sonofabitch *kara chogi*." Gone away. "He here this afternoon but now he gone. I don't know where."

One of the women shuffled across the courtyard to check the charcoal. Using iron tongs, she pried open the cover. The fire glowed brightly. She let the metal lid clang shut.

The edge of the full moon peeked over a tile roof.

"There it *is*!" Nam screeched. "The moon! Pretty soon foreign assholes kill Mi-ja." She clutched my sleeve. "You *do* something!"

"We *are* going to do something," I told her. "When was the last time the kidnappers called you?"

"You know. When they told you to go to top of Hooker Hill."

"They'll be calling again tonight," I said, "to give us instructions. You wait here. Ernie and I will handle it."

Slicky Girl Nam clutched her bare arms and shivered.

AT THE PHARMACY, ERNIE AND I PASSED A BOTTLE OF *SOJU* BACK and forth. I carried the .38 under my jacket, Ernie had his .45. Still, a little extra courage couldn't hurt.

I'd thought of having some sort of MP rapid-response team put at our disposal, but it wouldn't work. Wherever this rendezvous was going to be, Ragyapa would have lookouts. A bunch of clumsy cops barging in would be spotted for sure. We had no choice. Ernie and I had to handle the exchange ourselves.

"Where the hell did that goddamn Herman get off to?" Ernie asked.

"Don't know." I sipped on the *soju*. The fiery rice liquor burned all the way down.

"Maybe it's better without him," Ernie said. "If we took him along, there's no telling what he might do. The guy's totally unpredictable."

I stared at Ernie, trying to figure if he was joking. His expression seemed perfectly serious.

I handed him the bottle. As I did, the phone rang. I lost my grip and the *soju* crashed to the ground, liquor and crystal splashing everywhere.

"Shit!"

I snatched the phone off the hook. "Sueño."

"Midnight." It was the gravelly voice again. Ragyapa. "The Bridge of the Golden Tribute."

"Where's that?"

"You must find it."

It was already almost eleven. We had to drive back to the compound, pick up the skull, then make it to wherever in the hell this Bridge of the Golden Tribute was.

"I need more time."

"No more time! Midnight. Or the child dies."

The line went dead.

I OPENED THE DOOR OF THE ADMIN OFFICE WITH MY KEY AND switched on the lights. In front of the safe, I turned to Ernie.

"Do you have the combination?"

"No. I thought you had it."

"Shit. I don't have it either." I glanced at the clock on the wall. "No sweat. We still have an hour until midnight. All we have to do is track down Riley. He has the combination."

"Right."

We locked the office back up and headed for the Lower Four Club.

WE FOUND RILEY, ALL RIGHT. PASSED OUT IN A PUDDLE OF bourbon. When I slapped him a couple of times, he raised his head and groaned.

An old lifer at the bar named Kenny told us the story.

"Herman the German was in tonight. Paying for every round. Never seen him so generous."

"Which explains why Riley was putting it away."

"Sure," Kenny said. "He can't pass up a freebie."

I checked Riley's pockets, looking for his wallet. Ernie

finally spotted it on the floor beneath the cocktail table. A couple of dollars' worth of Military Payment Certificates and his weapons card and photos of smiling Caucasian faces were strewn all over the filthy carpet. But no safe combination.

"Enough of this shit," Ernie said.

We dragged Riley into the latrine and stuck his head under the cold water faucet. Finally, he sputtered to life. "What the hell?"

I slapped his cheeks. Hard. "Gimme the combination to the safe!"

"What?"

I slapped him again, maybe a little harder than necessary. "The combination, Riley. What's the goddamned combination?"

"Okay," he said in a hurt voice. "Why didn't you say so?" He reached for his back pocket. "It's in my wallet."

"No, it's not," I said. "We already checked there."

"Okay, then. I remember it. Just give me a minute."

Ernie shoved him back toward the water faucet and Riley started to spout out the numbers. I memorized them as fast as he said them.

ERNIE CLICKED IN THE TUMBLERS AND SWUNG OPEN THE HEAVY door. We peered inside.

"Son of a *bitch*!" Ernie shouted.

The safe was empty.

I swore and slumped down on one of the straight-backed chairs.

Once again, as it had done so often before, the jade skull of Kublai Khan had vanished. But this time, I knew who had stolen it.

An old lifer and an infamous black marketeer. The man

who'd treated Riley to so many drinks he'd passed out. The husband of Slicky Girl Nam. The father of the kidnapped Mi-ja. The man everyone in Itaewon knew well. Or thought they did.

Herman the German.

26

THE FIRST THING RAGYAPA NOTICED WAS HOW LARGE SHE WAS.
How unlike other women. This creature known as Lady
Ahn talked back when spoken to. And whenever someone
made the mistake of letting one of her fists swing free, she
punched the nearest of Ragyapa's disciples. Two of the
monks had to struggle to twist her arms behind her back.
They'd shackled her to the metal ring in the basement
floor.

She looked like a woman—the small waist, the large
breasts, the round hips—but she punched and spit like the
most ferocious of men. A she-tiger. Not at all like the com-
pliant little girl, Mi-ja.

Ragyapa wanted to meditate with this woman. The
monks took off her clothes and oiled her down but as soon
as they unbound her wrists she started fighting again. No
matter how often she was beaten, she kept fighting back.

Was it because of her royal blood? Ragyapa doubted it.
True royals have everything done for them—from birth

until death—and are the most docile people in the world. No, it wasn't her lineage that caused this woman to be so arrogant. It was the way she'd been brought up.

That was it, Ragyapa decided. She was nothing more than a peasant who thought too highly of herself. Trying to teach her proper behavior would be a waste of time.

He imagined her in the lotus position, oiled down, sitting across from him. Naked. For some reason the vision didn't excite him. She was too big, too gross, too full of her own desires.

No, the girl Mi-ja was much better. But she was growing weak.

Ragyapa ordered one more try with the big Korean woman. But this time, when the monks ripped off what little clothing she had left and pinned her down, she kicked one of them in the groin and bit into the ankle of another.

The men were enraged. They seldom meditated and had little control over their emotions. Should Ragyapa allow them to vent their foolish desires?

Ragyapa wavered for a moment, studying the woman called Lady Ahn. Her eyes flashed with hatred. Another foolish emotion. One that would take days—maybe weeks—to beat out of her.

No time for that, Ragyapa decided. In her present state, she held no interest for him.

Ragyapa flicked his wrist in a dismissive gesture. The two injured monks bowed deeply, showing their appreciation. When they dragged the big Korean woman away, she was still kicking and biting.

Later, while in silent meditation, Ragyapa heard her screams. All his disciples took their turns with her. Like a pack of beasts, Ragyapa thought, crawling all over her. His lips curled in disgust.

The monk in attendance rubbed oil on Ragyapa's body.

Ragyapa thought of the little girl. Finally, he motioned with his finger.

Mi-ja was brought to him. She was as listless as a puppet whose strings have been cut. But she was breathing.

The monk laid her naked body at Ragyapa's feet.

Ragyapa gazed down at her for a long moment. Finally, he reached forward and began rubbing oil on her flesh, hoping the soothing sensation would bring her back to consciousness.

It didn't.

He was forced to use the hot needles.

27

ERNIE WHIZZED THROUGH THE LATE NIGHT TRAFFIC AS IF HE had the entire transportation grid of Seoul preprogrammed into his brain. Headlights erupted from the dark, swerved, and disappeared behind us like swarms of fireflies. To our left was Seoul *yok*, the train station, with its huge Russian dome. Off to our right glittered the green lights of Namdae-mun, the Great South Gate.

I checked my watch. Twenty minutes to midnight. We had to hurry or the roads would be blocked by the curfew police.

My tourist guide to Seoul informed me that the Bridge of the Golden Tribute was located on the outskirts of the city, near the Han River Estuary.

I thought about Herman the German, a man I thought I knew.

He was a lifer like so many others. Hanging around Itaewon, living off his army retirement check and the few dollars he could hustle off the black market. It was an easy life. No worries. No job. His only commitment was to take a free military flight back and forth to Japan every ninety days to renew his three-month Korean tourist visa. Piece of cake. Sit in the Military Airlift Command terminal, sip coffee, shoot the breeze with the other lifers. A mellow way to pass one's golden years.

But then he complicated things by marrying Slicky Girl Nam. She brought the hammer down on him. Demanded that he increase his black market activities, bring in more money. She watched his hours. Didn't let him stay out all night carousing the ville. Kept him away from the young business girls who would wink and crook their fingers and make off with a few of those retiree greenbacks.

Slicky Girl Nam wanted those dollars all to herself.

And maybe she felt that she needed more than just the force of her personality to keep Herman in line. Maybe she felt that what their little family needed was a child.

The result had been instant responsibility for Herman the German. A guy who for most of his life had only two responsibilities: to make military formations every morning and to show up in the pay line at the end of every month.

It was clear to me now. Herman had wanted the jade skull all along. Maybe he had fantasies of smuggling it out of the country, selling it on the illicit art market in New York or in Europe. Taking the money and never returning to Korea. Never black-marketing again. Never again seeing Slicky Girl Nam. Maybe he grew tired of being knuckled on the head every time he spoke, of being humiliated in public, of being berated by a woman whose only accomplishments lay in the realms of prostitution and thievery.

But how had it all worked? Why had Herman entrapped us in all this? Why had Ragyapa kidnapped Mi-ja? How many people were being double-crossed? What the hell was really going on here?

Ernie pulled up to Sodae-mun, the Great West Gate,

the narrow stone edifice leading to the Bridge of the Golden Tribute.

"Where's the bridge?" he asked.

"Right at the next intersection," I said. "And at the third alley you come to, left for about a quarter mile."

He gunned the engine, cutting off a kimchi cab and flipping the irate driver the bird.

This entire mess started when Lady Ahn approached Herman the German about smuggling the jade skull out of Korea. Had she told him she didn't have the skull yet? That she was just making preparations so she could move it quickly once the skull came into her possession? Maybe. Or more likely, Herman had guessed. Maybe she'd been vague about the exact dates. And Herman would need exact dates to set something up. GIs left Korea only under military orders. With precise "will proceed" dates. Herman would have to know exactly when the skull would be available in order to set up someone to ship it out of the country for him.

When Lady Ahn couldn't give him a precise date, he'd known she didn't have the skull yet.

And then Ragyapa came onto the scene. Had he been following Lady Ahn? Yes. And when she approached Herman, Ragyapa waited until she was gone, then approached Herman himself.

I almost leapt out of my seat. That was it. Ragyapa and Herman were working together.

Ernie glanced over at me. "What's wrong?"

I explained my suspicions. When I'd finished, he slammed the palm of his hand against the steering wheel. "I'm going to *waste* me some goddamn Herman the German."

The alley narrowed, two cabs tried to squeeze past us without slowing, and Ernie scraped by them, grinding his teeth.

I should have seen it earlier.

When we made the first rendezvous with Ragyapa, Herman had been willing to let me go upstairs alone. Even though he knew Mi-ja might be there.

Maybe he had been afraid. But there was more.

Ragyapa's thugs had been waiting for us when we arrived on the ferry in Ok-dong. How had they known we were there? By torturing the Widow Fifi Kang. But how had they known we'd gone to Taejon? Only a few people knew. One of them was Herman.

And the clincher was the fire at the *yoguan*. Ragyapa and his boys had known Lady Ahn was there. They took a chance that maybe she had the jade skull with her. They were wrong about that, but they were right about her whereabouts. Other than me and Ernie, only Herman knew where she had been staying.

Herman the German had been working with Ragyapa. Why?

It was clear from our experiences on Bian-do that a foreigner like Ragyapa, even with the help of all his thugs, would never have been able to sail out to that hidden island and steal the jade skull from the monks on his own. Ragyapa must've realized that such a theft would take connections. Connections that only Lady Ahn could provide.

How much easier it would be to wait until she had stolen the jade skull, and then take it from her. And when best to grab it? When it came into the hands of Herman the German.

But why kidnap Mi-ja?

Maybe Ragyapa and Herman decided that Lady Ahn would need help. Koreans were certainly capable of helping her, but they all had connections in-country, debts to pay, families to support. Betrayal was a real possibility. The jade skull, once stolen from Bian-do, might never reach Herman the German. Or Ragyapa.

But who could help Lady Ahn? Who was trustworthy? Who had a reason to make sure that the skull reached the greedy hands of Herman the German?

GIs. No connections in-country. No families. No baggage of heavy indebtedness. And amongst GIs who had investigative experience? Who spoke the language? Who had CID badges that would help ward off the Korean police? Who was available right here in Itaewon, ready and waiting to be manipulated into a fool's errand?

The answer was simple: George Sueño and Ernie Bascom. At your service.

But they had to give us a reason to go along with such a dangerous mission. Money wouldn't be enough. Only one thing would be enough. Saving the life of a little girl. Saving the life of Mi-ja, Herman's own daughter.

The more I thought about it, the angrier I became. Herman had been working with Ragyapa all along. He had probably delivered Mi-ja to him. He had faked the anger at Lady Ahn in the subway, faked his hatred of Ragyapa and his thugs at the Temple of the Dream Buddha. But maybe there was one thing he hadn't faked. He hadn't faked his anguish at seeing her little ear sliced off and chopped up for dumplings.

I knew about the betrayal of children. When my mother died, my father took off and didn't return. Leaving me alone forever.

Had Herman been there when they'd chopped off Mi-ja's ear?

It was a question I was looking forward to asking him.

When the jade skull actually arrived in Seoul, I was the one who'd made the mistake of calling Herman. To lessen his anguish. To let him know that his nightmare—his daughter's nightmare—was almost over.

And what had he done in return? He'd notified Ragyapa of Lady Ahn's whereabouts.

Was it then that he decided to double-cross Ragyapa? Not to wait until we turned the jade skull over in exchange for Mi-ja, but to break into the CID office and steal the jade for himself?

Or was it Ragyapa who double-crossed Herman first? By snatching Lady Ahn at the *yoguan*? Ragyapa believed she had the jade skull with her. Herman would've been cut out of the deal if Ragyapa had managed to obtain the skull himself. Maybe it was the fire that made Herman decide to buy a few drinks for Staff Sergeant Riley, let him liquor himself up, and then steal the combination to the CID safe.

Double cross on top of double cross. Was that the ancient legacy of the jade drinking skull of Kublai Khan?

And now the skull was gone. Herman had it and he was running. And I was left with the rare honor of informing the murderous Ragyapa about that fact, while at the same time trying to keep Mi-ja and Lady Ahn alive.

All in a day's work for a U.S. Army CID agent.

I TOOK A DEEP BREATH, SMELLING THE SALT TANG OF AN INLET of the Han River Estuary. We were close to the bridge now. Very close.

Ernie turned off the jeep's engine, coasted next to a rickety wooden fence, and jerked back the emergency brake. As he chained and padlocked the steering wheel, I whispered in his ear.

"Let's check out the approaches to the bridge first."

He nodded.

This neighborhood of Seoul seemed to be ancient. The old homes were made of wood, and most had blue or red tile roofs. A few, especially those near the listless waters of the narrow inlet, were covered with straw thatch. As we stopped and peered around, we heard rustling in the straw.

"Mice," I whispered. "They bring good luck."

Ernie nodded.

As the pathway neared the river, the mud turned into a thick goo. It was hard not to make a sticking sound as we walked. The waterway was lined on either side with thick stone, like a canal. Spanning it was the graceful arch of a wood slat bridge. The Bridge of the Golden Tribute.

The bridge had been famous at one time. It was here that envoys from the Dragon Throne were greeted by officials of the Korean court at the end of their long journey from China. It was also here that the Korean king gave his approval to the annual caravan of riches that was sent as tribute to the Chinese emperor sitting on the Dragon Throne in the ancient capital of Peking.

Now the bridge was nothing but an eyesore in a slum. The wood was rotting. Lewd graffiti, scribbled in the Korean *hangul* script, scarred the twenty-yard span. Feces and stinking garbage and the corpses of vermin floated in the stagnant water below.

"Place smells like shit," Ernie said.

We checked the alleyways carefully. Empty.

Across the canal it was dark. We saw no movement.

"I'll go across and check it out," I told Ernie. "You wait here."

He stuck his arm out. "No. I'll go."

Before I could protest, he had scampered across the bridge. Wooden slats creaked under his weight. He disappeared into the darkness.

Five minutes later, he reappeared. He flashed me the hand signal for all clear.

Where were they? It was already two minutes past the midnight curfew. Did Ragyapa know Herman had stolen the jade skull? Were he and Herman already winging their way out of the country, laughing and sipping champagne? Were Lady Ahn and Mi-ja on their way back to their families? Or were they dead?

I didn't know the answer to any of these questions. All I could do was wait. It was four minutes past curfew.

Ernie found a secluded spot near a tiled overhang and leaned back into the shadows. I heard the cold metal clang of the charging handle of his .45 as he chambered a round.

The canal smelled rancid, the path was thick mud beneath my feet, the night was humid and starless and threatening to rain. Only the moon shone full. Dreadfully full. This would be our last chance to save Mi-ja. I settled back, reminding myself that I was part Yaqui Indian. Patience was bred into my bones.

But my sore muscles were all American.

We waited.

WATER SLAPPED AGAINST WOOD.

I peered around the corner. The monsoon moon glimmered off the greasy water, making the stinking little canal seem almost beautiful.

A boat was approaching. Full of men. Although they were rowing, I could make out an outboard motor in the back. One of the men, one near the front, had a head like a lightbulb. A turban. Ragyapa.

I motioned for Ernie to keep alert. They could also come at us from behind.

When the boat was ten yards from the bridge, I stepped out of my hiding place and strode to the center of the span.

The oarsmen brought the little craft to a halt. Ragyapa rose to a standing position, his legs braced wide, keeping his balance. An oily voice slithered through the air like an eel.

"Do you have the jade skull?"

That nailed it. He didn't know about Herman. How to play it now? How to keep Lady Ahn alive? How to keep Mi-ja alive?

"First," I said, "I have to see the woman. And the girl."

Ragyapa gestured with an open palm at the boat and spoke in his precisely pronounced English. "Do you think we could fit them in this? You have no choice. You must turn over the jade first, then we will release them."

"What guarantee do I have that you won't kill them?"

"None. But when I have the jade skull, I will have no reason to kill them."

He was lying. Their testimony wouldn't do much good if he escaped and left the country. But that was a big if.

One of his thugs steadied the rocking boat by gripping the stone wall. Silently, the monk hopped up on the wall and crouched there.

Ernie had a good line on him. I wasn't worried. But there was no sense putting it off any longer. I had to level with Ragyapa, strike some sort of bargain.

"Your friend," I said. "Herman. The one who was working with you." I waited. No emotion showed in the shadows of Ragyapa's face. "He has disappeared."

The crouching thug straightened and took a few steps toward the bridge. Off to the side, I sensed movement in the shadows. Ernie. I didn't look in his direction.

"Tell your man to hold," I told Ragyapa.

Ragyapa barked something in an indecipherable tongue. The thug froze, shoulders hunched, glaring at me.

Ragyapa spoke again. "What is this about Herman?"

"Earlier this evening, he broke into our office on the compound. Through trickery, he managed to obtain the combination to our safe."

"And the jade skull?"

"It is gone. He took it with him."

The thug didn't seem to understand, but his body tensed and he stood up straighter, glancing back and forth between me and Ragyapa, waiting for instructions.

Ragyapa's voice lowered, sounding now like a cobra in an ancient tale. "Where is Herman now?"

"I don't know," I replied. "He has disappeared."

He barked a sharp invective. That was all the thug needed. With no further order from Ragyapa, he charged up the walkway leading to the bridge.

I reached under my coat for my pistol.

Just before the thug hit the bridge, Ernie stepped from the shadows and smacked him on the temple with the butt of his .45. Somehow the man spun away from the blow and kept spinning until he grabbed Ernie by the neck.

A shot rang out. Red flame rocketed into the air.

Ragyapa shouted out more orders. The boat emptied. Like a swarm of locusts, his men clambered onto shore.

Ernie and the thug were still struggling. I propped my outstretched elbows on the railing of the bridge and pointed the business end of my .38 revolver directly at Ragyapa's forehead.

"Call them off," I shouted. "Now!"

Ragyapa stared at me for a second. Then he barked another series of orders. His men stood still. Ernie and the first thug were locked in an embrace, Ernie pressing his .45 to the man's head, the thug with a tight grip on Ernie's neck. They were frozen. Like two wrestlers in midbattle.

"We can stand here and slaughter one another," I told Ragyapa, "or we can try to find a way to work this out."

Ragyapa breathed in sharply. "What do you suggest?" he asked.

"First, I need your assurance that Lady Ahn and Mi-ja are still alive and that they will stay alive."

He shrugged. "We have not killed them."

"What proof do you have?"

"I will give you proof when the time comes."

"You don't need both of them," I said. "Let one of them go."

Like a teacher studying a student, Ragyapa stared at me

patiently for a moment, trying to decide if I was precocious or just noisy. "The child has already been freed."

"Where can we find her?"

"You will find her in good time. Enough of that. Now what of the jade?"

"I'm the only one who can catch Herman," I said. "You need to deal with me if you want the jade skull."

Slowly, Ragyapa nodded.

"Remember," I told him. "You will get nothing if Lady Ahn is killed."

"I will give you forty-eight hours," Ragyapa said. "By then, if you haven't found Herman, if you haven't recovered the jade skull, I will take it as a sign of bad faith and you will never see your fine lady again."

Forty-eight hours, I thought. Not much time. But he said that Mi-ja had been freed. That was progress. And I still had forty-eight hours to save Lady Ahn. If we were ever going to catch Herman, odds were that we would catch him early, in his first few frantic hours of trying to escape. If we didn't capture him early, we probably wouldn't capture him at all. The nightmare wasn't over yet but we'd passed the threshold of the full moon and still had hope.

"Done," I said. "Where will I meet you?"

He raised his forefinger into the night air. "That will remain my secret for the moment. I will notify you shortly before the meeting."

He didn't want to give us a chance to set up a police reception.

Ragyapa barked orders in his native tongue. The men on the shore hopped back into the boat. All except for the big thug still wrapped in an armlock with Ernie.

"Call your friend off," Ragyapa said. "He has a gun to my man's head. Tell him to point the gun at the sky, my man will let him go, and we will be gone."

Ernie tilted the barrel of the .45 skyward. The thug

snorted, stepped back, loosening his grip. He lowered his body and, like a leopard flipping an antelope, he swiveled and tossed Ernie head over heels into the air.

Ernie screamed and soared for a moment, flailing. He splashed into the rancid water below the Bridge of the Golden Tribute.

I pointed my .38 at the thug but didn't pull the trigger as he scampered down the edge of the canal and leapt onto the boat. Someone had already started up the engine and they were swinging in an arc, heading back up the canal the way they had come.

At the last moment, Ragyapa shouted up at me. "You wanted proof that she is alive. Here it is!"

At first my eyes couldn't focus and then I saw it. He was clutching hair in his fist, a head dangling below it.

Lady Ahn.

I almost squeezed off a round but then I realized that there was a neck below the head and her body was attached below that. Her arms bound. Her face bruised, lips puffed and bloody.

The outboard motor roared and Ragyapa and his boys sped off down the canal.

If I shot now they would kill her. Instead, I reholstered the .38. The engine noise faded.

I ran down to the edge of the canal, lay on the ground, and reached out my hand to the sputtering Ernie.

"Son of a *bitch*!" he shouted, as he splashed and kicked his way toward the shore. I grabbed his hand and hoisted him over the rock ledge.

He still held on to the .45. I grabbed the barrel and pulled it gently out of his grip.

Frantically, Ernie slapped at his face and his jacket and his trousers.

"Shit! Shit! Shit!" he said. "I'm swimming in *shit*."

He smelled like a sewer.

"We'll get you cleaned up, pal. Sorry that happened."

"Next time I see those assholes," he groused. "I'm gonna jack me some Mongolian dude up. I'm gonna jack me up a whole lot of Mongolian dudes!"

28

DROPS OF WATER FROM THE LEAKING FAUCET SPLASHED ONTO
Mi-ja's swollen tongue. It reeked of rust, but it had been a
long time since she cared. All she knew was that her throat
was burning dry.

Bound wrists throbbed beneath thick knots of hemp
rope. Her left ear still ached, as if some evil beast had
chewed it off just moments ago. Her sliced finger shot
globules of pain up the length of her arm.

She hadn't eaten in three days. She was still alert
enough to know she should be hungry, but the muscles
enveloping her stomach were clenched in a tight ball that
refused to relax or complain.

She heard footsteps.

As the wooden door of the bathroom creaked open, she
pulled as far away from the sound as she could. The chains
around her ankles rattled.

The door popped open. Mi-ja clenched her eyes tightly
shut.

The man squatted in front of her.

She relaxed somewhat. He was the oiler, the man who had prepared her before taking her to the leader. At least he wasn't the cutter. At least she wouldn't lose another ear or a finger or a toe.

She noticed he didn't have the bottle of oil in his hand. Why was he here?

The man checked her chains and the hemp ropes binding her wrists. When he was satisfied that they were secure, he smiled.

To Mi-ja, the smile was nothing more than the grimace of a skeleton. A death's head.

The man reached into his tunic and pulled out a handful of straw. The smell of it was strangely comforting to Mi-ja. She remembered the animals on her father's farm. The small black goats that were raised for meat. The large ox of which her father was so proud. And she remembered the tears that welled up in his eyes the day he had taken the ox to the market to be sold.

Had he cried like that the day she had been sold? Mi-ja didn't remember. So many things were fading from memory now. She tried to remember her mother's smiling face. It wouldn't appear.

The man squatting in front of her slid a long straw out of his fist. He held it in front of Mi-ja and smiled again. He opened his mouth, mimicking what he wanted Mi-ja to do.

At first she hesitated, cringing, turning her face away.

The man waited patiently until she looked back at him. Then he slid a cup of water in front of her. He pointed to the water and then he pointed to the straw.

Mi-ja understood what he was trying to tell her. She could have the water, but then she would have to open her mouth and accept the straw.

What was this for? Why did these mute foreigners want her to eat straw?

Mi-ja stared at the water. It looked like everything she had always longed for. Slowly, she nodded her head.

The man held the cup aloft, tilted it, and allowed a little water to splash onto Mi-ja's teeth. She tasted the wonderful wetness of it.

The man set the cup down. Then he held up the stiff piece of straw.

Mi-ja glanced again at the half-full cup of water. She was still dying of thirst. That little splash of moisture had only made her desire more rabid.

She made her decision. She must cooperate if she was going to be given anything more to drink.

She opened her mouth wide and said "aah."

The man slid the single strand of straw down Mi-ja's throat. He waited, making sure that she didn't gag. When he was satisfied, he reached down, picked up another dry twig, and slid it carefully down the throat of the helpless little girl.

After a small clump was in place, the man splashed a little more water down Mi-ja's throat.

Moisture seeped into the straw. It started to expand.

29

THE NEXT MORNING I WAS THE FIRST ONE INTO THE CID OF-
fice. I sat at Riley's desk, sipping on a steaming cup of
snack bar coffee, riffling through the blotter reports. No
word at all on Herman the German.

Last night, on the way back from the Bridge of the
Golden Tribute, Ernie and I had stopped at the MP Station. We started making calls, woke up a lot of duty officers—both Korean and American—but before we were
through, managed to put out a description of Herman the
German and a detention order for him at every port of
embarkation in the country.

There are no land exits from the Republic of Korea,
except by way of the Demilitarized Zone—and trying to
walk across the heavily mined DMZ is suicide. The officials at every other possible escape route, whether by air or
by sea, had now been alerted to collar Herman the German as soon as he showed himself.

It took us a few hours and it was exhausting work at that

time of night, but we had him. Herman was bottled up like a genie in a magic kingdom. And he wouldn't escape. Not in this lifetime.

The slack-jowled face of a hungover Sergeant Riley peeked around the doorjamb. "What the hell you doing in this early?"

"Trying to develop a lead on Herman the German."

Riley's stiffly pressed khakis crackled with starch. "Good. That lowlife ought to be locked up just for having bought me all those drinks."

"You don't remember, do you?"

Riley gazed at me, trying to focus. "Remember what?"

"Herman stole the combination to the CID safe from you last night. And then he stole the jade skull."

Thin lips tightened around crooked teeth. "Can I have my desk back now?"

"Sure, Sarge. Looks like you could use a little rest."

Riley sat down on the creaking wooden chair and started shuffling stacks of paperwork from one corner to another. "Jade skull. Stolen. All right. I get it. So have you found it yet?"

"We're working on it."

"How about that little girl?"

"Still in hostile custody."

"And the big girl?"

"Her, too."

Riley let his hands flop to the desk. "You and Ernie aren't doing very well on this case, are you?"

"Not very."

"Better get your ass in gear before the First Sergeant chomps it off."

"I need to talk to him this morning."

"About what?"

"About turning over Hatcher to the ROKs."

Riley's eyes widened. "Don't be messing with him

about that. The Eighth Army honchos have a case of the big ass about all these demonstrations. They say they're going to hold on to Hatcher as long as they want to and not be bullied into turning him over by a bunch of long-haired jerk-off students."

"Bullied? How can a thirty-thousand-man field army, with access to all the weapons in the United States arsenal, be bullied by anybody?"

Riley ignored the question. But the more I thought about it the more I figured he was probably right. The Eighth Army generals would see the demonstrations that way. Radicals trying to push them around. Everybody, no matter how much power they have, always thinks they're being picked on.

"Besides," I told Riley, "those students aren't jerk-offs."

"Of course they are. What are you, some kinda Communist?"

I took a deep breath. Time to make it official. "If Eighth Army doesn't turn Hatcher over to the Koreans before tomorrow afternoon, that nun he attacked is going to burn herself to death in downtown Seoul. In front of Buddha and everybody."

"How do you know this?"

"She told me."

"Christ, Sueño! If that little broad toasts herself, it'll start a goddamn insurrection."

"Just like those monks who burned themselves in Saigon," I said. "The government fell because of it."

"Have you reported this to Top?"

"No. That's why I want to talk to him this morning."

Riley stood up, confused, as if he wanted to go somewhere but wasn't quite sure where. "Yeah. You better talk to Top. Right away. You better."

I sat in a straight-backed chair across from Riley's desk and continued to sip my coffee. The ball was rolling now.

We'd see where it went. But before I could fully savor the turd I'd dropped into Eighth Army's punch bowl, Ernie stormed into the office, red-faced.

"Come on, damn it. The jeep's outside."

I set my coffee down. "What is it?"

"Disturbance in Itaewon."

WAILS OF ANGUISH ECHOED DOWN THE ABANDONED PATHWAY of Hooker Hill. At the top of the rise, we wound through narrow alleys until we reached the Temple of the Dream Buddha. Thick wooden double doors were ajar. A gleaming gold Buddha gazed calmly down on Slicky Girl Nam. She was hunched over what looked like a pile of rags.

Outside stood a red-robed monk, a Korean National Policeman, and a half dozen business girls roused by Slicky Girl Nam's screams. The women wore shorts and T-shirts, their arms were crossed across their breasts, and the flesh of their faces looked wrinkled and naked in the gray morning light.

The young policeman glanced at me suspiciously. He was probably planted here to protect the site until his superiors arrived. I flashed him my CID badge, which relaxed him a little.

In the middle of the pagoda, on the varnished wooden floor, lay the small unmoving body of Mi-ja Burkowicz, the adopted daughter of Herman the German and Slicky Girl Nam. Nam rocked back and forth on her knees, moaning as if someone was poking a hot poker into her guts.

Ernie flipped back the edge of his coat, clutched his waist, and swiveled his head, purposely looking away from the motionless child. "Shit!" he said.

That about summed it up.

I stepped forward into the pagoda and knelt to examine the girl.

"You no *touch*!"

Slicky Girl Nam's twisted face was red, as if the tears pouring from her eyes were hot steam. "You no *touch*!" she screeched.

I nodded and slowly moved around the girl. I could see that one ear was gone. But otherwise, from where I stood, she appeared to be uncut and unbruised. She wore red cotton pants and a matching blouse sequined with the faces of smiling rabbits.

I was searching for the cause of death. There was no blood. No mortal wounds. No marks around her neck. Then I saw them. The line of bruises around her wrists. And the single strand of straw sticking out of her nose.

I leaned over and peered inside the nostrils. Both were blocked with green hay. The bastards had suffocated her.

As if to confirm what I was thinking, Slicky Girl Nam reached out her wrinkled hand and touched the smooth flesh of Mi-ja's cheek. The child's pink lips parted slightly. Inside, her mouth and throat were also stuffed with straw.

Why kill Mi-ja this way? And then I remembered that Ragyapa was a Buddhist—or at least a member of some odd, perverted sect of Buddhism—and Buddhists must respect all living things. In Tibet, when it is time to slaughter a yak, they stuff straw down its throat and nose and let it choke to death. The animal suffocates, killing itself. So the owner won't be blamed for the sin of murdering another living creature.

But why kill Mi-ja now? Why, when I had told Ragyapa I would do everything I could to catch Herman and recover the skull?

But I knew the answer. Ragyapa had given us until the full moon to produce the jade skull, or Mi-ja would die. We hadn't made that deadline. He wanted to make sure that I believed he meant business.

He still had one more hostage, Lady Ahn, and his message was clear. If we didn't find the skull within the next thirty-six hours, Lady Ahn would suffer the same cruel death little Mi-ja had.

I knelt and spoke as gently as I could to Slicky Girl Nam. "We have to find Herman."

She looked at me blankly, waiting for an explanation.

"Last night," I said, "we were supposed to exchange the jade skull for Mi-ja. But it was stolen out of the CID safe. We couldn't make the exchange. We believe Herman stole the skull."

The flat muscles of her face writhed like a basket of pythons. Her rage-filled eyes spit fire. "That *pyongsin* stole jade skull?"

"He's not a cripple," I said. "He has the skull and he's running."

Slicky Girl Nam screamed a series of curses that thundered through the Temple of the Dream Buddha. "When I catch, I cut that son-bitch balls off!"

I stood up. Ernie clicked on his gum, shaking his head, no mirth in his eyes.

Captain Kim, the commander of the Itaewon Police Station, strode into the Temple of the Dream Buddha surrounded by his entourage. He stopped and glared at Ernie and me. "You two again. Every time there is a death in my precinct, you two seem to be nearby."

I didn't translate that into English. I was afraid Ernie would pop him. Instead, I stepped back and let Captain Kim take charge of the investigation.

It took four cops to pry Slicky Girl Nam away from Mi-ja.

WHEN WE RETURNED TO THE OFFICE, RILEY HAD ME LINED UP for three appointments. One with the First Sergeant, one with the Eighth Army Provost Marshal, and one with the Judge Advocate General's Office. They all wanted precise details concerning the upcoming plans of the little nun and the Buddhist hierarchy.

Luckily, they were so busy chattering amongst themselves about this new information, that they didn't have time to talk to me right away.

"You'll see them when they're ready for you," Riley told me.

Typical. Military commanders always start formulating their plans before they have all the facts.

While we were waiting we didn't twiddle our thumbs. Ernie made calls to the American side and I made calls to the Koreans, asking if anyone at the points of embarkation had encountered anyone matching the description of Herman the German.

He had only completed his third call when Ernie slammed down the phone. "Osan. The Space Available list. One guy signed up early this morning for a flight Stateside. Name: First Sergeant Herman R. Burkowicz, Retired."

I grabbed my coat.

"Where the hell do you guys think you're going?" Riley yelled.

"To collar a bad guy," I called back.

"But the honchos want to talk about this nun."

"You already know everything I know. If they don't turn Pfc. Hatcher over to the Korean authorities, she's going to kill herself tomorrow afternoon in downtown Seoul at the Gate of the Transformation of Light."

"They'll court-martial you if you don't show up for this shit," Riley hollered.

"What are they gonna do?" Ernie asked. "Send him to Korea?"

We ran outside to the jeep.

As we rolled out of the main gate of Yongsan Compound we swerved into the madly careening traffic of the

Main Supply Route. Thunder cracked. A flash of lightning sliced the sky.

"Looks like we're due for a little drizzle."

As soon as the words left Ernie's mouth, a whole world of water gushed out of the black heavens.

DRAPED IN HIS BLUE RAIN SLICKER, THE SECURITY GUARD waved us through the main gate of Osan Air Force Base. We followed the signs to the passenger terminal of the Military Airlift Command, parked the jeep, and ran inside.

The building contained only one large waiting room, latrines, and a snack bar off to the side. Before we talked to anybody, Ernie and I spread out and searched for Herman the German.

Ernie met me back at the Space-A counter. "No dice."

"I didn't think so," I said. "He wouldn't wait here where he could be easily spotted."

I flashed my badge to the Technical Sergeant at the counter. She was slender and her uniform had been well tailored and her complexion was like light cocoa butter. I gave her Herman's name. She thumbed through the onionskin sheets on her clipboard.

"He was here this morning," she said. "Signed up for Space-A and was issued a seat on the flight that left about a half hour ago."

"Damn!" Ernie said.

She kept licking her thumb and studying the manifest. "But he was bumped. Some ground-pounder from the Second Division showed up at the last minute with emergency leave orders. We had to pull Burkowicz off the flight."

"You mean he's still here in-country?"

"Sure is. Mad as hell when we pulled him off. Cursing about his rights as a retired service member."

"What rights?" Ernie asked.

She smiled. "None that I know of. Retirees have no

rights unless there's space available. And their priority comes right after cats and dogs."

"We called last night from Eighth Army CID," I said. "I thought you people were going to arrest Burkowicz if he showed up."

She shrugged. "Don't ask me. You'll have to check with the Security Detachment. They're down the hall."

"Never mind," I said.

Despite all our efforts, if there had been enough seats on that flight this morning, Herman would be on his way to the States with the precious jade skull of Kublai Khan stashed in a bag beneath his feet. So much for military efficiency.

I asked the Tech Sergeant one more question. "Are there any more flights leaving today?"

"None until tomorrow morning."

"Thanks."

I smiled at her but she didn't smile back. She was too busy looking at Ernie.

We grabbed a couple of trays at the small snack bar. I ordered a BLT, Ernie had a ham and cheese omelette with a side of hash browns.

"Worked up an appetite last night," he said.

I purposely picked a table next to a group of military retirees smoking and sipping coffee and bullshitting. Waiting for the next flight out of Korea.

We sat down, ate, and listened for a while. When they didn't mention Herman, I asked, "Anybody seen Herman the German around here lately?"

One guy with a bristly crew cut glanced over at me. "He was in here this morning. Didn't make his flight."

"So how is the old buzzard?"

"Seems okay. You know Herman. He don't talk much."

"I owe him a drink. Do you know where he's staying?"

"Out in the ville somewhere. That's all I know. He left

right after the Space-A call. If I see him, I'll tell him you're
looking for him."

"Don't bother," I said. "He already knows."

We gulped down our chow and left.

WHEN YOU WALK OUT OF THE MAIN GATE OF OSAN AIR BASE,
you walk into GI heaven. The village of Songtan-up is a
maze of narrow alleys lined with hotels and tailor shops
and leather goods emporiums and bars and chophouses
and nightclubs and brothels.

Just about anything a young man would ever want to
buy is available here. The best part is that none of it is
touted by Madison Avenue.

The monsoon rain had slowed to a drizzle. Just outside
the gate, an enterprising Korean vendor huddled beneath
an army-issue poncho, hawking flimsy umbrellas made of
bamboo and plastic. I handed him a buck for two.

Ernie popped his open. "The good thing about these
little pieces of shit," Ernie said, "is that they're disposable.
Don't have to worry about forgetting them in some barroom."

We wandered down the narrow lane, checking out the
shops. Most of the nightclubs were still shuttered and
locked.

"Should we canvass the hotels?" Ernie asked.

"I guess we don't have much choice. But we're going to
have to describe him to everyone. He won't be registering
under his own name."

"At least Herman's easy to picture," Ernie said. "A bowling ball with blubbery lips."

"That's him. I'll try to figure out how to say that in
Korean."

"You mean you don't know?"

"The word for 'blubbery' escapes me."

"You need to study harder, pal."

Ernie stopped in an open-front market and bought a couple of packs of the usual: ginseng gum. When we stepped outside, an old mama-san picked us up on her radar and started yanking on my sleeve, telling me she could introduce us to some "nice girls."

"We don't like nice girls," Ernie told her. "Only bad ones."

That didn't faze the old crone; she kept haranguing us. I was just about to push her out of the way when an explosion reverberated through the narrow alleys of Songtan-up.

"What was that?"

"A rifle shot," Ernie said. "Not far either."

Ernie shoved aside the persistent madam, and we ran toward the sound of the pop. Two more shots rang out.

"It's a fucking battle," Ernie said.

He fumbled for the .45 in his shoulder holster, pulled it out, and clanged back the charging handle.

THE SONGTAN CITY MARKET IS COMPOSED OF NOTHING MORE than a jumble of wooden stands covered with canvas. The stands occupy a spider's web of alleys in the heart of the city, and in their center is a circular intersection, the only open space in the market.

Huffing and puffing, we reached it in about two minutes. Ernie swiveled around, .45 at the ready, searching for a target.

A Korean National Policeman stood nearby, blowing shrilly on his whistle.

"Would you knock that shit off?" Ernie yelled.

The policeman ignored him.

An old woman wearing a white bandana huddled behind a pile of cabbages. I leaned toward her.

"Pardon me, Aunt. I am a policeman. Who was firing the gun?"

She pointed down one of the darker alleys. "I saw an American like you. Running."

"He went that way?"

"Yes."

"Why was he running?"

She clutched her elbows and shuddered. "Men were chasing him."

"American men or Koreans?"

"Neither. Some sort of foreigners."

I swirled my forefinger around my head. "Did one wear a turban?"

The wrinkles on the woman's face rose toward her forehead. "How did you know?"

I motioned to Ernie. We trotted into the alley.

30

ERNIE SAID THE SHOT WE HEARD WAS FROM A RIFLE. HE'D spent two tours in Vietnam and I wasn't going to argue with him.

But a rifle in Korea? There was total gun control in this country. Only the military and the police were allowed weapons, and the KNPs never used anything more than a sidearm. I thought of the M-1 rifle that had been stolen from the Korean policeman in the alleys near the Temple of the Dream Buddha.

Ragyapa. It had to be. But could he know about this lead Ernie and I had received little more than an hour ago?

We crept through the market, Ernie on one side, me on the other. Both of us with our pistols drawn.

Gloom filtered through canvas awnings. The vendors had faded back into the damp shadows. Carts piled with giant turnips and crates of mackerel on ice stood unguarded.

We were close. Very close.

Ernie motioned for me to halt and take cover. I obeyed. He scurried forward to a position where he had a good view of an ancient wooden apartment building with a walkway around its second and third story. Laundry fluttered from lines strung out the windows. The smell of boiling kimchi and charcoal gas wafted through the air.

Ernie crouched and watched, lost in thought. The barrel of his .45 caressed his lips.

Perhaps Ragyapa's showing up wasn't as miraculous as it seemed. There were only a few major points of embarkation from the Republic of Korea. The civilian ones included the international airport at Kimpo near Seoul and the ferry way down south in Pusan. Kimpo would be easy enough to watch. The major U.S. military point of embarkation was where we were now. Osan Air Force Base. There were a couple more bases farther south but Osan would be the quickest and the cheapest for Herman to leave the country.

Ragyapa must've stationed a man here, near the main gate. If that's what happened, Ragyapa and his boys would've been waiting for Herman when he was bumped from the Stateside flight and emerged from the main gate of the base.

Was Herman already dead? Did Ragyapa have the jade skull?

If so, he'd have no reason to turn Lady Ahn over to us alive. She was a witness. He'd eliminate the danger. He'd kill her.

Suddenly, from inside the building, another shot rang out. Ernie'd had enough of waiting. So had I. We charged forward, Ernie motioning for me to circle around the building and cover the back exit.

He kicked in the front door.

Ernie's .45 fired twice.

The sound of gunfire close at hand is enough to uncoil the innards of most mortals. Criminals usually scatter at the unholy sound of it. They like it when they're the ones wielding the firepower, but when the hot lead is directed at them, they turn into jackrabbits fast enough.

All hell broke loose in the building. A couple of rifle shots blasted straight into the sky, women screamed, children began to wail. The whole wooden framework seemed to shake, and the footsteps from within reverberated like a herd of panicked musk-oxen.

Before I could reach the rear alley, something slammed against wood. Rounding the corner, I saw short legs and PX-bought brown oxfords disappearing over the back wall. Herman!

I shouted and took a step forward but as I did, a gaggle of men exploded out the door. One wore a turban. Ragyapa. He saw me and hollered something that I couldn't understand. Next to him a man swiveled, and a flash erupted from the barrel of an M-1 rifle.

Something bit through the air above me. An angry bee moving at the speed of light.

I dived behind wooden crates stuffed with filth. Another bee bit into rotten lumber. Splinters erupted like a hive of tiny rockets.

My hand was shaking so badly, I could barely hold the .38. Somehow I pointed it forward, not having any idea where I was aiming, and pulled the trigger.

The recoil sobered me somewhat. I could hurt someone with this thing!

After that, all I heard were footsteps and shouts. A few seconds later, when I worked up the nerve to peer around a box of trash, Ragyapa's men were gone. In the distance, more KNP whistles shrilled.

Ernie erupted out the back door. Sweating. His head

swiveling back and forth so fast I thought he was going to unscrew his skull.

He pointed the pistol at me.

"Don't shoot!" I said. "It's me."

Ernie took a deep breath and lowered the .45. "Where'd they go?"

"Down the alley. But don't worry about them now. The KNPs will be here any second. It's Herman we have to find."

Herman must still have the jade skull. If he didn't, Ragyapa wouldn't be chasing him.

"The bastards *shot* at me!" Ernie said.

I stood up, dusting off my trousers. "You shot at them, too."

"But I'm a *good* guy."

"Sure you are, Ernie." I glanced at the damage the M-1 had done to the wood-slat wall and the crates. "I don't think that guy's zeroed his weapon."

Ernie examined the trajectory. "No. If he had, Uncle Snaps would've had to cough up all thirty thousand bucks of your Serviceman's Group Life Insurance."

The whistles of the KNPs grew louder. We didn't have time to spend all morning explaining to them what had happened.

Ernie helped me over the wall Herman had climbed. From the top, I pulled him over.

WITH THE KNPS ALERTED AND SWARMING AROUND THE VIL-lage, Ragyapa would be cautious. If Ragyapa got locked up for possession of an illegal rifle, Herman would be sure to make good his escape with the skull.

But that didn't mean Ragyapa would give up. His boys were out there somewhere, searching for Herman.

After climbing the wall, we checked with the owner of the hooch in front. He pointed us away from the market.

As we moved down the cobbled lanes, I stopped and asked every pedestrian and shop owner and street vendor I saw if they'd seen Herman. I used the description Ernie had given me. A human bowling ball, probably sweating by now and breathing hard.

It wasn't as if Herman the German was easy to miss. Almost everyone noticed him. They kept pointing us north, away from the market, away from the main gate of Osan Air Force Base.

Finally, we emerged from the alleys onto a main road. Across the street was the Songtan bus station. Nothing more than a half-acre blacktop area with a tin shack on the side for selling tickets.

As we darted across the street, dodging honking kimchi cabs, we scanned the crowd awaiting transportation.

I pushed my way to the front of the line. The ticket office wasn't much larger than a coffin. I leaned over and spoke through the little glass window to the sales clerk. She was surly and didn't remember anything about a foreigner buying a ticket. When I flashed my badge and pressed her, she told me she never looked at faces, only hands and change. Did you see any fat, pale hands with tufts of brown hair on them? No.

A dirty-faced girl with long black braids stood next to Ernie, holding a box of chewing gum and candy in her soiled fingers. They were haggling over the price of a double pack of ginseng gum.

The girl turned to me, probably hoping for another sale. I asked her about Herman. When I called him a bowling ball, she covered white teeth with dirty fingers.

"Oh, yes," she said, "the bowling ball man just got on a bus."

"Which bus?"

"Number nine. Already go."

"Where does number nine go?"

"I don't know. I never ride bus."

Ernie pulled a wad of gum out of his mouth. "Hey, this stuff is stale."

"No," the girl said, bowing. "It is very good gum. Number one."

"Shit." Ernie tossed the pack back to her, his face sour. The girl snatched the gum and slipped it carefully into her pocket.

We started to walk away. I had to find out more about bus number nine. The girl ran after us and tugged on my sleeve.

"Hey, I talk to you, you supposed to buy gum!"

I handed her a hundred won coin—about twenty cents—and shrugged her off.

A brown-skinned man in a gray coat and a gray cap stood near the street waving a red banner, guiding the buses in and out of the lot.

I asked him about bus number nine.

"Yes. It goes to Chon-an."

"Express?"

"No. Many stops."

"How many?"

"Three. Maybe four."

"Did you see a foreigner get on?"

"Yes. Bus driver laugh. Say he take two seats."

THE ROAD FROM OSAN TO CHON-AN IS PEACEFUL. A SPARSELY traveled two-lane highway frequented only by buses or open-topped tractors or the occasional country kimchi cab. Green rice fields spread out on either side of us, and the ribbon of blacktop was lined with quivering juniper trees. Villages appeared intermittently: straw-thatched roofs, women pounding laundry by a stream, farmers threshing grain in the open air.

None of this idyllic setting cut much ice with Ernie.

"I'm gonna *pound* that fucking Herman."

"Easy, Ernie."

"He did it to his own little girl. He let them take Mi-ja. Just so he could wrap his grubby paws around that damn skull."

"We don't know that for sure yet."

Ernie swerved the jeep around a slow-moving bus. "Now you're sounding like one of those lawyers over at JAG."

I checked the number of the bus. Not number nine. We'd be lucky if we caught up with it before it reached Chon-an. But Ernie was trying like hell. He held the speedometer at a steady eighty kilometers.

"Watch out!"

A thin man in gray tunic and pantaloons, back bent, hands clasped behind his back, sauntered across the road ahead of us.

Ernie slammed on the brakes, downshifted, and, once he was around the old man, gunned the engine and slammed it back into high gear.

"These pedestrians wouldn't last long in Seoul," he grumbled.

The sky was clearing. Monsoon clouds floated north-ward. In the fields, white cranes stepped gingerly through green rice shoots, searching for amphibians.

WE HAD REACHED THE OUTSKIRTS OF CHON-AN WHEN I SPOT-ted something rumbling ahead of us.

"That's it. Bus number nine."

Black diesel smoke spewed from the rear exhaust.

"I'll cut it off," Ernie said.

"Okay. But let's not get crushed beneath the wheels."

Ernie pulled up alongside the bus driver, leaning on his horn. I held my badge up and waved for him to pull over.

The suspicious-eyed driver glared, turned his eyes back straight ahead, and kept rolling.

"Son of a bitch won't listen to us," Ernie said.

"We don't have any jurisdiction out here," I said. "He knows that."

"Fuck jurisdiction!"

Ernie jerked the steering wheel to the right: The little jeep slammed into the front bumper of the bus. Sparks flew. Metal grated on metal. The driver above us cursed and honked his horn. Ernie swerved over again, bumping harder this time, grinding paint and metal off the side of bus number nine.

Faces gawked at us out the side windows. Ernie pulled in front of the bus and slammed on his brakes. We were bumped from behind.

"He's gonna run us over."

"No, he won't," Ernie said. "Killing foreigners causes too much paperwork."

Ernie was right. Gradually, the bus slowed, pulled over to the side, and came to a stop.

Before we could climb out of the jeep, the bus driver was already out of the door: red-faced, waving his hands, cursing. Spittle erupted from his mouth like water from a spigot.

He charged Ernie. I thrust my body between them.

The driver kept raving, cursing Ernie for being a reckless driver, and I held up my hands, bowing and apologizing profusely.

Ernie acted as if the driver didn't even exist. He pulled his .45, stepped around us, and climbed up into the bus. There were a couple of screams when the passengers saw the gun, but for the most part they took it well.

Ernie emerged from the bus about thirty seconds later.

"He's not here."

I started to question the driver about a foreigner, but he

ignored my questions and kept ranting about what a fool Ernie was. I didn't bother to translate any of it. Ernie just crossed his arms, the big .45 still clutched in his fist, and smirked.

I boarded the bus. The stewardess was a young girl of about sixteen with a red jacket and a helmet of black hair. I asked her if there had been a foreigner on this bus.

"Oh, yes," she said. "He took up two seats."

"Where did he get off?"

"In Pyongtaek."

I should've figured that. Pyongtaek was only a few miles from the village of Anjong-ri, which sits outside the big army helicopter base at Camp Humphreys. When he was in trouble, Herman always gravitated toward the military. He probably felt safer there.

"Was he carrying a bag?"

"Yes. He clutched it very tightly to his tummy."

"How big was the bag?"

"Round and big. Like his tummy."

I thanked the girl and apologized to the passengers for the inconvenience. They sat dumb, used to being pushed around by policemen.

The driver was still cursing, but he directed his invective everywhere but at Ernie. He was clearly intimidated. Either by Ernie's hard stare or by the .45.

Probably both.

We climbed back into the jeep.

"Where to?"

"Turn around," I said. "Last known sighting of Herman the German: Pyongtaek."

AT THE SMALL BUS STATION IN PYONGTAEK WE FOUND A STORE owner who had sold Herman a bottle of 7 Star Cider.

"He took a taxi," the man said.

"Which way did they go?"

"Toward the American compound."

This time Ernie managed to buy a pack of ginseng gum that hadn't already dried to bonfire kindling.

THE MPS AT THE FRONT GATE OF CAMP HUMPHREYS HAD JUST come on shift, so they didn't know anything. Besides, army retirees are a common sight in Anjong-ri. It's an out-of-the-way compound, the black-marketing is easy, and the village is full of cheap hooches and cold beer. The pot of gold waiting at the end of a military career.

Herman's trail was rapidly fading, but we decided to take one more shot. We drove onto the compound and checked at the Aviation Battalion's operation desk.

The sergeant behind the counter was helpful. "Army retiree, overweight, trying to catch a helicopter flight out of the area. Yeah," he said, "we had one who matched that description just a few minutes ago." He searched his manifest. "I checked his ID card myself. Name's Burkowicz, Herman R., First Sergeant, U.S. Army, retired."

Ernie nearly leapt over the counter. "Where'd he go?"

"Caught one of our routine medical flights. Chopper left here not twenty minutes ago. Heading to the H-105 airfield, Yongsan Compound, Seoul."

"Shit!" Ernie pounded his fist on the vinyl countertop. "Any chance of radioing them to turn back?"

"No way."

"This is official business," Ernie said. "Involving the crimes of kidnapping and murder. What's this 'no way' bullshit?"

The sergeant's eyes narrowed. "I said no way because it's not possible to turn the copter back."

"What do you mean?"

"Radio report came in just before you guys walked in here. They've already landed and . . . let me check here." He shuffled through a sheaf of papers. "The passenger disembarked, five minutes ago."

I thought about calling the MP Station in Seoul and sending a patrol jeep out to the landing pad. But it was too late. Herman had already hoofed it out the gate by now. He'd disappeared into the swirling madness of Seoul.

Ernie kept cursing. The sergeant behind the counter glared at him. I tried to make peace but my heart wasn't in it.

The ride back to Seoul was quiet. Except for the gears. Ernie kept grinding them.

Along with his teeth.

It was already late afternoon. We could've gone into the office, but who needed another ass-chewing from the First Sergeant? Besides, the groups of demonstrators holding portraits of Choi So-lan, the Buddhist nun, had grown. Traffic was backed up all along the MSR. Seeing the concerned faces on the small gaggles of women was depressing. Just another reminder of our failure.

We cruised into Itaewon, found a parking spot in one of the alleys behind the main drag, and strolled listlessly down toward the nightclubs.

The first few splats of rain hit the pavement.

Ragyapa was well hidden. So was Herman. It could take us weeks to find either one of them. Time we didn't have. Not if we wanted to save the life of Lady Ahn.

And meanwhile the clock was ticking for Choi So-lan, the nun who'd been attacked here in Itaewon. If Eighth Army didn't turn Pfc. Hatcher over to the Korean authorities—and turn him over soon—she would pour gasoline over her bald head late tomorrow afternoon and light it with a match.

All our effort in stealing the jade skull of Kublai Khan from the monks of Bian-do was for nothing. Mi-ja was dead. And now it looked as if Lady Ahn and the nun would soon meet the same fate.

A filthy street urchin tugged on my sleeve.

"Hey, GI!"

"Go away. We're busy."

"Somebody look for you. Behind UN Club. You go checky checky."

"Who is it?"

"I don't know. He say you come quick."

Ernie handed the boy a stick of gum by way of a tip and the dirty child scurried off.

"He didn't even ask for money," Ernie said.

"Somebody already paid him. So we might as well check it out."

Ernie patted the .45 under his jacket. "I'm ready."

Behind the UN Club, a maze of alleys stretched back to the Itaewon Market. A few droplets of light rain managed to penetrate the gloom. Our shoes sloshed in mud.

I heard heavy breathing, and then someone stepped out of a side alley.

Herman the German.

Ernie reached for his .45.

Herman raised his stubby arms. "Where the hell you guys been? I been waiting for you."

His eyes were still aggrieved and moist and his lips were as blubbery as ever. A large leather bag that looked as if it held a volleyball hung from his shoulder.

Ernie clanged back the charging handle of his .45.

"Turn around, Herman," Ernie said. "Slow."

He did as he was told and I slammed him up against the stone wall and frisked him. No weapons.

Herman turned his pleading eyes on me and clutched my arm. "You have to *hide* me, Sueño. They're *after* me."

"Ragyapa and his Mongols would only give you what you deserve."

"Mongols? Who gives a fuck about a bunch of Mongols?"

If Herman wasn't worried about Ragyapa, then who was he so frightened of? I shoved him away.

"Somebody's got you about ready to shit in your pants, Herman. Who is it?"

Even as I asked the question, I suddenly knew the answer.

Ernie screwed the nozzle of the .45 into Herman's ear. "Who's after you, Herman?"

"The Slicky Boys!" Herman roared. "Who in the hell else?"

31

# #

SLICKY GIRL NAM PLACED BOTH HANDS FLAT ON THE STONE floor—thumbs and forefingers touching—and bowed her head three times. She kept her skull pressed against the granite, waiting for permission to rise.

"It has been many years," said Herbalist So, the King of the Slicky Boys.

Slicky Girl Nam sat back on her heels, keeping her eyes demurely cast toward the floor. "Too long, Good Herbalist. You honor me by accepting this worthless old one into your presence."

The cavern was dark, lit only by flickering fires beneath simmering earthen pots. The odors of bat wings and ginger root and boiling deer antler wafted through the shadows.

"I have never forgotten your service to my father," Herbalist So told her.

"And I have never forgotten it either. At that time I was barely more than a child. But my friend Kimiko and I were your father's favorites. We served him well."

Herbalist So's father was the man who had established the slicky boy operation, the man who had organized all the Korean thieves who preyed off the compounds of the American military. He controlled their operations, stealing only what the Americans could afford to lose, ensuring long-term profitability for everyone.

When she first came to Itaewon, Slicky Girl Nam was only fifteen. Fresh-faced and shapely, she had been summoned to the presence of the King of the Slicky Boys. Even now she trembled at the thought of the power in the man's eyes—and the hot need of his hard body.

Although his son, Herbalist So, controlled a multimillion-dollar cartel of thieves, Slicky Girl Nam still thought of him as a boy. She always would. Because her finest memories were of the nights she had slept with his father.

Herbalist So seemed to read her thoughts, and was impatient with them. He used a less formal level of Korean. "You've come to me for a reason, Mother of Mi-ja. State it."

Slicky Girl Nam bowed once again. "I seek revenge," she said.

"Against whom?"

"Against my husband."

Only a slight rustling of cotton betrayed Herbalist So's shift on the hard wooden bench. He stared at her with dark eyes gleaming from a face as weathered as his earthen pots.

"A dispute between a husband and a wife," he said. "This is a very difficult thing."

"My husband, Herman the German, murdered my daughter. He killed my Mi-ja. All for greed. Because he lusted for possession of an ancient antique." Slicky Girl Nam straightened her back and stared directly into Herbalist So's eyes.

"You owe me," she said. "For years of service. First, for being your father's consort. And after he died, I became a streetwalker for the big-nosed GIs." She waved her arm. "*Thousands* of them! And when I was too old for even them, I took a job as a trash truck driver on the American compound and told you of the location of all the valuable commodities." She jabbed her thumb into her chest. "But did I ask anything for myself? No. You became rich, rich beyond imagining, and I received only a common wage."

Herbalist So's eyelids lowered. "You are forgetful, Mother of Mi-ja. Did we not forge a new set of documents for you to use in your marriage application? So your new husband wouldn't know you'd been a prostitute. So he wouldn't know how many times you'd contracted venereal disease. Or how many times you'd had abortions. Or how many times you'd been arrested for petty thievery." The craggy lines of Herbalist So's face set into hard ridges. "Don't tell me that we've done *nothing* for you!"

Slicky Girl Nam realized she'd gone too far. She lowered her face toward the floor. After a few moments, she spoke in a softer voice.

"You are correct, Good Herbalist. You have been good to me. Without you, I never would have found a husband. No Korean man would take me. But Americans are more easily fooled."

When Herbalist So didn't answer, Slicky Girl Nam knew that he'd been mollified by her groveling attitude. Still, she'd made her point. The slicky boy operation owed her for her years of hard work. Now was the time to ask for what she was due.

"I want to kill my husband," she said.

Herbalist So placed his large hands on his knees, rose from the bench, and strolled over to his simmering pots. He puttered with them for a moment, adding twigs to the fires, checking the tightness of the cheesecloth coverings. When he was finished, he returned to the bench. Slicky Girl Nam still knelt on the floor, her head bowed.

"It is always uncomfortable," Herbalist So said, "to kill an American. After all, we rely on them to provide us with the goods that are the lifeblood of our operation. A certain percentage of supplies and equipment pilfered is something they can tolerate. But to murder one of their own, this is something we always try to avoid."

Slicky Girl Nam looked up. "But you've allowed it before."

Herbalist So's face froze. He didn't answer. The exotic brews in his pots bubbled and occasionally boiled over. Flame sizzled.

"All you would have to do," Slicky Girl Nam continued, "is to find him for me. And when you capture my husband, *I* will be the one who kills him." She raised her gnarled fists into the wavering light. "With *these* hands!"

Herbalist So breathed out very slowly. "There is the matter of expense," he said.

Slicky Girl Nam lowered her head once again. "I cannot pay. My husband holds all the money. I have nothing."

"Of course," Herbalist So said. "You are but a helpless woman. Totally under the control of a strong husband."

There was mockery in his voice. They both knew that Slicky Girl Nam was only trying to drive a hard bargain.

Slicky Girl Nam knew what price she had to pay. It was huge, but what choice did she have? The jade skull must have tremendous value or all these men wouldn't be fighting for it so desperately. But for the moment—and maybe for the first time in her life—Slicky Girl Nam couldn't think of money. All she could think of was the tortured body of her adopted daughter, Mi-ja.

When Slicky Girl Nam finally spoke, she spoke very softly. "My husband has stolen an antique. It is very old and very valuable. For some reason, Buddhists from as far away as Mongolia are after it."

Herbalist So raised his bushy eyebrows. "What type of antique?"

"It is a jade skull."

One of the pots boiled over. Herbalist So rushed to the stone stove and snagged burning twigs. The flames lowered. He quickly returned to the wooden bench.

"The skull is yours," Slicky Girl Nam said, "as a gift, if you help me find my GI husband."

Framed by the ghostly shadows, a smile crossed Herbalist So's lips. He clamped his hands on his knees.

"So it will be," he said.

Slicky Girl Nam lowered her head three more times to the floor and backed out of the chamber.

32

PANTING AND SWEARING, WE DRAGGED HERMAN UP TO THE roof of the 7 Club. All the way, he kept swiveling his head, searching for the slicky boys, convinced they were about to pounce.

Actually, he was safe with us. I knew Herbalist So, the King of the Slicky Boys, and I also knew that So wouldn't get rough with Eighth Army CID agents except as a last resort. The slicky boys were patient enough to wait until they found Herman alone.

Why were they after him? That seemed clear. Slicky Girl Nam, one of their own, had decided to take her revenge on her husband, Herman the German, for the death of her adopted daughter, Mi-ja.

The rain was coming down hard now but the red tile roof of the fake pagoda atop the 7 Club protected us from its fury. We sat Herman down on a bench. I snatched the leather bag from his grasp and propped it in a corner.

Herman looked up at us, confused as to why we were so

angry. Ernie didn't say anything and before I could stop him, he crashed a right cross into Herman's face.

Herman cried out. Blood spurted from above his eye. Ernie punched him again.

"You son of a bitch! Your own daughter! I oughta *kill* you!"

I grabbed Ernie, held him. Herman didn't try to fight back, he just reached for his eye.

"Easy, Ernie. Easy."

Ernie stared glassily at Herman. I'd seen him like this before. Ernie was about to go berserk. Only one way to stop it.

"Take deep breaths," I told him. "With your nose. Concentrate on loosening the muscles of your neck. Let them relax. That's it. Now your arms. Okay, better." I slapped him on the cheek and peered into his eyes. "You okay now?"

Ernie spoke through gritted teeth. "Get that guy talking and get him talking quick."

I turned back to Herman. "You heard the man. Spill it, Herman. Everything."

"Fuck you guys."

Ernie exploded. He punched Herman and punched him again. I'd stop him for a second but then he'd wriggle free and lay another roundhouse on Herman's skull. Through it all Herman remained sitting, only occasionally covering his head. A reflex action. Other than that, he made no attempt to defend himself.

Finally, his knuckles raw, Ernie stopped punching and started reading Herman off. "You let them cut off your own daughter's ear! Then her finger. Kept her away from her mother for days. And then you let them stuff straw down her throat. Can you imagine dying like that? You're a dog, Herman. A fucking *dog!*"

Ernie's shouts became hoarse. The monsoon rain

poured down. Nobody downstairs could hear us, no one down in the street, no one in the buildings surrounding us.

When it seemed that Ernie's explosion was over, I spoke again to Herman.

"You ready now, First Sergeant, Retired? You ready to tell us what the fuck really happened?"

Slowly, Herman nodded his head. Droplets of blood splattered to the wet cement floor. "I'm ready," he said.

"And don't leave anything out," Ernie growled.

"I didn't know what the jade antique was at first. Something valuable, sure. Lady Ahn told me that. But I didn't know *how* valuable. Not until Ragyapa found me."

"How did he find you?"

"I don't know. Probably just asking the antique dealers in Seoul. They must've given him the word that Lady Ahn was planning on working with me. That's when he approached me."

Herman wiped a clot of blood from his eyebrow. "Ragyapa flew to Korea all the way from Hong Kong. He used to live in Mongolia, but not anymore. Because of the Commies."

Herman's eyes flashed up briefly. I wondered if he wanted approval for his grasp of international affairs. When he saw our faces, his lids drooped once again.

"Ragyapa told me that the jade was a carving of a head and it was owned by some old dude. Koobel Can or something like that."

"Kublai Khan," I said.

"Yeah. And it had been lost for centuries until some monks found it, and now Lady Ahn was going to swipe it from them."

Apparently, Herman didn't realize that the main value of the jade skull was that it was carved with a map of the whereabouts of the Tomb of Genghis Khan. I wasn't going to educate him. Instead, I asked a question. "Why didn't Ragyapa steal the jade skull from the monks himself?"

"He said it was protected by some mean mothers. Lady Ahn had an in, she was related to one of the monks or something."

"So it would be easier to wait until she stole the skull and then turned it over to you?"

"Right. We'd take it from her and split the profit. My end was going to be five thousand dollars."

Herman waited for us to whistle. Neither one of us did. He sighed.

"So I said, okay. Why not? But the problem was that Ragyapa didn't think Lady Ahn was going to be able to pull off the theft by herself. She needed help. If some Koreans helped her, it wouldn't take them long to realize how valuable the skull was. They'd rip her off before we had a chance." He glanced up at us again. "That's where you two guys came in."

"Why us?"

Herman shrugged. "You speak the language. You're good investigators. And you're honest."

I didn't thank him for the compliments. We'd screwed this case up so badly that I didn't think compliments were in order. Especially from Herman.

"But you needed a reason for us to help her," I prodded.

"Right. Ragyapa came up with it. Pretend that Mi-ja had been kidnapped."

Ernie couldn't stand it any longer. His fists clenched. "So you turned your little girl over to a criminal?"

Herman pleaded with his moist eyes. "He was *working* with me."

"And what about the ear, you dickhead?"

Ernie was becoming angry again. I patted him on the shoulder and leaned him back up against the railing of the pagoda.

"The ear was Ragyapa's idea," Herman answered. "I didn't like it, but he said it would really get you guys motivated to find the skull and free Mi-ja."

"That it did," I said. "Did Ragyapa do the cutting?"

"No way," Herman said. "He's a Buddhist."

"So who did?"

"I did it. The razor was real sharp. She didn't feel much."

Like an enraged jaguar, Ernie leapt across the pagoda. He smashed Herman upside the head, knocked him off the bench, and started kicking. Herman yelped and curled into a fetal ball. Ernie kicked the toe of his shoe into Herman's spine about three times before I could react. Using all my strength, I pulled Ernie off.

After I got them both calmed down, I sat Herman back up on the bench.

"Sorry for the interruption, Herman." I glanced back at Ernie. "It won't happen again."

Ernie leaned on the railing of the open-air pagoda, glaring at Herman, breathing hard.

Herman's peeved eyes glanced at him a couple of times and then turned back to me.

"I had to do it," Herman said. "It was the only way I was ever going to earn that kind of money. I did it for Mi-ja."

I let that one sit for a while. When Ernie didn't jump, I asked, "How so?"

"I was going to put the whole five grand in a certificate of deposit. For her college education." When he saw we weren't buying it, he kept talking. "They have fake ears nowadays. I've seen 'em at the One-two-one Evac. Or when she got older she could just wear her hair long. But how else was she going to get an education? My retirement check is three hundred bucks a month. I clear maybe four or five hundred more on the black market. Me and Nam were never going to come up with the kind of dough she'd need for college."

The rain kept falling.

"What about the finger, Herman?"

He let his head hang. "That hurt her more." A tiny serpent of drool slipped from his lips. "But it was only a little finger. She'd still be able to write and all that."

"Just get on with the fucking story," Ernie snarled. "Just get on with it."

Herman looked at me. I nodded.

"So you guys fell for it. And you went after Lady Ahn just like we hoped. And you helped her steal the jade skull. And when you returned back to Seoul you called me and told me you had it. I let Ragyapa know."

Now it was my turn to explode. I gripped the railing of the pagoda tightly, until the tendons in my arms felt as if they were going to snap. I relaxed, took a deep breath, and spoke as calmly as I could.

"And with that knowledge, Ragyapa attacked Lady Ahn in the *yoguan*?"

"Yeah. The son of a bitch double-crossed me. We were supposed to go up there together. Instead, the fire in the *yoguan* starts and I'm still waiting on a street corner with my thumb up my ass. He and his boys went alone. If she'd had the skull, Ragyapa would've kept it for himself."

"So when I told you the jade skull was locked in a safe place . . ."

"I figured you meant the CID safe and there was no choice but to grab it."

"What about Mi-ja?" Ernie snarled. "When you took off with the jade, you weren't thinking about her *education* then, were you?"

"That was a mistake," Herman said. "I guess the money got to me. But I didn't think Ragyapa would kill her. I mean, he's a Buddhist, you know. They're not supposed to kill anybody."

"Neither are Christians."

Herman stared at me blankly, not quite able to compute that one.

"How'd you find out that Mi-ja was murdered?" I asked.

"The lifers at the MAC terminal at Osan. That's all anyone was talking about."

"But you boarded that flight to the States anyway."

"I wasn't thinking clearly."

"You just wanted to make your getaway with the skull. And now you realize that's not possible."

"No. It's not."

"I'm glad you finally realize all this shit, Herman." I paced in a circle around the pagoda. "Once you make a full confession, you'll feel better. Probably won't even be slapped with much time in the monkey house. Koreans are lenient with foreigners. Especially former military."

"I'm not turning myself in."

Ernie bristled. "The *hell* you're not."

"I want to be there when you exchange the skull for Lady Ahn. I want to talk to Ragyapa one more time. About how he double-crossed me. About what he did to Mi-ja."

"Afraid that's not possible, Herman," I said. "You'll be in custody. Ernie and I will take the jade skull and make the exchange with Ragyapa for Lady Ahn."

"Not without me, you won't."

"Shit," Ernie said. "How the hell you going to stop us? We got the skull. We're going to kick your fat ass into jail. What the hell you going to do about it?"

Ernie snatched up Herman's leather bag and unzipped it. His eyes widened as he reached in and pulled out the heavy sphere inside.

It wasn't the jade skull of Kublai Khan. It was a patchwork of black and white pentagons. A soccer ball. Cut open.

I grabbed it and turned it upside down. Rocks clattered to the cement slab.

"You don't think I'd carry anything around as valuable as the skull, do you?" Herman asked. "I have it hidden in a safe place. So we got a deal? We go after Ragyapa and his Mongols together?"

Ernie's teeth sounded like iron spikes grinding on stone. I steadied him with the back of my hand.

We had no choice. Beating Herman wouldn't do any good. He'd proven he was impervious to pain. Cooperating with Herman the German, the only man in the world who knew the whereabouts of the jade skull of Kublai Khan, was the only way we were going to save Lady Ahn.

Even Ernie realized it. The grinding of his teeth slowly subsided.

I spoke first. "All right, Herman," I said. "We have a deal."

"Only one more thing," Herman answered. "You both stay near me, to protect me from the slicky boys. And you definitely don't tell Slicky Girl Nam where I am. After what happened to Mi-ja, she'll be out looking for me. With a knife. To cut my balls off."

"If she don't," Ernie promised, "I will."

33

HERMAN TOOK US TO THE PLACE WHERE RAGYAPA AND HIS BOYS
had been holed up part of the time while they held Mi-ja.

It was a ramshackle hooch, two stories, with a mangy
brown-and-gray mutt tied on a short leash in the central
courtyard. As we entered, the cur barked and bared his
yellow fangs.

The place was in Dong Binggo, the Eastern Ice House,
a district in Seoul not a half mile from Itaewon. During
the Yi dynasty, barges floated down the Han River from the
mountains to the north and unloaded blocks of blue ice for
storage underground. Later, the glacial chunks were
cracked open when the nobles at the royal court wanted
something cooled off. It was frustrating to realize that Ragyapa and Mi-ja had been so close to us. But if you drew a
circle on a map, using the distance from Dong Binggo to
Itaewon as the radius, you'd enclose thousands of tiny hovels like this one. All jammed together in an intricate, im-
penetrable patchwork.

Ernie knew what I was thinking. "There was no way, pal," he said. "No way we could've found them."

I grunted and swung a foot at the dog. He ducked.

The landlady was a wrinkled woman with two gray teeth drooping from purple gums.

"They go," she said. "Long time ago. They go."

I wheedled the exact date out of her. A long time ago turned out to be one week. Yes, she said, the little girl was with them. Still alive.

Of course they didn't leave any forwarding address.

We searched their rooms. Three of them. No kitchen. No bathrooms except for the *byonso* out by the front gate. The quarters were filthy. One room reeked of urine. A pee pot must've been spilled. Empty soda pop bottles and torn plastic wrappings with Korean lettering on them were scattered everywhere. Junk-food Buddhists.

Ernie and I squatted on the wood-slat floor and examined every piece of trash. Herman stood at the entranceway, eyes moist.

When we were through, we had nothing. No leads. No idea where Ragyapa and his thugs might've gone.

I stared at Herman. The unspoken question made him nervous.

"I don't know where they went. They didn't tell me nothing."

"What else do you know about them? Did they have associates? Koreans they talked to? Women?"

Herman shook his head. "No women. No Koreans." Slowly something dawned on him. "Only those other Buddhists."

"What other Buddhists?"

"Ragyapa talked about them one time. About how true believers in Buddha have friends everywhere. Even here in Korea."

"Why 'even in Korea'?" I asked. "Everybody knows there are plenty of Buddhists in Korea."

"But not his kind. Ragyapa and these guys, they were weird."

"Weird in what way?"

"Not like other people. Not like other Buddhists. A lot of little doodads that they carried around."

"Like what?"

"Like rattles. With strings on them."

Prayer wheels.

"And they were always joking," Herman said. "Laughing. Even drinking. They didn't seem like Buddhists to me."

"What'd they seem like?"

"Gangsters."

Ernie stepped through the rubble and rapped his knuckles upside Herman's head. "You left your kid with *gangsters?*"

Herman spread his fingers. "Hey. They said she'd be safe."

Ernie rapped him again.

Outside, I spent thirty minutes with the landlady, but she gave me nothing. Ragyapa and his boys had paid their rent in advance, stayed mostly in their rooms, and left without warning.

If she knew anything else, she wasn't telling.

AT A STONE-LINED ALLEY NEARBY, WE STOPPED AT A RED-LAC-quered shrine. Ernie and Herman waited outside while I slipped off my shoes, dropped an offering into a bronze pot, picked up three sticks of incense, and held them above my forehead. As I knelt and bowed to the gilded Buddha, I wondered if the Catholic saints of my youth were looking down upon me. If they were, I hoped it wasn't with loathing. I had enough people pissed off at me.

After replacing the incense in the embossed holder, I spoke in soft Korean to the monk seated cross-legged next to the bronze offering pot.

"Foreigners," I said. "From Mongolia. If they were followers of the Buddha, would they not have their own temples?"

The monk sat silent, eyes closed, and for a moment I thought he hadn't heard me. Or hadn't understood.

"Of course they would," the monk said in clear English.

I was startled, but recovered quickly. "Where would they go to worship?"

"There is only one temple in Seoul that follows the way of the Mongols. Same as the Tibetans, you know. Too much clanging of cymbals, too much ceremony, too many spangled costumes." The monk swiveled his bald head. "Don't you agree?"

"I wouldn't know."

"Yes, of course. Well, take it from me. They are much too ostentatious."

I was glad I hadn't sent Herman in. He wouldn't have understood this monk's English. Too ostentatious.

"Where can I find this temple?" I asked.

"You wish to worship in their way?"

"No. I am searching for someone."

"Ah, yes. Aren't we all?"

The monk gave me the directions. Bulguang-ni, a district outside the old stone walls of the city.

"The kings of the Yi dynasty didn't want them to conduct their business inside the walls of Seoul," the monk said. "Much too unseemly. All their goings-on."

"What types of goings-on?"

"Ugly things. Sacrifices. Orgies. Consorting with demons. The Mongols only just left barbarity, you know. If you can say they ever left it at all."

I dropped another coin in the bronze pot. It clattered loudly in the stillness.

"American money," the monk said. "Solid."

He smiled as I left.

THE JEEP ENGINE PURRED THROUGH THE OUTSKIRTS OF SEOUL, Ernie winding expertly through the thinning traffic. Herman sat in back, elbows draped over his thick knees.

During the ride, I ran it down—the way I saw the case—for Herman and Ernie. What it boiled down to is that by hiring Sister Julie and Hatcher to attack the Buddhist nun, Ragyapa had tried to create a diversion, a diversion that had two purposes. First, to divert the attention of Eighth Army. And, second and more important, to divert the attention of those powerful clerics who controlled the vast network of Buddhist organizations in Korea.

Since ancient times there had been many sects of Buddhism in constant competition with one another. One of the main divisions is between the Buddhists of Tibet and Mongolia, who believe in much elaborate religious display, and their more sedate brothers in China and Korea and Japan.

When Ragyapa arrived in Korea, he must've realized that the Buddhists in power here in Korea would never let him steal the jade skull, not if they understood its true value. Of course, the artifact had only recently come to light, after being forgotten for a number of centuries. Now was the time to strike, before it became common knowledge that the skull contained a map to the riches in the Tomb of Genghis Khan.

When Ragyapa's inquiries led him to Lady Ahn, he realized she was the ideal person to steal the jade skull from the monks of Bian-do. She had her own motives. She, of course, would be blamed for the theft. After that, if he stole the jade from her, he would be able to escape from Korea before the local Buddhists realized that the jade skull had fallen into the hands of a competing Buddhist sect.

There were two ways to do that. Keep the theft of the jade skull a secret, which was probably impossible. Or, better yet, keep the Korean Buddhist hierarchy preoccupied with an apparently bigger problem.

The bigger problem he'd invented was the vicious attack on a Buddhist nun by an American serviceman. And Ernie and I had fallen right into his plan.

The attack on the nun served another function, too. The demonstrations it ignited kept Eighth Army busy. Not all of our attention was focused on the kidnapping of Mi-ja. We'd pay enough attention to help Lady Ahn with the theft of the jade skull, but by the time Ragyapa took possession of the skull, Eighth Army would be in an uproar over the protests that would be sweeping the country.

It was a brilliant plan, and Ragyapa's timing had been perfect. Almost. My locking the skull in the CID safe — and Herman stealing it — had complicated things. But Ragyapa still had Lady Ahn. And with her, he could force my hand.

As far as I was concerned, Ragyapa was welcome to win this war. He could have the damn skull as long as I got Lady Ahn back. But I wouldn't hand the skull over to him on trust. To do so would sign her death warrant. He'd kill her for sure then, just to make certain there'd be no witnesses.

I'd have to get her back first.

If we could somehow find Ragyapa, surprise him, take Lady Ahn, and keep the skull, that would be even better.

I didn't see how, with so little time — only one more day — but we had to try.

Five miles north of Seoul, a sign slashed with an inverted swastika pointed the way to the Temple of the Endless Snow. The temple sat by a stream on the edge of the village of Bulguang-ni. The outside wall was streaked with dirt. Nestled inside was an ancient handcarved temple. In the rear were tiny rooms that probably served as monks' quarters.

A man in faded blue pantaloons and a blue tunic hobbled out into the courtyard and bowed to us. In Korean, I told him I wished to speak to the head monk.

"The monks have left," the man replied.

"Where'd they go?"

"Back to Mongolia. My wife and I are paid each month to preserve this place." He shook the wispy gray hair on his brown skull. "We don't get many visitors."

"Your payment comes from Mongolia?"

"Hong Kong now."

"Have there been any men visiting recently? Foreigners? Possibly Mongols?"

"No, sir. No visitors."

Ernie and I searched the grounds. The old man hadn't lied. The small temple seemed more like a poorly preserved museum than an active place of worship. Inside, the wood floors creaked, and demons snarled at us with fangs of faded bloodred. The place reeked of mildew. Rats scurried at our approach. The only sign of life was in the quarters out back. Smoke curled from a tin pipe chimney. An ugly woman hammered away at gnarled turnips.

I returned to the groundskeeper, scribbled my phone number on a scrap of paper, and handed it to him.

"If anyone visits, you must call me immediately. Police business."

His head bobbed like a pigeon. "Yes, sir."

We turned to leave. At the gate I paused, remembering one more question.

"These Mongolian monks, how long ago did they leave?"

The groundskeeper thought about that for a few seconds. "Hard to say, sir. My grandfather would've known exactly, but now . . ." He counted on weathered fingers. ". . . Yes, it's been almost a hundred years."

"WHERE IN THE HELL HAVE YOU GUYS BEEN?"

It was the First Sergeant, an angry flush of red shining from beneath his gray crew cut. We'd left Herman outside the CID office, handcuffed to the backseat of the jeep. As soon as he heard our voices, the First Sergeant had stormed out of his office and cornered us in the Admin Office in front of Sergeant Riley's desk.

Riley hunched over a stack of paperwork and started scribbling, hoping to be spared the blast of the First Sergeant's anger. Ernie pulled out a stick of ginseng gum, unwrapped it, and popped it in his mouth. The First Sergeant stared back and forth between us.

"I asked you two a question!"

"Relax, Top," Ernie said. "Your blood pressure."

"Don't give me that blood pressure crap, Bascom. Ever since you guys got back from Taejon you've hardly even bothered to stop back in the office and grace us with your presence. Isn't that right, Riley?"

"Right, Top." Riley continued to scribble.

The First Sergeant took a breath and continued. "First, that kidnapped kid gets murdered out in Itaewon. You don't have nothing to report on that, which is bad enough, and you don't have nothing to report on anything else you've been working on except for dropping a stray little piece of news on us. You two told Sergeant Riley that this Buddhist nun who was allegedly attacked in Itaewon—"

"Nothing allegedly about it," Ernie interrupted. "She was jacked up royally."

"Allegedly!" the First Sergeant roared. "It's *allegedly* until Pfc. Hatcher is proven guilty in a court of law."

"Asshole's guilty," Ernie said. "I saw him."

I elbowed Ernie. He shut up. The First Sergeant continued.

"And so you stop in here and give us that little tidbit of news that this Buddhist nun intends to pour gasoline over her head and burn herself to death. When is this supposed to happen?"

Ernie glanced at me. I'm the detail man.

"Tomorrow afternoon," I said. "At four P.M."

"Do you have any corroboration of that?"

"We'll have corroboration," Ernie said, "when her skin starts to crinkle."

"That's enough out of you, Bascom!"

Ernie chomped serenely on his gum.

The First Sergeant looked at me. "How do you know this?"

"We talked to her," I said. "Outside. During the demonstration in front of Gate Five."

The First Sergeant drew an involuntary breath. "You know demonstrations are off-limits to Eighth Army personnel."

Ernie sighed. "They surrounded us, Top. If it hadn't been for that little nun, George and I'd be dog food by now."

The First Sergeant thought that over. "Maybe better for the organization."

"Yeah," Ernie said. "A hell of a lot less trouble for you. You wouldn't have to deal with the truth so often."

"I said that'll be *enough* out of you, Bascom."

Ernie stood at attention and snapped a mock salute. I stepped in front of him.

"If the nun burns," I told the First Sergeant, "the whole country's going to erupt. It could even lead to armed insurrection."

The words "armed insurrection" forced the First Sergeant's attention off of Ernie and onto me.

"You really think they'd go that far?"

"There are more Buddhists in this country than any other religion. The Christians control the government and the military, but the rank-and-file troops are mostly Buddhist."

The First Sergeant slowly shook his head. "Maybe you're right, Sueño. All I know is that ever since we passed the word up the chain of command that the Buddhist nun was planning on torching herself, they've been on our backs wanting to know more. And what could I tell them? I had every MP patrol out, but we still couldn't find you."

"We were investigating, Top. You know that."

His eyes narrowed. "Maybe. So what does she want?"

"The nun?"

"Yeah."

"She wants Eighth Army to turn Hatcher over to Korean jurisdiction."

"That takes time. There are legal procedures. Treaty restrictions. We have to get clearance from the embassy."

"Tough shit," Ernie said.

I pushed him back. "Short-circuit the procedures," I told the First Sergeant. "The Eighth Army Commander can get on the horn to Washington, D.C., if he has to. Turn over Hatcher to the ROKs. Do it now. Today. Once we have the guarantee, Ernie and I will inform the nun."

The First Sergeant's freckled brow furrowed. He jabbed a finger at Riley. "You hold these two troopers *here*, Riley. You understand that, Staff Sergeant? Don't let them move!"

"Right, Top."

The First Sergeant swiveled and stormed off down the hallway.

Staff Sergeant Riley rose from behind his desk and tugged on the belt of his khaki trousers. "Well, I guess you both heard what the First Sergeant said. You know who's in charge, and you know who's going to enforce the order."

Ernie flopped down in a chair. "Bite me, Riley," he said.

Ten minutes later the First Sergeant came back. Eighth Army had approved it. Private First Class Ignatius Q. Hatcher would be turned over to the Korean National Police tomorrow at close of business. Four P.M. sharp.

"That's as fast as they'd move," the First Sergeant said.

"Assholes are stalling," Ernie groused. "Trying to save face."

The First Sergeant didn't answer. I motioned to Ernie. He stood up and we walked to the door.

The First Sergeant hollered. "Where in the *hell* do you think you two are going?"

I wheeled on him. "Somebody has to inform the nun about the turnover of Hatcher."

"We'll just broadcast it on radio and TV."

"No," I said. "She has to be told by somebody she trusts."

The First Sergeant thought about it. "You know where to find her?"

"Yes. We know where to find her."

"Good. Make sure she doesn't roast herself. Eighth Army's counting on you."

"Fuck Eighth Army," Ernie said.

ERNIE TOOK THE LONG WAY TO TOBONG MOUNTAIN, OUT THE Han River road toward Walker Hill. It made sense, because we fought our way out of the Seoul rush-hour traffic about a half hour sooner than we would have if we'd cut straight across town. Once we were in the countryside,—

Ernie made a beeline for Tobong-san. It was already dark by the time we reached the Temple of the Celestial Void.

An elderly nun emerged into the courtyard, hands clasped in front of her, and bowed.

"We have good news," I told her. "Concerning the nun, Choi So-lan. Eighth Army will comply with all her wishes. There is no need now for her to burn herself."

The old nun's shoulders seemed to sag. "You are too late."

Ernie understood the Korean phrase. He stepped forward. I held him back.

"She's already burned herself?" I asked softly.

"No. She has been taken away. For purification."

"Where?"

"I don't know. Secrecy is part of the rite. No one but the monks who will assist her are with her now."

"But we must talk to her."

"No one can. Especially not a foreigner."

"Not a foreigner? Why not?"

The nun tilted back her head, her eyes widened, and for the first time she stared directly at me. A red glow seemed to radiate from her pupils.

"Because you foreigners bring defilement. Everywhere you go. You defiled Choi So-lan. You defile everything."

Ernie looked at me with a questioning look, wondering what she had said. I didn't translate.

"You will never stop her," the old nun hissed.

She turned and disappeared into the shadows.

AS WE CUT THROUGH THE SWIRLING NEON OF THE CITY, GAG-gles of young men, and a few chicks, were hanging out at corners. They weren't your orderly demonstrators we'd seen earlier. More like street toughs. They waved photographs of the little nun over their heads and shouted anti-American slogans.

Ernie shouted back a couple of times, and I told him to cool it.

"If they don't like us *Miguks*," Ernie said, "they can go screw themselves."

"It's only because of what Hatcher did to the nun. That's what made them angry."

"It pissed me off more than it did them."

When we parked the jeep in front of the CID building, a bulb still shone in the Admin Office. Sergeant Riley sat behind his desk, his head lolling atop the ink-scribbled blotter. When he heard our footsteps, he jerked upright and rubbed his eyes.

"Been waiting for you guys," he said.

"More shit from the First Sergeant?" Ernie asked.

"No. Phone call. From your asshole buddy. Guy with a weird accent. Calls himself Rag Yapping. Or something like that."

"Ragyapa," I said.

Ernie and I both leaned forward. Riley smirked, delighted to be in the position of knowing something that we didn't.

"Spill, Riley," I said. "What'd Ragyapa tell you?"

"He said he's ready to meet and exchange the woman for the jade skull."

"Lady Ahn's still alive?"

"Heard her in the background."

"What'd she say?"

"She didn't *say* anything. She just screamed occasionally."

I didn't need any more detail. "When's the meeting?"

"Tomorrow afternoon. Four P.M. sharp."

"Four P.M.? That's the same time the nun torches herself."

"And the same time the Eighth Army honchos decided to release Hatcher," Ernie added.

"Yeah," Riley said. "It's almost as if this guy knew."

Ernie was impatient. "So where's this meet supposed to take place?"

"You'll love this," Riley said. "I don't know how he expects you guys to survive."

"Survive? What are you talking about?"

"The place you're supposed to meet. He made me write it down and spell it back to him so there wouldn't be any mistake."

Ernie grabbed for Riley's khaki collar. "Where, god-damn it?"

Riley brushed back Ernie's hand. "Take it easy, Bascom. I was going to tell you." He glanced down at his notes. "Guanghua-mun. The Gate of the Transformation of Light. Right in the heart of tomorrow's demonstration."

Riley smiled up at us.

"In the middle of a demonstration?" Ernie said. "We'll be killed!"

Riley smiled more broadly. "That's what I was trying to tell you."

Ernie turned to me. "It doesn't make any sense."

I waited, thinking it over. Then I spoke. "Sure it does, Ernie."

"How?"

"We're American law enforcement. In downtown Seoul tomorrow, in the middle of an anti-American demonstration, there's no way we can deploy any backup."

"That's for sure. They'd be stoned to death."

"And even the Korean National Police will be totally overwhelmed."

"When there's thousands of demonstrators out after their blood, of course they'll be overwhelmed."

"So setting the exchange up in the middle of a demonstration is a brilliant move. Tomorrow afternoon,

Guanghua-mun in downtown Seoul will be the most lawless piece of real estate in Korea."

Ernie let a long breath out between dry lips. "Strictly survival of the fittest," he said.

Riley barked a laugh. "For once, Bascom, you got it exactly right."

34

WE KEPT HERMAN THE GERMAN HANDCUFFED TO THE ROLL BAR of the jeep all night.

We parked in an unlit area behind the barracks and brought out a blanket for him, and even though he had to hold his arm straight up over his head, he spent a fairly comfortable night.

Why didn't we arrest him and book him and slap him in a holding cell at the MP Station? Because if we did, he'd never tell us where the jade skull was hidden. And without the skull, we'd never free Lady Ahn.

Ernie tried to wheedle it out of him by offering him a nice, comfortable bed in the barracks, but Herman wasn't going for it.

"We ought to just beat the crap out of him," Ernie told me.

I studied the scars on Herman's thick-boned forehead. He stared back at me impassively.

"It wouldn't do any good, Ernie," I said. "Herman will

turn the jade skull over to us, but he'll turn it over only when he's ready. Which is just before tomorrow's rendezvous. Right, Herman?"

He stared at me with his moist brown eyes. A bubble of saliva emerged from the corner of his fleshy lips.

As we walked to the barracks, another burst of monsoon rain splattered the pavement. By the time we trotted to the doorway it was coming down in torrents. The little canvas-topped jeep sat huddled beneath a deluge of mist and spray, as if it were at the bottom of a waterfall.

Ernie went to his room. I went to mine. All I could see was the beautiful face of Lady Ahn. Before I fell asleep, I cleaned my .38 three times.

THE NEXT DAY WE STAYED AWAY FROM THE CID OFFICE BY leaving word for the First Sergeant that we were still trying to contact the Buddhist nun to convince her to call off the self-immolation. We kept questioning Herman about the whereabouts of the jade skull but he wouldn't spill.

Two hours before the rendezvous, Ernie went berserk.

He punched Herman and kicked him, so enraged that I couldn't hold him back. Finally, he reached into his shoulder holster, whipped out the .45, and with a metal-on-metal clang, pulled back the charging handle.

He stuck the muzzle up against Herman's temple. "It's time, Herman. I want the jade skull. I want it *now*."

Sweat poured off Herman's forehead. For a moment I thought he was going to refuse like he had a hundred times before. But this time he changed his tune.

"Okay. It's in Itaewon. I'll show you where."

Ernie stuck the .45 back into the holster. "That's better. Let's go."

Ernie drove us to Itaewon. When we approached the nightclub district, Herman piped up.

"It's at Mama Lee's," he said.

Mama Lee. The biggest black marketeer in Itaewon. Why in the hell would he leave something so valuable with her? I swiveled in the seat. Herman saw the unspoken question in my eyes and answered it.

"She's the most reliable person I know."

Which maybe wasn't saying too much.

"I hope the fuck for your sake," Ernie said, "that it's still there."

Herman sat quietly in the backseat, head down, occasionally jerking his handcuffs apart, making the chain rattle, like a child fascinated by a toy.

Once inside Mama Lee's courtyard, it took us about thirty seconds to locate the jade skull of Kublai Khan. The most priceless Mongolian antique in Korea was in a leather bag, bound in cheesecloth, stuffed behind brown bags full of American-made PX goods.

"Business looks good, Mama," Ernie said.

"So-so." She tilted her gnarled hand from side to side. Puffs of smoke filtered through her snaggled teeth, like fire from a dragon's mouth.

Ernie lifted the jade skull up to the light and examined it. "Thanks for holding this for us."

"You take go," Mama Lee said. "I no like. *Chinguro.*" Creepy.

"Yeah, it's *chinguro* all right."

Ernie replaced the skull in the bag, slung it over his shoulder, and the three of us walked back to the jeep. We debated taking Herman to the MP Station and booking him.

Herman wasn't thrilled with the idea. "Hey! You guys can't do that. We had a deal."

"Fuck some kind of a deal!" Ernie said. "You had a deal with Mi-ja. To be her father and protect her. Instead you cut off her ear."

"That was business."

Ernie stepped toward Herman. I grabbed him and held on, feeling the jade skull pressing against my belly.

"Not now, Ernie. There's no time. We have to save Lady Ahn. And the nun."

Ernie took three deep breaths. Then he pointed at Herman. "As soon as this shit is over, we're booking your ass and the charge is going to be kidnapping and being an accomplice to murder in the first degree. You got that, you fat old lifer asshole?"

"I got it," Herman whispered.

As we shot through afternoon traffic toward downtown Seoul, Ernie had to swerve around groups of angry citizens, holding photographs of the little nun, throwing rotten persimmons at our jeep. I thought about what Herman had just said. It was the first time I ever remembered him answering a question with such humility in his voice. I looked back. His face was the same, aggrieved and worried, as always. But fat tears poured down his fleshy cheeks.

I didn't tell Ernie. It would've just pissed him off.

WE KNELT ON THE BALCONY OF A RED PAGODA THAT SAT ON A hill overlooking the T-shaped intersection in front of Guanghua-mun, the Gate of the Transformation of Light.

We had left the jeep in a narrow alley in a stone-walled residential district. Ernie made Herman move to the front seat and handcuffed him to the front roll bar.

"You can't leave me here," Herman protested.

"The hell we can't," Ernie answered. "You'll be safe this far from the demonstrators. They never come up here."

"But you promised I'd be able to see Ragyapa."

"Fuck that promise. You don't deserve shit."

Ernie lifted the thick chain that was welded onto the floorboard, wound it tightly through the steering wheel, and padlocked it. With Herman's wrist handcuffed to the roll bar, both vehicle and suspect were now secure.

As we walked away, Herman cursed and shouted at us, spittle erupting from his moist lips. "You can't leave me here, you bastards! Come back and take these damn handcuffs off!"

No matter how loud he shouted, I wasn't worried about anybody interfering. The local residents wouldn't want to become involved with some half-crazed foreigner. And the police would have plenty to do with the largest demonstration of the year—maybe the decade—about to begin right in the heart of their precinct.

From the vantage point of the pagoda, we could see streams of students moving in an orderly fashion toward Guanghua-mun. Armored riot-control vehicles and helmeted riot police had already taken up positions near the periphery. In case anything got out of control.

Russet-robed monks and gray-clad nuns knelt silently on the damp pavement. A lake of tranquility. I couldn't see Choi So-lan.

In the center of all this activity, the ancient stone gate loomed about fifty feet high. Atop it were bright green tiles, upturned at the eaves, and rows of porcelain monkeys, a simian honor guard designed to ward off evil spirits. Behind the gate were the manicured grounds of the old capitol building, built by the Japanese after their takeover of Korea in 1911. The domed building was still considered a reminder of colonization, and there was much talk about tearing it down.

Ernie watched the students. "They almost look like they're in military formations," he said.

"Close to it. Each university has their own student leadership council that organizes the students into groups. Boys march with boys. Girls march with girls. And the shock troops, the biggest and toughest boys, go in first."

All the students wore white bandanas across their fore-heads, knotted in the back. Korean characters were slashed across the front in black ink, but from this distance I couldn't read what they said.

Around a far turn, more battalions of students emerged, all heading toward the big open intersection in front of Guanghua-mun. Vehicular traffic had long since been blocked off. A wooden platform had been set up in front of the gate; student technicians fiddled with wires and speakers and amplifiers.

The sky was overcast, but no rain. Not yet.

I grabbed the leather bag from Ernie.

"I better take up my position," I said. "Ragyapa wants me right in front of the gate."

"Why don't you let me take it?" Ernie patted the .45 beneath his coat. "I'm better with this than you are."

"That won't help. Not with all these students. But speaking the language might make a difference. I know what to say to them." I stood and hoisted the bag over my shoulder. "Besides, if I act cool enough they just might think I'm a foreign correspondent or something."

"Did you bring a notebook?"

"Forgot."

"Well, then," Ernie said, "look studious."

And so I strode off toward the Gate of the Transformation of Light.

35

As I neared Guanghua-mun, the chanting of the students grew deafening.

"*Jayu mansei!*" Long live liberty.

"*Weiguk-nom chukko!*" Death to foreign louts!

"*Miguk-nom mullo kara!*" Yankee go home!

Although they were shouting all these terrible things, most of the students didn't even glance my way as I skirted their formations. But I felt as if I were tiptoeing past a giant tiger. His belly was temporarily full but if he became hungry and turned his green eyes on me, I'd be gulped down like a before-dinner aperitif.

Finally, I reached my position in front of the gate. I stood behind the podium, hoping no one would notice me.

I studied the area where the Buddhists had gathered. A sea of bald heads. There were too many of them and I wasn't high enough to see over the crowd. I couldn't tell if the little nun was there or not.

The buildings surrounding the intersection in front of Guanghua-mun were mostly deserted. But in a few of them, from high windows, people stared out at the crowd. In one or two windows I thought I glimpsed a glimmer of light. Maybe telescopes. Or photographic lenses. The secret police keeping tabs on troublemakers.

Suddenly, I felt naked standing out here. I wished we had set up a sniper in one of those windows. Ernie had promised to cover me, and I knew he would, but more students and more Buddhists were joining the swelling, noisy crowd every minute. Ernie would have trouble just keeping track of where I was, much less helping me if I needed it.

I searched for Ragyapa. So far nothing.

Suddenly, like a wave, the Buddhists rose to their feet, chanted for a moment, then knelt back down. The monks and nuns looked like a carpet of wool dotted with flesh-colored buttons. That's when I saw her. Choi So-lan, the Buddhist nun. She was in front with some large important-looking old monk who chanted and bowed to her. They were preparing her all right. Like a recipe: Marinate in righteousness before burning.

I wanted to charge over there, to give her the news that Hatcher would be turned over to them, to tell her that she didn't have to go through with this. Why hadn't I sent Ernie to do that? We'd been so nervous that we hadn't thought about it. Still, I had to stop her.

A door in an old wooden *yoguan* across the street slammed open.

Through it, Ragyapa shoving her from behind, stumbled Lady Ahn. My heart punched the walls of my chest like a clenched fist.

Even from this distance I could see she was a mess. Her hair exploded around her skull like uncut weeds. Her face was dark, shadowed, bruised. Her clothes were soiled and torn. If this had been a normal day, Ragyapa would have never dared to allow her onto the street. After one look at her, any self-respecting policeman would've investigated. But the rows of helmeted police had their eyes only on the surging demonstrators. None of them would break ranks; they'd be under orders not to.

Besides, what the foreign press called riot police weren't really police at all. They were conscripts in the Korean Army. After basic training, they were sent to the special riot police academy and taught how to wear gas masks and protect themselves with shields and wield riot batons. The riot police were soldiers, actually, and subject to military law and under the command of military officers. Most were from poor families, drafted when they were twenty years old. Few had any love for the wealthy students who would turn their backs on the money-making advantages of a university education to come out here and curse them for just doing what they were told to do.

It was an old story. Peasants against the Mandarin elite. And the Korean government wasn't above using class warfare to its advantage. The strong young peasant boys had been trained to beat up the uppity students.

I searched behind the *yoguan*. No sign of Ernie.

Ragyapa waved for me to come forward. His thug with the M-1 could be drawing a bead on me right now. No sense thinking about it. I walked forward.

Twenty yards in front of the *yoguan*, I stopped.

"Let her go," I said.

Lady Ahn didn't seem to know I was there. Her eyes were glazed. I'm not even sure if she knew where she was.

"Lady Ahn," I called, "can you walk forward on your own?"

She didn't move.

I unslung the bag and carefully set it on the wet pavement. "I'll leave the skull here," I said. "You let her walk toward me."

Ragyapa smiled. From out of the shadows of the *yoguan* emerged one of his Mongolian thugs. The thug held the M-1 rifle level, pointing it straight at my nose.

"That won't be necessary," Ragyapa said. "You will bring the skull to us."

I knew that if I stepped into the darkness of the *yoguan*, I'd never step out. Out here, if they shot me, someone would be forced to notice. The riot police would move. Ragyapa and his boys would never get away.

"No," I told Ragyapa. "We make the exchange right here. Out in the open."

From the corner of my eye, I saw something scurry along the side of the *yoguan*. Ernie, I thought, but I forced myself not to look.

"No!" Ragyapa said. "You will bring the skull to me now."

Suddenly, metal flashed from the sleeve of his coat. I saw it press up against Lady Ahn's side. She moaned. Then he lifted it. A gleaming dagger, pressed right into her throat.

"She will die," Ragyapa told me, "if you don't do what I say."

Behind us, student leaders started to rant into the microphones. They were criticizing the president of the republic. Calling him a lapdog of the American occupying forces. Accusing him of letting the filthy GIs get away with assaulting Korean women. Even innocent Buddhist nuns.

The students roared their approval. Off to the side, the riot police started to shuffle. Officers barked orders and the police repositioned themselves closer to the demonstrators.

I looked back at Ragyapa, into the evil in his eyes.

"If I step into the *yoguan*, she will die anyway," I said.

"If you want the jade skull, you will have to bring her out here and get it."

I knelt slowly, watching the M-1 rifle move with me. I reached into the bag and pulled out the jade skull. I held it high in the air and ripped off the dirty cheesecloth.

The light of the Seoul afternoon filtered through the intricately carved jade and brought the skull gleaming to life. It was like some precious emerald, filled with the grinning spirit of an ancient phantom of evil.

Ragyapa gasped. His gunman lowered his rifle.

"Put it down," Ragyapa hissed at me. "They will see it."

"If you don't want anyone to see it, you must come out here and take it. And bring Lady Ahn with you . . ." I gestured at the demonstrators behind me. ". . . or I disappear into their midst."

Ragyapa nodded, greed overcoming him. "Yes. Yes. Keep it lower. I will be right there."

He barked some incomprehensible order. From the darkness a hand emerged and handed him a white cloth. Hurriedly, he unraveled his turban, exposing his hideously scarred bald head. Then he wrapped the white bandana around his forehead and slipped off his coat. Suddenly, he had transformed himself into someone who, in the confusion of the afternoon, could pass for a student. I saw his plan. Once he had the jade skull, he could slip it under his arm and disappear into the vast legions of student demonstrators.

Okay by me, as long as he turned Lady Ahn over to me first. After that, we'd try to capture him in order to keep our promise to the nun. But Lady Ahn came first.

Ragyapa strode forward, tugging Lady Ahn after him. I lowered the skull and held it in front of my chest, hoping the M-1 marksman would think twice before pulling the trigger.

Moving my eyes as little as possible I searched for Ernie. Where the hell was he?

About ten feet from me, Ragyapa stopped. He shoved down on Lady Ahn's shoulders. Like a trained dog, she knelt at his feet.

Had he broken her will? After days of torture, it could happen to anyone. No matter how strong.

"Now," Ragyapa said. "The jade."

"Let her crawl forward."

"First you place the jade skull on the ground between us."

I thought it over. Probably as good a deal as I was going to get. And if Ernie popped a slug into the rifleman in time, maybe I'd even live through it.

"Okay," I said.

I had just set the jade down and Lady Ahn started to crawl forward when two things happened simultaneously. I heard a great grinding of gears and a woman's scream. Off to the left a vehicle careened through the dense crowd. Demonstrators, screaming, dove out of the way.

Over to the right, the officers in charge of the riot police had apparently become fed up with the students bad-mouthing their president. With helmets and face screens, shields and batons, the ranks of the riot police pressed forward. A Roman legion clearing the rabble.

Ragyapa snapped his head between the converging riot police and the madly rampaging vehicle.

Suddenly, I realized what it was. Ernie's jeep. But it wasn't Ernie at the wheel. It was Herman the German, holding his hairy arm high over his head, still handcuffed to the roll bar.

Somehow, he'd managed to scoot over far enough to wedge himself behind the steering wheel and start the engine. The chain welded to the floorboard was still preventing him from steering, but Herman didn't seem to care.

Every time he ran into something—a lamppost, the wall of a building, an iron railing leading to the subway—he backed up, stepped on the gas, and rammed forward. Like that, turning the wheel only a few degrees at a time, he had managed to zigzag all the way down the hill.

The radiator of the jeep looked as if it had been chewed by an iron-fanged dinosaur.

Herman butted into the last obstacle between him and Ragyapa: a stone pedestal that during normal afternoons supported a traffic cop. He rammed into it, backed up, turned the wheel as much as he could, then stepped on the gas again. This time he cleared it.

Making a long graceful loop, he swung through the crowd. Students cursed and leapt out of the way. The jeep picked up speed. Suddenly I realized what he was doing. He was heading right toward us.

I dived toward Lady Ahn and tried to lift her to her feet. As I did so a bullet rang out and ricocheted on the pavement behind me. The M-1 rifleman.

Meanwhile, the students had been preparing their response to the slow-motion onslaught of the riot police. In about a half dozen spots, flames ignited amongst the crowd of students. Upon a barked command, burning wicks attached to bottles filled with gasoline catapulted gracefully through the sky. Three crashed into the helmets of the riot police; each exploded on contact.

Whistles blew. Enraged, the riot police charged forward.

In the *yoguan*, I heard the sharp, compact blast of a .45. Ernie! Three, maybe four rounds.

As I lifted Lady Ahn to her feet, no more M-1 bullets exploded in our direction.

Ragyapa screeched and stumbled and crawled toward the jade skull. Lady Ahn seemed to come alive. She wrenched herself away from me and lunged for the skull.

Using her foot, she tried to shield it from Ragyapa's grasp. His fingernails scraped along her leg like claws. She screamed and recoiled against me. Herman and the jeep were heading straight toward us. I pulled her back, out of its path.

"Let me go!" she screamed. "The jade! I must have the jade!"

But it was too late now. Ragyapa was clutching the ancient skull like a football. He scrambled to his feet and looked back at the jeep.

I could see Herman's eyes. The flesh around them was contorted in rage. The mangled fender bore down on Ragyapa.

At the last second Ragyapa dived, rolled, and bounded back to his feet. Herman ground the gears with a great gnashing of iron, backed up, turned the steering wheel, and started after Ragyapa again.

Clutching the skull, Ragyapa took off like a hunchbacked football player. Herman roared through the crowd in his mad yet graceful arcs. People leapt out of his way. The battle between the riot police and the student demonstrators was in full force now. The noise was deafening. I'd tumbled down a rathole into hell.

"The jade!" Lady Ahn screamed. "The jade!"

I slapped her. "The *hell* with the jade. We don't need it."

At the moment, I was most concerned with getting out of there alive. Molotov cocktails were flying, the riot police were moving inexorably forward swinging their heavy batons, and behind them loomed the beetle-backed cavalry of the riot control armored personnel carriers.

A torrent of water lashed out into the crowd. Water hoses. A jet stream swirled past us, knocking us down. I yanked Lady Ahn to her feet again.

"Come on!"

Lady Ahn could barely walk. Ahead, I saw the canvas top of the jeep caroming madly through the crowd. We moved after it. I saw Ernie running out of the *yoguan*. Somehow, he spotted us above the sea of bandanaed heads.

When he reached us, blood pounded through the veins of his neck and his face. "I offed me a motherfucker!" he reported.

"The guy with the M-one?"

"Yeah."

"And the others?"

"Scattered."

"We have to get out of here."

Ernie looked at me as if I were mad. "What about the nun?"

I stopped. "Shit! I completely forgot."

"Come on," Ernie said. "There's still time to save her."

I started to move after him but Lady Ahn held me. "You go. I will stay here."

We were pretty far from the riot police. She'd be fairly safe. "Okay," I told her. "But keep moving toward that line of buildings. Get out of this area."

"Yes," she said. "I can do that."

My fingers lingered on her cheek. Then I ran after Ernie. She worried me. I knew she'd been hurt, and hurt badly, by Ragyapa and his boys. But she was still beautiful. And as soon as she'd gained her freedom, she'd regained that spark of dignity that she always carried with her.

People weren't even paying attention now to the fact that we were Americans. With the riot police on the rampage, everyone was too worried about his own safety to worry about us. The students were tough, well organized, and fighting back valiantly.

It took us two or three minutes to make our way past the

ranks of the riot police to the area occupied by the Bud-dhists.

They still knelt on the blacktop. A sea of tranquility in the violent chaos that raged around them. The little nun sat on a dais garlanded with flowers. A monk stepped for-ward, holding a can, and gingerly splashed gasoline over her bald skull. The little nun sat utterly still as the fluid soaked her robes.

Pungent fumes billowed in the air as I bounded for-ward.

"Eighth Army has released your attacker to the Korean police!" I called out in Korean.

The nun opened her eyes. She looked at me, puzzled at first, but then broke into a broad smile when she spotted Ernie. He stepped forward, reached in his pocket, and handed her a stick of ginseng gum. Without thinking, she took it in her small hand.

A disapproving murmur rumbled through the crowd of kneeling monks. The large, officious monk pushed in front of us.

"*Miguk salam yogi ei andei!*" he scolded. Americans aren't permitted here.

I bowed and spoke to him calmly in Korean. "Forgive me for intruding, sir. We are representatives from Eighth Army. Our Commander has recently seen the wisdom of your demands. The man who so cruelly attacked this nun has just now been turned over to the Korean National Police for prosecution and punishment."

Prosecution and punishment. I was proud of the vocab-ulary. Earlier today, I'd found both words in the same chapter of my Korean textbook. In Korean, the words are never split up.

The monk studied me. "It is too late. We do not have confirmation of this." He swiveled his head and spoke to the monk with the gas can. "Proceed."

When the monk raised the can, Ernie hopped forward, grabbed the can, and shoved the man back.

"Not on my watch you're not," he yelled.

As if they were one body, the kneeling monks rose to their feet and began waving their fists and hollering. I leaned into Choi So-lan's face, wiping gasoline out of her eyes.

"You don't have to die! The American who attacked you has been turned over to the Korean police. The man who paid him will be in our custody any minute. You are young. You must live. Buddha would want you to live."

She bowed her head and began to sob.

The head monk was sputtering now, waving his hands, yelling at his men to grab us. A few of the bolder monks pushed forward.

Ernie didn't need to understand any of the language to figure out what was happening. He poured gasoline onto the ground, and tossed the half-empty can at the approaching monks. Then he grabbed the little nun and jerked her to her feet.

"Come on, goddamn it! Run!"

And to my surprise, she did. Running along beside Ernie, sprinting away from the Buddhists, heading toward the maddening riot of the student demonstrators.

I trotted behind them, covering their retreat. One of the monks grabbed me, but I swiveled and kneed him in the stomach. A rush of air exploded from his mouth and he keeled over.

The other monks kept coming. I pulled out my .38 and waved it in front of them.

"Ha-jima!" I said. Don't!

The monks stopped in their tracks. I turned and raced off into the melee, following Ernie and the nun.

Around the perimeter, the advance of the riot police had stopped. More students streamed into the intersection in front of Guanghua-mun. The student leadership had probably held them in reserve. Their tactic worked. The tired police were being pushed back on all fronts. Some were down, others ran screaming, the flaming oil of the Molotov cocktails engulfing their heavily padded uniforms.

We searched for what seemed forever, making our way toward the careening jeep in the distance.

I ran next to Ernie. "Herman hasn't caught Ragyapa yet."

"Doesn't look like it."

Even above the noise of the screams surrounding us, we heard a thump. The roof of the jeep shuddered to a stop.

"Maybe he's found him now."

We shoved our way through the thickening, screaming crowd. The riot police behind us were in a panic, breaking ranks. Big armored vehicles, water hoses spraying, inched backward.

By the time we reached the jeep it was engulfed in a sea of people who were rocking it rhythmically back and forth. The nun shouted at one of the bystanders.

"What happened?"

"Some dog-faced American hit one of our demonstrators. A woman."

"Is she hurt badly?"

"They've taken her to a hospital."

People were ripping the canvas off the top of the jeep. Herman was inside, handcuffed to the roll bar, like a fleshy morsel inside a clam. He was screaming.

Ernie pulled out his .45. "They're messing with our prisoner."

I grabbed him. "Damn, Ernie. You're going to get us killed."

He swiveled on me. "They're going to kill *him*!"

I had no answer for that.

Choi So-lan shoved between us. "I will talk to them."

Before we could stop her, she plowed forward into the mob, head down, and burrowed her way to the front of the jeep. Holding her gasoline-soaked robes, she clambered up on what was left of the hood and waved her slender arms over her head.

"Listen to me, good people!" she called. The crowd continued to roar. "*Listen* to me!"

Gradually, a few heads turned. People elbowed one another, pointed.

"You all know who I am. I am Choi So-lan!"

A murmur went through the crowd, the name repeated from person to person. As the student demonstrators recognized her they stopped rocking the jeep.

"I am the woman who would be sacrificed today!"

The roar started to subside, the calls for vengeance against the foreign lout died down. Not everyone was paying attention, however. One man called for death to the big noses. Others shouted their approval. But people started to shush them, many wanted to hear what the famous nun had to say. The jeep's rusty springs gave out a final squeak. At last, the crowd quieted.

"The Americans have turned over my attacker to the authorities!"

A cheer went up from the demonstrators.

The nun pointed at the huddled mass of flesh in the jeep. "This born-of-a-dog foreigner must be punished." Another cheer went up. She raised her voice as high as it would go. "But not like this! He must be put in jail and tried for his crimes. Let not the foreigners say that we Koreans are barbaric. Let them not say that we tore a man to pieces without a trial!"

She pointed to the young men nearest the jeep. "You there, stand back! Allow the proper authorities to take this man into custody."

I grabbed the handcuff keys from Ernie and darted forward through the crowd. Leaning my body across the jeep, I unlocked Herman's cuffs, keeping my head down, hoping that at least some of the people in the back of the crowd wouldn't realize that I was an American.

"Keep your face down," I whispered to Herman, "and follow me. Don't say anything."

"I didn't mean to hit that girl—"

"Don't say anything, goddamn it, Herman. If they hear English it will just remind them that we're foreigners."

I jerked him out of the seat, threw my arm protectively around his shoulders, and, both of us bending low at the waist, we crouched our way through the crowd.

At just that moment a group of students managed to overcome the crew of one of the armored vehicles. Standing atop it, hollering, they turned the vehicle toward the line of riot police and started spraying them with water from their own hose.

A cheer roared from the crowd. A knot of students hoisted the little nun on their shoulders and swept her toward the site of this momentous victory.

Ernie joined Herman and me as we hurried through the crowd. "These kids think they're tough shit, but they're going to get their butts kicked," Ernie said. "They're just pissing off the man."

"Yeah," Herman said. "They ought to calm down."

Ernie slapped the side of Herman's head. "What about you, moron! Driving that jeep while it was still chained."

"I had to catch Ragyapa."

"But you didn't. Did you?"

"I came close. I clipped him a couple of times. And after I hit that girl he ran over here. Toward that *yoguan*."

It was the same *yoguan* where the M-1 shooter had hidden and fired on me. While Ernie and Herman were arguing, I'd been scanning the crowd, searching for some sign of Ragyapa. Some sign of Lady Ahn.

It was Ernie who spotted them first. "Over there. Up the alley."

They were under a lamppost. Lady Ahn on Ragyapa's back, clawing him like an enraged lioness.

"She's kicking his butt." Ernie's voice was filled with admiration.

"She ought to," Herman said. "By the time I got through with him, he could barely walk."

I sprinted forward, but my progress was excruciatingly slow. I had to push through tightly packed clumps of shoving students. I felt as if I were running through glue.

Another figure appeared in the light of the lamppost. A man. Holding a rifle.

"I thought you took care of him!" I shouted.

"Shot him in the arm," Ernie replied. "I didn't want to execute him."

"What about the damn rifle?"

"I took the magazine out."

But Lady Ahn didn't know that. The wounded Mongolian thug pointed the muzzle of the M-1 rifle into Lady Ahn's face. She stopped clawing and backed off, gasping for breath. Ragyapa hoisted himself to his feet. He started hobbling up the alley, clutching the jade skull. His hired gun covered his retreat.

"They're getting away," Ernie said. "With the jade skull."

"Let 'em go," I said. "Who gives a shit about it?"

Lady Ahn stood motionless, breathing heavily. Then she stepped up the hill into the darkness, after Ragyapa and the man with the M-1 rifle. After the skull.

"She's got balls," Herman said.

We finally shoved our way past the last of the demonstrators. The riot police were in total flight now. Their ranks had been broken. Many of them lay wounded and bleeding on the ground, their helmets and shields and batons scattered everywhere.

I felt sorry for them. Sure, they were the symbols of oppression. But in reality they were just a bunch of farmers, beaten up by a bunch of rich students. No one in the government, until now, realized how much rage the assault on the Buddhist nun had released. And no one had been able to predict that the riot police would be outnumbered ten to one.

Ernie once again pulled out his .45. "So we go after her?"

"Of course, we go after her. They'll kill her this time."

"Why the hell is she so crazy about the damn skull? The money?"

"It's more than that to her," I said. "It's the restoration of her family's honor. The restoration of her dignity."

"And she's willing to get *killed* for shit like that?"

Herman nodded vigorously. "Sure she is."

Without hesitation, Ernie slapped him once again on his round skull. "What the hell do *you* know about it, shit-for-brains?"

"Hey, I know a lot about that stuff."

"You guys argue on your own time," I said. We had reached the mouth of the alley. "Ernie, you take the left. I'll take the right." We didn't have any handcuffs—I'd dropped them at the jeep—so all I could count on was Herman's sense of honor as a soldier to stay with us while we were engaged in combat with the enemy.

"Herman," I said, "you protect our rear."

He nodded.

Ernie pointed his forefinger at him. "And remember, you're still our prisoner."

"Don't sweat it," Herman said.

We stepped into the darkness.

36

THE ALLEY WAS COOL AND DAMP AND THE WALLS LOOMED
over us like moss-bearded gods. Murky water trickled
through an open gutter, stinking of decayed flesh.

Covering one another, Ernie and I rounded one corner
and then the next. The sun had almost lowered and dark
clouds shrouded the rising monsoon moon.

When we rounded the third corner, we saw them. Ragyapa, Lady Ahn, and the thug with the M-1 rifle. The thug
aimed the rifle at Lady Ahn's temple, cursing softly, his
finger on the trigger. Ragyapa slumped on the cobbled
lane, moaning, rubbing his lower leg, the jade skull
plopped in a puddle in front of him.

Ernie whispered. "She doesn't know it's not loaded."

There was something I remembered vaguely from basic
training, about the M-1 rifle. Before I could voice my reservations, Ernie was on his feet, brandishing his .45.

"Freeze, assholes! And drop that rifle right now!"

The rifleman whirled. The shot sizzled through the air

and exploded in a cloud of dust in the stone wall two inches from Ernie's left ear.

That's what I had been trying to remember. Even though you pull the magazine out, if the bolt is forward, there will still be one round in the chamber. Ernie hadn't remembered. Some combat veteran. But at least the guy had missed. Otherwise, Ernie would be an ex-combat veteran.

No more bullets now. I leapt out of the shadows and charged.

The thug trained his rifle on me, pulled the trigger, but didn't have time to hear the metallic click. I barreled into him going about thirty miles an hour. He collapsed backward and I didn't give him a chance. I landed full force on top of him, my knee jamming into his solar plexus. Air exploded from his puffed cheeks, and I pummeled his face and kept pummeling until he went limp under me.

Then I turned on Ragyapa and kicked him in the leg. He howled. I kicked him again, then started punching, not caring anymore whether any of the monsters lived or died.

Ernie pulled me off of him. "Easy, pal. Easy."

Lady Ahn pressed against the wall, silent and wide-eyed. In the few seconds that the altercation lasted she had managed to grab the jade skull. Now she clutched it like an infant against her bosom.

For some reason the sight of her cradling that skull made me angry. Even now, I'm not sure why.

"Is that all you care about?" I yelled. "That goddamn skull?"

Her eyes widened even more, reflecting moonlight across the smooth flesh of her face. And then I realized that she was looking over my shoulder and I turned. So did Ernie.

Up the alley was a line of dark humps. Without any sound or hint of verbal signal, the humps rose, moved forward a few feet, and froze again. I wasn't sure if I'd imagined the movement. I turned and gazed at Ernie. He was just as confused as I was.

He motioned with his hand for me to wait, and trotted forward to the pedestrian lane that intersected the alley. Seconds later he returned.

"Troops." He whispered in my ear. "Combat soldiers. Not riot police. They're strung out all across the rise."

For the first time, it dawned on me what was happening. "They're moving down toward the demonstrators."

"You got that right," Ernie said. "And as quietly as death itself."

"We've got to get out of here."

"You fucking-A Tweety."

I glanced at Ragyapa and his thug. Both were hurt badly. When this riot was over, the Korean police would pick them up and probably deport them for being involved in the demonstration. I didn't want that to happen. Not until we could have them properly charged.

I searched their bodies hurriedly and found two passports. Both from Hong Kong, but both men had what seemed to be Mongolian names. I tucked the passports in my back pocket. Once I turned them over to the KNP Liaison, along with my report of their crimes, Ragyapa and his man would be locked up—and deported only if they were very lucky.

"Let's move," I told Ernie.

Lady Ahn had been listening to us. "Where?" she asked. "If we go downhill, we'll be with the demonstrators. It will be madness once the soldiers attack. Even being American won't save you."

"She's right," Ernie said. "We have to go uphill and slip past them somehow."

"All right," I said. "Let's do it."

"Where's Herman?" Ernie asked.

"Don't know," I said. "No time now."

Somehow Lady Ahn kept up with us, clutching the jade skull like life itself. When we reached a small pathway, Ernie checked both ways. The dark humps were still up ahead of us about twenty yards. We turned down the pathway, scurrying forward, looking for a place to hide. But there was nothing. Nothing but jagged stone walls and thick wooden gates shoved flush up against them. In the distance I heard movement. Gravel crunching. A long line of sound moving steadily toward us like a slowly cresting wave.

"They're coming down," Ernie said. "Hit it!"

He flattened himself facedown in the gutter against the wall. Lady Ahn and I crouched as best we could behind a wooden crate stuffed with rotting melon rinds. The biting aroma made me think of wine, somehow. Or champagne.

I had it all: a beautiful woman, moonlight, naturally fermented vino.

Soldiers in combat gear, holding bayoneted assault rifles at port arms, filed down toward the big intersection in front of Guanghua-mun. A few broke off from the main line and trotted down our alley.

There was nowhere to go. Nowhere to hide. I wrapped Lady Ahn's face under my arms and bent over her, pressing my lips into the nape of her neck.

The soldiers weren't fooled. I heard the footsteps stop right in front of us. Slowly, I looked up.

His face was a mosaic of rock-hard planes of stone, slashed with camouflage paint. A metal combat helmet shadowed narrow eyes. His body was lean and he wore combat gear that sat on him as comfortably as if he'd worn it all his life. Moonlight glistened off a patch on his left shoulder. A white stallion rising on a blue background. The ROK Army White Horse Division.

Judging from the number of soldiers I saw stretching

down the long pathway, they must've pulled a battalion strength—maybe a brigade—off the Demilitarized Zone just to teach these demonstrators a lesson.

The soldier didn't smile. He had only two stripes on his sleeve. A sergeant joined him. Soon an officer was sent for. A captain, upset by the intrusion.

I showed him my identification and started to speak in Korean.

"We are investigators for Eighth Army and—"

The captain slapped the badge out of my hand. "*Sik-kuro!*" Shut up!

Ernie stepped forward. "Who the hell do you think you are, Charley?"

A soldier jabbed a bayonet into Ernie's stomach, stopping just before breaking the skin, and backed him up against the wall. Ernie held his hands up and stared cross-eyed at the gleaming blade. Another soldier searched Ernie and took away his .45, holding it in the air, showing it to the officer. They found my .38 and the officer took that, too.

The officer barked a command. "You two stay here. And guard them."

Before I could speak again, the captain swiveled and stomped away to rejoin his troops. Soon, their footsteps faded and we stood alone with the two impassive soldiers.

In Korean, one of them started to speak to Lady Ahn.

"Is it true their dicks are as big as trees?"

She kept her head down. Not answering. The soldier kicked her lightly with his combat boot. "Come on. Stand up. We want to see what a foreign whore looks like."

Both soldiers laughed. Ernie bristled. The soldier pressed the bayonet deeper against his skin.

"Come on. I said stand up!" He pulled Lady Ahn to her feet. She pulled her shoulder away and stared at him, her face a mask of hatred.

"*Aiyaa*," the soldier said. "Prime meat. And you sell yourself for the Yankee dollar?"

I launched myself at him but he had been expecting the move and sidestepped me, ramming the butt of his rifle into my stomach.

Even as I curled over, I was angry at myself for reacting with pure emotion. For lunging at him, for leaving my midsection open. It was the move of an amateur. Now I was useless. I clutched myself and rolled up in a ball on the ground.

The soldier shoved Lady Ahn up against the wall, ripped open her blouse, and fumbled for her breasts.

"I found it!" he said. He pinched Lady Ahn's nipple cruelly, causing her to cry out in pain. "Large and brown from these foreigners sucking on it. It would make a good souvenir of our trip to Seoul, would it not?"

The other soldier laughed and barked his approval.

"Then let us take it with us." He lowered his bayonet and ran the sharp edge along Lady Ahn's pale flesh.

Once troops are turned loose on demonstrators there are no controls. They can do anything. Foreign reporters will know nothing about it. The whole thing will be hushed up by the government. But the students will know what happened. And demonstrations will subside for months—maybe years—afterward.

I tried to stand. Pain shot through my body. As if a two-by-four was sticking into my gut.

Ernie struggled but settled down when the other soldier nudged the bayonet deeper into his belly.

Lady Ahn seemed unafraid. With a sudden move, she twisted her body and raised her hands to scratch at the soldier. He was too fast for her. He shoved a powerful forearm under her throat. Slowly, he brought the tip of the bayonet closer to her bruised brown nipple.

It was as if a cannonball dropped from the sky. I

couldn't see anything clearly but somehow I knew, just from the large round shape. Herman the German had leapt off the top of the wall.

The soldier who had been groping Lady Ahn was now nothing but a crumpled, groaning mass beneath Herman's girth. The soldier with the bayonet in Ernie's gut turned at the noise, and Ernie reacted like a pissed-off tomcat. He punched and clawed at the guy, not giving him a chance to jab with his weapon. Lady Ahn pounded on him, too, and soon they had the soldier on the ground, hammering his skull into sawdust.

I crawled over and grabbed Ernie's feet. And Lady Ahn's. "Enough. Enough!"

They stopped pummeling the soldier.

Herman helped me to my feet. The pain was ebbing now. I was starting to breathe normally.

Lady Ahn covered herself as best she could with her tattered blouse. The jade skull was snuggled once again beneath her bosom.

"Let's get the fuck out of here," Herman said.

Herman bent over and snatched up one of the M-16 rifles. As we approached the next alley, I heard a rumbling sound.

"Armored vehicles," Ernie said. "We have to cross the next alley in front of them or the convoy will block our path."

We started to sprint, Herman huffing like a freight train. Before we reached the alley, the black front of the armored vehicle appeared. We were only a few feet away, but we weren't going to make it. Trash lay strewn around the pathway and Lady Ahn stumbled on something, I think the wreckage of a wooden crate. She tripped and sprawled forward, letting go of the jade, and crashed face-first into the mud.

The armored vehicle rolled slowly downhill.

Lady Ahn bounced back up almost immediately, gazing forward, screaming.

The jade skull skittered across the slick pathway like a soccer ball heading for the goal. It rolled in front of the armored vehicle, bounced, hit the metal floorboard, rolled again, and stopped just beneath the clattering treads.

In seconds it would be crushed.

Lady Ahn wailed and charged forward. I tried to stop her, but the smooth flesh of her forearm slipped out of my grip. When she reached the front of the armored vehicle, she dived, scrabbling forward, almost there.

We heard a crunching sound and saw what seemed to be a puff of green dust. And then a scream.

Lightning flashed. Thunder. And then a wall of rain hammered down.

My eyes were momentarily blinded by the lightning but then I focused. The long row of treads ground heavily across Lady Ahn's leg.

Only when the vehicle passed could we pull Lady Ahn out of the path of the next armored vehicle rattling down the lane.

A tiny sea of green gravel swirled in the running rainwater. It began to trickle like the tail of a comet into the dark gutter. I reached forward and grabbed a handful. The remains of the jade skull of Kublai Khan sifted through my fingers like the dust of a giant emerald.

The armored vehicle stopped. The hatch opened. Soldiers started to climb out.

"Pick her up! Carry her!" Herman shouted. "I'll cover you!"

Herman waved the M-16 he'd taken from the soldier he'd squashed.

Ernie and I did as we were told. We started trundling Lady Ahn away from the armored vehicle. Herman let go a burst of fire. The soldiers hopped back into the armored vehicle and slammed the lid shut.

At the top of the hill, I looked back down at the intersection in front of Guanghua-mun. Even up here we could hear the gunfire and the screams. The students were surrounded. The soldiers of the White Horse Division were cutting through them like hot bayonets through lard.

"I told you the government would get pissed off," Herman said.

Ernie slapped his head. "Shut the fuck up, will you?"

Lady Ahn's leg was mangled and bleeding badly. But she wasn't whimpering. I whipped off my belt and used it as a tourniquet. When I tightened it, she winced at the pain but didn't cry out. She seemed lost in a world of misery, and I don't think it had anything to do with her leg.

We wandered through alleys until we reached a section of Seoul where life was still somewhat normal. Waving the M-16, Herman stopped a cab. The terrified driver skidded to a halt. Ernie and I loaded Lady Ahn aboard and climbed in after her. There wasn't room for Herman.

"Report to the MP Station," Ernie told Herman. "You're still in my custody."

"Not the MP Station," Herman said. "I have some things to take care of first."

"I said the MP Station!"

Herman leveled the M-16. Ernie gazed into the barrel.

"Okay," Ernie said. "Maybe I was a little hasty. Where would you like to surrender?"

To my surprise, Herman answered.

"Itaewon. Tomorrow afternoon. Four o'clock."

Ernie nodded. "Sure. Any particular spot?"

"Yeah. The Virtuous Dragon Dumpling House, where they chopped up Mi-ja's ear. And come alone. You and George. No one else."

37

ERNIE HELD OUT HIS SHINY NEW .45 AND LET THE MONSOON rain splash off of it.

"Damn thing's too new," he complained. "No rust on it."

We stood under a storefront awning in Itaewon, across the street from the Virtuous Dragon Dumpling House.

"They're not supposed to have rust on them," I said. "It causes them to jam."

"An old wives' tale," Ernie said. "You have to work a weapon in, let it get dirty and muddy so all the gears mesh right."

"Pistols don't have gears."

Ernie stared at me. "That's the problem with you, George. You take all this technical shit too seriously."

I ignored him and studied the front of the Dumpling House. So far, Herman hadn't entered. If he kept his word, he should be here any minute.

Last night, when we arrived at the front gate of Yongsan

Compound, the MPs wouldn't let us through with an "unauthorized civilian" in the cab. I told them to go fuck themselves and forced the driver to take us to the 121 Evacuation Hospital anyway.

The emergency room nurse was also reluctant. But once she took a look at Lady Ahn's wounds, she went ahead and started working on her.

The doctors were worried that they might have to amputate Lady Ahn's leg. The decision would be made tonight. Luckily, they hadn't spared the sedatives, because Lady Ahn was still more distraught about losing the jade skull than about losing any part of her body.

We'd spent most of the day at the CID office writing up our reports and getting new weapons issued and taking a series of ass-chewings from the First Sergeant. He was pissed that we'd let Herman escape, pissed that we'd been involved with a civilian demonstration, pissed that a civilian woman had been admitted to a military hospital.

I reminded him a couple of times that if we hadn't stopped Choi So-lan, the Buddhist nun, from torching herself last night, the entire country would've become engulfed in an armed revolt. As it was, the students were put down and the nun escaped alive.

This cut no ice with the First Sergeant. It was all the military regulations we'd broken that gave him a case of the ass—and the explaining he had to do to the Eighth Army honchos. He almost restricted us to compound while all our actions were being "reviewed," but we talked him out of it by mentioning that we had a rendezvous with Herman the German this afternoon.

He wanted to know where, because he was planning on sending at least a platoon of MPs to pick Herman up. If the First Sergeant and the Military Police handled it in their usual clumsy way, Herman would smell a trap and bolt and we might never see him again.

When we wouldn't spill, the First Sergeant gave in.

"But you'd better bring him back," he told us. "And I mean tonight. And I want him locked up in the MP Station. You got that?"

We said yeah about eighteen times and he finally let us go.

It was a gentle rain that was falling on Itaewon. *Danbi*, the Koreans call it. Sweet rain.

The thick cloud cover allowed only a filtered gray light to illuminate the village. Wind whistled through the alleys. But still, Itaewon smelled of roses, as if the pattering rain had washed away all its sins.

My body ached and I was cut and bruised all over. So was Ernie. But we could operate. Operate well enough to wrap this case up once and for all.

A foot sloshed into a puddle. I elbowed Ernie. "It's him."

Like a fat shadow, Herman slipped into the front door of the Virtuous Dragon Dumpling House.

"Let's go."

We hopped across mud islands and entered by pushing through the steam-covered glass door. All the tables were empty. It figured, on an afternoon like this. We pushed through the hanging beads back into the kitchen.

The same cook we'd seen before, the one who had sliced up Mi-ja's ear and stuffed it into boiled dumplings, stood behind a cutting board chopping away with a hatchet. His grandson sat on a stool listlessly shelling peas, his bike with the big tin delivery box parked outside. They both looked up as we entered.

"Where's Herman?"

The cook nodded toward the side of the building.

There was a large patio area, used during the dry season, covered with a wood-slat roof and protected from bugs by rusty metal screens.

Herman sat at the picnic table in the center of the patio. Rainwater dripped down his round skull. From beneath his damp coat he pulled out the M-16 he'd taken from the Korean soldier last night. He set the rifle flat on the table, pointing it at us.

"Keep your hands in plain view," he said.

Ernie and I both stopped. I held my palms out. "This isn't going to do you any good, Herman. You can't hide forever. Might as well come in with us and get it over with."

Ernie sat on one of the wooden benches and leaned back, his elbows propped on the table behind him. "Yeah. What the hell's the matter with you, Herman?"

"A lot of things are the matter with me," Herman said, "but I'm going to straighten them all out tonight."

"Oh, yeah?" Ernie wasn't buying it. "After a lifetime of fucking up, you're going to set it all straight in one night?"

Herman nodded.

Ernie blew breath between his lips. "This I have to see."

Herman rose and kept the rifle on us as he moved us back into the kitchen. He handed the boy a note. The boy slipped into his plastic poncho, went outside to his bike, and sped off splashing through the rain.

Herman turned to the cook and handed him a pile of Korean bills. "It'll only take a few minutes, *ajjosi.*"

The man nodded, went out front, pulled all the shades, and put up his closed sign.

I started to become a trifle concerned. "You planning on shooting us, Herman?"

"Sit down against the wall." He pointed to a small bench. We sat. "Now pull your weapons out and hand 'em over."

"What the fuck?"

"Shut up, Ernie," Herman said.

With the M-16 pointed at him, Ernie shut up. He

pulled out his .45 and handed it butt first to Herman the German. Herman stuck the weapon in the thick leather belt enveloping his waist.

"What about yours?" Herman asked me.

"I'm not carrying."

Herman told me to stand. Holding the rifle with one hand, he frisked me with the other. Satisfied that I was telling the truth, he backed off and motioned for me to sit down.

"If you don't move," Herman said, "you won't get hurt."

It dawned on me what he was up to. "You want us as witnesses, is that it?"

"Sort of."

"What do you mean, sort of?"

"Well, you know how military guys are about ceremony. I'm no different from the rest."

Ernie guffawed. "I get it. What you really want, Herman, is a fucking honor guard."

"Yeah. I'm a veteran. I got the right."

Ernie started to rise. Herman lifted the M-16 and spoke softly. "But you'll be one dead honor guard trooper if you don't sit the fuck back down."

Ernie lowered himself slowly. "Okay, Herman. Okay."

Herman sat on the stool behind the cutting board, the hatchet in front of him. We waited in silence, all of us getting used to the situation.

"Who was the note for?" I asked.

"You know who."

"I do?"

"Sure you do. Think."

I thought.

Every player in our little drama had been accounted for. Little Mi-ja was dead. Ragyapa and his boys were being hunted by the KNPs, Lady Ahn was in the hospital. The Buddhist nun was reportedly back at her mountain temple.

Pfc. Hatcher was locked in some dank Korean dungeon. The KNPs were still holding Sister Julie. There was only one person left.

"Your wife," I said. "Slicky Girl Nam."

"Now you got it."

Ernie let out a whoop. "Has she got a case of the ass at you, Herman! Even with that M-sixteen, you're going to need protection."

"She's the one who put the slicky boys on my ass," Herman said. "And she's the only one who can call them off."

"You're more afraid of them," I said, "than you are of Eighth Army or the Korean National Police."

Herman nodded.

Outside, the rain started to pick up.

Five minutes later, someone rapped on the door. The owner opened it, said *"Oso oseiyo,"* and footsteps shuffled in.

Her head popped into the kitchen first. A wrinkled hand pulled off a broad-brimmed cap and a thick mane of gray and black hair cascaded to her shoulders. Slicky Girl Nam.

Her eyes were red with crying and blazed with rage.

"You son bitch!"

She charged.

Holding her small fists in the air, she smacked them into the side of Herman's head. His neck quivered, but other than that he hardly moved. She smacked him again and again and clutched his forehead with her claws, trying to pry his eyes out of his skull.

All the while, Herman kept the M-16 trained on me and Ernie, his finger on the trigger.

Ernie started to move. Herman snatched Slicky Girl Nam's wrist and ripped her fingers away from his eyeballs.

"Don't try it, Bascom," he said. Ernie sat back down.

Herman looked at Slicky Girl Nam. Her face was as twisted as a mask of the goddess of the underworld. "Not the eyes," he said. "That's the only place you have to leave alone."

When he let go of her wrists she started to pummel him again. She boxed his ears and punched his lips and smashed his nose. But she stayed away from his eyes.

Only when the laws of physics demanded that some part of his body give a little, did Herman flinch.

Slicky Girl Nam's rage was like the monsoon torrent growing outside. She scratched and clawed and punched until finally the strength in her arms gave out.

Then she stopped for a moment to catch her breath. Herman's head was bathed in blood. He had to wipe his face with the back of his fat knuckles so he could see, but he kept the M-16 trained steadily on us.

After catching her wind, Slicky Girl started cursing and punching him again.

We were both growing sick of it. Ernie spoke first. "Why don't you defend yourself, Herman?"

"I don't deserve it." More blows landed. "All I could think about was the money. So I sliced off Mi-ja's ear, convincing myself that it was for her own good. And I chopped off her finger, in one quick slice, hoping it wouldn't hurt too bad. But she screamed and cried for hours. Then I left her with those Mongols. They said they were Buddhists. They couldn't perform any butchery themselves. So instead they stuffed straw down her throat and let her gag on it until she turned blue.

"I did all that," Herman said, "to my own little girl. For money."

He shook his head in amazement. Slicky Girl Nam's punches were little more than taps now. Herman wiped the blood from his eyes once more and spoke to her gently.

"Are you tired, honey?"

"Yeah," she said hoarsely. "I'm tired."

"You rest for a minute and then you can use this." He pointed a bloody finger at the hatchet.

"What I do with that?"

"Don't you worry. I'll tell you. You just rest for a while."

Slicky Girl Nam breathed heavily.

"For Christ's sake, Herman," Ernie said. "You can't go through with this. Whatever you're planning."

"It'll be over soon. You just hold your position in formation like good soldiers."

Outside in the dining room, I heard the front door slam. Herman heard it, too.

"It's the owner," I said. "He's probably going to alert the police."

"I guess I didn't pay him enough," Herman said.

"I guess he got sick to his stomach hearing what she's been doing to you," Ernie said. "You have to stop this bullshit, Herman."

"Almost done," he said. "You ready now, honey?"

"I ready."

"Here, take the hatchet. Now after we're through with this, I want you to call off the slicky boys. Okay?"

Slicky Girl Nam gazed at the hatchet and then at the M-16. "Okay," she said. "I don't need them anymore."

"I'm going to lean my head down on the cutting board, honey, like this, so I can still keep an eye on these two guys."

"Okay, Herman," Slicky Girl Nam said. "What you want me do?"

"I want you to cut off my ear. Just like I did to Mi-ja."

Ernie and I leapt out of our seats. Using one hand, Herman raised the barrel of his rifle.

"Easy, boys. Steady in formation."

The gaping mouth of the business end of the M-16

looked huge from where we stood. We both slumped back down. Ernie cursed softly.

"Go ahead, honey," Herman said. "Cut off the ear."

Slicky Girl Nam licked her thumb and rubbed it on the edge of the hatchet. "It not sharp."

"That's okay, honey. You just push hard."

She placed the hatchet flat on Herman's head behind his ear. "Okay," she said. "Can do easy. You ready?"

Thunder blasted outside. Herman had to shout.

"Ready."

Slicky Girl Nam shoved the hatchet forward and Herman's ear tore off with an audible rip. Both Ernie and I leaned back.

The blast of the M-16 exploded inches from our faces. Ernie and I flopped off the bench and crashed to the floor.

I swiveled my head. A small hole gaped in the wall between us.

Herman's eyes were filled with tears, but he was still conscious. He sat back up. Blood gushed from his ear in a crimson stream.

"Sorry, you guys," he said. "Reflex reaction."

Ernie and I climbed warily back up onto the bench.

"Okay, honey," Herman said, breathing heavily. "Now chop up the ear in little slices, just like Mi-ja's ear was chopped up to go in that *mandu*."

Slicky Girl Nam seemed to have found her strength again. She chopped vigorously until Herman's ear lay on the bloody cutting board in shredded pieces. It looked just like the little ear we'd found in the bowl of steamed dumplings.

"How's that, honey?" Slicky Girl Nam asked.

"Good job."

All of Slicky Girl Nam's rage had disappeared. I'd never seen her so considerate of her husband. It was as if she'd finally gained respect for the old lifer. She glanced down at the sliced flesh.

"You want me to make dumplings?"

"No time for that," Herman said. "I've got to go now, honey. You take the rifle, keep these guys here. I hope you see now that I've paid for what happened to our little Mi-ja."

Slicky Girl Nam stared down at Herman's shredded ear. "You pay," she said.

Herman grabbed a wet rag and held it to the side of his head, stanching the flow of blood. "Give me ten minutes head start. Someday, when all this shit settles down, I'll come back for you."

Slicky Girl Nam's eyes welled with tears. "Okay, Herman," she said. "Someday you come back to Slicky Girl Nam."

Herman started to back toward the door. I reached in my pocket, pulled out a plastic bag, and slapped it on the bloody cutting board.

"Not so fast, Herman," I said.

The door was open, but Herman stopped. I pointed to the pile of green gravel in the plastic bag.

"I had it tested this morning, Nam. This is what is left of the jade skull of Kublai Khan. The problem is that it is not jade. It's glass."

"Don't believe him, Nam," Herman said. "You know you can trust me."

Ernie started to back away along the wall. Slicky Girl Nam's eyes narrowed and her finger tightened around the trigger of the M-16.

"He brought a phony glass skull to the demonstration," I told her. "Now that he's cut off his ear and he knows that you and the slicky boys won't be coming after him for killing Mi-ja, he plans to get the real jade skull and escape from the country. It was a good plan, Herman. If I hadn't grabbed some of this glass before the rain washed it away last night, you might even have pulled it off."

"Don't believe them, honey," Herman whined.

The front door slammed open, *"Kyongchal!"* someone shouted. Police!

Ernie leapt at Herman. In an extremely fast move for such a big man, Herman stepped back and slammed the door shut. Wood cracked against knuckles. Ernie howled in pain.

A dozen boots pounded into the dining room.

"Kyongchal! Umjiki-jima!" Police! Don't move!

I leapt at Slicky Girl Nam, grabbed the M-16, and wrestled it away from her.

Korean National Policemen stormed into the room, pointing guns at us. Hands were all over me. People shouted. Slicky Girl Nam screamed. I held the rifle over my head and hollered, *"Mipalkun honbyong."* Eighth Army MPs.

Captain Kim strode into the madness. The police stopped shouting.

"Herman *domang ka,*" I told him. Herman's running away.

The Itaewon Police Station commander pushed through the wooden door and peered outside. "He won't get far," he said. "Come on."

Ernie and I followed him into the muddy alley out back.

"Let the woman go!" Captain Kim shouted in Korean.

Once the policemen released her, Slicky Girl Nam took off like a hunting dog. We trotted after her.

She wound through alleys, heading toward the residential section, the general direction of her own hooch. On the hill above us, I spotted three or four men in sports training outfits darting in and out of alleys. Slicky boys. And then I saw Herman, twisting through narrow lanes, heading down the hill. The big man was slowing, totally exhausted.

"They're herding him toward us," Ernie said in admiration.

We were so close now, I heard Herman the German huffing and puffing. Ahead of us, Slicky Girl Nam was rapidly gaining on him.

Where three alleys converged, a huge puddle blocked most of the intersection. Herman plowed into it like a water buffalo charging a river. He sloshed forward a few steps, stumbled, and fell face forward. Slicky Girl Nam splashed in after him and leapt on his back like an enraged she-leopard. She clawed at his neck and they both twisted and growled and collapsed into the muddy pond.

Herman rose first, filthy rainwater sputtering off his lips. He punched Slicky Girl Nam in the nose and she slammed straight back into the puddle.

By now, Korean National Policemen had emerged from all the alleys. The slicky boys stood in the pathways above us, arms crossed, silent, observing. Herman pulled out Ernie's .45 and waved it in the air.

"Back off!" he shouted.

All the policemen leveled their M-1 rifles at him.

"Drop it, Herman!" I shouted, but I don't think he heard me. Instead, gripping the butt of the pistol in his two big fists, he crouched and pointed it directly at one of the policemen.

A shot rang out. Herman's bowling-ball body lurched forward. Blood blossomed between his shoulder blades. He swiveled, raising the pistol, and this time a volley of rifle shots whistled through the rain like wasps.

Herman jerked like a stung bear. Crimson gore gushed from five spots. He dropped the .45, stared up into space, and performed a graceful pirouette.

Slicky Girl Nam held up her hands but it did no good. Herman's body crashed down on top of her.

Ernie and I splashed forward. We rolled Herman off of Slicky Girl Nam and helped her to her feet. I knelt, probed my fingers into Herman's neck. No pulse.

Nothing.

Captain Kim barked crisp orders. Policemen approached. Four of them hoisted Herman's fat body into the air and carted it off through the muddy alleys.

Ernie gazed after them. When he finally spoke, there was awe in his voice. "Don't *ever* point your pistol at a Korean National Policeman," he said.

Slicky Girl Nam was shaking. She shrugged off my hand and marched over to the first policeman who had shot Herman. He noticed her standing in front of him with her feet spread and glanced down at her. She spoke first.

"Ku namja na ui nampyon ikun!" That man was my husband!

She'd been about to kill Herman herself, and now she was pissed because somebody else had done the job for her.

No emotion showed on the policeman's face.

Without warning, Slicky Girl Nam swung her small fist and smacked the KNP on the side of the head. The cop raised his rifle to ward her off but she kept coming, scratching and kicking and spitting.

Other policemen rushed over to help. Slicky Girl Nam smacked them, too.

Finally, they wrestled her to the ground.

A red-faced Captain Kim didn't hesitate when he shouted his commands. The policemen hoisted Slicky Girl Nam into the air, as they had done the corpse of her husband, and carted her off, too.

With muddy fingers, Ernie unwrapped a new stick of

gum, popped it into his mouth, and started chomping. "Hate to see a family destroyed like that," he said.

Blood swirled in the puddle around our feet.

"You're developing a conscience," I told him.

Ernie seemed amazed. "Me? No way."

We tromped back through the rain to the Itaewon Police Station.

38

THE DOCTORS AT THE 121 EVACUATION HOSPITAL CUT OFF LADY
Ahn's leg. Just below the knee.

When she was released, Ernie and I carried her out to
our new jeep and drove her all the way down south to the
ferry at Ok-dong. Ernie said his good-byes and strolled
away so we could be alone. I helped her to the loading
ramp. She had one crutch and was becoming pretty skillful
with it. She kept slapping my hand away.

"I will do it myself," she said.

Before she boarded the ferry, I told her that I wanted to
see her again.

"Why?"

"You should know," I said.

"Because you love me?"

"Because I'm starting to."

"Then stop," she said.

Normally, I wouldn't have argued. My pride would've

stood in the way. But this time pride didn't seem to matter. It didn't matter at all.

"Why?" I asked. "You know that we're made for each other. You're too independent for most Korean men. We could go together back to the States. You could be anything you wanted to be there. You could become someone important."

"I *am* someone important."

Heat swept over my face. "Yes. Of course you are."

"Don't forget that," she said. "And that's why I won't marry you."

"Because you're someone important?"

"Yes. And because I am royal."

I spread my hands. "Your family *was* royal at one time. Not anymore."

Her eyes shot bolts of anger into mine. "We are still royal. And that's why I can't marry you. It would defile my blood."

I thought of more words to say. A lot of them. But all of them were stopped by the knot in my throat. She had decided that she wouldn't stoop so low. Not as low as a GI. Not as low as me.

I envied her such arrogance. Life had punched mine out of me years ago. But she would need hers. I hoped it helped her as much as that crutch did.

I decided to settle for what I could get.

"If you ever come to Seoul, will you visit me?"

"No. I will never see you again, George Sueño."

She turned and hobbled up the loading ramp.

I stood and watched the ferry for a long time. Even as it pulled away, she didn't appear on deck.

When we drove off, Ernie didn't say anything. For the entire drive back, he didn't even click his gum.

———

WHEN WE ARRIVED BACK IN SEOUL, WE DIDN'T BOTHER GOING to the compound. Instead, we parked the jeep in Itaewon and slipped into the nearest barroom.

Like a pharmacist administering a drug, Ernie purchased a double shot of bourbon at the bar and set it on the table in front of me.

"You'll feel better after this," he said.

I jolted it back. Then I had another. Still, I didn't feel better.

"She'll change her mind," I said.

Ernie shook his head. "Don't count on it."

"There's got to be a way." Finally, it hit me. I clutched Ernie's forearm. "I didn't tell her about the jade skull."

Ernie blew breath between his lips. "So you figure that if we find the skull you can get her back?"

"Sure, I can."

"But for how long?" Ernie asked.

We let that question hang. I had a couple more shots.

After a while, we were reeling from bar to bar. Making a night of it. It was in the King Club that we saw her.

She was small, almost tiny compared to the business girls who surrounded her. She wore a blue cotton skirt that stopped just above her knees and a red-and-white polka-dot blouse. Atop her head, pulled down until it almost covered her ears, was a bright red cap with a fuzzy white tassel on the top.

When she approached us, Ernie waved her off perfunctorily but I grabbed his hand and made him look again.

Round balls of rouge exploded off the woman's cheeks. She smiled bravely but it seemed as if she was about to break down in tears.

We both recognized her at the same time: Choi So-lan. The Buddhist nun.

"What the hell happened to you?" Ernie hollered.

Her face fell. She covered her mouth with both hands, turned, and ran off toward the back of the King Club.

"What the hell did you say that for?" I yelled to Ernie.

Ernie could only point and sputter. "That was the little nun!"

"I can see that. Apparently, she's quit her job and now she's in Itaewon, looking for you. And you treat her like she's some sort of freak."

"She is! With that makeup and those clothes. She looks like a clown."

"So she's not up on the latest fashions. She'll catch up."

Ernie and I gulped down our drinks and walked over to the back hallway and convinced one of the business girls to go into the women's latrine and ask the nun to come out. About five minutes later she emerged, her face pink from crying.

We pulled her out of the King Club and down the street to a little bistro where it was darker and quieter. In a secluded booth, I sat her down next to Ernie and made her tell us what was going on.

"I quit," she told me.

"You quit being a nun?"

"Right."

"Why?"

"I don't know." She squirmed in her seat. "I want come Itaewon. I want see Ernie."

Her English was rudimentary, but better than either Ernie or I had suspected. Ernie finally overcame his surprise and even started being a little nice to her. He handed her a stick of ginseng gum and she chomped on it happily. When he bought her a cola, you would've thought he'd just presented her with a diamond ring.

After a while, they were sitting close to one another and chatting, and I decided to leave them alone. I tossed back a couple more shots and wandered off into the neon alleys of Itaewon.

After she had decided not to burn herself to death, the loss of face for the little nun—and for the Buddhist church—must've been difficult to bear. That plus the world she had experienced in Itaewon—and Ernie's hold on her—had been enough to make her decide to quit being a nun.

What would she do now? If she was relying on Ernie to provide for her happiness, she was in for a rude surprise.

I kept drinking and soon forgot about Ernie and the nun. I had problems of my own.

A vision of Lady Ahn's face started to float in front of me. Just out of reach. I stumbled after it. The face kept laughing at my foolish antics.

THE NEXT MORNING, ERNIE BEAT ME INTO THE OFFICE. I CAME in red-eyed and hungover, my head pounding.

"Where the hell did you run off to?" Ernie asked.

"I wanted to be by myself," I answered.

Ernie handed me a cup of coffee. I sipped on it. "How'd it go with the nun?" I asked.

Ernie shrugged. "So-so."

I knew what that meant. If Ernie hadn't gotten what he wanted, he'd be complaining.

"Did you take her to a *yoguan*?"

"Shit, no. Too expensive. I took her back to the barracks."

I nearly spit out my coffee. "Choi So-lan, the most famous Buddhist nun in the country, spent the night with you in the barracks?"

"She's not famous anymore," Ernie said.

I shook my head. "Not a nun anymore either," I told him.

Ernie grunted.

For some reason it depressed me. Talk about a long dismal fall.

Before we could finish our coffee, the First Sergeant called us into his office. He informed us that he had filed the paperwork with Eighth Army Finance to dock us for Lady Ahn's hospital expenses.

"It'll come out of your pay," he said. "Medical care for an unauthorized civilian." He almost yawned before he added the next sentence. "If it causes you any hardship, go see Army Emergency Relief."

Neither Ernie nor I saw another paycheck for three months. And neither of us went to Army Emergency Relief.

They could go fuck themselves as far as we were concerned.

THE STUDENT DEMONSTRATION WAS REPORTED IN THE WESTern press; there was even a blurb about it in the *Pacific Stars & Stripes*. But the articles didn't get the number of students killed right. Not by a long shot. Nor the number injured. They relied on government press releases which mainly told about the riot police who were hurt.

None of the soldiers of the White Horse Division were injured.

Except two.

THERE WAS A LOT OF NEGOTIATING GOING ON BACK AND FORTH between the Koreans and Americans. Neither side really wanted to see Pfc. Hatcher burned. The Koreans because they didn't want to endanger the millions of dollars in military aid they received from the U.S. every year. And the U.S. because, in the eyes of the Eighth Army honchos, what Hatcher had done wasn't so bad. After all, the nun hadn't even been raped or permanently damaged. Not physically, anyway.

But both sides had to go through the motions to assuage Korean public opinion. Everyone at JAG figured Hatcher'd be slapped with a pretty long sentence, but be let out after a few months for good behavior.

THE KOREAN NATIONAL POLICE CHARGED SLICKY GIRL NAM with assaulting a police officer, but didn't implicate her in the kidnapping and murder of her daughter, Mi-ja. We told them that everything she did was simply the performance of a good wife taking orders from her husband.

Even the assault on the policeman was a filial act: a faithful wife avenging her dead spouse. Captain Kim listened to that argument, but he wasn't going to take a chance on allowing any disruption of public order. Especially when that disruption took the form of an attack on a police officer.

Slicky Girl Nam was sentenced to ninety days in the Kyongki Provincial Prison in Suwon.

If we hadn't put in the good word for her, it could have been worse.

I MADE ARRANGEMENTS AT THE EIGHTH ARMY MORGUE TO OBtain Herman a brass plaque issued by the Veterans Administration upon the death of any honorably discharged veteran.

Herman's coffin was too wide for the narrow Korean vans usually used as hearses. Instead, we hired a truck.

Ernie and I rode in the truck into the countryside to the place GIs call Happy Mountain. We had no clue what religion Herman believed in—probably none—so we paid a Buddhist monk to wave some incense over his grave.

We buried Herman right next to his adopted daughter. I figured it was too late for her to mind.

Nobody else was there and nobody said a eulogy. Both Ernie and I knelt and touched the sod atop Mi-ja's grave.

As we walked away, Ernie stepped over to Herman's eternal resting place. He gazed down at the fresh soil. Then he spat on it.

RAGYAPA AND WHAT WAS LEFT OF HIS THUGS WERE PICKED UP by the Korean National Police. Charges were filed concerning the murder of Mi-ja, and they were awaiting trial in less than a week. Both Ernie and I would have to testify and Ernie, especially, was looking forward to it.

"They have all those cute chicks taking dictation."

The Korean prosecutor told us we didn't have to worry about Ragyapa getting off. "The last Korean citizen tried for a major crime in Mongolia was given fifteen years."

"What's that got to do with it?" I asked.

The prosecutor's eyes widened. "We'd lose face if we gave one of their citizens any less."

He had a good point.

THAT NIGHT ERNIE AND I HOPPED FROM ONE BAR TO ANOTHER throughout Itaewon. Even though there was much laughter and many business girls and rock and roll blaring so loudly that it rattled my skull, I still could think of nothing other than Lady Ahn.

We sat at a cocktail table in the UN Club, a little candle flickering between us. Ernie slapped me on the shoulder. "Get over it, pal. If she don't want you, she don't want you. There's plenty more."

I nodded dumbly and sipped on my shot glass full of bourbon.

"I've made my decision," I told Ernie.

"What's that?"

"Tomorrow we drive out to the jail in Suwon."

"To see Slicky Girl Nam?"

"Right."

"What the hell for?"

"There's still something missing."

Ernie thought about that for a moment, sipped on his beer, and peered at me cagily. "The jade skull of Kublai Khan," he said.

I nodded. "You got that right."

Choi So-lan, the former nun, entered the club, found Ernie, and clung to him fiercely, warding off all the business girls. It would be a long night.

39

#

THE MONSOON RAIN HAD LET UP, THE BLUE SKY WAS CLEAN, and blue jays chirped in the rustling elms that lined the road to Suwon. Ernie downshifted the jeep's engine as we pulled up to the chain-link fence surrounding the cement block walls of the Kyongki Provincial Prison.

When we entered the visiting room, Slicky Girl Nam was already sitting on the other side of a flimsy wooden partition. She wore a shapeless gray smock, her face was scrubbed clean, and her hair was tied back in a neat bun. We sat down on the splintered bench opposite her.

"How it hanging, GI?" she said.

She asked us if we had cigarettes, but neither one of us had brought any. A mistake. She pouted and looked away from us.

"We came to see how you were doing," I said.

"Better if you bring GI *tambei*," she said.

I handed her a five-dollar bill. "Here. Buy some."

She studied the bill, then stuck it in her brassiere beneath her smock. "GI cigarettes better," she said.

We chitchatted for a while, not wanting to come right out and say why we were here, which was to find out if Slicky Girl Nam knew anything about the whereabouts of the jade skull. After the death of Mi-ja, Herman had been frightened that his wife would try to take revenge. And he had been even more frightened of the slicky boys. But he had never wanted to cut Slicky Girl Nam in on the money he planned to make from the jade skull. Still, she might know something.

She asked me about Herman's funeral, and I did my best to try to make it seem better than it was. Ernie became restless and started fidgeting in his seat. I figured I'd better wrap this up.

"Did you search your hooch?" I asked Nam.

"For the skull?"

"Yeah."

"Of course I search. I search everything. Nothing there."

I noticed a smudge of charcoal on Nam's fingers.

"You have to change your own charcoal here?" I asked.

"Yes. No Herman anymore do it for me."

She hacked out a laugh, and as I gazed into her dark eyes it hit me. The whole scheme. Herman's plan to get away with the jade skull of Kublai Khan.

I sat up and leaned toward Nam. Even Ernie noticed my excitement.

"The night Herman was killed," I said, "he was heading toward your hooch?"

Slicky Girl Nam thought about that. "Maybe. He go that way."

"When you received his note asking you to come to the Virtuous Dragon Dumpling House, you were at home, weren't you?"

"Yeah. I at home. We play *huatu*." She slapped her hand down, mimicking the action of playing Korean flower cards.

"Was the floor warm?"

She gazed at me, puzzled. "Of course it warm. After Herman run away, *ajjima* next door start change charcoal all the time."

Her voice trailed off and her eyes widened. She stood up. So did I.

"You son *bitch*!" she hollered. "You no can go. You no can go without Nam go with you!"

I motioned for Ernie. "Time to head back to Seoul," I said.

Ernie looked back and forth between me and Nam. "What the hell's going on?"

"I'll tell you when we get in the jeep."

Slicky Girl Nam started to climb across the counter. A female guard ran forward, grabbed her by the shoulders, and shoved her back.

"You no slicky from me!" Nam yelled. "It mine. You got it? I put up with that Herman son bitch for *too* many years. It *mine*!"

Three guards had to hold Slicky Girl Nam down as we backed out of the room.

WHEN WE WERE ON THE ROAD HEADING BACK TOWARD SEOUL, Ernie swerved around a line of slow-moving buses. "What the hell was Nam so worked up about?"

"About the jade skull," I answered.

"I figured that much. But we still don't know where in the hell it is."

"We do now."

"How do you figure?"

I explained it to him.

One thing had always bugged me: Why had Herman

boarded a military airplane at Osan Air Force Base with the jade skull in his carry-on luggage? Surely he knew that we would notify the Military Police in Japan or Okinawa or wherever his first stop was. Boarding the plane and arresting Herman and confiscating the jade skull would be a snap. Once he got on that plane, he was trapped.

But maybe he didn't have the skull.

Maybe he had ditched it somewhere and was carrying a soccer ball full of rocks, and if the MPs arrested him they'd find nothing illegal on him. Ernie and I would look foolish. Herman would be released, and the First Sergeant might not believe any of our theories concerning the whereabouts of the jade skull of Kublai Khan. Ernie and I might even come under suspicion for the theft ourselves.

Herman would be able to return to Seoul, wait until things calmed down, and smuggle the skull out of Korea at his leisure.

But where had he hidden it?

I remembered the first night we went to his hooch, how Slicky Girl Nam had punched him around for forgetting to change the charcoal and keep the *ondol* floor warm. Now I knew why he forgot. He'd been with Ragyapa, slicing off Mi-ja's ear.

And later, at the Beik Hua Yoguan, even when we had a hot tip concerning Lady Ahn's whereabouts, Herman was more concerned about getting back to the hooch and changing the charcoal.

At the time, I thought it was because he was frightened of Slicky Girl Nam's wrath. Now I had a different theory. He didn't have the skull then but maybe he had other things to hide.

Ernie slapped his hand on the steering wheel. "The son of a bitch hid the skull beneath the charcoal!"

"That could be it," I said, "that could be where he kept his stash. And maybe that's why he didn't want Nam—or anybody else—to change the charcoal."

"And when Slicky Girl Nam searched her own hooch for the skull," Ernie said, "she was so used to having a hot floor that she didn't think about the charcoal stove beneath the floor."

"Right. And all the time we were chasing Herman, the skull was sitting there keeping warm."

"And when he left the Virtuous Dragon Dumpling House, he was heading back to Slicky Girl Nam's hooch to pick it up."

"That's what I figure."

"So we'll have to find out."

"That we will."

THAT NIGHT, ERNIE AND I HIKED FROM THE COMPOUND TO Itaewon and climbed the fence around Slicky Girl Nam's hooch. We slipped through the darkness to the opening that held the charcoal. When I pulled up the metal lid, a red glow sparkled.

We had to be quiet because the *ajjima*, the old neighbor lady who lived next to Slicky Girl Nam, had taken it upon herself to guard the hooch.

Ernie found the metal pan and the long steel tongs that were used to change the charcoal. I stuck the straight tongs into the perforations of the burning charcoal briquette. When I had a good hold, I pulled it out. Ernie slid the pan under it. I dropped it in, and plucked out the second briquette.

We shone the beam of our flashlight into the steaming cement hole.

"There it is," I said.

At the bottom of the hole was another cement disk. On it was a flat hook. I examined the tongs. The handle had been hammered and bent slightly. It looked like just wear and tear, but I figured Herman had fashioned the tool precisely. I turned the tongs around and stuck them into the hole, handle first.

The bent handle fit perfectly into the metal hook of the disc. I lifted it out. Solid. About four inches thick. Below it was another disc. This one made of metal. I started to lift it out. It was heavier than I expected.

With a scraping sound, a rusty metal cylinder slid out of the bottom of the concrete stove. I set it on the ground. Ernie tapped the lid, and licked his fingers.

"Not hot," he said.

The bottom of the cylinder was even cooler.

"Must've cost Herman a fortune to have this made," Ernie said.

I nodded.

A rock fell off the stone wall behind us.

Ernie wheeled and reached for his .45. Like big cats, three slicky boys landed in the courtyard.

I didn't give myself a chance to think but charged them head on, swinging the metal tongs in front of me. The first slicky boy ducked. I lost my balance and slammed into the wall.

The slicky boys slipped clubs out of their belts and closed in on me. A chink of stone exploded into dust when Ernie fired the .45.

"Don't move, assholes!" he yelled.

Lights clicked on throughout the neighborhood. I grabbed the metal cylinder, stuck it under my arm, and Ernie and I backed out of the courtyard.

Once we were in the alley, we started to run.

We scurried through the maze of Itaewon's alleys and made good our escape into the traffic of the Main Supply Route.

The cab driver was too frightened to ask about the rusty cylinder cradled in my lap.

IN ERNIE'S ROOM BACK AT THE BARRACKS, WE HAD TIME TO examine the contents of the metal cylinder. Wrapped in asbestos was the jade skull of Kublai Khan. Also a wad of Korean and American money and an American passport. Herman's face frowned out of the passport, but the name under the face was phony.

Ernie counted out the money and handed me half. "Beats Army Emergency Relief," he said.

I touched the skull with my fingertip.

"No way," Ernie said.

"No way what?"

"No way are you going to use that thing to get Lady Ahn back."

"And what makes you think I won't?"

"Because I won't let you."

"Bullshit."

Ernie shoved my shoulder. "That's right. I won't let you make a fool of yourself."

He was starting to annoy me. "I'll do any goddamn thing I want to do."

"No. You won't."

The tap on the side of my head stunned me. When my mind cleared, I realized it was a punch. The best Ernie had. He held both fists up, bouncing on his toes.

"Come on, goddamn it! Come on!"

I stepped toward him, more surprised than angry. "You'd punch *me*? Just to keep the jade skull?"

"Not to keep the jade skull," Ernie answered. "But to keep you from chasing after a woman who intends to use you. And then toss you aside."

"You're full of shit."

"Not me. *You're* the one who's full of shit, Sueño."

I took another step toward him. Ernie snapped out a jab, but it wasn't strong enough to slow me down. I had three inches and twenty-five pounds on him. He landed a couple of punches. I threw him back up against the wall and cocked my right hand.

He was open. I could have pulverized his jaw, but I didn't do it. He was like family to me. The only family I had.

Slowly, I dropped my fist.

Ernie smacked me again. "Go ahead, goddamn it! Fight! You want to throw your life away on some broad who doesn't give a fuck about you? Then fight!"

I stood with my hands at my sides, glaring at him, expecting him to punch me again. He did.

This time my jab shot out with a life of its own. And another and another. Ernie staggered back under the onslaught. My right caught him below the eye and I felt flesh and cartilage and bone beneath my knuckles.

I didn't like the feeling. It was like beating up your little brother.

Ernie was dazed, his eyes glassy. Still, he kept bouncing on his feet, holding his fists up. I didn't want to hit him anymore. I hadn't wanted to hit him in the first place.

I turned and walked out of the room. He didn't follow.

It was raining again. I didn't think about where I was going, but my feet moved with a will of their own. In a few minutes I looked up in surprise. I stood surrounded by the flashing neon of Itaewon.

I entered the first nightclub I saw and reached across the bar for the nearest bottle.

WHEN I WOKE UP, I WAS IN MY BUNK BACK AT THE BARRACKS. How I got there, I didn't remember. It was still dark. I wanted to vomit, but figured I'd better take a leak first.

I slipped on my shower shoes, opened the door to my room, and slapped my way down the hall.

Spec 4 Jorgenson, the CQ, Charge of Quarters, slouched in a big chair in front of the entrance to the barracks. His khaki uniform was as wrinkled as if he'd slept in it all night. Which he had. He roused as I approached.

"Sueño," he said, rubbing his eyes. "Did your partner ever find you?"

"What do you mean?"

"I mean Bascom left for Itaewon after you did. Said he was going to look for you."

I rubbed my head. "I don't know if he found me or not."

"Tied one on, eh?"

"Yeah."

"So anyway some chick came looking for him."

"What chick?"

"You know. The little one. With the real short hair."

Choi So-lan, the ex-nun. Her hair had started to grow out and she'd stopped wearing her cap.

"I hope it was all right," Jorgenson said. "I let her in his room."

"You did?"

"Sure. I'd seen her here with him before. You know, spending the night. I figured he wouldn't mind. And she was crying and all. I didn't want her sitting out here in the hallway bawling."

I grabbed him by the lapels and pulled him to his feet. "Gimme the key!"

"Sure. Sure. It's on the ring here."

He rattled a loop lined with about fifty keys.

I snatched it out of his hands and ran for Ernie's room. In the dark I was fumbling with the keys, trying each one. Jorgenson approached with his flashlight.

"Here. Let me do that."

He found the right key and opened the door. I switched on the light.

Ernie wasn't in his bunk. The blankets hadn't been mussed. Still out in Itaewon, I figured.

It was the wall locker I was worried about. Ernie had an extra bolt on it and a double padlock, always bragging that it was burglar-proof.

The padlocks hadn't been moved.

But the hinges lay on the floor in pieces. Someone had patiently scraped off the thick layers of olive-drab paint and unscrewed the hinges and pried them off. The door of the locker was slightly ajar.

"Shit," Jorgenson said. "I didn't know she was a slicky girl. I thought she was his girlfriend."

"Did you see her leave?"

"No. She must've slipped out the side door."

A drop of rain splatted on my leg. The window was open, the screen set on the floor below it.

I peered into Ernie's locker. Jorgenson shone the flashlight in. Propped up on a set of folded fatigues was Herman's phony American passport and the wad of Korean and U.S. bills. I counted them. They hadn't been touched.

But the jade skull was gone.

Jorgenson reached in and lifted out a felt purse. "What's this?"

I snatched it out of his hands and examined it. I saw the neatly embroidered Korean lettering: Choi So-lan.

I pulled back the strings of the purse, opened it, and turned it upside down. Out fluttered two handfuls of freshly shorn black hair.

"Looks like somebody cut their hair," Jorgenson said.

I nodded.

"Not that chick who was looking for Ernie?" Jorgenson

asked. "If she cut off this much hair, she must be bald by now."

I nodded again, thinking of Choi So-lan. Of Lady Ahn. Of Mi-ja. Of Kublai Khan's jade skull. "I think you're right, Jorgenson. She's bald all right. As bald as a Bride of Buddha."

About the Author

MARTIN LIMÓN grew up in Los Angeles county, just fifteen miles south of City Hall. He retired from military service after twenty years in the U.S. Army, including ten years in Korea, and now lives with his wife and children in the Seattle area. His first novel, *Jade Lady Burning*, was a *New York Times* Notable Book of the Year. He is also the author of *Slicky Boys*, which has been optioned by Paramount.